THE WEST HAVEN UNDEAD

THE WEST HAVEN UNDEAD BOOK 3

THE WEST HAVEN UNDEAD

NICK SAVAGE

4 Horsemen
Publications, Inc.

4 Horsemen Publications, Inc.
1497 Main St. Suite 169
Dunedin, FL 34698
4horsemenpublications.com
info@4horsemenpublications.com

Cover by J. Kotick
Typesetting by Autumn Skye
Editor: Blair Parke

Library of Congress Control Number: 2022951990

Paperback ISBN-13: 978-1-64450-790-2
Hardcover ISBN-13: 978-1-64450-895-4
Audiobook ISBN-13: 978-1-64450-792-6
Ebook ISBN-13: 978-1-64450-791-9

DEDICATION

*For my wife, who helps me fight
the demons in my head.*

Table of Contents

CHAPTER 1

"Our voice is more than the sound it makes.
The manner in which we use our words speaks volumes."
~D. Childers~

Thick white clouds drift in the sky above as the wind adds a welcome breeze on this late summer's evening. Connor DeSalvo, a young man of twenty years whose ruggedly handsome looks are accompanied by shaggy, sandy brown hair, stands in his backyard, baseball in hand. He throws it ten or so feet toward his cousin, Scarlett McAllister.

"Easy, Con," she pleads, shaking the pain away from catching the ball barehanded. "You aren't in baseball anymore. And I never was." She flips her long, copper-red hair behind her shoulder before tossing the ball back.

"Sorry," Connor says, chuckling. "You don't have to do this with me, ya know." He underhand tosses it back to her.

She makes the easy catch. "I know. But what else do we have to do?" She squints her eyes and scrunches her freckled nose as the setting sun beams down one last time for the day. "Plus, Jack would've liked this." Her aim gets away from her as she tosses the ball back to him.

Connor dives for the ball, catching it as he lands on his side. Scarlett hurries to him in a panic. "You okay? I'm sorry."

Connor sits up. "As you said, you never played ball."

A smirk overtakes her lips. "I didn't think I could hurt our high school's golden boy at his own game."

"Again, as you said, I don't play anymore. That and those days are behind me now. High school is behind you, too, now. Maybe it's time I move on." Connor's gaze turns to the distance.

"What does that mean? Move on?" Scarlett's voice grows a little stern.

"Box up all my old baseball stuff. Toss it in the garage or attic. It's not doing me any good now," Connor says, trying to convince himself. "I am not that guy anymore. None of us are who we were even a year ago." He brings his gaze back to her.

"But who you were got you to who you are," Scarlett states, attempting to convince him otherwise. "But it's your choice. My recommendation, sit on it for a while."

A three-mile-long stare overtakes him. "You know he broke a car window once?"

"Who?" Scarlett is not following her cousin's thoughts.

"Jack." He turns to her for a moment. "We were tossing a ball around. Nothing unusual. But one got away. Went through a car window. Passenger side, if I recall. He was so scared. Felt so guilty."

"What happened? He never said anything to me," Scarlett says, taking a seat on the ground next to Connor.

"Nothing. I sent Jack inside the school. Snuck some money in the glove box, hoping it would cover the repair. I told him never to mention it; I guess he didn't if you didn't know." Connor holds back a smile.

"Do you think you'd both be playing ball if he were still … here?" Scarlett's eyes turn to the sky.

"I think we both would have been expelled for drug use." He stops and turns back to her. "When he got arrested, he told me they busted him for drugs."

Scarlett nods. "I remember."

"But we never did any," Connor continues.

Scarlett nods once again.

"Then, I got expelled for testing positive." Connor stands up and starts strolling away from the house.

Scarlett joins her cousin. "All news we already know."

"But that cop, Espinoza ... he knew Jack would test positive. That's why the other cop, the one that wound up dead, told me what he did…" Connor's thought escapes him.

"What other cop?" Scarlett tries to keep up.

He shakes his head. "There was a cop who told me Jack's house was known for drugs. Well, he said the Taylors ... as in the whole family. But they weren't known for drugs. They didn't do drugs. It makes you wonder how many drug tests are false. Just telling the Normals that a Legend's among them."

"But Max Espinoza left. Allison told him to leave town after what happened with Mrs. Waldgrave and Mrs. Espinoza," Scarlett recaps. "I think that everything is over. We made it through. Didn't we?"

"How many of our family and friends have died in the last two years, Scar?" Connor quickens his pace.

"You want a number, or is that rhetorical?" Scarlett keeps in step with him.

"My mom and dad, Jack, his parents, Bri's mom, Mrs. Espinoza." Connor tosses up his fingers.

Scarlett is quick to interject. "I wouldn't call a teacher who kidnaps our friends a friend nor family."

"Fine," Connor concedes. "But in two years, we have had more people die than others experience in a lifetime. I think that whatever has been happening in West Haven is far from over. Honestly, Scar, I think all those things that have come our way ... I don't think they'll ever stop."

Scarlett grabs his arm to stop their walk. "Then what do we do now?"

"Besides learning to deal with what comes next? We get my girlfriend to talk to me again." Connor stops walking away from home and starts returning there.

"Yeah, 'cause getting Allison to do something she doesn't want to is always an easy task." Sarcasm drips off her words.

"I guess I'll save that for another time," Connor concedes.

"Say we do get her talking to you again, then what do we do?" Scarlett ponders.

"Then the question turns from 'what do we do' to the ancient Latin question for the ages, '*quo vadimus?*'" Connor lets a smirk escape.

"What the hell is that?" Scarlett does not entertain his language skills.

"Where are we going?" Connor replies.

"I thought we were going home? We're like ten steps away," Scarlett answers, oblivious to his translation.

A chuckle starts to sound, but he cuts it short. "That's what it means. What we do after we get Allison talking to me again can only be answered when we know where we are going."

"I assume the 'where' in your question is somewhere more profound than a vacation," Scarlett quips.

"Something like that." And with those words, his mile-long stare returns.

The reds, oranges, and yellows of fall have started infiltrating the deep green leaves on the maples, oaks, and elms comprising the dense forest. The fallen leaves reflecting the moonlight above add to the warm hue of the umber ground. The minimal clouds that litter the night sky crawl by in the almost still air.

Oil lamps that line the main road light a small town of two-room homes and a few businesses. Two bright-burning sconced torches frame an entryway to signal an open tavern. The music and jubilant laughter inside echo far into the distance, beckoning weary travelers.

The sleeping forest begins to rouse, causing small animals startled awake to scurry off, looking for new, safe beds in which to rest. The low branches of trees shake, sending leaves to the ground. Suddenly, incomprehensible, pained moans can be heard as a man stumbles out from the thicket of foliage, collapsing onto the dirt road. His torn rags collect dust as he struggles to stand up. His weathered face and barrel-chested body, covered in scrapes, cuts, and bruises, speak of a man whose apparent fifty-plus years have been anything but kind. He runs his filthy, white-gloved hands through his matted, slightly salted, dark brown hair, which shines crimson in the moonlight. He drags his left foot, hobbling toward the light of the town.

The forest behind him settles as its creatures again find sleep. The leaves rest on the ground as the branches come to a standstill. Even the clouds above seem to sleep in the night sky.

Inside the local tavern, townsfolk celebrate. The barkeep pours a steady flow of brown liquor and ale. Rejoicing patrons fill the wood tables and booths. A minstrel, positioned in the corner, plays joyous songs on a harpsichord, singing along in an equally celebratory fashion. A table away from the musician sit two guards in uniform, resting Brown Besses at their side, ready if needed.

A man and woman dressed in brown cloth robes nurse their drinks in a corner booth. They keep to themselves, watching the festivities unfold. The man's black hair and scar, which runs above and below his right eye, lend him a menacing look. In contrast, the woman's pale gray eyes and silver vixen hair balance the pair in a peaceful aura. To the casual observer, they would appear to be enjoying the night in silent reverie. Still, if one stared long enough, they might see something more—if they knew what to look for. If one were wise enough, they might see these two staring at the other while their lips hardly move, almost as if they mumble to each other in silence. As far as these two patrons know, even if someone saw their lips move, the guests of this establishment wouldn't know any better.

A skinny man with a slight potbelly stands from a center table. His 6'3" rangy stature towers above the rest of the crowd. He waves his thin arms, which look as if they may fall off his shoulders at any moment, in fluid, hypnotic motions to silence the crowd. His gaunt face smiles a black-toothed grin through a long, patchy goatee. The minstrel fades out his music. The barkeep finishes pouring a lager, wipes up a small spill, and, after slinging the rag over his shoulder, gives his full attention to the man. A short, stout man dressed in a well-tailored, button-down vest, seated next to the scrawny, pot-bellied man, glances at his pocket watch before sliding it back into his pants. As he stands up, a rehearsed smile breaks out across his face. He outstretches his arms, palms toward the people around him. Barely five feet tall, he looks up to the man that towers over him.

The tall, lanky man raises his stein of ale, and the crowd follows suit. He turns to the group that now encircles him. "When we first settled here, there were no roads. There were no homes. Just forest." He scans the crowd, watching the eager anticipation in their eyes. "But we found a clearing and said, 'Yes! This is our home!' We built homes and a general store. We built a pub!"

The crowd cheers.

"We built a community where we can feel comfortable—a place to keep us safe from the growing dangers around us. A haven to raise our families. A place we can call home!" He takes a deep breath and raises his glass higher. "And we couldn't have done it without this wonderful man." He puts his hand on the shoulder of the well-dressed man.

The crowd raises their glasses higher. The man takes a deep breath, but the end of his toast is interrupted as the bloodied man from the forest crashes through the tavern doors. His outstretched, gloved hands reach toward the distant bar top as he falls face-first onto the floor. An ornate, jeweled amulet spills out from under his rags, its silver chain clinging around his neck.

He lifts his head off the floor. His swollen eyes remain closed as he mutters one word, "Uisce."

The crowd stands in stunned silence. Unsure of what to do, they stare at the man who interrupts their night of joy, dismissive of his foreign word.

The misplaced man and woman from the corner booth stand up and rush to the fallen traveler. The woman sees the amulet as she leans down. She places it back inside the man's shirt, but not before glancing at the sapphires and amethysts that adorn the outside of the silver amulet. She sees something inside but can't make out what the charm encases.

The man hoists the bloodied stranger onto his lap. "Water!" He calls out to the barkeep or to anyone who may listen. But his call for help falls on deaf ears. The patrons remain frozen in confusion, staring at the situation unfolding in front of them.

The village guards rise from their booth, Brown Bess in hand. One runs out the doors as the other takes careful steps toward the downed man.

The woman screams out, "Someone get a glass of water!" Almost in unison, the disgusted crowd rises and exits the bar. "Now!" She turns back toward the bloodied outsider. She examines him, searching for severe wounds hiding beneath the dried blood and dirt.

The barkeep pours a goblet of water and brings it to them. Without stopping, he sets it down and continues straight out the front of the tavern.

The woman pours some of the water into the man's mouth. She tilts his head back, forcing it down his throat. He coughs, bringing awareness back into him for a moment.

"An oiread sin corpán marbh," he gasps, looking into the robed man's eyes.

The woman turns to her companion. "Dead bodies?"

The robed man flinches as he catches a static, shock-like jolt while wiping some dirt from the bloodied man's face. He looks toward the woman. "December, what do we do?"

The silver-haired woman looks at the bloodied man, stroking his matted, knotted hair. "I think we listen, Raymond." She looks at the guard standing beside them. "Something for the man to eat, please."

The guard disappears behind the bar, leaving only the bloodied man, December, and Raymond in the room. "Start from the beginning," she urges.

The bloodied man strains with every word he speaks. "Níor thosaigh siad ach ar troid." December looks to Raymond, who shakes his head.

December looks back at the man. "What did? What started fighting?"

The man continues as he stares off beyond the ceiling. "Is ar éigean a d'ealaigh mé."

Raymond looks to December for a response. "He's not answering me."

Raymond chimes in quietly, "Legends wouldn't do this."

December continues staring at the man. She gives a dismissive head-shake. "Of course not." The man collapses into her lap. "Not without good reason, that is." She shakes him enough to get him to open his eyes again. "Where were you?"

The weakened stranger does not respond to her words. His eyes are red and weary. "Tá an oiread sin comhlachtaí fuilteacha ann. An corp."

December squints, trying to figure out the meaning behind his words. She whispers to herself, "What bloodied bodies?"

Raymond scans the room. Finding it still empty, he turns to December. "Let's get him back."

The guard re-enters empty-handed. "Best not to move him. He needs further examination. I couldn't find any prepared food."

December takes off the man's gloves to look for wounds or signs of what might have happened or where he may have been. After pocketing the gloves, she holds the bloodied man's hand in reassurance as he falls back unconscious.

The guard kneels down and puts his bare hands on the man's face. He gently pats the side of the now-unconscious man's face, but he doesn't stir. The guard tries rattling him awake. "Sir! Sir, can you hear me?"

The traveler stirs a bit and opens his eyes to see the guard holding his face. Dark gray smoke starts to seep out from between the man's face and the guard's hands. He pulls away in pain. He stares at the bleeding burns that line his broken-skinned palms, still smoldering from the moment of contact.

December releases her grip on the fallen man upon seeing the burned hands. She seems unsurprised by the lack of damage on her hands but is more surprised by the damage done to the guard.

The burned guard gets up and runs toward the bar. He sticks his hands in the cool water of the sink. "What in God's name just happened?"

December looks at the guard, searching for an answer. Raymond slips the amulet from around the traveler's neck and tucks it into his pocket while the guard tends to his wounds. December opens her mouth to speak when a well-decorated officer struts into the bar, followed by the other lawman from before. The new lawman is the apparent ranking officer now.

In his freshly pressed clothes, the ranking officer takes a striding step toward Raymond. He stops only a foot short. The menacing look on his unblemished, smooth face tries to intimidate Raymond as he stares down. "He needs to come with us."

Raymond stares up at the guard. His skin has taken on a pale, slightly bluish translucence, far more intimidating than the baby-faced guard. "He can't stand."

The officer takes a deep breath and places a hand on his sword. December sees this and sets the man's head down. Before Raymond can react, she positions herself between the officer and Raymond. The lack of space forces him back a few steps.

The man looks past December toward Raymond, who is still seated. "That is of no concern to you."

December smiles and bats her eyes at the officer. "Now, good sir. There's no need to try and intimidate us by heaving your..." she pats his chest "...well-sculpted manhood out and placing your hand on your sword, as if we desire some sort of confrontation."

As she speaks, Raymond discreetly reaches under his robe and pulls out a small cork and vial from a hidden satchel. His pale blue skin's transparency has grown more noticeable—the circulatory system beneath shows a little more. With his other hand, he digs a long fingernail into the bloody man's arm. He draws a few drops of blood, but the man remains unconscious.

The officer's tone turns patronizing. "Little miss, batting your eyes at me will win you no favor. See, a strange man, who happens to be covered in blood, stumbles into a tavern, and you are quick to protect him. Maybe you know something about this man that we do not?"

Raymond moves the uncorked vial just out from behind his robe. A small trail of smoke seeps down the vial, up the bloodied man, and into his mouth. The smoke stops pouring out from the vial and finishes the journey into the man's mouth. Preoccupied with December, the city guard doesn't seem to notice the event happening beneath him.

December responds, trying to stall for time so Raymond can complete his work. She smiles at the man. "Patrols follow a man on the verge of death into a bar and threaten those trying to save him. Maybe you are trying to hide something?"

The patrolman shakes his head, letting out a soft laugh of annoyed amusement. He whips out a Flintlock and smacks her in the head with the butt of the gun. He attempts to move around the dazed December, but she shakes it off in time to grab him by his face, clawing her nails in. He drops his gun and screams as blood seeps from where she dug in. A cracking sound emanates from beneath her hand. Blood rushes out faster as she lowers him to the floor before letting go.

The guard lays unconscious, bruises forming around his eyes and the bridge of his nose, marring his once smooth face. She turns to Raymond. "We need to get out of here!"

A gunshot rings out.

Both Raymond and December turn to the other patrol officers. The man with the burned hands is fumbling with his pistol while the other has his pointed at them. December disarms the one officer with blinding speed, sending his gun flying across the tavern to land under a wooden table. Raymond lifts the unconscious man, as if he is weightless, and begins to run out the door. His skin regains opaqueness with each step. December turns her head to the two standing officers, both of whom are too stunned at the display of speed and strength to follow them out.

A dense growth of trees protects a nondescript log cabin. No trail leads up to the porch. No exterior sign that this cabin exists in these woods. No porch sconce. Only one chair. No place for a wagon or horse to stable. The forest has swallowed this dwelling. The windows flicker with the faint glow of candlelight escaping through the drawn curtains and shades.

The interior accommodations are a little more lavish. The dark mahogany, book-filled, shelved desk with a matching chair, side shelving units, custom made to match, and a four-post bed fill one of the smaller rooms. Raymond sits at the desk, thumbing through books sprawled out in front of him. He glances at the amulet over and over, as if the object is taunting him.

The other bedroom has a wooden rocking chair next to an easel. A draft in the room threatens to send a loose piece of parchment on the easel to the ground. An oval-shaped outline of a head, roughed out by December, is now earning its eyes in light charcoal strokes. On a small table next to her sits more charcoal. She looks back to the small bed against the opposite wall fitted with sheets. Resting on it is the bloodied man, now washed and clothed. He sleeps peacefully, resting on the bed. She pulls one of the man's gloves from her pocket and curiously examines it.

Raymond finds nothing more than carvings and set jewels as he inspects the amulet. He studies it for some intricacies to identify this piece but is unsuccessful. No buttons. No latches. No hinges or any mechanism to open the charm. Its jeweled silver cage forever protects the polished amber.

A deafening, whooshing sound fills the air from out of nowhere. Raymond drops the amulet onto the desk and holds his ears.

Inside the other bedroom, December drops the glove, and the man's eyes open. He sees December frozen in confusion and pain. She turns to him, but he snaps his eyes closed, feigning sleep.

Raymond grabs a thick, closed tomb from a shelf in front of him. He opens it up to a dog-eared page. Raymond's eyes grow wide from the words he reads. He grabs an open book from the desk, flipping a few pages to a drawing of an amulet. This amulet is not jeweled like the one he holds, but it is still made of carved silver and houses an amber stone. The muscles in his face tighten more and more as his head bounces back and forth between the two books. With each passing paragraph, his face turns a darker shade of bluish red as his veins bulge from his forehead, threatening to burst at any moment.

He looks out of the bedroom door into the hallway. The random flickering of the candles turns rhythmic. He takes an almost relaxing breath and watches the flames as they rise, fall, and flicker in their sing-song pattern, as if they have a consciousness of their own. The color of his skin slowly returns to normal.

Back in December's room, her attention turns toward the flickering pattern as they silently call to her. The man in the bed watches with one eye open. December stares into the distance, listening to the silent conversation of the flickering lights. After a moment, the pattern changes rhythm and quickens its pace. December unclips and rolls up the canvas. She turns to the man in her bed, whose eyes are again closed. Satisfied that he is still asleep, she rushes to Raymond, leaving the dropped glove on the floor.

As she turns the corner into Raymond's room, she opens her mouth to speak, but no words come out. No vowel or consonant sounds of any sort usher forth. Only the sound of wind exiting and a rasping sound, like a pebble hitting a window. Raymond tries to respond, but he, too, only sounds passing air. He tries to scream, only to make the noise of calm wind. They both look around, trying in vain to yell. A realization hits December, and she stops. Her eyes widen as she realizes that the unknown man is alone. Raymond follows behind her as they hurry back to her room, leaving the amulet unguarded.

They run into her room to find an empty bed. No mysterious man sleeps soundly. No man at all. The glove she dropped is missing as well. She looks down at the parchment canvas in her hand. Raymond turns point and runs back into his room. The books on the desk are unmoved. Nothing is out of place, except for the amulet. Raymond pushes the books on his desk around, throwing them on the floor. The sound of a small stone smacking against glass chimes out each time a book hits the ground. Raymond frantically continues searching for an amulet he knows is gone.

December enters Raymond's room, causing him to stop. Raymond turns to December. However, they can only stare at each other, overcome by panic. No amulet. No voices. No idea who the man is, where he came from, or where he is going.

Allison's eyes shoot open. "That was strange." Sleep weighs heavy on her as she reaches into the nightstand beside her bed and pulls out her leather-bound parchment journal. Though the bookmark is nearing the end, she opens to a blank sheet and begins by noting the time illuminated in green neon from her alarm clock radio—3:50 a.m. She jots down details from her dream with a speed that matches how fast they are fading from her mind. This routine has become ingrained in her from nineteen years of vivid, troublesome dreams. Well, at least as long as she remembers dreaming in her nineteen years.

She hears that distinct sound again. The same noise rang through her dream—a pebble hitting the glass of her bedroom window.

She ignores it for the moment to continue writing what she can. The details fade as she tries to capture all her dream in the journal, leaving her with only broad strokes of what played out in her subconscious.

She lays back down in bed after tucking her diary away into her nightstand. Before she can settle in, another pebble smacks her window. Out of the habit from her morning ritual, she grabs her phone off her nightstand and sees eighteen missed calls from the same person—Connor.

"Allison Petrovsky! I can see the light on your phone! I know you're up!" Connor attempts a whisper from outside, but his volume is loud enough to border on shouting.

Allison shakes her head, forcing down a slight smile. She pushes her pink cotton sheets and black comforter off herself. Standing up, the young Petrovsky straightens her skull-print pajamas and steps to the window, running her fingers through her bright pink, pixie-cut hair.

Opening the window, she sees Connor looking up from below, wearing his now outdated varsity letterman jacket. The moonlight of night's approaching end shines down on him.

"It's like four in the morning. What is it?" Allison tries to keep her voice down, lest she wake her father.

"Your hair! The red. The black. The long. It's... it's…" Connor stands befuddled, staring up at her hair.

"No biggie, Con. Decided it was time for a change." Allison brushes it off.

"It's very ... different." Connor snaps back to the moment. "But it's so you. I love it."

"Thanks. Now that you've complimented my hair, can I get back to bed?" Allison's patience wears thin.

Connor's hands form an oval around his mouth, attempting to direct his voice her way. "You haven't returned any of my calls. I wanted to make sure you are holding up okay."

"I fell asleep early. I work tomorrow," Allison stops herself, "tonight. Like, after I go back to bed and wake up, I work at five. Stop by the store, and we'll talk or whatever. I'm going back to bed."

Connor's hands drop from his mouth as Allison ends their brief conversation by shutting the window. She pulls out a flask from between the bed frame and mattress. Unscrewing the top, Allison takes a couple of big swigs with an ease far more fitting for a seasoned drinker than a nineteen-year-old. After tucking the flask back in its hiding spot, she rests her head on her pillow. Allison lies staring at the ceiling, rubbing the pair of onyx-crusted pentacle earrings she's worn every day since Connor gifted them to her for her eighteenth birthday. She remembers simpler times before the existence of vampires, werewolves, undying, and other beings stole her youthful innocence. She drowns herself in those thoughts as sleep washes back over her.

Back outside, Connor stands below her window slack-jawed. Shuffling his feet back to his Camaro, his shoulders fall in dejection. He knows Allison knows it's been more than just today that she hasn't returned his calls. They both know that what her mind struggles with affects them both, thoughts of a lost life that has pushed her to solitude. She keeps her desires for another woman near her feelings on being a vampire—both filed away under D for denied. They are emotions Connor feels should be dealt with while still fresh, but each person must learn to live with themselves in their own way. So must she.

Halfway through Allison's front yard, he hears the faint yet distinct sound of a match bursting to life with flame. Startled, he turns to see Vistrus standing on the front porch, lighting a cigar. He extends a second stogie toward Connor.

Connor stares at the gesture, unsure of what to do.

"Interesting times, you could say." Vistrus puffs his cigar. Smoke circles his head, as if the universe is giving Connor a strange sign out of a video game that this man has something worthwhile to share. Connor listens to the universe and grabs the cigar.

Cut and ready to be lit, Connor glances at Vistrus for a cue on how to hold it. "Interesting times indeed, Mr. Petrovsky."

Vistrus notices Connor's uncertainty. "Never had one before, Mr. DeSalvo?"

Connor shakes his head.

Vistrus holds out another match to light Connor's cigar. "Puff, but do not inhale. These are meant for flavor."

Connor puffs as Vistrus lights up his cigar.

Vistrus looks up at the night sky while he continues his late-night smoke. "Do not worry about college."

Vistrus's words cause Connor to tense up. Falling from would-be star freshman to expelled pariah still weighs heavy on his shoulders. He waits a moment to see if Vistrus will add to his minimal dialog, but he does not.

"I'd like an education. I hear it's important," Connor half-jokes.

A hearty laugh escapes from Vistrus. "Education is about more than just textbooks and classroom lectures. You can read, can you not? Then pick up a book and learn. Life educates in more than one way."

"So I'm finding out. It's just so…" Connor's thoughts trail off as he searches for the perfect word.

"Surreal," Vistrus offers up.

Connor nods. "Yeah, surreal."

Vistrus huffs out a sad smile. "But it is not. What is happening now is as real as it gets. There is nothing surreal about anything you all are going through."

"I wouldn't know." Connor puffs on his cigar with increasing confidence.

"She will come around. She is going through a tribulation of sorts." Vistrus scruffs Connor's hair. "You know, your father would kill me if he saw me give you a cigar."

Connor's face turns a heavy shade of sad. "It's not fair. What happened, you know?" He tries to hold back his emotions as tears claw their way to his eyes.

Vistrus taps his cigar to drop a chunk of ash. "Do I have to tell you about life and being fair?"

Connor shakes his head. "No. Still sucks, though."

"That it may. For you. For your cousin Scarlett. Right now, something sucks, as you put it, for my daughter on a whole other level." Vistrus lays out the reality of their current situation.

Connor looks to his elder. "I know." A thought hits the young man, forcing him to let out a small huff. "You know, even if my father were here, he couldn't be mad."

Vistrus raises a brow. "Why is that?"

"I'm an adult—a man. No longer under his control." Connor pauses for a second. "Or, wouldn't be anyhow, if he were here."

Vistrus nods and smiles. "Now, continue to act as such, and learn to be more so a man each day. Your actions now will shape your future in The Nation. That is something Nick and I both believe you have a strong place in. Especially in the Kipling Society."

"Kipling Society?" Curiosity floods Connor's face.

"It has been a while since I talked with you about the Societies." Vistrus takes a puff to give Connor a moment to soak it in. "Are you in?" A straightforward question, yes, but his tone was anything but asking.

Connor hesitates as he takes a deep breath. His voice lowers as if others might be hiding around, listening. "I'm in because of his age and his cunning."

Vistrus's smile lifts his head. "Because of his gripe and his paw. That is the call and response of the Kipling Society, your society. Also, the only time you will hear me utter your response."

"Yeah, Grandma Eleanor wrote that on my graduation card. You told us about it all in your basement, or music room, or whatever you call it." Connor tries connecting the dots.

"It is from *The Law for the Wolves* by Rudyard Kipling. Each Legend is represented by a society named after a poet. Thus, our answer. Remember?" Vistrus relays the knowledge to the young DeSalvo.

"So, what is your Society? Your call and response?" Connor's curiosity bests him.

Vistrus takes a puff from the well-enjoyed cigar. "See, an education without a text." He smiles. "Coleridge Society. Even in a private moment, you must ask the question. The answer shall never be uttered without first being asked."

Connor's brow furrows. He does not understand the need for such a formality in present company. Still, Vistrus's philosophy on education weighs fresh on his mind, so he will learn to adhere to this ritual. "Are you in?"

"I am in a night chilly and dark." Vistrus lets those words sink into Connor's head. "If you ever ask and those words are uttered, then the person is in the Coleridge Society."

"And I respond with mine," Connor begins to speak.

"Not always," Vistrus interrupts. "Never feel compelled to answer the question when asked. If you do not feel safe answering, then do not. Trust your instinct. If you do not wish to respond to their call, remain silent. If you ask the question, they will know you are in. It is not a requirement to identify your society. The general acceptance is you do not answer back unless you are in the same society."

"Generally," Connor confirms that minute detail.

Vistrus nods.

"Am I allowed to ask what your response back would be? If he said he was in the chilly night first..." Connor inquires.

"The night may be chilly but not dark." Vistrus draws Connor's attention deeper. "But you are never to utter those words in response back. You shall never pretend to be something you are not within The Nation, even when there are those hunting us."

Connor's eyes lock on Vistrus. His breath escapes him as his lungs tighten for a moment, unable to catch any air.

"Before your parents passed, Ken found the notebook that kept you so occupied." Vistrus puffs his cigar.

Connor begins to rock back and forth on his feet. Feelings of adolescent guilt fill him with nervous energy. "I didn't think it was real. I didn't know what to think when we figured it out."

Vistrus smiles at Connor's instinctual defensiveness. "Young man, you need not defend your actions. It is understandable. We have all been there. The ludicrousness of first thinking you might be a Legend. Who would you tell? Who would believe you? If only we as parents did a better job than our own."

"Why bring it up so long after the fact?" Connor finds steeled nerves, a regained confidence that has not gone unnoticed by Vistrus.

"How you cracked the code. It brought to light a growing problem for The Nation. The Council noticed."

"I studied the book. The code-cracking was mostly Allison, actually." Connor gives credit where it's due. "Collectively, Al, Scar, and myself, but she fit the pieces together."

Vistrus smiles at Connor's ability to step away from praise when not earned. He can tell Connor has more to say.

"But the blond man is dead. So is Linda, and Max left town. Isn't the problem over?" Naivety drips from Connor's words.

"Getting rid of a few bad seeds does not cleanse a poisoned tree. You found the problem as the problem found us. Now we have to see how deep its roots grow." Vistrus looks up at the starry night sky.

Connor stands, taking in the overwhelming complexity of the whole situation. Frozen in thought, he is unsure of what to say or how to react..

"It is a lot to chew on." Vistrus extinguishes his cigar by flicking out the cherry a few times. "Drive safely, Mr. DeSalvo. I am sure I will see you soon."

Connor nods as he watches Vistrus enter his house, leaving many questions to float through Connor's head. Lit cigar in hand, Connor walks to his car. Leaning against the driver's side door, he looks up at the vast expanse of the night and enjoys the rest of his smoke in peaceful solitude, pondering his new thoughts.

Duncan Elias, decked out in his hand-decorated leather jacket, torn blue jeans scribbled upon with permanent marker, and an NWA shirt, sits on The Attic couch. Sprawled out on two of the three cushions next to him is Rex, a scrappy-built, oily-haired teen that fits every stereotype of slacker metalhead, fully equipped with a tattered, stained, just-this-side-of-dirty grime punk shirt and unwashed jeans, exuding the smell of teenage boy. Duncan manages to find comfort squeezed in his corner. On the adjacent chairs sit the rest of his old crew. Tonight, Duncan's old entourage replaces his new normal of Bri, with Scarlett and Connor's occasional appearances. The leather-clad headbangers and punks choose to embrace the rebellious side of their teen years.

Airs of old familiarity and discomfort waft through Duncan's mind of the growing notion that he joined his buddies here tonight out of some attempt to save fading friendships by rehashing the exact motions of their past. This night seems to embody the old saying, "You can never go home again." Here Duncan sits with them all, his crew from last year and countless years before, trying to make every night the apex of their glory days. Though, in his mind, Duncan knows that what stirs is not nostalgia yearning for what once was but the fading energy flickering out of what still is, as it slowly dies its tragically unhip demise.

Each passing moment in Duncan's head tells him that this group of friends, as loyal as they are to each other and he will always be to them, have lost the need to keep him near—or at least he has lost the need to keep them close. Duncan feels he is no more the lost soul wandering the lonely boardwalk of life, looking for what will indeed be accidental, misdirected guidance or, worse, intentional manipulation that will ultimately lead to their downfall. Duncan is not some lost boy with a desire to never grow old, for he does not mind what the world has shown him through Brianna. Here he sits, visiting a not-so-distant past and the old friends who still dwell there. He takes a tiny morsel of solace, knowing their time will come when they each stray from the path that longs for eternal youth.

Those sitting on the chairs talk amongst themselves about whatever topics force words out of their mouths and into the other's ears. The people on the chairs have always been the nameless sheep to Duncan. Not that he doesn't know his friends' names, but just that they are those in a flock that will remain so until they form some semblance of self-realization. It's not that Duncan thinks they are bad people for being lost. They are good at heart—just misunderstood, which was the invisible force that attracted them to each other and forged the bonds of friendship so long ago. Really, it is this person he shares the couch with that matters to him—the lost soul of the group still getting treated like the runt of the litter. The one who latched onto the friendship that Duncan offered when they first met and whose loyalty had only strengthened with each passing day they hung out. Times changed, though, as love entered Duncan's world. Love or lust or teenage hormones taking control— whatever it was—drove a wedge between the bromance that Rex felt they had. Their friendship has sprung a leak, causing the hull to fill with water and forcing it to sink while no one notices. While Rex may feel that Duncan has abandoned the ship, Duncan knows that Rex hasn't found the lifeboat of new friendships already in the water, waiting for him to board.

After an extended silence, Rex gives Duncan a stern kick in the thigh. "It's nice ta have ya back, dude." Rex's deep-dish Chicago accent makes everything dese, dems, and doz—not to mention the nasally Chicagoland Mahm instead of the proper, softer Mom. That's just Rex, Chicago-born and bred until life relegated him to the suburbs.

Duncan looks around; the uncomfortableness presses outward from inside him. "Sorry, it's been so long."

Rex rests his hands behind his head. "Got a new guitar an' amp. Figured it's time ta start a new band or somethin'." His thoughts escape him as he adjusts his red, plaid bandana. "Maybe do a solo prahject…"

Duncan looks at the stage that sits empty tonight. "What happened to The Crap Bags?"

"Crapped out, Dunc's," Rex winks. "You need ta do vocals for me."

"So much for goin' solo," Duncan reminds.

"Whatev'." Rex puts up his defenses.

"That an' I hold a tune like a fork holds water," Duncan jokes.

"But forks can't … ah. Gotcha." Rex sinks back into the couch. "No matter. Still think it'd be cool," he continues, again adjusting his bandana. Rex watches Duncan struggle to find old, familiar comfort in the company of his crew. "We missed ya a laht, Dunc. Hangin' out wit your girl, you missed a laht."

Duncan inhales the stale air of The Attic and looks around at his longtime friends, oblivious to his presence. Duncan wonders if, perhaps, they are not unaware but instead ignoring him as punishment for finding enjoyment outside their little, rebellious clique. "I can see they miss me … horribly."

Rex turns to see what Duncan sees. "Well, I miss ya, man. If dat counts for somethin'."

Duncan turns to Rex, who again futzes with his bandana. "Always messin' with that thing. If it doesn't fit right, they make more."

"Nuh. Dis is my signature look. It might be small, but it's all I gaht." Rex presses down on it, securing it in place for another moment.

"Don't sell yourself short, man. You're more than this. More than where you're headin'. Look, I think you might like Bri and her friends if ya gave 'em a chance."

Rex wiggles his back to adjust the cushion beneath. "You sayin' we expand our circle?"

They both look at the others, still ignoring the two of them.

"Somethin' like that, Rex." Though Duncan has thoughts more akin to bringing Rex to them instead of them joining the group.

"Speakin' of," Rex furthers his thought as he contemplates sitting more upright, "one of dem..." Rex waves a hand at the others, "...is bringin' a new guy in. From what I hear, he's in ta some next-level shit."

Duncan shakes his head. "How many times I gotta tell ya, ya ain't going anywhere but nowhere with that stuff. And goin' nowhere's not where it's at, dude. You're better than that, and you know it."

"Not like ya care anymore," Rex shoots back.

Duncan feels the sting of those words. He understands the reason for the shot, but knowing why someone shot you doesn't make it any less painful.

"I can't stick around to meet this new guy. Why don't you hang out with us? Meet Bri. Like I said, give her a chance," Duncan implores, standing up.

Rex looks up at him, having resigned to staying in his prone position. He stretches out his legs, dominating the entire couch. "Can't t'night. But yeah. Let's." A weak smile starts to form before dying off.

Duncan nods his head from the heaviness of newfound guilt weighing down his eyes. "I'll text ya."

As Duncan disappears into the crowd of people dancing and drinking to the house music or conversing at high-top tables, another body emerges. A man a few years older than the rest—not older enough to stick out like a sore thumb, but older enough that one might question the agenda of such an individual. His light brown hair combed neatly to the side, with a line buzzed into the part, is a stark contrast to the crowd he is here to meet. His dark green and blue plaid flannel is buttoned up and tucked into his dark blue denim jeans, free from fraying or tears. Even his face is clean-shaven and his eyebrows well-groomed. His black combat boots laced high are freshly polished as if to say nothing about him is less than perfect.

He makes an abrupt stop in front of Rex and his remaining friends, one foot snaps to the side of the other in a military-like fashion. He scans them over as they continue chattering, unaware of his presence.

Rex turns his head just enough to see he-who-stands-there out of the corner of his eye. Rex watches as the stranger stands, hands clasped behind his back and shaking his head at the sight before him. Rex is familiar with the look of disappointment on another's face. He has seen that look countless times before on those who don't— or refuse to—understand the life Rex wants to live. However, there is another look on this stranger's face, a look that grabs Rex's attention, causing him to sit up and turn forward to face this man. A move that does not go unnoticed by this newcomer. He returns the gesture with a slight nod.

The stranger's lips let a small smirk escape before he clears his throat capturing the rest of the teens attention.

"So … this is what I walk into? I see I have my work cut out for me," he scolds.

Rex stands up, stepping toward the unknown man. "Who da hell are ya, coming at us like dat? You lookin' to get funny?"

The man doesn't flinch. He moves his face closer to Rex, but the rest of him remains still and calm. He speaks with a slow and deliberate inflection, each word is as determined as the last. "Sit down, boy, or I'll sit you down."

A crushing defeat pushes Rex back down on the couch.

The man turns to one of the others. "Is this what you think is acceptable? Mingling with the likes of those?" He gestures to the strangers around the venue. "You will never be any better than you are now if all you do is sit here with these undesirables. Doomed to forever be what you are." He scans the crowd, and anger fills his eyes. "Come with me. Now." The words are a command, not a request.

The stranger turns around, and the boys follow. Rex stands from the couch. He feels compelled to follow them despite an instinct whispering to him, urging him not to go. Rex whips around to see if Duncan is still within his eyesight. He is not. Rex, unable to listen to his resistance, dashes to catch up with the rest. His only wish is that Duncan was with him.

Scarlett McAllister lies in bed, trying to find the sleep kept at bay by abstract thoughts of life, love, and her unknown future floating through her mind. She flips and flops back and forth, wrapping her blanket around her tighter and tighter, burrito-ing herself in. Struggling against the grip of the comforter, Scarlett frees her arms enough to shift to a position deemed comfortable for a few moments. Speculations about the little cousin she'll never meet stray to the front of her mind. The potential, tiny family member is now being looked after by her parents in some fantastical, clouded paradise. Ponderings stalk her brain about the reasons behind her aunt and uncle's murders, causing another sleepless night since the incident. She can't help but wonder why her life the past few years has been surrounded by death, death that has avoided her since her parents; that all gets overtaken by a curiosity about when the grim reaper will try to claim her.

Her position has become uncomfortable now, so she turns the other way to stare at her closet door, standing ajar. The darkness causes her still-adjusting eyes to play tricks on her. She watches the closet door in morbid hopes of seeing some boogeyman hand creep out from within. As if to give no reprieve from her reality, the realization hits that there is no boogeyman. Not to her and her family, at least. They are the boogeymen, or the rest of them anyhow.

A disheartening weight sinks in that, if Scarlett never transitions, she may never get to know what sort of monster she is or was meant to be. Then she quickly corrects the words in her head that only she heard. Not monster, but a human with an exceptional, autoimmune response. As suddenly as sleep can overtake someone, it can also leave. That last thought has swept away any slumber that may have been sneaking in. Her clearing mind reminds her that they are not boogeymen—that they do not like to be called such names. She doesn't think anyone would. Such names do not intend to invoke a sense of peace and calm.

A passing thought in her head whispers that perhaps her parents' deaths were related to the recent ones. Her thought dissipates like a gust of wind that blows apart freshly raked leaves. The reality is that there is no connection—that her musings would be uncomplicated fantasies to tie a bow of simplicity around complex events. But now she lies awake, staring at a boogeyman-less closet with a crowded mind, trying to find sleep that is farther away than it was minutes ago.

A distinctive chime from her phone causes sleep to sail farther away from the port of her mind. Scarlett gets out of bed, walking a few steps to grabs her phone off her dresser to see a text.

[Allison: You up?]

A quick reply, and Scarlett is back in bed, phone in hand. Before she can even settle in, her phone starts to ring. "Strange night to need me. I couldn't sleep," Scarlett answers the call.

"Connor just left, well, not just left..." Allison plays with her birthday earrings Connor gave her, "but yeah, that's not why I called."

"You can't just drop a bomb like that and then expect me not to say anything. However, in the spirit of good sportsmanship, we will get to that later," Scarlett says, tucking herself back under her covers.

"I had another dream." Allison keeps it short.

"We all dream," Scarlett retorts, lost to her reference.

"Remember? At my house ... that morning, like forever ago?" Allison tries to jog Scarlett's memory.

"Oh, yeah." Scarlett's excitement begins to shine through. "Your disturbing dreams and journal. You finally letting me into your weird little world?"

"Only if you stop calling it weird." Allison sits up in her bed. "So, it's not like the dreams are just dreams. These are different. I have normal dreams. Nice, little movies I watch while I sleep."

"Interesting description, but I get your point," Scarlett interjects to let Allison know she's listening.

"But some dreams, like the one I woke from, are different. They aren't nice, little movies. They're…" hints of hesitation seep into Allison's words, "I don't know."

"Describe them however you can. Obviously, you need to talk, and I'm not getting any sleep until you do," Scarlett urges.

"Like I'm watching a concert, or play, or whatever. Like I'm there." Allison shifts around like a cat on its back. "Maybe I'll just go back to bed."

Scarlett stands up, taking a few paces. "Nuh-uh, girl. You called me. We're doing this. We all have realistic dreams. What separates this from the rest of your dreams, besides the realism?"

"I can smell, feel, hear. All of my senses are active in these. I know they're just dreams, but after finding out my mom had them, too, it's made me want to talk more about them," Allison admits, finally finding a little comfort.

"I take it your dad hasn't found a therapist yet?" Scarlett slows her pacing.

Allison shakes her head. "I haven't bought it up, brought it up, whatever, since that day. So, no."

Scarlett sits on the edge of her bed. "What happened in the dream?"

Allison takes a deep breath. "It was old. Like, I dunno, medieval times or something. And I knew two of the people."

"Who?" Scarlett squeaks out.

"I don't know. I couldn't place them. Something was off. They were younger in my dream than in real life, but I couldn't place their faces. Just that I knew them." Allison describes her dream best she can remember. "See what I mean? How could I know they were younger than in real life if I couldn't place who they were? Are?"

Each new detail causes Scarlett to shift in her bed, like a cat kneading the blanket before lying down. Her eyes grow ever bigger over the possibilities running through her mind, regarding everything Allison's dreams might be and what she could do to help her friend.

A heaviness sets in Allison's speech as she slows to a finish. "Did you keep up with all that?"

Scarlett shakes her head, forgetting that Allison is not in the room with her. After what Allison thinks is a pregnant pause, Scarlett finally speaks, "Yes. That is a wild dream."

Allison seems disheartened. "Scar, it's not so much about the dream. I could smell the woods, the fire burning in the cabin. I could smell the mold in the bar and the stale yeast in the beer."

"And why won't your dad find a therapist who is versed in your special condition?" Scarlett settles back in bed.

Allison shakes her head. "I don't have any condition. You all are still crazy if you think I'm some vampire." Allison takes a moment to wait for a response, but Scarlett remains silent. Allison resigns, continuing, "He won't say. But do you think we can look into it? Find out if there is something there to be found or whatever?"

Again, Scarlett nods, but this time she remembers she is alone in the room. "Of course. It'll be fun. Remember the excitement when we broke the code in those notebooks? The butterflies rising in your stomach. That feeling like you can't control your arms 'cause we wanted to scream in joy at making progress? That's what this will be like!"

"Um," Allison hesitates, unsure of Scarlett's enthusiasm, "remember the dark road that Connor took? How he almost failed out of high school and lost his scholarships? How not fun that was for him? It almost killed him."

"Yeah, yeah, yeah." Scarlett waves off her friend's concern. "We're not like him, Al. It's not going to kill us."

"If you're sure you want to help. It might be nothing, ya know." Allison offers Scar another out.

"But what if it is something? That's what I'm talking about! As you always say, Betty White up." Scarlett throws down the gauntlet.

CHAPTER 2

"The most damaging lies are the ones we tell ourselves."
~I. Petrovsky~

Eleanor's hair waltzes in the breeze as she strolls the local nursery's flower selection. Hair whose gray has all but pushed out the last of the remaining traces of brown, hair belonging to a woman who has grown only more graceful in her age and wears her color just as well. She sways on her feet, humming "Greensleeves" as she smells an assortment of daisies.

A stock worker replenishing the flowers nearby takes note of her musical selection. "A little early for Christmas music, isn't it, Mrs. DeSalvo?"

Eleanor's face lights up with a frail smile. "Oh dearie, it was something much sadder and more melancholy long before someone commandeered it for a holiday tune."

"I did not know that. Always something to learn from you," the employee replies, bobbing her shoulders in amusement. "Anything I can help you with today?"

Eleanor shakes her head as she whispers the tune for the employee's ears, "Alas my love, you do me wrong/To cast me off discourteously/And I have loved you well and long/Delighting in your company."

A nearby voice joins in. "Greensleeves was all my joy/Greensleeves was my delight."

Eleanor stops singing upon recognizing the voice, a voice she hasn't heard in too many years to count. She freezes in the uncertainty that she may be wrong but also holds still by the possibility that her memory serves her correctly.

"You always did love your daisies," the man says, stepping closer to her.

Eleanor turns to see a man with broad shoulders and a sturdy build. A man over six feet tall whose weather-lined face has held onto his almost crimson-red hair color far too many years longer than it should. A barrel-chested man who doesn't need the flannel shirt he wears to inject thoughts of an outdoorsman into a passerby.

"Bishop? How long has it been?" Eleanor feigns a weak smile.

"Too long." Bishop lets that linger for a moment.

He watches as the employee behind Eleanor finishes stocking the new selection and moves from the aisle.

Bishop lowers his voice to a whisper so near imperceptible that any casual observer would think he is mouthing words to himself. "I heard. My condolences."

Eleanor squints her eyes in suspicion. "Your condolences are a little late. That shouldn't surprise me, though," she returns in similar hushed tones. "What are you doing here?"

Bishop turns to what Eleanor thought was an abandoned flatbed. "Picking up some large pavers. Redoing the driveway."

"I mean, in West Haven." Eleanor's tone shifts to no-nonsense. "You can't come back after all this time."

Bishop lets out a laugh that, to the people in the store, seems sudden and without prompt, but to him and Eleanor, it has a purpose. He returns to talking at a conversational volume. "I am my own man, Eleanor. I'm not back for you. Though with what's happened the past few years ... strength in numbers and all."

"Just like a light fairy. Disappear when no one is looking and reappear just the same." Eleanor shakes her head.

"Sometimes..." Bishop double-taps his nose with his index finger, "when they are looking." He then points it at Eleanor. "What seems like so many years for some is nothing more than passing time for others." He stops for a moment to try and capture his words, but he already spoke. "It was nice seeing you again, El."

"Take care, Bishop," she replies in a tone more suited for a business meeting than a run-in with an old acquaintance.

Eleanor turns back to her daisies. Bishop pushes the overstocked flatbed with the ease of a much younger man. Eleanor relaxes her shoulders as the distance grows between the two of them. A slight tension in the corner of her eyes pushes back countless years of emotions and memories she has yet to deal with.

Scarlett and friend-turned-frienemy-turned-friend-again Brianna Waldgrave sit in a booth at Scarlett's tchotchke-splattered work, Manic Mondays, sharing an appetizer of cheese fries. This is one of those restaurants that decorates the walls with gaudy items purchased from random yard sales. The kind of restaurant that hangs a jackalope next to a billiards rack for no reason, except to fill space and seem hip and relevant. They both casually watch the televisions in the bar as commercials play between the evening news, talking of a lethal batch of heroin that has hit the streets. Televisions surrounded by mounted faux animals and paintings custom-made for this location but still aren't of remarkable quality—all decor enough to give the just-this-side-of-Western-style wooden construction a little more life to the restaurant.

A few cowboy hat-wearing bar guests further drown their sorrows with each sip of their beer. But today, Scarlett is off from work and doesn't have to pay them any mind. Plus, a more imminent matter dominates the air. Bri tries to stay tuned in, but a cloud of melancholy hangs over her in a fog thick enough that Scarlett has taken notice.

Scarlett's copper-red hair falls in front of her face as she chows down on a cheese-smothered French fry. "She's not talking to Connor. Hell, she's barely talking to me." She brushes the wisp of hair off her face to keep from covering it in cheese. "I mean, we talked a little last night, but..." Scarlett chews on her thoughts as to whether she should share Allison's dreams with the object of her newfound desire, "it was personal. You understand."

Brianna nods, pulling a simple black hair tie from her purse. "Here. Keep your hair and food separate." She forces a smile. "Plus, it shows off your freckles."

Scarlett uses her freshly napkin-wiped hands to toss her hair up in a messy tail. Shaking her head, she replies in skeptical hesitation, "Really? My freckles? Such a love-hate thing with them."

"I used to be so jealous," Bri admits with a stunted laugh. "Own what you got."

Scarlett amuses herself with the thought that both Bri and Allison have tried to build some self-image confidence in her. To not necessarily flaunt but be proud of what she was born with is not a thought that usually runs through Scarlett's mind.

Bri sips her soda. "Returning to topic ... barely is better than not at all. I haven't spoken to her since ... that night."

"Yeah, well, doing what she did isn't something to be taken lightly." Scarlett throws another fry down her gullet.

"Which part?" Bri asks with raised brows as she hushes her tone. "When, like, she confessed her love for me in front of Connor? Or where she..." Brianna lets her sentence trail off. The thought of not just Allison's actions but also her dying mother weighs a bit too heavy to finish her words.

"Both, I guess. But I was thinking the second thing might be the more whelming, overwhelming. Whatever." Scarlett sips her soda, turning her attention to some eye-catching commercial flashing across the screen. Two bar guests at the far corner booth sitting across from each other catch Scarlett's attention—her high school alma mater's maintenance man, Raymond, and the school lunch lady, December. Both sit in quiet company to the other while occasionally jotting down thoughts in the margins of books that lay open on the table. Raymond seems to be engrossed in the text's pages.

"I used to think people who worked at a school just kinda lived there. Save your mother," Scarlett says, looking at Raymond and December.

"I've found a lot of kids think or thought that, or something like that at least. That is until they come to my house and see my mom outside school. I guess it's strange to a lot of them," Bri spouts off. Then it hits her, "Saw."

Scarlett knows things take time to sink in. Some events sink in right away. Even so, it takes time to change what you have spent your whole life accustomed to saying or doing.

Scarlett waits a moment to respond, letting Bri pull herself out of her haze. "We're used to them in that environment. At school. We think of them only as educators. Once we see them elsewhere, it has a strange way of forcing our minds to realize that people exist with these full lives outside of where we encounter them," Scarlett adds.

"Sonder, Scarlett," Bri smiles.

Scarlett tilts her head in confusion. "I know you said a word."

"It's the feeling you described. A realization that people you don't know, or the people that pass you by, have full and rich lives outside yours." Brianna offers up a rare moment of intellect.

"Sonder? Interesting word." Cautious words from Scarlett's lips.

"Thanks. Saw it on an Instagram meme." Bri's somber tone over-shadows her gloating.

Scarlett's mind relaxes upon realizing Bri isn't shining with a moment of brilliance but a remembrance of Instagram. Then a thought passes through her mind that those two things don't have to be mutually exclusive.

"What made you say all that stuff?" Bri asks, shoveling a heap of cheese fries into her mouth.

Before Scarlett can answer, their conversation is interrupted by an unexpected kiss on Brianna's cheek. Bri turns to her boyfriend, Duncan, and the fog of melancholy that had settled around Bri dissipates at the sight of him. Brianna and Duncan are the perfect picture of an odd pairing. Brianna, with her trendy clothes radiating clean-cut living, paired with a wholesome appearance, either accompanies sheltered naivety or covers up deep-seated internal conflict. Then there's Duncan, with both his clothes and pointed teenage frustration that screams defiant rebel, covering up a misplaced inferiority complex about being intelligent.

He takes a seat next to his girl as Scarlett excuses herself for a moment. "Just gotta say hi to a few people."

Duncan nods at her before turning to Brianna.

Scarlett takes cautious steps to approach December and Raymond. Neither seems to notice her, as they have become engrossed in the news story that still carries on about the bad batch of drugs. A hesitancy in her step has her questioning if she should say hello to them outside of school. She treads forward anyway, trying to calm the nerves that have stirred up. Both seem unaware as they scribble on their books, attempting to catch every word the news anchor says. Scarlett's curiosity gets the best of her, so she sneaks a peek at what they are writing and reading. Neither the language written nor read is English; it is one that she doesn't even recognize. No familiar words in Spanish, French, or other romantic languages. No Cyrillic symbols to indicate Russian or other Eastern European languages. No characters that look any-thing of Asian origin either. The letters are Roman. The words, though, are unrecognizable. One word does stick in her mind amidst the sea of jumbled letters. Not for any reason, other than it is the first she can make out in Raymond's less-than-legible hand-writing on the bottom corner of the page, in different colored ink than the rest: *Adeirrig.*

"Mr. Raymond," Scarlett says, trying to be as non-startling to the pair as possible.

Shaken from their concentration and unawareness of her pres-ence, Raymond and December slam their tombs shut and turn to her. After their moment of shock and surprise passes, a smile crosses both of their faces.

A soft, pleasant voice sounds inside Scarlett's head. "Hello, Ms. McAllister."

"It's nice to see you two ... ya know ... outside of school. I wanted to thank you. Both of you." Scarlett begins fidgeting with her hands.

Raymond's voice echoes in her mind. "No need to thank us. There are bigger things in store for you than detention for a little misunderstanding."

Scarlett looks back at Brianna and Duncan, watching them cozy up. She turns back to December. "Can I ask you something?"

"Ask what you want. Just know that the answer may not be what you want to hear." The tones of December's warning are most pleasant in some contradictory way.

Scarlett whispers, "How do you guys do that?"

Both Raymond and December smile and look at each other. Raymond turns to Scarlett, "One day, we may tell you. But here and now is not the time or place."

December's soothing tones ring in Scarlett's head. "Just know that we have been around longer than you can imagine. We observe everything."

Raymond takes the reins. "This town of ours, West Haven, has a lot more hiding under its surface than what you and your friends experienced over the last two years."

Scarlett goes to speak out loud but is cut off by December's whispers inside. "When the time is right, you will know. For now, we have our own concerns to attend to."

"One good turn deserves another," Scarlett starts. "Anything we can do to help?" She gestures to Bri and Duncan, oblivious to the world around them.

Raymond smiles. A smile that would otherwise look pleasant, save for the scar that runs through his right eye, lending him a menacing look. "Find your own voice. Then, perhaps, you can help us find ours."

December smiles. "It sure was nice seeing you, Scarlett. Take care now." She turns to her notebook but doesn't open it.

Scarlett catches her drift but is still lost on Raymond's final words. "You too. Sorry to interrupt."

Scarlett walks back to her friends, her face scrunched in confusion and embarrassment at the strange end of their conversation.

She sits back down and tosses a fry in her mouth, interrupting Bri and Duncan's make-out session.

Duncan pulls his lips off Brianna's. "What was that all about?" He returns to nibbling on Bri's neck.

Scarlett thinks a little too long about her answer. "Started as a thank-you for some help they gave me a while back."

Duncan again pulls away. "How'd it end?" He resumes with butterfly kisses.

"Not sure. I thought they were really nice. They seem really nice. But, I don't know." Scarlett has lost herself in her thoughts.

Scarlett relaxes a bit more as Brianna pushes away from Duncan.

"So, like, what, Scarlett? Spit it out," Brianna urges, sipping her soda. "How do you even converse with people who can't talk? The silent people."

"I like to think we had a good talk, but … something seemed off," Scarlett admits.

Duncan leans in and whispers, "Are they … ya know?"

All three stare at Raymond and December for a moment before turning their gazes back on each other.

Scarlett hesitates with the truth. "I don't think so."

Brianna hears the pause in Scarlett's words. "Duncan, dear, this is all way new to us. We can't know for sure. If they say no, they could be lying or reluctant to be upfront with that sort of information. If they respond properly to confirm, then we can assume yes. But even so, they may know stuff they shouldn't, ya know?"

"Legends or not, something tells me they won't be helpful to us anymore. Not like they were in school," Scarlett admits. "But only time will tell."

Duncan wraps his arm around Brianna's shoulders, extending his other across the booth back, "Well, if they are creatures of Legend and won't be on your side, which is fucked up if you ask me, at least know that I got you covered, even if I'm just a Normal." Duncan upturns one side of his lips as he nods his head. "I find that those who should be family are ofttimes the farthest thing from. And sometimes, those friends who seem to have the least in common with you are the most reliable."

Bri kisses him on the cheek. "Just look at us."

Scarlett nods. "He's a little too rebel, and you're a little too 'OMG.'"

"Oh, my God, Scarlett, I am so not," Bri blurts out.

Duncan and Scarlett toss each other a glance and giggle at Bri's expense.

"Either way, whatever they think…" Bri waves a hand in December's direction, "doesn't matter. Or at least it shouldn't matter. We have bigger problems to worry about."

"What's that, love?" Duncan steals a sip of her soda.

"Allison."

"The seeds are planted, but they have yet to grow," Vistrus says as he takes a seat in his antique, gold-riveted, red velvet chair. He reaches into the custom-made humidor stationed next to the chair on an end table. A pentacle-inspired symbol carved into it accents the rich coloring of the wood. Each point of the star is a clearly defined triangle, with depth on each side of the raised centers that peak and fall on the left and right sides and the bottom—a three-lined rise in each point. Those raised points are the basis that forms the outline of a simple house—floor, wall on each side, and an A-line roof. In the center of the pentacle, and thus the star's center, is an equal sign carved in relief fashion—encircling it all in a burn pattern.

"I have always loved that box," Nick admires the humidor.

"Calling it a box is like calling the *Mona Lisa* a doodle. This humidor is a work of art itself," Vistrus defends, handing Nick a cigar.

"I still think the symbol of The Nation on a humidor is flaunting what you are," Nick points out as he sits back on the couch next to the end table, making the marble ashtray in front of the cigar box an easy reach for both.

"Not flaunting. Pride. I do not hold Normals to substandard levels. I am proud to be the Legend I am," Vistrus responds, raising the right corner of his lips.

"I'll grant you that." Nick drops the subject. "Connor seems to be taking nicely to the idea. When I first talked with him, he was confused. He couldn't understand why they expelled him for testing positive. Or, I should say, he was confused about testing positive."

Vistrus nods. "Connor will make a fine addition. He is an intelligent young man who has come a long way."

"What about the others?" Nick puffs his cigar.

Vistrus shakes his head. "We cannot approach Ms. McAllister yet. She still has not transitioned. We do not even know which society she belongs to."

"What about your daughter?" Nick moves forward.

Again, Vistrus shakes his head. "I have my reservations about her."

Nick puffs again. "Your daughter? You can't protect her from danger her entire life."

"It is not that," Vistrus exhales. "I fear she is heading down the same path as her mother."

A tense look of concern overtakes Nick. "Her dreams are haunting her?"

"I was hoping she would be able to use them for good. Use them as Inessa first did..." Vistrus pauses his thought. He is unsure how to continue without possibly degrading his wife's memory. "You have been in this town longer than I." Vistrus waits for confirmation.

Nick nods his head. "Not much. You and Inessa arrived while we were in the beginning stages of setting up the West Haven council."

"And you never found it peculiar they had not set one up before that?" Vistrus tosses out bait to see what bites.

Nick shrugs. "I guess The Nation never deemed it necessary before."

Vistrus waits, studying Nick's eyes and facial expression. He looks for some minute gesture or tick that says he is not telling the truth. Vistrus listens to Nick's heart rate and breathing—a thump-thump of calm, collected honesty accompanies steady breaths. Vistrus trusts that Nick knows nothing of the old council. He realizes that if he can tell anyone about his discovery, Nick might be the only person he can trust.

Vistrus stands up and puffs his cigar a few times, filling the air around him with smoke. "Let us take a ride."

Nick adjusts his pants and shirt as he stands. Cigar in his mouth, he takes a puff as well. "Where are we heading?"

Vistrus smiles before leading the way. "It is a surprise."

As night settles on West Haven, the customers inside the record store Allison helps manage transition from the Barry Manilow, Maroon 5, Ariana Grande crowd to ones more styled in ripped, black jeans, flannels, and a palette for more politically charged, angry lyrics.

Allison doesn't hear the ding of the door chime as she hits play on the store's sound system to blast out the I Wrestled A Bear Once song "Smells Like Kevin Bacon" on a playlist she made for nights here. Filled with tunes by other talents like Igorrr, Tomahawk, Death Grips, and more, Allison makes her later-night customers feel more at home than the music played during the day.

After starting the song, she turns around to find Connor standing at the counter. The unexpectedness of someone standing there knocks Allison back a step before she laughs it off. Out of the corner of her eye, she sees two guests perusing the aisle with their backs turned to her.

"Got a moment?" Connor asks more out of politeness than the thought that she might not.

"I'm pretty busy, Con." Allison grabs a bottle of blue spray cleaner and a rag to begin wiping down the counter.

"You're not that busy, Al. It's been almost two months." Connor bobs his head, trying to make eye contact with her. A feat she is avoiding. "I have to get updates on you from your father. He's a nice guy for talking with me but gets weirded out when I try to make out with him." Connor was hoping for a laugh, but it only agitates her more.

Allison finishes wiping down the counter with such speed, one might think she was going to burn a hole into it before slamming the bottle down and tossing the rag to the ground, saying, "I don't need people to look out for me. I'm not some mental patient who needs tending to, attending to, whatever. I don't understand why the hell everyone is making such a big deal out of what happened."

Connor scans the store, but the only other people are the two that snuck in ahead of him. He leans toward her, lowering his voice, "Two months, love. Two months I've done my damnedest to give you your space. But it's been long enough. You haven't talked to anyone: Scarlett, Brianna, me, no one."

Allison locks eyes with him. "I haven't talked to you."

Her words hit hard. They are simple on the surface, but Connor can read between the lines into the subtext.

"So, you've been talking with who? Bri? Scarlett?" Connor's voice raises a bit.

"Scarlett ... sometimes. All right." Allison's agitation continues to grow. "She's the only one who isn't treating me like a basket case. The only one who understands it isn't a big deal," Allison shoots back.

"Not a big deal!" Connor raises his voice a little more. "You..." Connor catches himself and calms down before continuing in a much quieter whisper, "killed someone. You confessed your feelings for someone else in front of me. Never mind that it was Bri."

Allison frantically waves her finger between the two of them. "This. This right here is why I haven't returned your calls. What I said about Bri was just words. Just stuff flying out of my mouth while I did what I did. It didn't mean anything. All right? Just something to get me through the moment."

Connor's eyes grow wide. "And what you did..."

"Was justified," Allison finishes for him. "Had I not done what I did, she would have tried to kill us all. Had I not gotten the jump on her, who knows if she would have me ... on me ... jumped me. Whatever!" She calms her voice down. "The things she would have done to us. The things she had already done to Bri's mom. The things she could have done to you, Connor. What sort of pain, torture, and whatever other word fits here would she have inflicted on you?! That's not the kind of thing I want to think about or picture in my head. So yeah, what I did was justified. It was no big deal."

"And the hair? You loved your cut—the red with black tips. That was you—all of junior high and high school." Connor's concern sounds in his shaky voice.

"And that's all over. I figured it was time for something new. As I said, it's not a big deal." Allison smiles.

"Keep telling yourself that," Connor mutters but not under his breath enough. "We're here for you, but we can only push so much…"

Allison interrupts, "Then stop pushing." Allison stiffens up. "Look. I gotta start closing everything down, get out the new inventory. I'll call you tomorrow or something. We'll go out to the car show."

"What car show?" The confusion washes across his face.

"Ducky's is starting up their car shows again. Tomorrow is the grand reopening or whatever." Allison begins organizing the area behind the counter.

"We haven't been to a car show since junior high. Why start now?" Connor looks around, like he missed something in their lives.

"'Cause they have them again. Aren't you listening? It's something different than the same ol' same ol' of hanging out at The Attic." Self-righteousness slipping out in her tone.

"We like The Attic. We miss The Attic. We miss you, Al." Connor leans on the counter.

"Could you not do that? I just wiped it," Allison begs, re-wiping the counter. "Sucks, doesn't it?"

"What?" Connor takes her bait.

"Not having someone return your calls. Not having the person you love reach out to you when they are dealing with something. Being shut out of the big moments in their life." Allison shoots those words at him.

Connor knows the bullets are his to take. "I didn't know what was going on then. None of us did. I'm sorry I acted that way. Doesn't mean you have to, though."

Allison freezes, unsure of what to say. She stares at him, unblinking.

Connor waits for a response that Allison does not return. He turns away, dejected. "I do like the hair. It's pretty punk." He walks out of the store without a formal goodbye.

Allison watches as he exits through the door. "I miss you, too," she mutters.

The two people who have their backs to them turn and approach the counter. Allison lifts her head to see familiar faces, albeit out of place.

A look of misplaced recognition is plastered on Allison's face as she furrows her brow. She catches an elusive memory that tries to escape her grip; her dream of the two people losing their voices shoots fresh into her mind as she recalls her conversation with Scarlett. Allison opts for a casual approach, knowing that telling people she has had limited encounters with that she dreams of them would create a most awkward situation. "Aren't you my lunch lady and the janitor who tried to cover my ass?"

Raymond and December smile and nod. Raymond places his eclectic selection of CDs on the counter. He sounds his voice in Allison's head. "That pulling and pushing inside that you feel, the constant nauseousness, that will go away. The damage you are doing to those around you, though, may never heal."

Allison stops ringing up his purchase. She freezes, staring down at the counter, unable to look at him. A million thoughts start running through her head with memories of that night: the blood spraying about; the cracking sounds of bones crunching under her normally petite frame; the life that she caused to fade right in front of her eyes. It is a feeling she wishes she didn't have to feel. A sensation that nudges at her every waking moment since that night. A sense that invades her sleep, haunting her dreams. Every moment of every day, her mind replays that prom night. But these two, standing in front of her, couldn't know what she felt then and still feels now. Allison doesn't see how.

"You have no idea what you are talking about," Allison says and stares at the register, continuing to ring their purchases at a slow pace to see if she can fish out what they know.

A softer, gentler tone sounds inside Allison's mind. "But we do. We know more than you realize."

Allison, fighting back welling tears with every breath, looks up at them. "But you're just high school employees."

Both December and Raymond gesture as if they were chuckling, but the only emanating sound is air leaving their lungs.

December pulls out her wallet. "Our only form of communication is to talk to you with only our minds. Do you think we send telepathic communication to everyone we meet or only a select few? Do you really think we are *just* high school employees?"

Allison takes a moment to think about those words.

Raymond lifts a finger. "We know you took her life."

Allison again hangs her head.

Raymond continues, "We know why. We know why it had to be covered up. Justified or not, it is an event that will weigh heavy for far too long. Here's the harder pill to swallow." He pauses to ensure what they say takes root in Allison's thoughts. "It may happen again. You must face what happened in order to find a way to learn to live with that because, at the end of each day, you are either in or you are out. So, you have to ask yourself, are you in?"

Allison looks at him. She hears the words but isn't sure if he is asking the question or something else lost on her at the moment.

"Well, are you in?" Raymond repeats in her mind.

Allison looks around the store to make sure it is empty before answering, but even so, she hunches over and keeps her voice low. "I am in a night chilly and dark."

Raymond's voice answers back, "With the breath from their pale faces."

His words resound in her mind, words she has not heard yet. She knows he is in The Nation but does not know what kind of Legend he is. She knows she has much to learn still but feels the need to know if December is also in.

"Are you in?" Allison keeps her voice low for the off chance someone is in the store.

December lets a welcoming smile come across her lips. "I am in as they put out the star-light."

Again, words that Allison has yet to hear. She doesn't know what they mean, but there is a feeling of relaxation starting to crawl through her stomach that, despite knowing Connor, Bri, and her father are Legends, there are others out there. Allison's loneliness may have solace yet if she can admit the truth about herself.

CHAPTER 3

"How can we look to the past for guidance
to what is right, knowing now that
so much of it was wrong?"
~V. Petrovsky~

The calm atmosphere of the cemetery and fluffy clouds dotting the blue sky fill Scarlett with a sense of calm as she reads the words etched on her parents' tombstones: Hillary McAllister, Devoted wife and loving mother; and James McAllister, A family man. There are no burials in progress in some distant part of the cemetery. The silence surrounds Scarlett with a sense of security she has not felt for some time. In this moment, the last living McAllister seems to be the only breathing person.

The lack of dates on either stone is something that Scarlett used to wonder about. A missing detail that adorns so many other tombstones was, at one point, a great mystery; now it seems engraving a Legend's lifespan on a headstone would not be well-received. So, her curiosity sits more on when they might have been born.

These little moments with her parents are the only time she has with them. Time has buried whatever memories of her parents she stored in the far reaches of her mind, too deep to recall.

Scarlett leans against her mother's stone, getting dirt and dust on her work uniform. It's her peculiar way of cuddling with someone who can no longer hold her.

"This whole thing: The Nation, being who we are, seeing them do what they do—it is all so much. Allison ... my Al, killed someone. How is she going to deal with that? How can we help her deal with that? Especially now. She has avoided any conversation, dodged any mention of it since that night. The Nation, whoever they are, already seemed to have swept it under the rug of justifiability, but something seems wrong. I feel like The Nation is a lot of talk about doing things, but when it comes time to do those things they talk about ... that's all they are. Talk and no show. Bark and no bite. I don't know. All I know is that so far, I sat by as Mr. P. covered up the deaths of multiple people on multiple occasions. Something feels off. But what the hell do I know? I'm nineteen and just learning these things about myself."

Scarlett watches a murder of crows fly overhead. The stillness of her surroundings envelopes her as her mind begins to stir.

"Bri and I have grown closer again. It's funny. Now that high school is over, I think there is a lot that could have been different. I wish there were some things that, well, *were* different. Jack, his parents not being killed. I'm not sure what's worse, the fact that he died or the torture he went through, endured, and suffered before being killed.

"So many things, Mom and Dad. So much has been going on. Allison admitted she was in love or loves, or whatever, with Brianna. Even Bri is worried about her. Al won't be around her just as things are starting to feel like the good ol' days. Ya know, before high school tore us apart. I feel like she is making me choose between her and Bri. Not so much in words, but I can feel it. Make sense?"

Scarlett takes a deep breath as her thoughts escape her.

"But on the other hand, Al is having me help her with her dreams. I never told you guys about them. I never really knew, so." Her thoughts on introducing this topic to her parents wander away. "Anyway, her mom had dreams; they think it's what drove her mad. Except now, we are learning things. That maybe her mom wasn't so crazy after all. I'm gonna help her decode 'em. Delve into her subconscious and face the beast within." Scarlett scrunches her face. "I don't think Al would have liked that word choice. It'll be inter-esting, for sure. She worries that if we get too involved, we could end up like Connor did, or almost did ... whatever. I told you about that, though. I don't think we'll get that bad. We're stronger now than we were. But isn't that the way it goes?"

She huffs out a small laugh as she stares toward the sky. Her thoughts linger in the space beyond the clouds for a moment before returning her gaze to the tombstones.

"Work's slow. Got off early, so I thought I'd swing by. In case you were wondering why I was here on a Saturday."

Scarlett continues filling her parents in on the thoughts invading her mind. The sky above stays calm in some cosmic effort to keep Scarlett grounded. She wraps up her conversation, feeling more unsure about the uncertainty of it all. She knows her parents aren't answering her, but still, talking through things out loud with them helps her process everything ... most of the time. She isn't sure if it is the current state of things, the fact that high school is over and behind them, her coming to terms with all her friends being Legendary, that she still hasn't figured out what type of Legend she is, something still heretofore unseen, or a mix of things. But Scarlett leaves the cemetery feeling less accomplished, more unfocused, and further from an idea of what to do than when she walked in.

She stands up and looks down at her parents' stones. "One day." She places a hand on each of their tombstones for a moment. "I love you, Mom and Dad."

Rex and his three friends sit crowded but at attention on a dilapidated couch. The couch stuffing peeks through where the fabric has worn out. The middle bows in—from a few feet away, it looks like a crooked smile. In the otherwise nondescript room, pacing in front of them is the man who commanded them here—Ashby. His military-style mannerisms dominate every action. He looks around the room, taking in the collapsed ceiling's decay, overturned table, and battered walls. This room is the epitome of the opposite one would think a person with Ashby's apparent discipline would step foot into.

Ashby's leather bomber jacket is puffed out a little in the chest. He stops pacing and turns to the boys. "There are things in this world that, frankly, are not long for it." He pulls down his jacket zipper with a slow, deliberate motion. "But you four…" He makes eye contact with each of the boys on the couch. "You all are worthy. I can see the potential within you."

Rex adjusts his signature bandana before raising an unsure hand. "Um, worthy of what? I heard ya had some next-level philosophy on life and drugs. I'm just here for the goods, dude."

A wry smile crosses Ashby's face. "I am glad you mentioned those. What I have is not just some drug. It is a trial. A test of constitution. To try the endurance of the human body by bringing you to a higher level."

Each of the boys exchanges glances. The uncomfortableness of the situation makes them shift in their seats, as if adjusting their bottoms will make the situation less surreal.

Ashby continues pacing. "For too long, I have watched my people be pushed aside by those who think they are like us. For too long, I have seen my brothers lose out on opportunities to those lesser than us. I am part of something whose only desire is to bring us back to our rightful place at the top." The volume of his words increases in direct relation to the passion growing as he speaks. "No more shall we sit and watch as others thin out our kind. No more will we sit back as lesser beings quietly invade our cities like cockroaches. We are the ones who have worked and fought and struggled to survive while they come here and leech off what we have built."

The boys all find themselves nodding along to his words—enamored by the intense fire in his speech. Rex, however, tries not to raise his eyebrow. He sees his friends eating every word Ashby spits out for them, like a mother bird regurgitating food for her young. Rex turns back to the speech so his eyes do not wander.

Ashby stops pacing and breaks eye contact with the group. Reaching into his inside jacket pocket, he pulls out a small, leather, zipped-up case. He opens it to reveal four syringes filled with a liquid, the color of which is unlike anything the boys have ever seen before. The hue is something like a swirling blue, somehow translucent and opaque at the same time. He sets it on the only upright table in the room, which wobbles from a bent leg but can still support the lightweight pouch.

Ashby takes a syringe, holding the needle's point upright. "This is the test. No one wants to be unworthy. The people I represent, those that call each other brothers, have all passed this test. I know you all will, too."

He pushes the syringe's plunger, enough for a bit of liquid to shoot out. He hands one syringe to each of the boys. "No need to tie off. Just do what you do."

Each of them holds the needles to their arm, hesitant. Rex looks up. "Ya don't look like anyone who'd … partake. So, why offer?" Then a thought crosses his mind as the glaring differences between them and this stranger light up the room. "Why do ya want to join us?"

Ashby nods his head. "I was like you once. Without direction, wandering aimlessly in a world with which I was so angry for no reason—rebelling every chance I could, if only for rebellion's sake. This..." he gestures to the moment around them, "will be the last time you feel the sting. The last time you ever think about mirrors and lines. The last time anything goes into your body that is not meant to be."

Rex nods his head at those last words, fidgeting with his bandana.

"But this..." Ashby throws up a finger to the ceiling, "this is meant to be."

Rex watches as his friends all inject the strange and unknown liquid into their arms. Again, he wants to run but doesn't. Instead, he succumbs to the pressure of his peers and is the last to inject. A warm pulse creeps through his body, filling every nook and cranny until a cozy feeling washes over him. He leans back in his seat. His body feels lifted, as if floating on a cloud. His eyes start to close.

Just as suddenly as the liquid warms him all over, it changes. The warmth rips itself away. The cozy feeling of floating has hit the ground at terminal velocity. His pupils widen as they fix their gaze on one of his friends. The world around Rex pulsates and breathes as if the walls, floor, and furniture are alive. But even as his surroundings inhale and exhale, it is the changing features of his friend from which he and the others can't look away. His eyes are locked as his friend's skin stretches and pulls taught. The stretch marks forming before his eyes, the veins that bulge through the surface, trying to explode all over the world around him, and the long hair thinning, exposing scalp, have Rex's mind running in circles, trying to rationalize what his eyes are taking in.

"It hurts!" his friend screams as his skin pulls so tight it is almost transparent.

The other two friends turn to each other, unsure of what is happening, smiling as if this is just some strange, psychedelic effect of the drug, but they do not laugh.

"Someone help!" Rex's friend continues shouting, arching his back in pain. He lunges at one of his friends and grabs them by the shoulders. "What is happening?!" His grip tightens, and a sharp, loud snap resonates through the room.

Unintelligible screaming is all that his friend's mind can produce as he lies on the ground, unable to move his arms. The last of Rex's group steps in to protest the happening. "Dude, bro. You can't do that." He pushes out his arms to shove the transitioning friend but does not budge. The newly hypertrophied muscles hold him in an unmovable defense. In turn, he pushes his friend, unaware of his newfound strength. His friend slams against the wall and slumps down. The newly minted Legend turns to Ashby, growling, "What have you done?"

"Discovered that you do not have what it takes." Ashby pulls out another syringe, this one filled with a clear liquid. Stepping toward him, he says, "Come here. I will help you." His words carry a cubic-zirconium authenticity.

Rex's friend turns to him, desperation in his eyes. "Run!" He grabs Ashby like a rag doll, tossing him through the unsteady table. Rex seizes the opportunity, dashing for the door. Ashby springs up, undaunted by being thrown, and lunges for Rex. Ashby reaches out to grapple Rex around the neck but only manages to grab his red bandana. Ashby tosses the cloth to the ground, but before he can reach out again, the transitioned one grips Ashby, ripping away his chance at stopping Rex. Rex opens the door as cries for help from the floor flood his ears. Rex sees his friend unable to move from two broken collarbones. His friend who hit the wall drifts in and out of consciousness. Rex stops for a moment, deciding if he should stay.

"Run!" His fully transitioned friend roars again.

The last thing Rex sees is his friend, in all his hulking form, bent down over Ashby, who holds up the syringe, jabbing it into oversized muscles. Rex slams the door behind him as he runs off. He knows what he saw was more than some effects of the drug. As Rex runs down the dark hallway, his mind can't separate fact from drug-induced fiction.

Vistrus and Nick sit in Vistrus's office at the West Haven Museum of Natural History & Art. Years here have filled his office shelves with books on various topics and framed pictures of him and his deceased wife, Inessa, him and Allison, and one of Inessa holding Allison. His desk is clean and organized; even the stack of acquisition papers needing signatures sits in a pile off to the side—all nothing more than work to keep him busy the following days.

Nick runs his hand through his receding gray hair, giving it a wild look that isn't too far past his growing impatience. Vistrus can already hear Nick's heart pounding harder in his chest but is still determining if it is beating more from guilt Nick is hiding that he didn't detect earlier or something else.

"What was so important that you had to wait 'til we were at the museum to tell me? Time may be on my side, but I don't like being dragged along." Nick runs his hands back through his hair, trying to straighten it.

"Hypothetically, can you think of why The Nation would hide something from The Council?" Vistrus throws out.

Vistrus continues to listen to Nick's heartbeat for a telltale sign that his earlier deemed innocence was false. Not that Nick has ever given Vistrus a reason to think he was anything but forthcoming and honest, but new information means having to look at things in a new light. Not everything, nor everyone, will look good under all the lights.

"The Nation is a governing body. They've been around longer than we have. If secrets were kept, they have their reasons," Nick raises a brow.

"If that secret was related to West Haven, do you not think it would be important enough to fill in at least The Council members?" Vistrus continues.

"Get to the point," Nick urges, his heart pounding with more anger than before.

"Something is going on with The Nation." Vistrus does not hear the cryptic tones coating his words.

"Choose your words wisely. We are both on The Council. We have obligations," Nick warns.

Vistrus hears Nick's heart start to calm. His blood pressure settles back down as the thump-thump of his heart softens. Perhaps his loyalty to The Nation, while strong, is not as blind or unquestioning as Vistrus thought.

"I understand. And you will do what you must. But a part of me thinks we were not the first Council," Vistrus continues.

"Without proof, baseless accusations can be grounds for your removal from The Council," Nick amends his warning.

"What if I had proof? What if I could show you something that, at the very least, raises doubt?" Vistrus stands from his chair.

Nick also rises from the opposite side of the desk. "If you are able to raise a doubt, I will keep my thoughts out of The Council's ears for now. If such proof exists, then my thoughts on The Nation may undergo a forced reevaluation."

"Then it is time." Vistrus exits the room. Nick follows Vistrus down artifact-filled halls with vaulted ceilings, covered in masterfully painted murals. They stop at an elevator labeled "Employees Only" not far from the Egyptian sarcophagi on loan. Nick scans his surroundings, giving in to a sinking feeling that not all is well.

"I need to know this is going somewhere, Vistrus." The irritation swells in Nick's voice.

The elevator doors open, and Vistrus steps inside. "The walls in this place have ears. We are almost there."

Nick steps in, and the doors shut. A short ride later, they emerge in the museum's temperature-controlled vault facilities.

"Few are allowed down here. If anyone stops us, do not speak," Vistrus warns.

Nick heeds Vistrus's words with an understanding nod.

A relatively short and uneventful walk later, they find them-selves in the rear of the vault—storage for the replicas and unim-portant set decorations. A fortunate place of relative needlessness because, even if employees were lurking around at this hour, they would not be in this spot. Vistrus has since cleared away the cob-webs that once took hold of this area.

The cyclopean architecture comprising the vault's back wall is different from the poured concrete of the rest. Vistrus makes quick work, finding the spot where he first removed weakened mortar from the wall to forge a finger-sized hole, leading to the hidden switch. One that leads to a long-forgotten door, that is until Vistrus read his wife's diaries.

As the stone door reveals itself from hiding, Vistrus can hear the excitement build in Nick's heart with each passing breath.

The smell of lingering mildew and dust assaults their nos-trils while they walk down the hall. Vistrus shuts the secret door, hiding them from the outside world and shrouding them in dark-ness so complete that neither man can see, despite their heightened sense of sight.

Nick stops. "What is this? I can't see."

Vistrus taps the screen on his phone to start the flashlight, illu-minating the hallway enough for them to traverse to the other end. "This should do."

An amused huff escapes Nick. "Been a while since I was unable to see in the dark."

Nick looks around the hallway constructed from the same cyclo-pean architecture as the door and a sloped cobblestone walkway leading down to what seems like a dead end. This dead end changes the architecture once again. No longer are the stones cyclopean. Large solid blocks of marbled lime and obsidian serpentine stone-work comprise this wall.

Vistrus again reaches for the switch to open yet another secret door. He can hear Nick's heart beat ever stronger. The blood rushing through his veins creates an ocean wave sound in the room's back-ground, a sound they can listen to because of their Legendary disposition.

Vistrus turns to Nick. "Are you ready?"

Nick nods while keeping his stare on the wall in front of him as the second secret door creeps open.

Vistrus motions for Nick to step into the darkened room first. "After you."

Connor pulls into a parking spot overlooking the car show. At the bottom of a tiny hill about twenty feet high sits the restaurant that hosts tonight's event, an old Chicagoland one-off called Ducky's. The place is an old-school-style hot dog joint with tiled floors and walls. The tables look like they came straight out of some 1950s diner. A line of people stretches from the register to food pickup, overlooking the kitchen.

This line to the pickup area is where Connor ends up, while Allison and Scarlett search for an open table on this crowded night. By the time Connor walks up to the girls with food in hand, they have yet to secure a spot.

"Eat and walk?" suggests Connor.

Scarlett nods in defeat. "Always fun to be hanging out at the other end of my work parking lot."

"It's a strip mall with restaurants on each end. It's not like we're close to your work." Allison heads to the side exit.

"If I can see the building, I'm too close," Scarlett jests as they step outside.

"Then pay attention to the cars. After all, this is a car show," Connor offers up, finding themselves amidst the custom cars.

The group takes a few moments to appreciate all the cars on display. Various makes and models, from modern to classic and vintage, fill the main lot. Some car owners show off their superior sound systems with short blasts of music. Others are hopping around on hydraulics. The majority of car owners opt for the classic show model of clean, custom paint jobs, custom trim, souped-up engines, transmissions, nitro-burning, etc. Any way it goes, the music blares out of the restaurant's exterior speakers, reminding customers of the 1980s and '90s hair metal and grunge greatness.

Scarlett eyes a shiny purple muscle car whose enhanced engine juts through the roof, flames shooting out the custom tailpipe. "Talk about souped-up."

"Souped-up for sure. That engine and flame kit costs more than the rest of the car," Connor notes.

"Supercharged. Not souped-up," Allison interjects, admiring the car's modifications.

"Same thing," Scarlett responds. "Supercharged. Souped-up."

"Actually, not. The term 'souped-up' dates back to pre-hot rods, having equestrial roots." Allison has earned both Connor and Scarlett's full attention.

"I don't think 'equestrial's' a word, but we follow ya," Connor offers. "Go on."

"An-y-way, the Webster people added the term to the dictionary around 1910 or so. Owners used to illegally drug horses to make them perform better for races back in the early 1900s. They called it 'giving the horses their soup.' Thus, 'souping them up.' So yeah. Thanks for coming to my TED talk," Allison finishes, turning back to the display of cars.

"How the hell do you know that?" Connor wraps his arm around her.

"Daddy told me after he tweaked something on his Porsche," Allison gloats.

"I think equestrial shall henceforth be a word," Scarlett declares. "Of or having to relate to something equestrian."

"Wouldn't that just be equestrian, then?" Connor tries to confirm.

But before Scarlett can respond, a familiar voice calls out to them, "Scar, Con, Al!"

The three of them turn to see Brianna waving as she weaves through the crowd to meet them, Duncan in tow.

Scarlett tries to sneak a glance at Allison to see if she is alright, but her stare fixes on Brianna. A strained look is painted on Allison's face, as she fights the mental demons still haunting her. A need within her rises to somehow absolve herself of her actions against Linda Espinoza, though Allison rationalizes her actions as justified, since Linda killed Sylvia, Brianna's mother. A desire within that Brianna understands what Allison feels, and a small part of her hopes Brianna feels the same.

Allison is lost in her thoughts as she watches the world around her play out like some movie on an old silver screen. She hears the voices, but the words are blurred. There's nothing but background noise as she tries to focus all the rage that led to months of isolation and feelings so indescribable that she has yet to put them into words. Besides ignoring her friends, her only action of note is the radical change in hair color and cut. Then she notices Brianna smiling at her and, like a bolt of lightning, all the voices around her flash into sharp focus.

"I love the new hair, Al," Brianna compliments, running her fingers through it. "And the bleach and color didn't even damage it."

Allison stands in shock. The feeling of Bri's hand through her hair sends a tingle down her spine. An excitement she thought she was ready to deal with but not now, not at this moment in a very public, very crowded place. She jerks away from Brianna.

"I'm sorry. Didn't mean to…" Brianna holds her hands to her side.

Allison is quick to shake her head. "It's not … just unexpected. I'm glad you like it."

Allison attempts to regain her calm and grab control of her emotions, but every little noise around her seems to make things worse. The sound of the cars revving their engines, the thud of hopping tires smacking against the pavement, and the bass pounding from the speakers, yelling about how it's eighteen and life to go all overtake her senses, amplifying every slight sensation. Connor wraps his arm around her to calm her down, only agitating her more. She pushes him, doing a quick turnabout, and begins hiking up the hill away from her friends.

"Allison!" Connor calls after as he begins to follow.

"I'm sorry. I didn't mean to. I just liked her hair," Bri apologizes, unsure of what she did wrong.

"It's cool. She's still a little on edge about things." Scarlett tries to clarify while chewing the last of her fries.

Connor jumps the last half of the hill and lands a few feet from them. Not as graceful a landing as he had hoped for, but being cool isn't a terrible concern of his right now.

"That was quick," Scarlett notes, slurping her soda.

"I don't know what to do. She won't talk to me. This night was her idea." Connor shrugs, lost for words.

Duncan finishes the last of his fully loaded Chicago-style hot dog. "Let me give it a swing." He licks his fingers clean as he treks up the hill to Allison.

Duncan is quick to track the not-so-quiet sounds of her rapid, labored breathing and panicked moans as she sits against the tire of some random car with her head between her knees. He approaches but doesn't say anything or even clear his throat to draw her attention. Duncan finds a seat on the ground against the car across from her, facing each other. This way, he can keep her company while she works through her attack.

He does notice that her skin is tightening around her cheeks and eyes. He watches as tiny red veins overtake her nose, a feature he's only seen in old-aged alcoholics. But then he notices her skin pulling tighter as her nose starts sinking into her face right before him. Blood begins dripping from her mouth. Slow at first, like a trickle from a leaking pipe, but within a few seconds it turns into a small stream. A few teeth tumble out as her hysterics take to new heights. Duncan watches as her hair thins but otherwise stays short and pink.

While Duncan was privy to her last transition, he did not have the chance to observe it from such an academic viewpoint.

"I understand why you feel the way you do about her." Duncan remains calm and clear in his words.

Allison lifts her head enough to be able to look at him. His words seem to start sedating her breaths.

"She is beautiful. She's not as dumb as she comes across, but she acts that way 'cause she's conflicted ... confused about life. But I think you know all that."

Duncan continues as he watches Allison's transition slow its progression.

Allison continues keeping an eye on Duncan, listening to his words. She doesn't notice ... or chooses to ignore ... in her peripheral vision that Raymond and December slow their pace as they walk past. Their heads look in Allison's direction, but they don't stop. They do not check up on her to make sure she is okay—a signal that they either trust Duncan will handle the situation aptly, they hold a metaphorical, bright neon sign glowing the word "apathy," or they figure she does not want the added attention. Either way, Allison is okay with their passing.

"Society has these expectations, and as much as they're changing, they're staying the same. It's no easier coming to terms with these feelings that are different or new nowadays than it was ten or twenty years ago. Even if society is shoving it down everyone's throat that it's okay to feel any way you feel, each of us knows the ways those around us will feel. Or at least think they know the way those around will feel." Duncan continues laying it on thick for her.

"How … would … you … know?" Allison whispers through heavy, pained breaths.

Duncan lets out a slow smile. "I know. Everyone has the same, initial, preconceived perception." He gestures to his leather jacket, metal T-shirt, ripped jeans, and flannel.

Allison's migraine brought on by her transition strikes down her attempt to smile. She turns her head to the ground and grabs it with hands that have varicose veins covering a vast majority of the surface and thick, long nails that could rend flesh.

Duncan continues, "I had a crush on this one guy. Long before I ever admitted it to myself. Something I'd never tell my family. Stuff like that is kept on the down-low."

A hushed gasp is heard close by as feet stop in front of them. Duncan looks up to see Rex.

"No," Rex mumbles with squinted eyes. His focus wavers as much as his unsteady feet. "Not here. Not again!" He points at Allison with a swaying finger.

Allison looks up without thinking. "Go away," is all she manages to get out before he interrupts again.

"Your face! Ya got no nose! Is dat what he'll become?" Rex looks to Duncan for answers.

Duncan hops to his feet, grabs Rex, and moves them so he can no longer see Allison.

Duncan takes a good look at Rex's glassy eyes and observes the constant scratching at his arms. "I won't become dat," Rex blurts out as Duncan tries to steady him.

"What are you on?" Duncan holds Rex back from peeking at Allison. "Hey! Rex! What you on?"

Rex cannot keep a steady gaze on Duncan. "I dunno. I was dere. Den he started changin', man. Like, like it was all a movie or somethin'. Den I see her."

Duncan gives Rex a slight slap to grab his attention. "Leave her out of this."

"It's like everyone's a monster, man. Dis is so not cool." Rex laughs at the absurdity of his words. He goes to adjust his missing bandana. Upon realizing it's gone, he looks at the ground around him to see if it is there.

"Hey, Rex! Where's your signature cloth?" Duncan scans the ground with him.

Rex again runs his hand through his hair. "I dunno."

Duncan grabs Rex's arm and sees fresh track marks. Rex pulls away as a realization washes over his face. "She's a vampire! Dat's what he was tryin' ta cure."

Duncan shakes his head while steadying Rex's stare on him. "No, she isn't. She's not some make-believe creature. She's not a fairy-tale monster or boogeyman or some other crazy storybook creation. She's having a bad day. She fell in some mud and needs to wash her face. Understand?"

Rex shakes off Duncan and backs away to stare slack-jawed at Allison. "Bro. You left me with dem. Ya don't understand. Monsters don't exist. Or dey shouldn't, but dey do. Dey do when ya take what I've taken. Ya left me when I needed ya, man. All for what?"

Allison snares her thinned lip, growling. Rex continues, "Some blonde piece? Ya left me with things that I shouldn't see. No. Things that shouldn't be, but dey are. Dey are, man!"

Allison lunges at Rex. Her fists land square against his chest, flinging him back onto the hood of a silver sedan. Rex's head connects against the windshield with a loud thud.

Before either Rex or Duncan can react, Allison pounces on top of him. "Don't you dare say we should not be." A mixture of drool and blood spills from her mouth onto Rex's face. She presses a thick, claw-like nail into his cheek.

Tears stream down Rex's face as an uncomfortable laugh creeps out. "My eyes show me da truth. Dat I am meant to be. But I see things dat can't be real. Vampires? Monsters? I dunno, Duncs. Duncs, ya don't know. Ya don't see what I see, do ya?"

Duncan stares at the two of them, trying to decide his course of action as he stands beside Allison.

Rex's laugh turns to a pleading. Tears continue streaming down his face. "Ya left me for some flavor of the month. Ya threw me out like yesterday's garbage."

Allison rolls Rex off the car and onto the pavement. "No one is garbage. No one."

Rex stands up, unsteady on his feet. He stares past Duncan as his eyes dilate, and his skin loses color. An ungodly noise emanates from his chest, a noise so distorted and vile that Allison and Duncan stare at each other, unsure of what to do. Again, the noise emanates, and Rex lurches forward. He bends at the waist, mouth open, toward the ground as the noises continue. Noises so twisted and scrambled that Duncan and Allison are rendered motionless. Rex stumbles away from them as the noises continue, his throat joining in the demon-summoning orchestra playing within him, like a reject sect of Tibetan throat-singing monks. He does not vomit, though. The dry heaving seems to be all he has.

Allison hides her face back between her knees as Rex distances himself. She sits, weighed down in confusion by his words. Her mind is heavy, trying to understand the meaning of them. She struggles to breathe under the significance of the events.

Rex points at her. Words escape through his dry heaves. "He said … dere will … be a reckoning. Dat da … cure … is comin'." Allison can't even lift her head to look at him.

Duncan shakes free from his motionlessness and fixes himself between Rex and Allison. "We'll talk later, Rex. No one's abandoned you. Just keep your mouth shut." Duncan watches Rex stumble off, mumbling to himself.

Meanwhile, inside Ducky's, a tall, lithe man standing around six foot three stands on a chair, towering over the patrons. His long hair and tattered Skid Row tour shirt lend him a retro badass vibe that has stuck with him since the band was all over the radio waves. He holds a microphone to his mouth with one hand and waves his other arm in the air.

Connor, Scarlett, and Brianna finish the last of their meals from a corner table as the awards begin for the night's show. Scarlett notices only a few booths from them, next to a window, sit December and Raymond. She smiles at them, nodding her head. Raymond nods back, his scar making the friendly gesture seem more ominous than it should. December gives her a courteous smile before both return to their hot dogs, fries, and bottled beer. Scarlett recognizes that her silent acquaintances seem not to want any attention, so she leaves her acknowledgment at that.

The music on the speakers dies down as the microphone's power is turned on. A muscular man of short stature donning dreadlocks and a Dr. Dre shirt stands on the floor next to the announcer, holding an award. On the table next to him sits a box with a few trophies to be awarded.

A raspy voice, with as much energy as he is tall and his hair long, rips through the speakers, "It's been too damn long since we've had a car show here!" The crowd cheers as he holds the microphone to them. "Thank you all so much for making this return so amazing! And thank you to Ducky's for making this our home!" The tall man's energy invigorates the crowd. "We are keeping all our old categories for awards. That said, let's get this show goin'!"

As he looks down at the trophy handed to him to read the category and winner's name, written on a Post-It stuck to it, Rex crashes through the door, blood and spit still smeared on his face, stopping himself on the first table he can and sending the table's food and drinks plummeting to the floor. The dry heaves subside as the table hits him in the chest.

The seated patrons are too busy trying to avoid the soda, ketchup, and other condiments being spilled on them to say anything to Rex.

The rest of the crowd turns their attention from the ceremony to the disturbance.

Rex waves his arms as he sways back and forth while getting back up. "Dere's ... a ... a ... a monster! A monster thing! Dey exist!"

The urgency in his voice sends red flags up for the group of friends. The rest of the crowd remains ignorant of life's greater secrets.

"A dead-alive woman, man! Like, a She-thing!" Rex tries to urge the crowd his way, but his intoxicated demeanor ruins his credibility.

Except Connor, Scarlett, and Brianna know very well who he is talking about. Connor stands up and makes his way to the interruption. Scarlett tosses a glance toward her elder Legends.

Raymond and December both eye each other. December turns to Scarlett and gives a discreet shake of her head no. Both she and Raymond look out the window next to their booth. From their vantage, they can see the silhouette of Duncan up on the hill but not of Allison.

Scarlett knows that despite their rejection, she must go with Connor. She and Brianna are quick to catch up as Connor drags Rex outside.

Connor notices the dilated pupils, colorless skin, and breathing that is too shallow for having just been so excited.

"Bri, go get some water, a soda, something for him to drink," Connor commands.

Brianna runs off to grab her cup for a refill.

Connor holds up the boy as they walk to the side of the building.

"Wait here for Bri. We'll be right around the corner," Connor informs Scarlett.

Scarlett nods her head before he turns out of sight.

"What did you see?" Connor shakes Rex to gain his attention.

Rex's focus improves for a moment. "Dey look like dat vampire from dat old, creepy flick." His eyes grow big. "But worse, man. No nose. Blood just pouring from its mouth." He wipes his face to show the blood on his hand. While staring at his hand, a switch flips inside his mind. "I am meant ta be. I was told! Dat's what he told me! But Duncs left me. He shouldn't have!" Rex fades his speech by the end. His gaze fixes downward, past the ground to whatever might lie below.

Connor tries to remain calm, but his nervousness causes his heart to race faster. He can feel his muscles begin to enlarge.

Connor notices Rex losing focus and fading from consciousness. He plants a firm slap on his cheeks to wake him. "Hey! Hey! Stay with me! Where did you see this!?"

Rex turns his head in the direction of the hill. His arm is too weak to point as he attempts to wave it in that direction. "Up by da cars, dude."

Brianna and Scarlett turn the corner and pour water into Rex's mouth. He gulps it down, regaining some awareness.

Rex struggles to give an appreciative nod. He regains his footing, though still unstable. "Watch out for da monsters." His words turn inward as he continues babbling, "He'll tell me who is not meant ta be. I'm meant ta be. He said so. Never mentioned da monsters, Ashby did." Rex throws his hands to his head. "Wow. I think I overdid it, man." He stumbles off toward Allison and Duncan.

The three of them stare at each other, unsure how to handle this situation. Scarlett points at Connor and Brianna, then points up the hill, telling them to find Duncan and Allison. She then motions she is heading back inside for something.

Connor and Bri take off toward the crazy stranger. Connor catches up with a blinding speed, even unexpected to himself, though Rex is already standing back at the cars where he saw Allison's transition, towering over her and Duncan.

Inside Ducky's, Scarlett stands tableside to December and Raymond, "Please! We don't know what to do!" Her plaintiff cries fall on deaf ears.

Raymond stares out the window at the scene unfolding up the short hill. December looks at Scarlett, but the young McAllister's head is silent.

Scarlett furrows her brow as she stares back at December. "I don't know if you can hear me," she starts in her mind, trying to project her words into December's head, "but that guy is drawing attention to Allison. If she gets outed, you know as well as I do that people will not be kind or worse."

She waits, hoping for a reaction that never comes. Decembers give a sad smile as tears begin to well in Scarlett's eyes.

"Fine," continues Scarlett. "Sit on the sidelines and do nothing. I thought you were with us."

Raymond turns his attention away from the window to Scarlett. "It is not a matter of being with or against you. There are no sides here. It is a matter of learning how to live in your world and dealing with things yourself."

"So that's it!" Scarlett shouts in her head. Tears start to fall. "You just brush us aside?"

December loses her smile. "We are not brushing you aside. We have our own worries that, believe it or not, have nothing to do with you or this immediate situation. We can't risk anything."

"Your own worries?! Don't we all? Some people still find it within themselves to help others. I guess that is too much to ask from you, though," Scarlett scorns before turning away.

As she exits the restaurant, December's voice sounds in Scarlett's head, "Breathe slow. Remain calm. Think about more than the immediate problem. You have this. You don't need us."

Back on the hill, Duncan stands to block Allison from Rex's view. "What are you doing, bro?"

"Someone needs to see dat I belong. Proof dat I do belong. Proof dat da monsters are real." Rex's swaying worsens.

Connor and Bri both step toward Rex.

"Don't call my friend a monster. You have no idea who you are messing with," Bri threatens in a tone beyond the cruelty that even her popularity exuded.

Connor pushes Rex against the car. "Ever call my girl a monster again, and I'll make sure that every person you pass on the street can only respond to you the same way."

Rex sobers up for a brief moment as the gravity of Connor's words sinks in. A meek chuckle escapes him as the false sobriety wears off. "I need ta belong somewhere. Ya don't understand."

Connor shoves Rex out from between the cars, causing him to stumble. Rex loses his footing and hits his head on a car in the next row, leaving a nice dent in the side.

He falls to the ground but, despite his efforts, can't get up.

Connor turns to Allison still seated on the ground with her head between her knees. He sees her thinned hair and the thick, claw-like nails on her bony hands. He starts to rub her back in an effort to calm her.

Duncan steps to Rex, still struggling to get to his feet. "Rex, my man. I told you to forget what you saw because you didn't see anything. Why couldn't you just leave well enough alone?"

Rex's drugged-out stare turns to desperation. "What's happenin'?" Rex collapses back to the ground, wavering on the brink of unconsciousness.

Allison's pink hair thickens back up. Her claws recede into her nail beds. Her mouth again cries tears of blood as her teeth grow back. "Shouldn't it hurt more? I don't understand."

Connor hugs her tight. "I love you, Allison." He rocks her back and forth as she transitions back to her Normal state.

"Con, bro, we need an ambulance," Duncan pleads.

Connor turns from his love to see that a small crowd has formed around them. "You heard him! Someone call 9-1-1!"

His words resonate with the crowd. A stranger pulls out their phone to dial emergency services.

Whispers can be heard among the crowd of the absence of said monster or whatever Rex was trying to describe in his tirade. After a few moments of scene-watching and rubbernecking, most of the crowd has dispersed. Allison stands up to see her friends all around her, concern evident on their faces.

Brianna reaches into her purse. "Your mascara is running." She hands Allison a compact mirror and mascara.

Allison takes it from her. "Thanks."

Ambulance sirens creep above the music as they approach from the distance. The remaining crowd next to Rex has died down to two concerned citizens. Raymond and December walk past the group of teens.

December's voice whispers in Scarlett's head, "Told you you'd be fine."

Scarlett knows they may have saved face for the time being, but she is not looking forward to what tomorrow may bring.

The ambulance does its duty and loads Rex onto a gurney. After taking what non-committal statements they can from witnesses, they close the doors and speed off, causing the remaining stragglers to disperse.

Brianna and Connor stare at Allison, sharing the same concerns for her well-being. More than that, though, all the young adults standing here realize that this thing making them so unique and different will become a crippling burden if they can't learn how to control it.

Nick steps into the pitch black, but before his eyes can attempt to adjust to the darkness, Vistrus flips a switch, flooding the room from the many tiny overhead lights. A few have burnt out or stopped working; the remaining more than make up for the illumination. Nick finds himself surrounded by the same marbled serpentine stone as the wall leading in. A barren room whose two long walls tilt fifteen degrees backward as they rise ten feet gives the ceiling more space than the floor. Judging from first glance, Nick estimates the longer walls to be about twenty feet while the two shorter walls are about ten. Nick studies his surroundings, but he does not see any windows, ventilation shafts, or even another door that would indicate this ever connected to something. No. Every instinct within him yells that this place was never intended to be found, except by those who knew it was here.

"Where are we?" Nick turns to Vistrus.

"I can only imagine it was a council chamber of some sort. A place from before our time here," Vistrus ponders.

Nick shakes his head, turning back to admire the room's architecture. "Impossible. I was on the first Council set up here," he dismisses.

"That is just the thing," Vistrus starts, "I do not think we have always been called 'Council.'"

Vistrus inspects the dust and dirt that has settled on the floor. He studies it to ensure that the only tracks since he first discovered this room are his and now Nick's.

"Poppycock. If you think finding an old room, as mysterious as it may be, is enough to levy the accusations you did against The Council, you best prepare for severe consequences," Nick warns.

"I have a trusted source. One who would not lie to me. One that would never steer me wrong. My source may be misunderstood, but I understand." Vistrus paces back and forth with determined steps.

"Who is this source you speak of?" Nick watches Vistrus pace.

Vistrus stops. "One that will remain anonymous as long as I can keep it that way." Vistrus resumes pacing.

The scowl that crosses Nick's face says he is anything but sat-isfied with that answer, but he will have to be okay with it for now. He begins following Vistrus's regimented pacing. "So, what exactly do you think you know?"

Vistrus's tone becomes even more serious than usual. He calms his breathing and heart rate before speaking. "There was a council before us by a different name. One that, after being killed off, has been erased from our history and memory. It seems that the person responsible for the erasure did so against their better judgment. Though, they just followed orders. It seems this Nation of ours might be different than they portray themselves."

Nick lets the weight of those words sit on his shoulders as he tries to remain tall. He knows that if there is any truth to Vistrus's theory, whatever they uncovered cannot be brought to anyone else's attention.

"Who else have you told?" Nick's words are hesitant and cautious.

Vistrus says nothing and only shakes his head.

Nick nods back in understanding.

"I do not think we should tell anyone. In the spirit of total hon-esty, it took me a while to even tell you. I was unsure if there was someone I could tell," Vistrus admits.

Nick looks around. "I need to sit. This is too much to take in standing." He finds only the floor.

Vistrus hushes out a laugh, followed by a half-smile. "I know exactly how you feel."

Nick returns his attention to Vistrus. "Then this is our little secret. I will not even tell Eleanor. You tell no one."

Vistrus raises a curious eyebrow. "But your wife is second in command."

Nick gives a slow nod of acknowledgment. "Plausible deniability."

Vistrus takes over the thought. "So, none of The Council are to be informed then?"

Nick nods his head. "The less that know, the better. When the time is right for others to be informed, we shall both know it as so."

Vistrus takes his turn to nod in understanding. "Then this is our place. From here on out, we shall not step inside except with each other. No one by themselves and no one else."

Nick extends a hand to seal the gentleman's agreement. "Agreed."

Vistrus shakes Nick's hand. Both men take an audible, deep breath. They know that what they agreed to do is something neither knows anything about, but, at the same time, both acknowledge The Council may not be as trustworthy as they'd like to believe. They also realize that after decades spent on the West Haven Council, The Council may have an entirely different agenda than what they put forth. Which, of course, makes them question what their role in all of this might be.

Nick looks to the ceiling. "That just leaves one burning question."

Vistrus raises his brow in acknowledgment.

"If this chamber is as old as you, and now I, suspect it is, when were the lights added?"

Vistrus, too, turns his gaze upward. "And why?"

CHAPTER 4

"I am not sure we can anymore."
~N. DeSalvo~

The evening sun casts rays of varying reds and purples through Eleanor's kitchen window. Steam rises from the bowls of cheesy mashed potatoes and sauteed asparagus next to a two-liter of cola, teasing Connor's senses. He leans his elbow on the table, holding his head in his hand. His other hand sneaks stalks of asparagus as his grandmother pulls out the potato flake chicken from the oven. As she sets the tray to rest on the stove, the front door swings open.

Scarlett skips in a bounding fashion. After taking off her shoes, she hops into the kitchen. "Smells wonderful, Grams." She kisses Grandma Eleanor on the cheek, wrapping her arms around her for a huge hug.

Eleanor smiles, returning the hug. "Careful, dearie. Likely break a bone you keep hugging that tight."

Scarlett releases. "Sorry, Grandma." She turns to the table, snatching up a piece of asparagus. "I thought you had to work tonight, Con?"

Connor lifts his head from his hand. His face hides the frustration he feels. "Someone wanted to close. I wanted to talk to Grams."

"Telling Grandma about how your girlfriend is switchin' teams?" Scarlett plates herself some mashed potatoes.

Connor nods his head to Grandma, who plays deaf to Scarlett's words. "We hadn't gotten there yet." A strained look on Connor's face sends his head back into his hand.

Scarlett pours herself some cola. "So, ya haven't told Grams? Did ya at least sort things out with Al?"

Before Connor can respond, Eleanor chimes in, "I do like that little girl. Is everything okay with you two?"

Scarlett swallows a mouthful of potatoes. "She's been going through things. She's having a hard time accepting certain parts of her life."

Eleanor nods as she washes the dishes used for cooking. "Turning into adults can be difficult. Very confusing times, figuring out who you are compared to who you thought you were. It was for me. Everything's changing. Especially for those who are In."

Scarlett nods and looks at Connor, whose lack of reaction has her a little concerned for their future. "There was an incident right before graduation."

A sad look crosses Eleanor's face. "I know. Allison and the teacher."

"But it wasn't her fault." Scarlett snaps to defend. "Or, at least, she didn't mean to do it. You know … kill her."

Eleanor nods, drying her hands on a towel.

"She's been having thoughts. Feelings about a girl I don't think she's ready to face. Especially this girl," Scarlett says, sipping her cola.

Connor tilts his glance their way. "She won't talk to me about it. I've tried giving her space but nothin'. We all even went out the other night, still nothin'."

Eleanor takes a seat. "Car show. I know." She begins passing out chicken breasts. "Whether she meant to or not, she did kill someone. That is something she has to face every day, every time she looks in the mirror. It is a weight that stays with you. A burden she has to learn to live with. But it is something that she must figure out. This other thing. This girl. I might be old-fashioned, but love is love. I might also be biased, but you are a catch, Connor." She lets the first words sink in for a moment before continuing, "Here's the rub, my bias toward you, my being old-fashioned, doesn't matter. Whatever she is feeling isn't about you or me. It's about her. Now, the relationship you and her share is about both of you. The question is, what are you two going to do together?"

"What's there to do? I can't exactly puppy-dog-eye and smile her back to my side," Connor says, cutting into his chicken. "But I don't want to lose her."

"Let me back up a bit." Eleanor smiles, biting into her dish. "What events led to ... Allison taking a life?"

Connor scans the room as he prepares for what he has to say. He must relive the events of that night if his grandmother is to understand the entirety of what went down. As he scans the room, he misses something outside. A figure lurks on their lawn, camouflaged against a tree. A large, statured figure of some strange, mythical, Paul-Bunyan-like proportions, covered with bark-like skin and ivy-esque hair wrapped around it, making it much more imposing. But Connor does not see it. Whether it be from scanning too quickly, the creature's camouflage, or another reason, he misses it.

Connor takes a deep breath. "It went like this." He swallows his bite of food. He starts with the relevant details leading up to the night. "We had this thing we called Operation Cobra Kai. By the time prom night rolled around, we already knew that Mrs. Espinoza was kidnapping students. We traced it back to a test Jack and I took. But after he died, we knew we had to do something. That Council you all speak so highly of wasn't doing anything. Operation Cobra Kai was our little way of making sure Jack didn't die in vain. So anyway, Scarlett, Allison, Brianna, Duncan, and I all pull up to Bri's house in the limo.

"That's when we noticed the police car parked outside Bri's house. That exact vehicle marked with the same number 51 had harassed the Taylors and been responsible for their deaths. We had planned for Operation Cobra Kai to transpire a few weeks after prom, but we all knew. We could feel it—some primal rage inside us as we exited the limo, shouting that it was happening now. Then, we heard the screams from within the house. The sounds of bodies crashing against walls pierced our ears—the high-pitched, jarring noises of glass shattering and wood splintering.

"On a side note, Duncan had never really seen the full extent of anything before that night. He knew something bigger was

happening. He wanted to be an ally. But he couldn't have compre-
hended the entire scope," Connor fills Grams in. "We were supposed to have some backup. Some people who Duncan rolled with
who were cool. But he lost his phone.

"Us Legends and Duncan burst through the front door, hoping
to thwart whatever violence was happening inside. But as we burst
through, there was no crime to stop. It had already been done. We
were stuck, frozen in our tuxes and prom dresses from the carnage
before us. The first thing I saw was Mrs. Waldgrave lying on the
floor, her lifeless eyes pleaded to save her. Her mouth screamed
silently for help, but we were too late. Her skin was scaled with
thick brown-grey bark where Ms. Espinoza had not hacked it off.

"Some third victim I later recognized was the weird hospital
nurse from my father's mugging, lying face down across the room.
But that memory is not as vivid as the feral look in Ms. Espinoza's
eyes as she towered over Mrs. Waldgrave's body, machete in
hand, spatters of blood decorated her body like a Jackson Pollock
painting. Her eyes forever burned into our minds. She had the eyes
of someone beyond redemption—the eyes of someone who knew
nothing but pure hate. Any normal feelings she pretended to have
while teaching Advanced Biology were gone. No traces left. The
open-mouthed, ear-to-ear smile of a madwoman cemented the
entire image like a shadow on a wall after a nuclear flash."

Connor's eyes squint as he tells his grandmother the horrid
details from that night. "The smell of iron from the blood, mixed
with whatever had been cooked in the kitchen earlier, filled the air.
That Officer Max Espinoza, the man responsible for kidnapping,
torturing, and ultimately killing Jack and his parents, was the same
as me. The long hair that covered his arms, the tufts on his hands
and face. Max laid against the wall, covered in blood, unsure if he
was dying or not, unable to move.

"I don't know what it was. I'm not sure if the scene was too
much for Allison to comprehend, if it was her feelings for Bri
coming to a rolling boil at the sight of Mrs. Waldgrave lying dead,
the collective loss of everyone over the past year, or a combination
of it all, but she snapped. She went from her normal short-fused,
yet fun-loving, anger to a full-blown vampire, or whatever we're

called, in the ten feet between where she and Ms. Espinoza stood and Al killed her.

"That transition wasn't painful for Al, not like it is for us. She didn't seem to notice, just that her head hurt. In those few steps to reach the person responsible for the violence surrounding us, Allison's lips had thinned. Her nose had withered away. The thin, petite frame we all know was replaced with muscles large enough to scare even a professional wrestler. The blood that poured from her mouth as her teeth trickled out didn't faze her. Allison's mind was laser-focused on Ms. Espinoza.

"Ms. Espinoza had raised her machete into the air and began to strike down on Allison, but she stood no chance. Allison plowed into her, slamming her to the ground and sending the machete flying.

"We all just stood in shocked awe, shocked at what we were seeing. Allison lost it. She pummeled Ms. Espinoza with side fists to the face, screaming about her love for Bri and taking it all away. The snap and crunch of bone continued as Allison hammered away at Ms. Espinoza's face, beating her beyond recognition."

Connor turns to his grandmother, tears falling down his cheek. "It was a most explosive way to have her self-realization. But honestly, I don't think it would have happened had that whole night not happened the way it did."

Scarlett, too, tries to eat the chicken with tears running down her cheek. The memories of that night are still too fresh in her mind to want to relive them again.

The lurking figure outside still watches them—eyes on Eleanor as the group sit ignorant of its presence.

Eleanor looks at both her grandchildren. Her face starts to move as if words are forming, but she remains silent. Both kids sit in silence and return to eating their food. They both hang their heads in shame.

"She cares about you, young man. She cares very much. And if I were to fathom a guess, I would say her internal conflict isn't about how to break things off with you but what she thinks you must think of her after that night. I think she might need you more than she lets on." Careful words spoken from years of experience.

"But she won't talk about it. And she barely talks to me at all," Connor resigns.

Eleanor takes a scoop of mashed potatoes. "Have you tried the back door?"

Connor and Scarlett both shoot looks at each other, unsure if that is serious.

"Um, why is that important?" Connor quickly defends. "And why would you want to know?! That's personal and not something a grandmother asks her grandchild!"

Eleanor laughs at their teenage minds. "I meant ... another way in. Perhaps a direct approach isn't the best means to connect with her."

Connor points at her, embarrassed by his previous words. "That makes more sense."

"But most importantly, be sensitive to her needs," Eleanor advises.

"Of course, I wouldn't be any other way. I want her to be happy. I'd like it to be with me. But more than that, I want her to be happy." Connor washes his words down with a sip of his soda.

The unseen figure outside slinks away from the tree and the house. With every step, the vines and bark-like skin disappear and look more human. The dim glow of the distant streetlamps only cast a silhouette, hiding any features from the group if they were to perchance glance out the window.

Duncan rubs his hand over his shaved head while he chews on everything he wants to say to Rex, trying to filter out what might best be kept either for later or to himself. Rex may have been on more than one chemical at the car show, but Duncan knows Rex knows what he saw. Duncan squeezes his forehead together with his left hand, moving it to rub his eyes. He looks up as the elevator doors open and shakes his head to bring himself back into the moment.

Stepping off the elevator, he finds himself in the psych ward of West Haven General. After chatting up the main station nurse in the middle of the floor, he waits for Rex in the common area. Looking around the dingy yellowish brown-and-tan walls in need of a touch-up, he sets his eyes on a table filled with old magazines, classic novels, and a few decks of playing cards. He laughs to himself as he observes the few patients sitting in this room, all with their eyes glued to the wall-mounted television, watching some soap opera. Behind a locked cabinet is a shelf filled with board games so old, worn, and abused that the chance of any game containing all the necessary pieces to play is slim to none. Judging by the layer of dust on the padlock, Duncan thinks the patients have long since figured that out.

Duncan grabs a deck of cards and starts shuffling while he waits. Before his mind has a chance to wander off farther into anything else, Rex stops in the doorway to the room, wearing a hospital gown and plastic patient bracelet. He holds a pack of cigarettes in his hand. "Nice ta see your abandonment isn't total." Rex eyes Duncan's shuffling. "We don't have chips."

Duncan stands from the couch. "I haven't abandoned you. The others, sure. Never you. I'm just broadening my horizons. You should try it sometime." Duncan looks at the pack of cigarettes Rex holds. "We have smokes."

Rex steps past the threshold, shaking his pack of cowboy yellows. His Chicago accent is as thick as rush hour traffic, "What's dis den? Come to claim me for your new crowd? Or, is da wayward Duncan returnin' home?"

Duncan takes a seat across the table from Rex. "I came by to check on you. You didn't look so good the last time I saw ya." He begins to deal the cards.

An indignant laugh escapes Rex as he speaks, "Yeah, I don't remember much from dat night." He eyes his hand, tossing out one smoke.

Duncan takes a deep breath, raises his eyebrow, and lurches his head toward Rex. "What do you remember?" A simple question to gauge if Rex is lying about not remembering or has some sort of amnesia—selective or otherwise. Duncan calls Rex's smoke, tossing one into the pot. Duncan holds a jack/two off suit. Not a winning hand by any means, but it is the hand he dealt himself, so it is what he must play.

"Nothin' from da night. Earlier in da day..." Rex lets his reply trail off. "Flip 'em." He taps the table for the flop.

Duncan knows he has to play his cards right, so he calls on nothing as well. He needs to keep hidden the world that few outside The Nation are privy to. More so, he needs to know if keeping their world hidden will even be an issue at this moment.

"What happened earlier in the day?" he says, flipping over the cards. First, an Ace hits the table, followed by a king. A weight hits his chest. He knows this is not looking good for him. He flips the third card of the flop. A two. At least he has a pair and a possible straight draw. Though, neither are a good bet at this point.

Rex eyes the cards in his hand and the flop. "We got a hold of a new batch. Real primo grade. But it did'n' hit right. Somethin' felt off. But good." He looks at Duncan as he tosses two cigarettes into the pot.

Duncan looks for a tell in Rex. "I told you all to stay away from that stuff. Messes with your head." Now he knows what drugs they took. Now he knows why Rex was so unsure on his feet. He needs to press further to see if any memories are stirring in Rex's mind. Duncan matches the bet. "Who gave you the new stuff? What else can you recall?"

Rex's breathing grows heavy with irritation. "I don' remember his name, man. He just kinda showed up, an' we were wantin' a fix. Las' thing I remember was walkin' to Ducky's. Da sound systems from da cars were poundin'. Makin' me feel like a wave, man. I'm tellin' ya, dis stuff was like nothin' I ever felt before. It was heavy. Burning from my insides. Den, I wake up here." The agitation of not knowing shows as he shivers and fidgets. "Da turn?"

Duncan looks down and delivers the turn—a ten. A queen on the river will give him his straight. His bottom pair is worthless, as Rex is almost certain to hold something better. His mind stirs, trying to decide if there is anything more Rex isn't saying. "I know you've been wondering why I went for Bri," Duncan begins.

"Who?" Rex asks, revealing no memory of their previous conversation.

"The blonde," Duncan clarifies for his friend. "She is straight. No needles. Nothing hard. She's a good person."

"We're good people," Rex is quick to defend.

"She doesn't self-destruct. Not like you all, anyhow. Not like I did…" Duncan pauses in his words as he looks around the ward's common area.

Rex leans in, whispering, "So, ya found little Miss Perfect. No time for da rest'a us."

Duncan turns to his friend. "That's not what I said or implied. She is far from perfect. And if she were another person, she could just as easily end up in a place like this. Despite what you might think, you're still my friend. You OD'd. I wanted to make sure they were treating you properly in here. I know how poorly they look upon addicts." Duncan watches Rex's chest start heaving up and down, trying to control his anger. "They'd rather treat people with mental disorders. People who want help and can be helped."

"Five smokes! You gonna call or be a lil' bitch?!" Rex throws five cigarettes into the pot, sending a bunch flying off the table. "I'm not some loser addict. Just a strange batch is all. Prolly tainted. Doc told me I have some sorta amnesia."

Duncan casually matches the bet before picking up the deck to deal the river. "Yeah, tainted. What other reason do you have for your memory loss? I mean, do you think these people think drug addicts are worth helping?" Duncan continues goading as the river shows—a three. "You think you're worth helping, right? Then show them you are."

Rex starts to tear up. His mind is bogged down by the torrent of emotions raging inside. "It was dark blue, bro. And light blue."

Duncan tilts his head, unsure of what to make of that statement.

"I seen it brown, tan, reddish, hell, even black. But blue? I don' know what we were thinkin'. I don' even know if da others are okay. I can't remember, Duncs. You gotta believe me."

All the weight that Duncan carried through this visit lifts away in Rex's words. Duncan sees the desperation and panic in Rex's eyes.

Rex leans in. "Dude, I know we all done things in our youth. But dis. Dis wasn't even next level. Dis was levels beyond next level."

Duncan takes a deep breath, looks down at the cards on the table, and gestures for Rex to take his turn.

Rex throws his entire pack on the pot. "I do remember. Da guy kept callin' it some sorta test. Somethin' about separatin' us from da unworthy."

"He gave you a test?" Duncan laughs. "Like fill in the bubble with number two lead?"

"No." Foggy memories of the day's events leak into Rex's mind. With a sudden jerk, he shifts his gaze around the room, trying to focus on the memories. "Da test was da drug. He kept sayin' it would separate us from anyone unworthy. I'm sure of it, I think. Damn it! I can't remember." Rex's emotions gain momentum, causing him to stumble around the room. Rex starts swiping at his arms and chest. "It's so hot again! Make it stop!"

Duncan grabs Rex, moving him to a chair. He would like to think that whatever Rex feels is all in his mind, but he feels the heat emanating from his friend. He knows whatever Rex took is not meant to be recreational. If Rex's recollection of the name is correct, it could be a terrible sign for his friends and their families. Duncan wants his friend to get better by getting the treatment he needs, but a rational part of his brain feels guilty because it hopes that the memories of their encounter from that night never return.

"It burns! Make it stop!" Rex screams, his attention turns to the nurses running into the room. Rex sees the pills and syringe in their hands. "No! I'm not crazy! Da fire!"

Duncan stands, moving away from the nurses. "I don't know what happened?"

The nurses grab Rex, who has become more combative by the second. "Duncs, ya gotta help me!"

Two of the nurses direct Rex out of the room. The third stays behind to escort Duncan after he gathers the pot of cigarettes.

"Did anything happen that caused him to have an outburst?" the nurse inquires.

Duncan shakes his bald head. "We were just playing cards. I flipped the river and then…" he lets it trail off.

The nurse looks at Duncan. "I'm so sorry. Ever since he first came to, he has been spouting off about burning inside. All he has is a mild fever."

"I think those drugs may have been tainted or something," Duncan offers a reasonable explanation.

The nurse nods their head. "Is there anything I can relay to him after he calms down?"

Duncan picks up the cards Rex was holding—pocket kings. "Just tell him I'll be back to visit."

Duncan throws the pocket kings back onto the table as he exits the room. A winning hand on his part, even if the outcome was a little overplayed.

Scarlett sits at the dining room table with a blank notebook in front of her. The one they stole from Max Espinoza sits next to that. A couple of pens and sharpened pencils stand at the ready. She has cleared off the rest of the table, making it both ready for work and distraction-free.

After a moment, she pushes away from the table and skips to the kitchen. She reaches into the fridge and grabs a couple of soda cans. As she closes the fridge door, the front door opens.

"You'd think my father wouldn't leave the diaries in his desk drawer, especially after hiding them like he did for so long," Allison calls out, kicking off her shoes. "Connor still at work?"

"He's not here, and if he's not begging you to talk, then I'd say work," Scarlett quips.

Allison lets out a small laugh while shaking her head. "Where we doing this?" She holds out armfuls of books and diaries.

Scarlett walks back to the table, placing a can of soda on the pile of books Allison carries. "They're your dreams; tell me how to begin."

After Allison drops the books and diaries onto the table, she pulls the tab on the soda, and the hissing sound of escaping carbonation resonates through her ears. "Hell if I know. I'm just the girl with the dreams. No idea what to do with 'em."

Scarlett purses her lips to the side in thought. "Well, how long have you had these vivid dreams?"

Allison takes a seat at the table. "Long as I can remember. But…"

"But what?" Scarlett urges, sipping her soda.

Allison looks at the supplies lined up on the table. "All this? I'm starting to think it isn't real. Or that it's not needed."

Scarlett ceremoniously pushes aside the notebooks, pads, pens, and pencils. "Then let's just talk about them. Is there a time when they seemed more real than others?"

Allison perks up. "Actually, yeah. Right around the time Jack was abducted."

Scarlett waves an upright palm. "Then let's start there."

As if that little bit of guidance to Allison's rise in lucid dreams was the nudge she needed, she pulls in her chair, ready to talk. "Started with a dream about Mrs. Waldgrave. I saw her death."

"You saw who killed her in your dream?" Scarlett tries to clarify as she jots down notes.

"No, no, no. It went like this," Allison begins. "I was standing outside Bri's house. You know, in the dream.

"The night was dim. Not a lot of light. I peered into the house as if I was watching zoo animals in a cage. Didn't care if anyone saw me. Didn't even cross my mind. Mrs. Waldgrave floated around fluid-like. It was typical of her hippie, tree-hugging ways, mixed with having drunk one too many martinis. The scene was normal. While she dusted knickknacks, Mrs. Waldgrave looked at me, and that somehow pulled me inside. I realized I could no longer see myself. The dream had become first person as Mrs. Waldgrave led me into the kitchen smiling. Everything seemed kosher." Allison remembers this being a calm moment in the dream. "But just like I was shoved into the house, the mood changed as fast from Pleasantville to chaos and frightened pleas." Allison describes in vivid detail the claws that rendered Mrs. Waldgrave's flesh, tearing away chunk after chunk 'til only bone was left. Then the one word she spoke in the dream, "Why?"

Scarlett has stopped taking notes. Now, she sits slack-jawed with unblinking eyes as Allison finishes describing her dream.

"So yeah, there was that one," Allison speaks as if giving a play-by-play of a missed television episode. Allison waits to see if Scarlett has something to say, but she remains motionless, staring. "So, I think we know what that one meant. Looking back, it's pretty obvious, I think."

Scarlett nods her head. "Yeah. I think we got that one covered. But how does your mind know these things?"

"That's the mystery. I guess some things you just know," Allison offers up a convenient explanation.

Scarlett scrunches her face, shaking her head. "Nuh-uh. People don't just know things. They can infer and be correct. They can observe, but they don't just know. Knowledge is not innate."

"So, what's your explanation then?" Allison relaxes in her chair, chugging her soda.

"You've seen things. You might not have known what you saw, but you've seen them. Your mind remembers. Your mind sorts it out. They say that when people have tense dreams, it's their mind's way of sorting out problems, so they don't have to deal with them while they're awake." Scarlett flips through one of the books Allison brought, searching for a passage. "Here, I'm not making it up." Scarlett plants her finger on a paragraph.

Allison takes the book and reads the passage. "So, it might be a starting point. But it doesn't mean anything."

"Don't be so defeatist," Scarlett urges.

"I mean, all right, at night, we look at the stars, right," Allison begins.

Scarlett nods, not wanting to disrupt Allison's flow.

"We know they are stars—giant balls of gas. But you and I know nothing about what type of gas they are comprised of, composed of, whatever. We know nothing about the infinite planets that circle those stars. And you and I know less of the moons and space surrounding them." Allison lays out her metaphor with surprising clarity. "Right here..." she gestures to the supplies now littering the table, "we are staring at the night sky."

Scarlett smiles, a glint of hope in her eye. "But like the night sky, and by that, I mean the books on the table, the answers lie within. We just have to look through a telescope."

Allison smirks. "I hope you're right."

"Have you had any dreams that, looking back, haven't been explained away by life events?" Scarlett picks up a random journal.

Allison rummages through the books until she finds her sleep journal, typically housed in her nightstand. She picks it up and begins scanning the pages while Scarlett searches for a needle in a dreamland haystack.

Her eyes light up as she slams the dream journal on the table. "Here. This one!"

Allison pulls it back, not seeing that Scarlett is reaching for it, too. "This one was really weird."

"Good start. Draws me in," Scarlett eggs her on.

"You were in it," Allison teases.

Scarlett smiles as Allison's face falls flat. Scarlett loses her smirk just as fast.

"You were dead." Allison hesitates to gauge Scarlett's reaction.

She sits there listening, waiting for something more to go on.

"We were in a forest, and others were there. They were chanting. It was all very supernatural." Allison keeps it vague.

"Like Sam Winchester *Supernatural?*" Scarlett tries to clarify.

"Not quite. But yeah, I guess. I mean, they wore robes and stuff," Allison continues. "But that's not the worst part."

A loud rapping at the door stops Allison from continuing to try and decode her cryptic dream. She hops up. "I'll get it." She approaches the door, paying no attention to the shape outside the window. She swings the door open to find Brianna standing there. Allison's newfound, borderline jovial mood in taking a step to seek help experiences a quick downshift to uncomfortable. Her eyes shoot toward the ground and watches Brianna's feet shift up and down on her toes, waiting for some invitation inside.

"How ya been?" Brianna whispers in an attempt at casualness.

Allison's eyes shift upward but stop at Bri's hands swinging at her side. "How you holding up with everything?"

"Well, dead parent and all aside, I have some news." Bri cuts through the small pleasantries to the heart of her visit.

Allison steps aside and motions with an outstretched arm for Bri to enter, who tilts her proverbial hat as she does.

"It's nice to see you again, Allison." Bri's soft-spoken words of honesty.

"Where's Duncan?" Allison feels her heart flutter as she asks.

Bri's voice rises so Scarlett can hear, "That's what I came to talk about."

A momentary smile escapes Allison's lips. A brief second of happiness, though she knows she misunderstood Brianna's words. Allison knows that she loves Connor—that Connor holds her heart in his hands, but there is that all-tugging string that Brianna unknowingly plucks whenever she is around.

"He's done something, I think. To protect us or stall so we stay hidden. But, like, you guys need to know," Brianna cuts to the chase.

Allison's butterflies fluttering about her stomach have died and fallen flat with those spoken words. That momentary release from the torment she feels about herself, about her recent treatment of Connor, about her conflicted feelings toward Brianna— the love-hate-love that consumes her—fades to black. She once again feels surrounded by all that she wishes was gone. She reaches into her back pocket and pulls out her flask as she catches up to Scarlett and Bri.

Bri is already relaying the earlier events of the day from the West Haven General psychiatric ward. Allison tries to listen. She wants to soak in every word that Brianna says and notices the way Brianna twirls her hair every time she mentions Duncan's name. She sees the smile that Brianna tries to hide in describing what she believes are acts of love for her and her friends. Every hair twist and hidden smile are more reminders to her that Bri will never reciprocate these latchkey feelings tearing Allison up inside; they are hers alone. As much as she loves her boyfriend, there is a part of her that will go untouched, and until those feelings resolve, she may never feel whole.

Allison chugs the rest of her flask while Brianna continues regaling the story. The warming sensation of alcohol washes over her—relaxing and soothing, like seeing an old, much-needed friend. She smiles and nods at Scarlett and Bri, excusing herself to the bathroom.

She closes the door and leans against the sink, listening to the laughter from the other room. Her breath sits heavy in her lungs; she pushes it all out as a tear rolls down her cheek. Pulling out her phone, she texts Connor.

[Allison: When you coming home?]

She stares at her phone as if Connor sits at work holding his phone, waiting for her to text or call. Each second seems like a million. Each breath takes every ounce of energy to keep closed the floodgates of frustrated and confused tears trying to gush out of her eyes.

Her phone chimes. She lights up the screen to read the preview of Connor's response. His words read like a savior in dark times.

[Connor: Just pulled in.]

Those three little words wash away all the confusion she feels. All the time she spent avoiding and pushing him away seems to be all for nothing in those three little words. She knows he will be there for her and help her feel whole again. He is her guiding light on the dark, lonesome road she is walking. She hears the front door open and close. She looks past the opaque composite bathroom door, picturing him in her mind. She hears him say hi to Scarlett and Brianna, asking where she is. A muffled response causes footsteps to head in Al's direction.

She answers his knock on the door by pulling him in and flinging herself into his arms.

"I need you," she whispers as her lips caress his ear. A gentle bite of his earlobe leaves no doubt in his mind about what is on hers.

He kisses her back, making up for the time between her senior prom night and now. The feel of her on his lips washes away all the time he spent trying to reach out and talk about the words she spoke and the violence she committed. At this moment, he feels a tightness in her touch. He knows it has been a few months since they last had the pleasure of feeling the other's skin. Many weeks since they last spoke for what anyone would consider a real conversation—more than just him on bended knee, pleading for her to communicate with him before being pushed away. Even though her arms are wrapped tight around him, pressing her body against his, he doesn't feel her quiver. He doesn't feel the passion they once shared not too long ago. No flirting to make up for lost time. He feels the mechanics of someone going through the motions, trying to cover one thing with another.

Allison leads her man to his bedroom, kissing him ten times between each step they take, with a passion in her touch that goes past lust and love. An uncontrolled pattern in which she plants her lips on him, a new experience, unlike any foreplay or flirting they have done before. He knows it is her in front of him; it is his love who once had an A-line haircut of red and black that is now pixie and pink. But the girl whose misdirected anger found direction for a few macabre moments has not come home since. He worries that she may never fully return. Connor sees before him a grown woman, a woman who wanted to have accomplished more than what her life had led her to at this moment. This embrace by his heart's love is suffocating. It is not the familiar love he knows that grips him. The face and the voice may be Allison's, but mannerisms and idiosyncrasies are slighted, just different enough that he knows something is off.

She shuts his bedroom door behind them, taking off her shirt, not waiting for him to make a move; she will make it for him. He stands a foot from his bed, slack-jawed and unmoving. Her eyes give a sultry squint as she lowers her head. A dog-sly smile crosses her face as she takes swaggered, deliberate steps toward him. With one finger, she closes his jaw, moving in to give a firm bite to his bottom lip.

"Ow." Connor puts his finger to his lip, checking for blood.

Allison's smile deepens. "Don't be such a wimp." She shoves him backward onto the bed.

Connor wants to enjoy this moment. He wants to be taken and take, but every fiber of his being tells him she is not here, not mentally anyhow. That what she is taking charge of is not him but something still eating away inside her brain.

Allison takes a small leap, her diminutive frame landing on top of him. She moves in for a deep kiss, and her tongue dances with his.

A thought reveals itself in Connor's mind. If she is using him to work out some issue, who is he to deny her methods? As much as he would like to be user-friendly to her, he knows her. She is not some random stranger looking for strange. She is his Allison, his tiny cup of adorable, sugar-coated anger, rebellion, and rage. She is not a sultry minx to be used as she is trying to be now. He realizes, though, that this may be her finding out who she is. She may be trying something new to see if it suits her. If it is something else, he would never forgive himself for not asking.

"What's going on, my love?" Connor breaks the moment, stopping her in her tracks.

Allison moves toward his MP3 player dock and turns on some alternative pop sung by a smoky, sultry female as far left field from her usual selection as one can get. "Enjoying a moment."

Connor sits up in his bed. "One that began before I came home, apparently."

Allison does an about-face, turning away from him. "I was just trying something fun." She grabs her shirt off the ground and pulls it over her head. "God, can't you just be in the moment?"

Connor tilts his head like a curious dog. "It didn't feel fun. You felt angry. Distant." He hears the thump-thump of her heart beating harder and faster with each passing beat. He knows his heart is also starting to kick up, if he can listen to hers. He must remain calm to keep her calm; if he transitions, she will, too. He does not want to add that to his already full plate, but her heart kicks up more and more as she decides on her words.

"What the hell does that mean?" She spits at him, her hands shooting to hold her head. "God, this hurts!" she yells to the room.

Connor hops to her and pulls her to his side on the bed. "Just breathe, baby."

She lowers her hands and looks at him with snaring teeth wiggling her mouth. "Guys can be such … such … babies sometimes. I'm sitting here, trying to do stuff that should have you all excited…" she looks down at his lap, "but nothing."

He holds her tighter. "I am all for that. But your mind is not here. It's a thousand miles away. I don't know where, but far from this room."

"So what?!" she snaps as her teeth start falling out. Her skin begins tightening. "Can't you just be a distraction for me for a night? Just something I can use to clear my mind?" Tears start falling down her face. Her hands wrap around her head once more. "God, why does this hurt so much?!"

Connor pulls her tighter, trying to calm her down once more. "If you want to talk about what's on your mind, then perhaps after, we can distract you further from it."

His words, or something in her mind, slow her heart. He feels the pounding begin to soften as he embraces her. "I love you, Allison. I always will. Whatever is on your mind, when you are ready, I am here for you. You are the most important person in the world to me."

He feels her heart soften and slow more and more. The sound of blood rushing through her veins fades from his ears. The distant sounds of Scarlett and Bri chuckling over some unheard words fade out as he calms himself. For the first moment tonight, and in months, he feels Allison relax in his arms. Her tension softens so much that she is being held up solely by him. He is okay with this.

She looks up at him. Her teeth and skin have returned to normal again. "We're going to have to talk about some things, huh?"

Connor lets out a quiet laugh and nods his head. "Come on, love. Let's go get some food."

Allison gives a meek nod as they stand up.

Upon exiting the bedroom, they see Bri walking to the front door. "Leaving so soon?" Connor asks, his tone indicating she should stay.

Bri turns to him. "Gotta bail but had to share some news. Scarlett'll fill you in." She turns to Allison, trying to keep her mood light. "Nice seeing you. It'd be nice to catch up next time."

Allison moves behind Connor to wrap her arms around him. Kissing his ear, she eyes Brianna. "Sure. Soon."

"Be good, Connor," Bri bids, shutting the door behind herself, leaving the three of them to keep each other's company.

Connor grabs a soda from the fridge and finds a seat at the table, joining Scarlett and Allison. "That thing that just happened, Al. That's what I'm talking about."

Allison shrugs him off. "Later, Con. Just having fun."

"An-y-way," Connor deliberately changes the subject, "What we got here?"

Scarlett gathers a few things around her. "Al's dreams seem to be more than dreams."

Allison nods. "Yeah, they're all prophetical and stuff."

"You mean prophetic, Al," Scarlett corrects.

"That's what I said, prophetical," Allison clarifies.

"No, I mean you mean prophetic. No -al," Scarlett tries again to eschew obfuscation.

Connor looks up from the notebooks to interject. "Actually, Al's right. Prophetic would mean they have been proven to be prophetical. Since they haven't, they're just prophetical. Even though she was making it up, she happened to be right."

Allison sticks out her tongue at Scarlett. "See, Lil' Let, I'm prophetical."

"Either way, skimming over all this stuff, I don't think it's a good idea," Connor says, killing the jovial mood.

Scarlett and Allison both slump, defeated.

"Come on, cuz, why?" Scarlett implores.

Connor puts the notebooks down, shaking his head. "Look at what happened to me. We know that if we're right, and we tend to be, interpreting Allison's dreams can lead us down a deep rabbit hole. I almost lost everything I had worked so hard for."

Connor takes a chug of his soda, giving Scarlett a chance to respond. "We already lost everything. Neither you nor I have living parents; she's got one..." she points to Allison, "your college schol-arship went out the window. What do we have to lose?"

Connor looks toward the ceiling, searching for an answer. "It ... can put you in a dark place. Lost in a world that may or may not exist, and it's hard to pull yourself out. You invest all this time and energy into it that you realize if you're wrong—and you don't want to be wrong—but if you are, you're not sure how to come back."

"So, what do we do?" Allison raises her hand as if she were still in class.

"You two tread lightly. I have to work early tomorrow. I'm heading to bed." Connor stands from the table.

"They got you working a lot lately," Scarlett notes.

Connor nods. "Apparently, work forgave all the time I missed while looking for Jack once we found him."

"So?" Scarlett prods for more.

"Now they have me making up for lost time." He smiles through his words.

"No good deed, huh?" Scarlett snips.

"No good deed what?" Allison looks at Connor.

"Goes unpunished," Connor finishes the saying while planting a kiss on Allison.

"What goes unpunished?" Allison is not following.

"No good deed, Al. No good deed." Scarlett's amusement fades to irritation.

"Can I spend the night?" Allison tilts her head to Connor, giving puppy-dog eyes.

"I assumed you would," he says with a smirk, turning to his room.

"Connor's not gonna be any help." Scarlett points out the obvious to Allison.

"What do we do now?" Allison gestures to the notes in front of them.

Scarlett scans the room as if others might be hiding, waits till Connor shuts his door, and lowers her voice, "We continue ... without him."

"Even if it leads us down a dark rabbit hole?" Allison asks.

Scarlett holds a long stare at Allison before giving a soft nod. Scarlett starts reorganizing the books in front of them while Allison pilfers the liquor cabinet for leftovers from before Connor's parents passed away. She returns with two shot glasses and a bottle of rum. Allison fills what space she drank out of her soda can with said rum. She pours a shot for each of them and raises hers up. "To new adventures."

Scarlett smiles and clinks her shot glass against Allison's. "To new adventures."

The two of them skim through the journals as they sip on rum and cola. After some time and a portion of the rum disappearing, Scarlett stops her search. "You guys are Russian, right?"

Allison turns to Scarlett. "At least as long as you've known me."

"Speak it?" Scarlett turns the diary to Allison.

"Nemnogo." Allison looks at the book.

"That's a yes?" Scarlett hopes.

"A little bit." She looks at the page in front of her. "Dad never really taught me much. He said it was important for him to plant roots when he came here. He doesn't speak it much. All I can do is order some food and ask where the bathroom is. What am I looking at?"

Scarlett points to the words "Faoi Dhó Duine."

Allison shakes her head. "That's not Russian. Not sure what that is."

Scarlett adds, "So, Russian, it is nyet."

Allison rolls her eyes at the horrible pun. "No, it is not. Google it."

Scarlett pulls out her phone and types it into the search engine. She scrolls useless search results pertaining to Irish proverbs. "I don't know what your mom was into, but it's something Irish. I-rish we had something more."

Allison puts down the journal and takes away Scarlett's soda. "You're cut off. No more drinking and no more puns. You're a bit extra right now."

Scarlett throws up her defenses. "I'm extra? You're extra. We have to learn Irish to crack this code. That's extra."

Allison lets out a laugh. "Yeah, it is. We're lost in space. I think we've peered down the telescope enough for tonight."

Scarlett nods her head in the direction of Connor's room. "Time for a little er-ee er-ee?"

"That's your bed squeaking noise? You need to work on that. And no, I think I am going to take off. Let him sleep." Allison's adventurous tones are replaced with something sullener.

"You okay to drive?" Scarlett's concern spills out.

Allison nods as she gathers her books. "As good as I ever am. I'll see you tomorrow.

CHAPTER 5

*"The past had its moment, as will the future. The present is the
moment we must be concerned with."*
~E. DeSalvo~

The moonlight shines through the curtains of Vistrus's office. A small desk lamp helps illuminate the otherwise dim room. Vistrus, sipping on a glass of dark cherry red Cabernet, thumbs through a few of his wife's diaries that have sat untouched on his desk for months, undisturbed since the first time he had to break the unspoken promise a diary author asks of would-be readers— to stay away. The one person she trusted to respect her privacy while alive now invades thoughts once written for her eyes only. He again flips through entry after entry about The Mind, the Faoi Dhó Duine, and ramblings of chess and its importance. A sense of betrayal haunts him after rummaging through her past thoughts once more because these words were not meant for him. For if they were, in a diary they would not be placed.

He stumbles across an entry that rings familiar while searching through a volume new to him. He is positive it was in another diary—confident this volume has been untouched by him.

The empty Mind holds only the white. One half white. One half nor right. The empty Mind is not so right. Nor is it white. Green and black. Black and

green. Serpentine. Holds only the Faoi Dhó Duine.
The Mind is empty. My mind's not empty. All alone
surrounded by stone. Surrounded by those at home.
At home in stone. The stone is home. He understands.
He is my man. My man with a plan. I am the plan. I
know it's his land. This land. This land is our land.
My land. The Mind's land is his land. My land first,
but he does not know. The Mind is like a snake. It
slithers away in darkness. Hissing, tongue out, until
it is safe. My love. My love. Falling away. Further
away. So close. Just out of reach. No matter how
far. No matter. Forgotten matter. Resting. Waiting.
The Mind sits empty. Almost. But now it can shine.
The Mind I made so it can shine. Darkness. Light.
If you please. Darkness if you don't please. These.
Almost. Almost.

Those words weigh heavy on his mind. He knows he has heard
them before, or at the very least, something near identical. The
journals he hides in his floor safe now sit on his desk. He is left to
search the volumes he locked away in his desk drawers, but there
is nothing but space where the books should be. He stares for a
moment. He short-jumps from his chair to the wall. His fingers
flip through book spine after book spine, searching for the diaries he must have misplaced. His heart starts racing as he comes
across a missed volume. Upon opening it, the handwriting looks
like Inessa's, and the dates coincide with others. He must have misplaced this one. Though it does little to calm his nerves about the
lost tombs, he manages to find an entry from Allison's infancy.

Two words catch his attention, sticking out like a severed thumb
laid out on an empty, stainless steel table, waiting for some hand to
attach to. The *Clochnawa* and The *Adeirrig*—two words that shoot
the sound of his racing heart straight to his ears. Words he has not
heard uttered in casual conversation in over a hundred years make
his skin start to recede, hair thin out, and muscles hypertrophy in
uncontrollable ways he has not felt in many more. His lifetimes of
experience have taught him to take slow, deep breaths. He shuts
his eyes and concentrates on the sound of his breathing. He drives

out of his mind the sound of the ocean that echoes through his ears from surging blood. Pushing aside the pain from his transition, which has been reduced to an annoyance of deep sleeping limbs over time, he can concentrate on his breaths and those two words.

He opens his eyes and looks back at the page. Even a Legend as old as Vistrus knows only rumors and hearsay surrounding The *Clochnawa* and The *Adeirrig*—two Legends that exist only in myth. Two Legends that exist within The Nation for the same reason as the boogeyman exists in the Normal world. They are nothing more than a way to keep those who have newly transitioned from telling others. A stop-gap until they learn that others are not like them. But those two Legends have been all but forgotten. His mind rushes back to rumors he heard as a young boy in Russia and faint memories from early childhood. Spotted memories filled in with what his subconscious finds suiting.

He looks to the start of the passage, keeping control of his breathing.

> I spy with my little eye. Why my eye? Why can't I? Why my little eye? The Clochnawa was there. Was I there? Was I here? My hair is here. No, it is gone and back again. When will it end?

Vistrus stops reading the passage, the words that had once floated through his wife's mind written on the page. He flips further into this volume. His heart pounds upon finding the passage he read months ago.

> My new mission started. The beauty of the swirling green-and-black walls was indescribable ... The Mind is black-and-green marble.

How did the book end up misplaced?

Vistrus keeps this passage open as he references the one he read a few moments earlier, one written much earlier, though no more cryptic or maddening. He reads what she wrote over and over again, trying to compare the two passages, one scribed with only a bit more clarity than the previous. The clarity in the latter coincides with Inessa's real-life downward spiral that led to her demise. He knows he is missing something that connects the two besides the apparent content. Her writings are a direct reflection of her mental state at the time. He wonders if he ever knew his wife as intimately as he once thought. Musings invade his mind of if, in the end, she was the same person he traveled halfway across the world with or just a shell of her former self. Then it hits him. A mental lightbulb switches on as he realizes that both the snakes mentioned in the earlier passage and the swirling green and black referenced in the latter are allusions. He wonders why she would feel the need to make such coded references to something as mundane as serpentine marble in a diary. His skin crawls with the possibilities of what might make her feel so unsafe that she had to resort to vague references in her journals.

He tries to force his mind back to when she was alive, of happier times when Allison was still in diapers and Inessa had moments of clarity. A warm sensation washes over him as his wife comes to life again in his mind's eye. Her smiles and mesmerizing eyes make Vistrus feel a certain sense of safety he hasn't felt in close to eighteen years. He tries to recall any conversation that might give him a clue as to why these passages, the entirety of her entries, are nothing more than obtuse references that seem more like code than anything she could reference back to at a later time.

The echo of the front door slamming shut pulls him out of his memories. He opens his eyes to find himself again surrounded by the remnants of Inessa's abstract ramblings in his study. Something he will have to try to piece together at another time.

"Daddy?!" Allison shouts. Her stomping feet echo through the house.

"You have not been home for a few nights," he responds, spinning his desk chair to face the door of his study.

Allison enters the study, letting light from the hall flood the room and reveal the full scale of the clutter surrounding Vistrus.

She hugs tight the books she holds in her hands. "Been working on a few things."

She returns her mother's thoughts to the empty shelves as if having been checked out from a library. She slings her backpack from around her shoulder, pulling out the dream theory books to re-shelf them. All done in a strange silence as if she is avoiding late fees from the school library.

"Did you leave the house with those?!" The words may have formed a question, but their tone held a different tune. A low, deliberate no-nonsense that only a father who already knows the truth can achieve. Allison comprehends that to answer with anything but the truth, the whole truth, and nothing but the truth will be met with something less than desired.

"Been working on something over at Connor and Scarlett's house," she responds. She turns to her father, whose one-eyed stare burns a hole through her. "We wanted to see if Mom's old diaries could help me with my dreams. Connor says my dreams are cryptical." She watches her father's head tilt. "No, wait." She searches for the word she knew earlier. "Never mind. My dreams are something. I can tell ya that, Dad."

"Who saw those books?" Again, his tone warns against any attempt to deceive.

"Connor and Scarlett. Well, and myself, of course." She looks for a smile on her father's face but sees only stoicism. "No one else. Not Bri or Duncan or anyone. Honest. I mean, Bri stopped by, but that was for something else entirely."

Vistrus relaxes his demeanor, letting out a deep breath. He reaches out his arms. Allison embraces her father for a brief hug, but he holds her tight.

"What's going on, Dad?" Allison pulls herself away.

Vistrus scratches his head. "I am not entirely sure, but these books, nor the content within, can leave this house. Whatever you have found, that is to be the last of it. Leave her diaries alone. Until I find what I am looking for, forget that you ever read these. Understood? I am changing the hiding spot of my desk key, too. Maybe now you will not find it."

Allison feels the tug of youthful naivety leaving her body, never to return. "Understood." The air in the room clears as the conversation concludes. A smile sneaks across his face. "I am glad you are safe. I am starting dinner in a bit. Are you going to be around?"

Allison nods, trying to get past the uncomfortableness of her uncertainty about what transpired. "I have to work an overnight shift tonight, but I'll be around for dinner."

"Overnight?" her father inquires.

"Inventory night. Late-night snacks will be provided by the owner. So, yay." She feigns excitement.

The sun shines down on Eleanor's garden in a blinding array. The few clouds above seem to concentrate the light, making the midday twice as bright. The spry Eleanor squats down, hand pulling weeds out of her daisies. Her soiled gardening gloves protect her hands from the spiny leaves of the stinging nettle.

She hums the familiar tune of "Greensleeves": "Your vows you've broken, like my heart/Oh, why did you so enrapture me?/ Now I remain in a world apart/But my heart remains in captivity."

"It's a little early for Christmas music, Grandma Eleanor." Connor approaches from the backyard's side gate.

Eleanor leverages her hands on her thighs to help boost her up. She shakes her head. "You youngins' all think it's about the holiday." She sees him as he steps out of the sun's blinding light. His face is a little more pale than usual, lacking of color that lends an ill tone. "Looks like you caught something. Go grab yourself some water."

Connor shakes his head and checks his reflection in the window. "I feel fine. I'll grab some drive-through after I leave."

"What brings you by this afternoon?" She eyes her grandchild.

He looks around as if searching for an answer. "Must've forgotten. Blame it on the sick."

As Eleanor squats back down to return to her weeding and gardening, a silver amulet set with amethyst and sapphire stones falls out from her top. It swings a few times on its silver chain as she tries to catch it, then quickly tucks it away.

"Nice necklace," Connor notes with a casual tone, taking a seat at a frosted glass-topped patio table.

"Thanks. It was a gift." Eleanor smiles, looking into the past.

"From Grandpa?" Connor's interest grows.

She stares into her past while continuing to pull weeds. "No, this was given to me by someone I knew long ago. An old," she searches for a specific word before settling on, "friend."

"Friend, sure." Connor's accusatory tone does not go unnoticed.

Any part of Eleanor's mind that lingered in her distant memories rocketed back to the present. "Young man, you might be an adult, but do not forget that I was young once, too. Your grandfather might be the love of my life, but he was not my first." Eleanor is quick to put young DeSalvo back in his place.

Connor shifts to a humbler tone. "This other friend, who was he?"

Eleanor smiles as she turns from her work. "Just someone from another life. Someone who would have made for a far different life had things been ... well ... different."

Connor sits up a little straighter. His words come slow and deliberate. "Do you ever wish that life was with this mystery man?"

Eleanor shakes her head. "Life works out the way it does. I am not one to reason why. At least not anymore."

A distant sound of an approaching car driving down the street pings his ears. He stands from the chair. "I have to go."

"Did you remember why you stopped by?" Eleanor asks as he exits the yard.

He turns back for a moment. "No. But it is always nice to see you."

Connor disappears behind the fence, leaving Eleanor to tend to her garden.

A few moments later, the gate opens again, but this time Scarlett and Allison enter, laughing over some funny quip unheard by Eleanor. Scarlett has a shoulder bag flung on her right side.

Once more, Eleanor rises from her work, this time taking a seat at the table. She has resigned from doing what she set out to, for the moment anyhow.

"Hey, Grams," Scarlett chuckles, "Al and I have a question. Shouldn't take long."

Eleanor tosses her gardening gloves on the table. "I'm retired, dear. It's not like I have places to be. Lemonade?"

They nod as Eleanor disappears inside for a few moments before emerging with a tray holding a lemonade pitcher and three glasses.

"Okay." Scarlett pulls out a chair and takes a seat. "So, Al's been having dreams."

Eleanor pours their lemonade as Allison settles into her chair. Allison nods while eying the concrete at her feet for something to keep her from looking at Eleanor.

Scarlett continues, "We think they mean something."

Eleanor's lips pull upward on her face as she prepares her words. "All dreams mean something, my dear."

"Yeah. No. I mean, Al had a dream a while ago where someone killed Ms. Waldgrave," Scarlett tries to clarify.

"In which someone," Eleanor corrects.

Scarlett stops her thoughts, lost in Grandmother's words. "What?"

Eleanor shakes her head. "Never mind." She weighs in her thoughts. "Her mind is dealing with the loss. She was there. So were you. I would not be surprised if you had a dream or two about her demise."

"But she had the dream like a year before she died." Scarlett pulls out Allison's dream journal from her bag. "See, she keeps them written down."

Eleanor is happy to grab the book from Scarlett. She has a smile on her face as she begins scanning the pages. "I assume your father has not let you talk to someone before this, Miss Petrovsky?"

Allison slinks further into her chair. "No. He thinks I'll end up crazy like my mom."

"He's worried, dear. He doesn't want to lose his only child." Eleanor tries to comfort her.

Allison lifts her head to look at Eleanor. "Have you ever killed anyone?"

Eleanor shifts back in her seat, forcing a smile at the audacity of the young lady's question. "The world is a strange place. There are things you accept even when evidence to the contrary is nestled away somewhere in the recesses of your mind. There are things people assume about those around them ... family, friends, and strangers alike. They assume these things because to think other-wise would make the world a far more unnerving place."

The girls give Eleanor their undivided attention, but Scarlett's scrunched face indicates that she does not understand something.

"Last Christmas, you overheard us talking about how your Aunt Tracy was pregnant when she died. Then we told you about the prophecy of the Grey Fairy," Eleanor begins as the girls remember that night. "We mentioned that Legends could only bear one child because of the damage the hormones cause to the mother's body."

Both girls nod their heads as they follow along.

"You accepted what you had been told. Just as you accept that Connor is your cousin." Eleanor tries to get them to the point.

"Yeah, so?" Allison misses it.

Eleanor chuckles. "If Connor and Scarlett are cousins, then that would mean I had two children since her mother and Connor's father were siblings."

Scarlett's eyes light up. She opens her mouth to speak, but another voice chimes in, "Are you telling me we aren't actually cousins?"

Their heads all turn to find Connor standing behind them, slack-jawed.

"You look much healthier. Feeling better so soon?" Eleanor notes the color that has returned to his skin.

"What? Yeah. I'm fine. What is this that I am walking into?" Connor holds solid in his befuddlement.

"I'll make this quick since the point is to another. Legendary families throughout the years have had to combine in order to appear more like Normals. Too many one-child families started to look strange centuries ago. But that doesn't mean you aren't family. It's about more than blood relations," Eleanor explains.

"That's a thin excuse for blatantly lying to us all these years," Scarlett scolds.

"Survival. It is the number one rule. It may seem thin, but only because my explanation is lacking at the moment," Eleanor defends.

"There's so much explaining to do, Grams." Connor finally breaks his pose to sit in the last open chair.

Scarlett ignores Connor's objection. "What does any of this have to do with what we were talking about?"

"Just as that news has stirred emotions inside you that were otherwise resting and happy, answering her question may stir emotions. Is that something you are ready to do?" Eleanor sits up in her chair.

Scarlett and Allison stare at each other in a futile attempt to send some telepathic confirmation that they are ready. Scarlett hears the desperation screaming in Allison's eyes, so she turns back to Grandma Eleanor. "Why not? It's not like things can go back to Pleasantville."

Eleanor adjusts herself. "Almost every adult you know in The Nation has, at one point or another, taken someone's life."

The ten tons of bricks that is their new reality smack the three young adults square across their chests. Scarlett and Connor stare past their grandmother to the abyss beyond. Their mental faculties try to comprehend the totality of her words. They sit, frozen, as their new reality envelopes them in the darkness of death and what their futures now inevitably hold.

Allison bends over in her chair while grotesque, guttural noises emanate from her bowels and throat. Connor lifts her chair, moving her to the grass so as not to need to clean the patio. As he sets her down, a sound that could summon demons erupts from her while she gets a second look at this morning's breakfast. The rest of them stare at her as her inner demons make a physical appearance. A few moments later, she regains control of her abdominal muscles. Still clutching her stomach, she admits, "I don't want to do that again."

"Just a little throw-up, Al." Scarlett misses her meaning.

Eleanor pats her granddaughter on the shoulder. "Not what she meant, love. But that is the reality you wanted to know." She walks to Allison and squats beside her chair. "Here's the rub: If you can stomach this and understand that the vast majority of us who have, have done so out of self-preservation, like yourself, then you see that we are not the creatures from film noir and horror stories; we are only ourselves."

Allison sits up a bit, tears in her eyes. "I don't want to be this."

"Not all vampires, as you still call them, want to be like this. But you are. We Legends have our crosses to bear. We must learn to live with the harsh lessons life throws our way. The fact that you reacted the way you did, Miss Petrovsky, shows you are ready to deal with what you have done. Hopefully, you can move forward." Eleanor attempts to give Allison a morsel of comfort.

"So, why tell us all this, Grams?" Scarlett interjects with a raised hand.

Eleanor stands from Allison's side. "Because her mother's dreams led down a dark road. I cannot tell you what to do with your life. I cannot direct you on how to live. But I can try to best prepare you to face what life throws your way. If I can do that, walking dark paths may be a little brighter than if I hadn't."

Connor hears Eleanor speak of Allison's mother's dreams. His face tightens, holding back words while she speaks. In the moment of silence after she stops, he lets his thoughts rush out. "I told them not to look into her dreams. I told them that she is fine, that she is not her mother. I told them that going down an unknown road can be completely unhealthy. But here they are, asking for help. And you're offering it? Grandma, come on! You can't condone her exploring dreams that have clearly affected her and others in her family? It's not like these are normal."

"Enough!" Eleanor shouts with force enough to frighten all three teens. "They are grown women. You may want what is best for her. We all do. But you cannot dictate what they do. You cannot control how they live their lives. Did you not hear what I said? You can only prepare them to make their own choices. Here's the sad reality, Connor; her mother, Inessa, was not driven mad by her dreams. Dreams, even in Legends, do not hold mystical powers that induce insanity. They are just dreams. Nothing more. Nothing less. While Miss Allison here may have dreams that prove true, there are no demons that will hunt her for looking into them."

Connor stomps his foot. "Fine, but I am saying it now. This is not a good idea. If something does happen to her, it will be your fault!" He tries to stare down his grandmother, finding she is immovable.

"Did you finally remember why you stopped by?" Eleanor's words are sharp and pointed.

Connor stands, confused at her question. "I'm going. I can't be here right now."

The three women watch Connor fling his arms toward the ground in frustration with each petulant stomp of his feet as he marches away.

"He might be right, but this is your choice to make." Eleanor watches her grandson disappear around the house.

CHAPTER 6

"Cultural roots are always bloodstained.
How we tend to them tells more about us now
than our ancestors ever could."

~V. Petrovsky~

I nessa Petrovsky stands in a dark room with only a dim spotlight shining down on her. Even with her eyes having had time to adjust to the low lighting, all she can see is a group of five silhouettes seated behind a long table. The dark stone floor is still wet and chilled from the snow trying to melt beneath her bare feet. She tries again to catch a glimpse of The Body members before her.

A voice from the shadows speaks, *"Это не то, к чему следует относиться легкомысленно."*

Inessa nods her head, still unable to make out The Body members, but she figures if they wanted her to see their faces, they would have either had some lighting or picked a different Legend. She lowers her hand to her side. *"Lightly is anything but how I would take this."*

"Вы понимаете все, что мы просим от вас?" A different voice asks of her.

Inessa nods her head. *"I understand."*

The center of the five Body members speaks, *"Все?"*

Again, Inessa nods her head. *"All of it."*

She sees the heads turn to each other and nod in unanimous approval.

"What about my betrothed?" Inessa speaks in hesitant, hushed tones. "He knows nothing of this ... The Body, what we do, why I am going."

"Да. Ваш суженый," a new voice speaks as the shadow nods its head. "Он будет на теле. Вот почему мы сказали ему, что он переезжает в Соединенные Колонии."

"I thought the United Colonies were already set. Why the guise of relocating there to set up a new Body?" she inquires, still unmoved from her dim spotlight.

The last of the Body members yet to speak rises from his seat. Still enveloped in the darkness, his thick Russian accent coats his English. "Events are in motion—events that will lead to a formation of a new country. This will present the perfect opportunity to make this move. If you are to investigate the incidents as we have discussed, this will be your cover."

Inessa takes a deep breath as shivers run through her spine. "I wrap up dealings in New York. Then to the land of Checagou in Illinois territory."

Again, the man speaks in accented English. "Are you ready to say goodbye to Russia?"

Inessa thinks for a moment, contemplating the life they ask her to leave behind.

"Так?" Another voice speaks. The shadow of his hand turning palm up can be seen.

Inessa swallows her doubts and nods her head. "да."

Again, the thick Russian accent ushers the English language. "Good. You set sail in two days' time. May you be protected on your voyage."

Before she can respond, a figure emerges from the darkness behind her. With a swift yet friendly motion, the stranger places a black cloth bag over her head. They usher Inessa out of the room as the spotlight fades to black.

The early morning sunbeams shine through the kitchen window, casting a light on the stack of scrambled eggs in the center of the table. Vistrus listens to radio news on his cell phone, finishing the herb-roasted potatoes that accompany breakfast.

The radio host spreads his news through the phone speaker. "The drug epidemic ravaging the Chicago suburbs has hit especially hard in the town of West Haven. Authorities still have not found the person behind the batch of heroin responsible for twelve deaths and counting, with others recovering in the hospital."

Vistrus finishes pouring himself a cup of black, dark roast coffee as Allison trudges into the kitchen, tapping away on her phone.

"You look like the living dead. No pun intended." Vistrus shuts off his phone radio.

Allison yanks out a chair, collapsing into it. She replies with a grunt as her head hits the table.

He places an empty plate in front of her. "Late night?"

She lifts her head only enough to rest her chin on the tops of her hands. "No. Early day. Gotta cover at the store." She lifts her head to free her hands. Shoveling some eggs and potatoes onto her plate. "What you up to today?"

Vistrus chews his food. "Long day of work. Will you be okay to feed yourself?"

"I think I've mastered hand-to-mouth coordination." She laughs. "Breakfast food is much better when it hasn't been sitting out for hours."

Vistrus shakes his head. "Who would have thought?" He checks his Breitling watch. "I have to run. Can you put breakfast away?"

Allison nods her head, continuing to munch away on the eggs.

"And dishes?" He takes one last sip of coffee.

"Sure," she says with a full mouth, causing bits of egg to fly out.

"It is nice to see how you have matured," he says while smiling, heading to the door. Turning back to look at his daughter. "Sometimes I wonder what I did to raise such a good girl."

Allison listens as he exits the house. She slows her eating as she waits for the purr of his Porsche's engine to leave the driveway. Satisfied he is gone, she hops out of the chair, phone in hand, and springs down the hall.

[Allison: All clear. Dad served breakfast if you're hungry. Door open.]

She stands in her father's room, snapping pictures of everything—his bed, the way he laid out the pillows, the arrangement of everything on his dresser, nightstand, and anything else that is not permanently in its place.

"Love the pj's, Al," Scarlett jokes. She holds a plate in her hand, topped with the morning selection from the kitchen.

Allison jumps back. "Damn it, Scarlett! I didn't hear you come in."

"Where we at?" Scarlett looks around the room. "Doesn't look like you did anything."

"Just finished with pictures." Allison holds up her phone.

"For what?" Scarlett downs a bite of potato.

"Make sure everything is put back in exactly the right place." Allison taps her temple. "He'll notice any little change."

"Do you really think he hid the key in here?" Scarlett scans the room for unlikely hiding spots.

"I've already checked his reserve spots he thinks I don't know about." Allison begins searching.

"If he thinks you don't know, then wouldn't he have used one of them?" Scarlett joins the search.

"Paranoia?" Allison offers.

The two continue combing his bedroom but come up empty-handed. They carefully put everything back in its proper place, as depicted by Allison's surveillance pictures.

"What about his cigar box?" Scarlett suggests.

"His humidor? No way," Allison shoots her down. "The metal could affect the flavor. He would never jeopardize his stogies."

Scarlett heads to the living room. "But that's what would make it the perfect hiding spot."

A light bulb goes off for Allison. "Girl, you might be right."

They stand at the humidor, admiring the beauty of its smooth wood finish and carved emblem; its meaning still alludes Allison. Scarlett examines the box like a child trying to understand the intricacies of a masterpiece like "A Sunday Afternoon on the Island of La Grande Jatte" by Seurat.

"So … just open it?" Allison asks as if Scarlett has some transcendent wisdom to defer to.

"I've never smoked a cigar before, let alone touched a humidor." Scarlett takes a step around the box, visually examining it.

Allison shrugs her shoulders, then lifts the lid but only finds a few cigars and space enough that her father will refill sooner than later. "I can see the bottom. Nothing here."

Scarlett looks inside to confirm Allison's findings. She sees that the bottom of the inside is not flat. Each side of the humidor is raised an inch or so. Tiny holes have been drilled into the raised flooring.

"Check the sides," Scarlett commands.

Both girls inspect the sides of the box to find two tiny drawers. They find that inside them are two little moist bags to help maintain humidity in the humidor. Scarlett also discovers the key squirreled away under a bag.

She holds up the key. "Let's do this."

Allison nods in agreement. "Now is the tedious part."

"Nice word, Al." Scarlett is taken aback a little by Allison's use of vocabulary.

"Thanks. I know words," Allison jests.

The two girls unlock Vistrus's desk, remove the diaries, and begin scanning each page into Allison's laptop via an external scanner.

"If your father's paranoid enough to lock these up, you'd better turn off your Wi-Fi. With everything we know, imagine what we don't," Scarlett cautions.

Allison heeds the warning and disables the Wi-Fi. "How will I e-mail you these files if Wi-Fi is disabled?"

"I guess turn it on for the e-mail, then turn it off. I mean, you'll have to turn it on when you go on social media, so yeah. Just don't leave it on. And password-protect the files," Scarlett offers.

"With what password?" Allison shrugs.

Scarlett ponders Al's words for a moment. "West Haven Undead."

"Seriously, Scar. West Haven Undead?" Allison reiterates in disbelief.

"Yeah, Alli," Scarlett's faux irritation frosts her words, "West Haven Undead."

Both girls laugh, relieving some of the task's anxiety.

"Sounds like we're in a gang or a rock band or something." Allison smirks.

Scarlett's eyes light up. "If you think about it, we kinda are. I mean, The Nation, any secret society, is nothing more than some sort of gang."

"And we are a small offshoot, the West Haven Undead." Allison laughs. "Except, I'm not some blood-sucking vampire. And we don't know what you are."

Scarlett chuckles. "I never said we were good at being Legends or whatever. And while a vampire isn't what you are by traditional notions, you are a Legend."

Allison's light-hearted mood washes away. "Not if I can help it. Let's finish this up."

Scarlett heeds Allison's cue and keeps the talking to a minimum as they continue scanning each diary, page after page. No time to read the contents. Allison takes full command of scanning. Scarlett attends to putting the breakfast leftovers in the fridge and washing and drying the dishes. The hours continue ticking away as the girls take breaks only to eat once more and use the restroom. Night falls before either of them realizes it, but they accomplish their mission. Allison scans the last page of the books. They place them back in the desk drawer in the proper order and lock them back up.

Time must have evaded them longer than they realized. As they exit the home office, they hear the sound of the front door opening. Scarlett pockets the key as Allison runs to hug her dad—a hopeful distraction for Scarlett to return the item.

Vistrus hugs his daughter. "How was work?"

"Slow. Another clerk wanted the hours, so I came home early. How was your day?" Allison leads her father into the kitchen.

"Long. I am famished." Vistrus opens the fridge and pulls out some burger patties. "How are you, Miss McAllister?"

Scarlett skulks around the living room, trying to make no noise as she opens the side drawer of the humidor. "Good. I like the carving on this box. Very cool stuff."

Vistrus sets down a pan on the stove. "It is the symbol of The Nation."

Scarlett gently shuts the drawer, returning the key to where Vistrus thinks it is hidden. "What does it mean?"

"What do you mean, 'what does it mean?'" It means The Nation," Allison offers from the kitchen.

Scarlett enters the kitchen, sitting next to Allison. "All symbols have meaning, Al. They aren't just cool designs."

Vistrus flips the burgers. "Are you sure about that assumption, Scarlett?"

"Safe bet, I'd say. Most flags are made of strips that are representative of something from that culture. Then some symbol on those. This can't be too different," she backs her thoughts.

Allison pipes up, "Like the stars represent the states, and the stripes represent the original thirteen settlements."

"Colonies." Her father is quick to correct.

"Same diff," Allison defends.

"Close enough." Vistrus smiles, opening a new bottle of cabernet sauvignon. "You are in The Nation, after all. You should know your roots."

Scarlett raises her hand next to her face. "Mr. P?"

"Yes, Miss M." His response a reminder he does not like the initial-only name. He nods to the fridge, motioning for Allison to grab the burger condiments.

"I'm not in The Nation. At least, not yet," Scarlett admits.

Vistrus adds cheese to the burgers. "You may not know what society you belong to, but your parents were both in. You are, too."

Her brow furrows with a lost sense of wonder as she nods in agreement.

He plates up the buns as the cheese finishes melting on the burgers. He hands each girl their plate so they can add ketchup and mustard to their burgers.

Pouring his nightly glass of red wine, he continues, "Each point of the star represents a society within The Nation. No specific point has a designation, only that each society is represented. The Coleridge Society, which are those you have come to call vampires. The Kipling Society represents those like Connor. Poe represents fairies, both light and dark. Tennyson for the Undying, and Frye for those we call the Clochnawa."

"The Clock-na-what?" Allison repeats.

Vistrus holds up his finger. "We will put a pin in that for the moment. If you notice here..." he points to the star's center, "there is an outline of a house. That stands for the unity of the five societies under a common cause. The equal sign is that no society shall have a higher, weighted input than another. Finally, the circle around represents that we are encompassed as one, hidden from the rest of the world. But the societies exist because of a need for a common cause."

"But I don't understand. Are you, we, us, whatever, older than those poets?" Allison poses a valid question.

Her father huffs a proud laugh. "Yes. We predate them by many, many years. Before the societies started being named for poets, they were named for colors, and before that, the elements."

"But there were only four elements: air, fire, wind, and water," Scarlett observes.

"Tell me you all didn't have 'heart' like that old cartoon," Allison says through a bite of her burger.

Their observations and apparent casual acceptance of the societies amuse Vistrus. "No, The Nation did not inspire *Captain Planet*. At the time of the elements, there were six societies. But sadly, one of the Legends was realized as nothing more than a myth."

Both girls sense a tone in his voice not to press that matter further. Scarlett's curiosity takes the floor. "What were the other two elements then?"

A half-smile at not pressing the matter crosses his face, but he answers anyway. "Space and time. The meaning of those two has been lost for ages. Now though, we prefer the high society of the fine arts. Poets were the agreed-upon form."

The girls sit silent, contemplating the meaning of everything they just heard. Once again, their world is changing, never returning to what it was before. A comfort rests in each of them that at least this new information is just that, meaning to their world without the consequence of losing a loved one.

Vistrus turns the radio app on his phone back on. The news station once more ushers forth news of the drug epidemic.

"We know a kid who almost died from that," Allison blurts out.

"Yeah," Scarlett confirms.

Vistrus tightens his posture. "You girls are not…" He lets his statement deliberately trail off.

In unison, both girls give a chorus of negative confirmation that they are drug-free.

"Wouldn't touch the stuff. Needles give me the willies," Scarlett finalizes her stance.

"Dad, I don't even know what the stuff looks like. I'd assume black." Allison feigns knowledge of drug culture.

"Blue," Scarlett adds while taking a bite of food.

"It is good to see we raised you right. The stuff is brown to black," Vistrus informs them.

"Yeah," Scarlett agrees. "We had a cop give a lecture on it when we were in junior high. But this stuff is blue, so I've been told."

Concern crosses his face as his memories recall the writings within the notebook Connor stole. Thinking about his conversations with the Taylors, his interest turns to alarm, knowing this is not a drug. The cure is on the street.

CHAPTER 7

*"It's what they're telling us
that has me concerned."*
~J. Taylor~

Scarlett finishes tapping her employee number on the computer screen, officially ending her shift at Manic Mondays. Another workday behind her with no plans for the evening except to be by herself. Some much desired alone time. A familiar voice sounds in her head as she grabs her wallet from the host stand.

"Glad we caught you. Do you have a few minutes?" the gentle, ever-friendly voice of December pleads within her mind.

Scarlett turns around, forcing the corner of her lips to turn upward as she says out loud, "Nice to see you two. Care for a walk? I was just about to leave." Her tone was not asking but telling them they had to follow if they wanted to speak with her. Scarlett feels justified in her emotions, as December and Raymond were the ones who left her treading deep waters at the car show.

Outdoors, the early autumn air, starting to cool, is still comfortable enough to not need a light jacket, except for those moments when the wind kicks up. They take a lackadaisical stroll through the lot toward the strip mall sidewalk, away from traffic and limiting prying eyes and ears. They continue alongside the 24-hour big-box chain that fills the retail space once held by a now-defunct department store chain. On this slow night, the few cars in the parking lot fill the otherwise empty space around them.

"We weren't always like this, you know." December dives right into whatever it is they need to tell Scarlett.

"Weren't always like what? The kind of people who sit on the sidelines as others need help?" Scarlett whispers back in her mind.

"Deserved, but you have to understand. We can't expose ourselves. Or risk exposing ourselves," December tries to defend in her silent voice.

"Understood. But while you sat on the sidelines refusing, or unable, to help another Legend, she was being exposed in the worst possible way." Scarlett's internal whispers begin to rise in volume.

Raymond's mind-voice chimes in. "The kid doesn't remember what happened. He has other concerns on his mind than trying to prove vampires exist, at least for the moment."

Scarlett slows her pace, turning to Raymond. "How do you know these things? How do you know that Duncan's friend doesn't remember or that he has more important things going on? Are you some sort of eyes and ears of West Haven?"

Scarlett turns back to her after-work saunter. Raymond and December match her pace.

December's voice again sounds in Scarlett's mind. "If we find anything, we tell The Council. But there are things even they do not know."

"It sounds like you are about to tell me these things that The Council doesn't know. Why tell me?" Scarlett watches as a man loads groceries into his trunk.

She realizes that to this man with his groceries, the three of them are just out taking a quiet walk. This man is blissfully ignorant of the conversation taking place that only they can hear. It makes her wonder how much out there she cannot perceive as it transpires around her.

"Because," Raymond takes over, "one day, you will understand why we do the things we do. One day you will be in such a position yourself to make hard choices."

"Then why not tell me then?" Scarlett's indignation grows.

December butts back in. "We're telling you now because of how we acted. And it helps to understand where we come from to better get to where you are going."

"Where you come from is important?" Scarlett lessens her tone.

"Where we come from is where you come from." Raymond sounds his internal voice. "Haven't you wondered how this all began?"

Scarlett's mind pulls away from the conversation to the discount party and clothing store on their right. A combination she never quite understood, but the store has been here for as long as she can remember. If a store that combines fashion and party supplies can somehow make sense enough to survive, then she hopes whatever knowledge they are about to impart on her will be of some comfort. "Genetics. Al's dad told us all about it."

An airy sound escapes Raymond's throat as his chest makes the motion of a hearty laugh. "We could talk once. A long time ago. We were ill and looking for a cure."

Dying grass and weeds creep into the dirt roads of this tiny Boii village, searching for water. Wailing cries of agony emanate from the little, one-room homes made from brick and mortar, whose roofs are in dire need of repair. The darkening sky above begins to take away any illumination from the man pushing a corpse-topped wagon. The gangrenous bodies piled on top display stunted limbs, faces distorted by withered noses, and cystic-like bulbs, the discoloration of their skin, eyes, and teeth present even before death.

Rain begins to trickle down from the sky above, cutting the drought that has cursed this town. The cart passes a relatively quiet home sitting at the epicenter of this plague. If the rain was not picking up at an increasing speed, the cart-pusher might have checked inside for any survivors, but he can always come back tomorrow.

Inside the dwelling, three infected people sit around a small fire, heating a cast iron pot. Boils cover their faces, accompanied by lips thinned out to almost non-existence. Their eyes protrude from their orbitals, ready to pop at any moment. Teeth jut out from their mouths in all directions.

The fingers on the woman's hands are withered and crooked, barely able to stir the contents of the vessel.

A man of short stature presses his hands against the ground to gain leverage so he can stand. He wobbles a few times as he rises—a simple task proving more difficult with every movement. He hobbles over to a small ledge. His hands, no longer able to securely hold the three wooden cups he grabs, hug them against his chest. Back at the fire, he drops the cups on the ground. The other two each pull one closer to themselves.

The woman continues stirring the pot. "Je to připravené?"

The stocky man walks past his tossed cups to a locked trunk in a darkened corner of the already dim room. He shakes his head, snapping out a response, "Ne." He darts his finger to the tiny cauldron, then, with it still pointed, makes a stirring motion. "Pokračujte v míchání."

The woman turns back to stirring the pot; light from the fire reflects off a jeweled amulet that hangs around her neck. The same amulet that December stole from the strange man in Allison's dream, though the amber inside does not swirl. Tears pool in her eyes. She turns to the man sitting at her side. "Rajmund."

He turns to her. The scar that runs above and below his eye is visible through the dying skin and bulbous growths. She nods her head to the pot. "Jsi si jistý, že to bude fungovat?"

Rajmund nods his head. "Ano, Dášenka." The smile on his face is less than convincing. Dášenka looks back to the pot as she continues to stir. Rajmund puts his withered hand on her shoulder. "Tohle musí fungovat." He stares at the mixture cooking over the flame. A determination in his eye that all hope he holds resides within the cast iron.

The other man kneels next to a chest, fumbling with a crude lock and key. His hands too damaged from this disease to hold anything with ease. He drops the key a few times before managing to find a way to ease it into the lock. A twist later, the lock opens. He lifts the lid to pull out a smaller wooden container. After shuffling back to the fire, he removes a piece of metal from the box—a black substance with bits of silvery-white creeping through the surface. He takes great care, dropping it into the liquid as Dášenka keeps stirring. The man pulls out another object from the box, while silvery and metallic, is grayer than the other. Again, he uses caution placing it into the mixture.

Both Rajmund and Dášenka look at the man. Rajmund is first to speak. "Co to je, Pasha?"

Pasha shakes his head, waving off the question. Taking the ladle from her hand, he fills his cup. Rajmund and Dášenka hand him their cups to be filled. A little liquid remains in the pot. The color has darkened from the coating of the metallic rocks placed into it. Though the substance is darker, an iridescence glows from the liquid—a luminescence that sends a hesitancy through Rajmund and Dášenka. They stare into their cup of glowing concoction, unsure if drinking it will help cure their affliction.

Pasha raises his wooden cup. "Na Zdravi."

Eying the other for some approval, Rajmund and Dášenka raise theirs with a bit of hesitance. They both reply, "Na Zdravi."

Pasha puts the cup to his lips, taking a sip to show his seriousness. As Rajmund and Dášenka start to drink theirs, Pasha gulps down the rest of his. The others follow suit.

Moments later, a terrible pain begins to tear its way out of their stomachs. All three fall over, gripping their abdomens, begging the pain to stop. The clawing, cramping, stinging pains that burn within them spread like wildfire through their chests and into their arms and legs. They all begin to seize, thrashing around, unable to control themselves. Rajmund's arm smacks against the cast iron pot simmering on the fire. The sound of his cracking bone reverberates through the small, one-room house. His forearm flops about as bone juts out of the compound fracture. The pain continues as their cries of agony drown out the screams from the other townsfolk. Tears run down their faces as they plead for the torment to stop. Their gangrenous skin starts flaking off. Wrinkles form on the now sagging flesh of what was once young, smooth skin before the plague stole that from them. Then the burning pain starts to subside. A torturous tearing that grips every fiber of their being replaces their momentary reprieve. They can't help but watch as their skin begins to tear away from the bones, revealing the muscle beneath.

A building pressure within Rajmund's head swells. Screams escape his mouth, trying to reduce the pain any way he can, but the pressure keeps building. He hears a slow popping and crackling within his head. Then his right eyeball shoots out of his head. Still connected to the optic nerve, it hangs on his cheek, looking down at his body decaying as he slowly dies.

Their screams fade as pain overtakes them. A strange light-gray mist emanates off their bodies, swirling around before floating toward Dášenka. The peculiar mist swirls around her amulet as their world fades to black.

Silence. The pain has left. There is nothing to see or hear. A deep sleep envelops them. Each is unsure if they are alive or dead. More silence. A chill washes over them as they lay. All three of them are motionless in their slumber.

Then the silence is broken. A voice pierces the abyss to announce that they are deceased, "Mrtvý. Spálit."

It commands to burn what is there. But in Dášenka's mind, if she can hear the voice, she is not deceased. She most decidedly does not want to burn. Dášenka opens her eyes to see a man setting fire to the house. She can feel the heat from a much larger fire. She tilts her head to a window to find the entire world engulfed in flame. Every house in her village is ablaze. The stranger leaves the house, satisfied that it will burn. Dášenka rises to her feet and grabs Rajmund, trying to wake him up. She slaps his cheek, calling to him, but no sound ushers forth. Her voice is gone. Making no progress by hitting him, she drags him out of the house. Rajmund slowly wakes as his back is drug across stone and grass. The heat from the fires warms him at an alarming rate. They make their way to safety, avoiding those who would rather see them burn.

They look each other over. No withered hands. No rotting flesh or hanging eyeball. No disheveled teeth. No pain to subdue them. They are whole again, though without a voice.

Rajmund looks at the burning house and tries to speak, but nothing comes out. He points, gesturing over and over to the burning doorway engulfed. Dášenka knows Rajmund wants to go back for Pasha, but there is no way past the spewing flames.

Dášenka looks at her amulet. She sees within it, dancing about, the swirling gray mist that rose off their bodies as they laid in agonizing pain.

Scarlett stands slack-jawed at the story they told. "Where the hell is Boii?" are the first words to escape her lips.

Raymond and December silently chuckle. "Modern-day Czechia," December replies inside Scarlett's mind. "Not the take-away we thought you'd have."

Scarlett shakes her red hair, trying to get a mental grasp on this reality. "How did you figure out what was in the amulet?"

Raymond resumes his slow stride. "About five years later. Though that story is not related to our condition." Before Scarlett can respond, Raymond tells her, "If you are the only one talking out loud, anyone who hears you might think you have lost your mind."

Scarlett shoots him an evil eye.

December chimes in to her mind, "All he means is you can think what you want to say. We'll hear it just fine."

Scarlett hops to catch up and keep pace with them as they stroll past Ducky's and back toward Scarlett's work. "All right. Wait a minute. I'm not even Czech. You can't have me believe that all Legends are from Czechoslovakia or descendant from you." She pauses as a light bulb goes off in her head. "Wait! Are we related? Are you like my great-great-grandparents or something?"

Decembers gives a slow shake of her head. "We were simply the first." She motions to herself and Raymond. "Us and Pasha. We never saw him again. We know he survived, though."

Scarlett's eyes light up. "How?"

"Rumors of a man. Stories. He went to any plague-stricken village he could find. He would peddle his cure to those who would buy. Left the country and made his way across Europe. But the plagues died down, and as they died down, so did the stories. We do not know if he is even still alive, but we assume he is," December regales her tale.

"How could you know for sure?" Scarlett inquires further.

"The amulet." Raymond keeps his response short.

December tosses him an upturned eyebrow. "What Raymond means is that the amulet I was wearing was stolen from us. It holds our 21 grams. If the amulet is still intact, then Pasha is still unable to stay dead. As are we."

"That's a good thing, right? I mean, not being able to die," Scarlett clarifies her words.

"You earn a respectful appreciation for a few things when you live as long as we have. One is being alive; two is knowing you can end that on your terms. As long as the amulet is lost, we can no longer be in control of the second," Raymond answers.

The three of them stop at December's car. December speaks up again, "We need the amulet so we can again be in control of our own lives, Ms. McAllister."

Scarlett tries to absorb everything from this evening. "So many questions that I can't even think of what to say."

December smiles. "Then ask when you think of how to say the words in your head."

"Why tell me all this?" Scarlett blurts out.

Raymond nods his head. "Because of what happened over there." He points to Ducky's. "What happened to your friend is not just your problem. It is also not just our problem. It is everyone's problem. But December and I cannot handle every problem that involves a Legend. We have our own dangerous waters to tread."

December jumps in, "And while we have no issue helping where we can, what is more important is helping you learn to swim in your seas." She tightens her lips, holding back a smile. "We would not have let you and your friends drown."

They open the door to get in their car. Scarlett still asks one last question. "When did all that happen? You know, you two and the other guy."

December looks to Raymond. He gives a slight tilt of his head before taking his seat and closing the door. December glances back at Scarlett before taking her seat. "Long ago."

The car starts, and they drive off, leaving Scarlett standing alone outside her work.

CHAPTER 8

"Children are the universe's way of saying
humanity's problems will continue."
~B. Scott~

T he delicate jawline on Inessa's face clenches tight. Her scrunched and squinted eyes accentuate already prominent cheekbones. She scribbles in her diaries with lightning speed. Tiny baby Allison cries in the background in infantile attempts for more food, attention, or whatever other things her undeveloped brain doesn't know how to verbalize yet for her needs. The melancholy in Inessa's eyes betrays her apparent youth with a sadness that comes only from age and experience.

She continues jotting down thoughts as she talks to herself, seeking to distract from her crying infant.

So many years. So, so many years. How did I not see? How did I not know?

Baby Allison's cries grow louder and louder, pulling Inessa's thoughts away from her writings and the same wooden desk that Allison will come to know as she grows older. Inessa turns her head to the office door. The wails from the child fill the silent hallway behind it. The young mother looks down at her watch—11:48 p.m.

"Late night again, love. When will you be home?" she whimpers. "I just need some peace and quiet, please, Allison."

As if the tiny baby could hear the words, her crying begins to fade. Inessa creeps into the child's bedroom to make sure everything is okay. No smells that only a baby could make permeate the room. Nothing seems out of place. Just a sleeping baby who stayed up far too late. A peaceful smile crosses Inessa's face, though she wonders if she is not the mother she should be. A seed of doubt that every mother feels at one point or another has planted itself. She wonders if she should have rocked her child to sleep again … again. She knows attending to every little whim can develop bad habits in the child. Still, she is Allison's mother, and what sort of mother ignores a crying child? Vistrus has told her countless times in the past year and a half that she is a good mother. She tries to believe him, though she has her doubts.

Now that baby Allison is back asleep, Inessa returns to her diaries. She takes her seat, trying to get her thoughts back to where she was. She is quick to regain her place and jots down more musings.

> Their voice is gone. I think I know where. Not here. There. Close by, not here. Their voice. Not a choice without it. Taken away. Met a four. Never met the five. No longer alive. No longer on fire. The fire consumes if it were alive. Shall it be alive, or shall it remain at rest? What's best, the fire knows. The fire says no.

She stops writing to shake her head. Her eyes tighten, unsure if she is about to cry or just frustrated. "How will he ever figure this out? I sound crazy, but I know who killed them. I know who it was and when and how, but the why."

She starts a new paragraph in her diary.

> Why the body count? Why leave the bodies out? Protect the home. Protect those that grow. Nations rise, and nations fall. One responsible. The one behind it all. If I should fall. Chess. Like a queen. Or a pawn on a kill. I know the reason why. Why they all died. Why? Why? I. The Mind. The Mind protects her, the Faoi Dhó Duine. The hand shall light the way. Why don't they care? What isn't there?

Erase it all. Erase the fall. Erase the past. Repeat the last. Hide it from all. Except from me. Under his nose. Under his toes. My love. Under it all. It is him, I know. I know why. But will they listen? Will they care? Do I dare? I must...

A gentle knock on the office door distracts Inessa from the recesses of her mind. Vistrus stands holding a Chinese take-out container. A fork sticks out, tempting Inessa to eat.

"How are you feeling, my love?" Vistrus extends the food her way.

Inessa takes one last look at her journal before closing it. She knows what she wants to tell him. Even after all the past decades of hiding the truth from him and staying on mission, Inessa knows he is trustworthy. It is not from lack of trust but out of concern for his livelihood that she has not betrayed The Body's trust for over two hundred years. She knows she completed her mission long ago, but what she found and what The Body tried to sweep under the rug—or didn't care enough about to look into by creating The Council—has kept her on guard. She repeats his question in her mind, "How am I doing?"

"Conflicted," she starts, scrunching her nose. She knows that every word has to be something. Some clue without doing the "there's-something-I-have-to-tell-you-but-can't-tell-you-so-keep-guessing-'til-you're-right" dance because that is a coward's way of telling someone something they shouldn't. The Nation's secrets are not hers to share.

Vistrus steps in, handing her the food. "Conflicted about what?"

"No, not now. Now, we enjoy some food." Inessa lifts a fork full of noodles to her mouth. "The bodies have long since laid to rest."

Vistrus takes a deep breath, widening his eyes. He sits on a small love-seat opposite the bookshelves. "What bodies, my love?"

Inessa shakes her head. "These are some good noodles. I love Chinese night." She looks around the room, searching for something. "How about a game of chess while we eat?"

Vistrus chuckles. "Certainly have been talking about it a lot lately. It has been many years since we have played. It would be my pleasure."

Her wandering eyes focus on her husband. "A game to keep the mind focused. You never know what's coming from strange angles."

Vistrus closes the diary and looks past the drawn curtain of the window. "What the hell was she looking into?" He, again, reads an excerpt from her diary.

> *Hide it from all. Except from me. Under his nose. Under his toes. My love. Under it all. It is him, I know. I know why. But will they listen? Will they?*

"She knew ... something," he whispers. "But what?" He stands from the desk and begins pacing a few steps. "She was the only one to know about the room in the basement." A realization strikes him. "The room under my nose and under my toes! Now I must figure out the 'he' that she wrote of. And, of course, the 'they.'"

He stops pacing and places the diary back in the locked drawer. "My darling, Inessa, I wish I had figured out what you had been trying to tell me back then. What made you so scared that you could not tell me?"

Connor stops outside his house. He stands at the door, wanting to go in. He knows nothing terrible, horrid, or macabre awaits him inside. It is that every time since his prom night, when he is alone, a feeling grips him, telling him there are scenes inside too wretched to see. At first, this feeling was a paralyzing fear, but it has since calmed down to nothing more than horrid memories flashing through his mind countless times, memories that he wishes he didn't have to keep. He knows they are his to bear. There is nothing special about this moment. He isn't coming home from prom; all he did was finish a mundane night at work. Perhaps it is how the breeze blows across his hair or that no lights are on inside, even though Scarlett should be home. He knows this is nothing more than another turn of the knob to enter his home, a solitary moment as uneventful as his shift spent at the pet store. He pushes the memories of that night aside and turns the knob.

Life had thrust homeownership and adulthood upon him in the blink of an eye, but the annoying habit of kicking off his shoes and letting them land where they may has stuck with him. He sees further down the hall a dim light peeking out from under Scarlett's door. A weight lifts from his chest, one that lessens a little each time he proves his past experiences wrong. He breathes a little easier than moments ago. One last grasp of uncertainty wraps itself around him. He gives the door a soft knock, but no response. He feels his heart start to race. He knocks again, a little more forceful than before. Still nothing. He finds himself in the same place he was about two years ago. He wonders what happened, why, and how it all went wrong. He hears his blood flow through his veins as his skin tightens around muscles starting to bulge. He slows his transition. The excruciating pain from his first transition has since died down to somewhere between bearable and overwhelming. Right now, he can control it. He does not want to get caught by surprise by whoever is behind this door. He tries not to think about the worst-case scenario of what has transpired on the other side.

He takes his time turning the knob, careful to be as quiet as a roach on the wall. He opens the door with a slow, deliberate motion. Sounds of clicking and tapping with underlying distorted droning pierce his ears. His mind skitters about, searching for what could be making those noises. His head peers around the door to see the believed nightmare playing out in his mind, but finds only Scarlett, headphones blaring, tapping away at her keyboard.

For the second time since coming home, he feels the weight of a thousand elephants lifted off his chest. His breathing relaxes as he transitions back to Normal. He creeps up behind Scarlett to sneak a peek at what has her so engrossed. Staring at the screen, he sees words and phrases organized in some fashion, reminding him of research done from the stolen notebook. Though, now, he is not familiar with the terms she writes. The few he catches a glimpse of before she closes the window to go back to another file are *The Mind, Faoi Dhó Duine, Chess?* Then, in parenthesis, Scarlett typed in the words *Why this game? What's the significance?* After that, she has the word *Clochnawa*. Again, in parenthesis next to it, she wrote *not common, but strange.* The only other phrase Connor manages to see before she minimizes the window is the word *Adeirrig.*

Connor pulls her headphones away from her ears, sending her arms flailing. After her brief moment of heart-racing false danger, she smiles. "What's up, cuz?" The words dart out of her mouth a million miles a second. Her head bobs side to side, surrounding herself with the open files on her screen as she maximizes the window.

"What you working on there?" Connor waves his hand at the screen.

"Just some research. Been pretty engrossed all day. So little to do and so … no. Wrong. So much to do..." Her focus, again, is on the screen and not on her cousin. Caffeine from the three empty Carmine Bovine energy drink cans beside her keeps her eyes wide and wild. "But this stuff really does give you energy," she says, trying to force out a few more drops from an already empty can.

"Yeah..." Connor rolls his eyes, turning his thoughts elsewhere, "got me through finals."

Scarlett turns back to the computer screen, placing her headphones back over her ears before he has a chance to continue his thought. She continues scrolling through the diary entries, music blasting in her ears.

Connor reads the scanned entries from Allison's house. He knows Scarlett and Allison have chosen to ignore his warning and dive headfirst into helping Allison with her dreams and her late mother's internal thoughts.

"Got a moment to talk?" Connor pulls one of her ears free from the industrial music playing on her computer.

Scarlett points to the screen. "Not really. In the zone right now. All of this."

"It shouldn't take long," he tries again.

"Can't we talk about it later? I mean, this is a lot of stuff to get through, and I wanted to finish a few more today, well, tonight, before I head out." Scarlett is oblivious to Connor's needs.

"That's what I wanted to talk about," he tries again to capture her attention.

Still not catching the tone in his voice or the meaning behind his words, she says, "If you want to help, pull up a chair. We could make a thing out of it, but I gotta get back to this. We can talk later. You're coming with us, right? Of course, you are. What am I saying? You wouldn't miss a chance to see Al."

Connor's patience with Scarlett's hyper-caffeinated state has worn thin. His shoulders slouch as he turns to leave her to her vices.

Scarlett continues skimming the notes of the diaries, unaware of her surroundings, the proverbial clock ticking away.

The cold, sterile halls of the hospital seem even more sanitized by the fluorescent lights overhead. The walk to the brown steel, handle-less doors at the far end of the freshly painted white walls, marred only by the intercom on the right, is anything but welcoming. Brianna grips Duncan's hand as they stop at the West Haven General Psychiatric Ward entrance.

Duncan presses the call button to be greeted by the nurse, "May I help you?"

Duncan looks upward, waving at the camera tucked away in the ceiling. "Here to visit with Rex. I should be in the ledger of allowed visitors."

Duncan turns to Bri, who stands wringing her hands. "Nervous, my love?"

She forces out a meek smile. "A little. Never been inside one of these before."

"It's not bad. Mostly drug problems and eating disorders. They leave you alone," he finishes as the door buzzes, signaling to stand back.

From the inside, a ward nurse opens the door. Duncan motions for Brianna to enter, but she rejects the chivalry. Duncan nods at her decision, stepping into the psychiatric ward first.

Brianna looks around at the yellowing walls and brown trim needing a deep cleaning. She catches a glimpse of a woman too thin to stand, being pushed around in a wheelchair. Bri averts her eyes, not wanting to stare. Now she sees the industrial tile below her feet, speckled and tinted yellow from years of wear and tear. Even the grout screams in desperation for new life.

Duncan leads her to the common room, where she can breathe a little easier as the carpet gives a homey illusion to help pacify lingering anxiety. Talking heads on the television again speak of the ongoing drug epidemic sweeping West Haven.

Duncan points to the screen, whispering to Bri, "That's what all this is about. Right there."

Bri's eyes lock on a stock graphic of brown liquid in a needle next to the news anchor's head. "Then why aren't we looking for that? Why are we in here when the drugs are out there?" Her words are quiet but not hushed enough.

"'Cause I'm in here," Rex interjects from the doorway. Still dressed in his hospital gown and plastic patient identification bracelet, his skin is oilier than the last time Duncan saw him.

Duncan stands to greet his friend. "You don't look so … clean."

Rex smirks. "Ya'd be dirty, too, if ya knew what summa dese inmates did in da shower." His Chicago accent grows thicker the more time he spends in the psych ward.

Bri gags at the thought. "That's … not pleasant." She stands to greet Rex as well.

"I see ya brought yer girl," Rex remarks. "Always saw ya 'round da halls at school. Yer skin use'ta be smoother. Tough times for da popular kid?"

Bri lowers her head. "Something like that."

Duncan turns his attention back to the news clip. "That stuff is still out there. I don't like seeing you in here."

Rex relaxes his guard just a little. "Yeah, well, I don't much like bein' in here. But in here is not out dere. Catch my drift?"

Yes. Duncan catches it. Inside the ward is clean, or at least clean from drugs. Rex may not have been a straight-laced, sober-fun boy, but everyone has their breaking point. That point where fun, no matter how dangerous, crosses a line into too far. His line was what put him in here. Rex knows that while hygiene might be taking a back seat, at least he is safe.

"So, the showering or lack thereof?" Bri raises her hand.

Rex sits across from them, leaning in. "Makes me look crazy. I don' wanna leave. As long as dey think I can't take care'a myself, I'm Ponyboy."

"Ponyboy?" Bri repeats, lost on the meaning of the reference.

"Golden, Blondie. Golden. As in, ain't leaving here. Three hot ones a day an'a clean bed." Rex leans in further. "I still don' know why she's here, dough? We gonna try an' all fit in da broom closet?" A devilish smile crosses his face.

Bri shivers in disgust. "Gross! Duncan, say something!"

Duncan gives Rex a gentle punch on the arm. "Not cool, bro. Not cool."

"But funny, righ'?" Rex pushes the boundaries of the moment.

While nodding his head in agreement, Duncan says, "Not at all, bro."

Bri slinks back into the couch, resigning to the moment's awkwardness.

Rex laughs. "She's cool, Duncs."

Duncan can see Brianna shift around in her seat, trying to find comfort in the otherwise uncomfortable moment. "So," Duncan begins, changing the subject, "last time I saw you, you mentioned something about a 'cure.' Do you remember anything more?"

Rex leans back in his chair, trying to summon the repressed memories in his mind. "Not really. Dat whole night comes an' goes in flashes."

"Where were you guys when he showed up? Was he straight dealin' at The Attic?" Duncan presses.

Rex pipes up a little, "No, we all met up dere. I remember dat. Must'a left at some poin'." Rex loses his thought. "It's all so fuzzy."

"It couldn't be too far from Ducky's. You made it there." Duncan tries to jog his memory.

Rex stares at the floor as flashes of memory blink in his mind, "No. Some new place."

"There's no new place in town. Not any place worth going to. If there were, I'd know." The self-righteous tone in Bri's voice throws back to her old clique.

Rex shakes his head. "Not new new. Diff'rent new. Da place itself was all run down. Dilapidated an' stuff."

Duncan and Bri share a look to see if either knows where this place is, but neither does.

"Where is this place, Rex?" Bri chimes back in.

"I can't remember. I don' even know how we ended up dere." Rex starts getting agitated.

"It's cool, bro." Duncan reaches out to calm Rex down. "Does the name Ashby mean anything?"

As if hit by lightning, Rex freezes in place. The mention of the name strikes a chord of terror inside his mind. His stare becomes more than a mile long, looking out to a place he thought he'd forgotten. After a moment of them all sitting there, Rex takes a sudden breath, his first since Duncan mentioned the name.

Out of the corner of her eye, Bri watches as a young woman, aged beyond her years, enters the common room. Her shifty eyes examine all corners of the room, searching for something that is not there. Bri scoots closer to Duncan. She watches as the female patient stops a few inches from the TV, tilting her head to stare into the screen's pixels. Bri taps on Duncan's leg. He grabs her hand and holds it tight.

Rex catches the memory that he was searching for. His eyes widen as he recalls more from that night. "Dere was somethin' 'bout him. Like an atmosphere, or whatever it's called. He had dis perma-grin on his face. Not like a creepy one dat screams pedo. Like subtle. You had'ta look for it. But when he showed us da stuff. It was dere. Somethin' wasn't right. It shouldn't be blue. But he promised it'd be like nothin' we ever did before."

Rex stops to read Brianna's reaction, but she remains all ears. No disgust or judgment shows on her face—only a willingness to listen, mixed with some distraction. He continues, "We were tyin' up our arms an' he started yappin' away about da cure. How dis was going to separate da men from da men."

"Men from the men?" Bri questions.

Rex shrugs his shoulders, shaking his head. "I guess one was a capital M. I dunno. But he was sayin' dis was da new way. Workin' from da bottom up." A realization hits him. "I didn't realize I was da bottom."

"You're fine, bro," Duncan assures.

"Da burnin' finally stopped like a day ago. I mean, it wasn't constant. Like, only when I got agitated..." Rex's thoughts trail off.

Duncan leans into Rex. Bri notices a slight twitch in the patient at the television and senses something is off but convinces herself it is just the setting. She sees the girl grip something tucked under her shirt. The patient is very subtle about it. Bri raises her hand at her waist. "Guys?" she whispers, trying to gain their attention without signaling to the girl, but they ignore her words.

"Where can I find him?" Duncan asks.

Bri notices the girl's hand creeping under her shirt to whatever she is hiding. Her hand tightens its grip around it.

"Hey, Rex," Bri again tries to interject her concern.

Rex ignores Brianna to address the vagueness of Duncan's question. "Find who?"

Bri watches as the patient's head tilts ever so slightly to their conversation. "Guys," Bri tries again to point out her concern.

"What, Bri?" Duncan's irritation is evident in his tone.

At that moment, Bri retreats to a quiet place in her head, a place she can feel safe within these walls of psychiatric minority. The lesser approved way of thinking that, at this moment, she feels a part of. She points to the girl by the television. "I think we have company." The volume of her voice is faint enough that Duncan has a hard time hearing her, and Rex misses her entire response, even though he is only a few inches further.

Duncan scans the girl out of the corner of his eye. He nods her way so Rex can make a more informed decision on the situation. Rex glances at the television, then at the patient before returning to the conversation.

Rex repeats his question, "Find who?"

"Ashby," Duncan says.

The girl below the television lunges at Rex, pulling out what she concealed in her clothes. Her scream alerts the nurses at the main desk, who all rise and hurry to the room, sedatives in hand. The female patient lands on Rex, trying to plunge the paper-folded and sharpened shiv into him. Bri rips her off of Rex, but the blade has found its way into his chest. The patient fights back against Bri, but her petite size belies her Legendary strength. One of the nurses rushes to tend to Rex's bleeding wound while the others sedate and further restrain the girl.

"You leave him alone!" the female screams as the nurses strap her in a jacket. Her eyes struggle to stay open as the sedative takes effect. "Vampires are all around! The undead. You'll see. He'll save us all." Her words die down as the drugs take over.

Rex hears her words while the nurse places butterfly stitches on his wounds. "I remember now."

The nurse helps Rex to his feet before turning to Duncan and Bri. "I think it's time you guys leave."

As the nurse walks Rex out of the room, he turns back to his friend. "It made me see things. Made me believe dey were real."

"Come on, Rex." The nurse tries to calm him down. "Let's get you to your room."

Bri and Duncan stand in the middle of the common room, given the evil eye by the one nurse behind the desk who guards the door lock.

"We're not undead or vampires," a dejected Bri whispers to Duncan. "I have an idea, though. Let's go."

They leave the chaos behind and take their leave of the ward. Buzzed out the main door, they find themselves locked out and in the sterile halls of the main hospital.

Allison lies in bed, holding her phone. Her calm and peaceful look contrasts her wild, short, pink hair. She pulls her covers up to her neck, all snuggled in, save her arms and hands. She starts texting.

[Allison: Just getting ready to fall asleep. Wanted to say goodnight. Love you.]

She hits send and puts the phone at her side, not on the charger. She tightens the blankets around her, keeping an eye on her phone in hopes of a response. The seconds tick away as the backlight dims, and her phone screen turns to black. She thinks of the reasons why he might not be near his phone. Countless reasons, none of which are an affront to her or their relationship, but something in her mind picks at her. She wants to hear from him. She wants to see the icon on her phone light up to indicate he has seen her text and that he loves her too. She knows he does. She knows that even after her confession for Brianna, he stands by her side. She recalls her conversation with her guidance counselor—that relationships are changing. And as they change, the definition of what comprises a relationship changes. She wonders, as she continues to stare at her blackened phone, if he might be open enough to challenge the terms of their relationship.

Sleep starts to weigh on her eyelids, causing her thoughts to wander, becoming more abstract. She tries to will the sleep away, but it proves too strong a foe. The world around her closes in on her phone until, inevitably, sleep wins.

A gentle breeze blows across the open flatlands, spinning the tiny weathervane atop a small two-story cyclopean stone house. A fence, constructed in the same manner as the dwelling, runs along it. Behind the house, a few cattle and horses graze. A young woman, whose immense beauty rivals the nature surrounding her, and a young man of broad, lumberjack proportions rest upon a degrading wooden bench overlooking the field. The sun shines golden rays upon the earth around them as the evening twilight makes its nightly appearance.

The man holds her hand between both of his. Her emerald green eyes make hesitant contact. "I have to end this. We cannot see each other anymore, Easpag."

A tear hovers in his eye, threatening to unleash a cascade down his face. "I can offer you everything. All that you will ever need. I have never done you wrong."

The young woman looks down at her hands; the sadness in her eyes darkens the world around her. The clouds above begin to gray as she stares into the possibilities of her future.

"Everything isn't enough. I do not desire one who will give me everything. I desire one who wants me to be myself, Easpag. Someone who understands I am my own, not a prize to be kept and shown off." She looks up at him as she finishes her words.

Easpag's eyes narrow. His jaw clenches over and over again as if chewing her words. He looks toward the sky to see blackening clouds gathered overhead. A lone raindrop lands on his cheek. "I never thought you were a prize to be flaunted. Won, yes, as every man must win a woman's heart. Never to be put on display. I do not understand."

She pulls her hand out from between his, grabbing his attention from the heavens. "I have to tell you something." An evenness in her tone sets in as deafening thunder booms over them. Rain starts pouring down, but neither one of them moves. "It is different with him. Feelings. Emotions."

"I have feelings and emotions. I thought you did for me as well," Easpag flails his words.

"I do. There is a part of me that feels I always will—on some level. But it is impossible for me to continue this life like this. I must make a choice. Not making a decision will do no one any good. I do love you, Easpag. I also love Nioclás."

Lightning flashes above them, illuminating the darkened sky. The roaring thunder that follows rumbles the earth at their feet.

"Nioclás," Easpag grinds out through his clenched teeth. "There is nothing so special about him that I cannot provide."

The young woman inhales. The rain eases for a moment but still showers down. "It is not about being provided for, Easpag. It is so much more. I love you. I have said that. What I feel for Nioclás cannot be described. I wish I could give you reasons. There's a part of me that wishes this was another life. One where we could be together. But it is not."

Lightning strikes the field before them, shaking the earth and rattling their bench. The heat from the strike warms the air around them—the rain intensifies again.

"I am to marry Nioclás, Easpag." Her eyes connect with his. Even as the heavens rush over them, she can see the tears falling from his eyes.

Lightning strikes all around them, over and over, lighting the world that moments ago turned black. The thunder above rolls continuously, a droning below the news his mind is trying to grip.

"Maybe in another life, things between us could have been different. In a different time, perhaps, we could have worked. But I can no longer deny my own heart. I cannot be sorry for that, but I can feel bad. And I do, Easpag; I feel terrible. One day, though, you may find happiness in your own way."

A final bolt of lightning strikes down, forking to hit both the woman and Easpag. They disappear in a puff of steam formed from the rain and heat. The thunder shakes the world, sending the house crashing to the ground.

Allison's eyes shoot open. Her heart races, pounding in her chest. She can hear each beat as it strikes against her insides. The adrenaline coursing through her veins chases off any sign of sleep. Her mind tries to find the source of what rattled her awake. She looks out her window, but the world is calm, no water raining down nor puddles on the ground. She finds nothing out of place. She runs her fingers through her hair in an attempt to regain her bearings.

She eyes the nightstand, knowing that this dream must be remembered. So, she does what she always does—starts with the time, 3:40 a.m. She feverishly scribbles down every moment of the dream she can before it fades from her mind. After a page and a half of capturing fleeting memories, she lays back down.

Her eye catches the dim light from her phone, alerting her to some notification. She taps the screen to find a text.

[Connor: Sleep well, love. Talk tomorrow.]

As if a sleeping pill were kicking in, slumber calls her again. All vivid memories of the dream washed away in Connor's five simple words.

CHAPTER 9

"If to cease means to stop,
why doesn't decease mean to unstop?"
~A. Petrovsky~

D uncan's trademark leather jacket and ripped jeans, paired with his Run DMC throwback shirt, are always the contrast to Bri's baby blue cashmere cardigan and flowing skirt, topped off with a white derby hat. They sit in the West Haven mall food court, the odd couple they are, happy as clams sharing some fast food that passes for Mexican cuisine.

They people-watch as groups of teens pass by, some of whom have suspicious twitches and wandering fingers. Other youths, of course, are there to enjoy time away from home and prying parental eyes. Then there are the moms who scurry along, trying to wrangle little ones while holding onto their shopping bags. For these two young lovers, this moment is theirs, just a couple of kids feeding each other a burrito and nachos while sipping a soda—not a care in the world.

Except for the big one—the mysterious man named Ashby, who wandered into town peddling a blue liquid he calls "the cure," a problem they would prefer not to think about for a moment. The scratchy eh-hem of Connor clearing his throat forces them to dwell on said problem.

Duncan gives a nonchalant turn of his head to see Connor holding a bag from the same fast Mexican place. "May I sit…" Connor gestures to an empty chair, "or are you going to try and feed me?"

"Nice shirt. New?" Duncan points to Connor's screen-printed shirt promoting some heavy metal band while popping a nacho into his mouth.

Connor dumps his food from the bag. "Yeah. Came in today." He unwraps his supreme loaded burrito and chomps down on it. "Whatcha guys doing, besides feeding each other?"

Through a sip of her drink, Bri says, "People-watching."

Connor raises an eyebrow. "People-watching?"

"People-watching." Duncan's tone indicates that this should be standard practice. "Like that kid over there." He nods to a stranger across the court.

"What about him?" Connor bites into his burrito, causing a bit of cheese sauce to drip down his hand.

"What do you see?" Duncan urges.

"I dunno. He's alone. Head hanging down like he's looking at his cell phone in his lap," Connor observes, wiping his hand.

"But his phone is on the table. His hands are hanging down at his side," Duncan points out. "What about his dirty clothes and unkempt hair? Who's he remind you of?"

"Your other friends!" Bri's over-enthusiastic response causes Duncan's face to scrunch. A moment not lost on her. "Sorry, I just meant that he's probably going to end up a statistic, whereas you got out of that group. You are doing something."

Duncan takes a deep breath. He mulls over the words in his head before speaking. Both Connor and Bri can see the wheels turning in Duncan's mind and don't dare put a stick in the spokes. After a few moments of careful contemplation, his lips part. "That's the thing. People always say shit like that. 'Just another statistic,' or 'I don't wanna become just a statistic.' And people get all sad that things like that happen—that people lose battles with whatever they were fighting—drugs, cancer, abuse, depression, or whatever. Or that they die in a car accident because they were, or got hit by, a drunk driver. Then they all say stuff like, 'I can't believe they became a statistic. They deserved better.' But that's the thing. In the end, we are all just a statistic of some sort. We all die. We all lose battles of some sort in our lives. What people always imply in those greeting card sentiments is that the statistic is a sad one. People who get degrees and become millionaires are just a statistic. Same with those who become famous or stay in anonymity. Everyone, at some point in their life, and especially at the end of it, is nothing more than a byline somewhere."

"What does that have to do with the price of rice?" Connor swallows the last of his burrito.

"It means that people feel bad for the inevitable. Feel bad for the fact that society lets bad statistics happen. That people think their parents were so flawless, despite their own numerous flaws inlaid in them by their parents, and so they try no harder to raise their kids better than their parents did. No adjustments for current views, morals, technology, dangers, or whatever. They just half-ass their parental duties. Then blame the kids when they grow up and start tweaking out in a food court mall, placing no blame on themselves whatsoever because it's more convenient to believe a little lie than face the truth that they were only half the parent they could have, and should have, been." Duncan finally takes a breath.

"Everything okay at home, baby?" Bri finally chimes in.

Duncan lets a weak chuckle escape his lungs. "Five by five, Bri. Just think that society needs to take a long, hard look in the mirror and have an honest conversation with itself."

Connor raises his hand by his face as if in class. "Um, he hasn't moved since before you launched into your *Good Will Hunting*-esque monologue."

Duncan and Bri exchange a concerned glance and simultaneously rise from their chairs. Connor follows suit and stands up, finishing the last half of his soda in one long sip. The three of them dump their food, place the trays on the dirty shelf, and walk to the teen.

"Bro, you all right?" Duncan looks the kid up and down.

"Hey, man." Connor shakes the kid's shoulder.

The stranger turns his head up to them, his pupils fully dilated, and all tone faded from his skin. "I belong."

Brianna steps forward. "Belong to what?"

The kid turns to Bri, but before he can say a word, he collapses, smacking his head against the table with a thud audible even in the white noise of the food court.

Duncan sees the marks on the kid's arm, surrounded by a blue stain. "Let's go! Now!"

They look around at the apathy of those around them. No one notices that a kid is passed out in a mall. As they pass a few tables down, Bri turns to an older lady sipping a hot tea. "I think that kid needs help. Can you call someone?"

The lady directs her attention toward the unconscious kid instead of the tea she cupped in her hands. She turns to ask Bri a question, but they have moved on. Bri turns back to see the lady pull out a cell phone to dial what Bri hopes is 911.

The food court doors open to the parking lot, which backs up to the main road and the car dealership across the street. Duncan turns left as Bri continues straight.

Bri turns back. "Car's this way, dear."

Duncan motions his head. "This way."

Bri, with Connor in tow, catches up to Duncan. They walk a bit away—close enough to monitor the exit but far enough away, tucking themselves behind some shrubs that one would have to be looking for them to find them. It doesn't take more than Duncan lighting a cigarette for the distant sound of ambulance sirens to hit their ears.

Duncan takes a drag. "Connor, did you see the blue stain on his arm?"

Connor nods his head. "What was that?"

Bri watches the distance for the approaching medical responders before answering, "Drugs, Connor."

Connor turns to Brianna. "How the hell would you know? You've never touched the stuff."

"She's right. At least, I think she's right. We went to visit Rex in the hospital," Duncan starts.

Before he can continue, Connor interrupts, "Who's Rex?"

"The dude from Ducky's." Duncan is quick to remind. Connor nods in confirmed remembrance. "He was freaked out. Hardcore."

"So what? He's a druggie. It happens." Connor is quick to dismiss.

"So's no," Duncan scorns. "Of all my old friends, he's the only one worth anything. He needs us, and I need to be there."

"Yeah, Con. Don't be so quick to judge," Brianna jabs.

"That's funny coming from you, Bri," Connor jabs back. "But you're right. Contempt prior to investigation and all."

Duncan nods. "I thought I was the only one who knew what that meant."

"I said it to the team once," Connor reminisces as sorrow creeps in. "We were all standing around watching Coach talk to a cop. Ended up being the beginning of a bad year."

"Jack?" Duncan's one-word question causes Connor to retreat further into his memories.

Connor nods. "It was the event that started it all. Before that day, we were just like you. Normal. We were happy. Then all this started, and here we are."

The EMTs hop out as their ambulances roll to a stop in front of the food court. The lights blare, but they silence the sirens.

"Can someone tell me what that contempt thingy means?" Brianna waves her hands at them.

"In a nutshell, it means I shouldn't have judged Rex before I knew the full story. Just like that kid inside will be judged for circumstances beyond his control, or for the circumstances leading up to what caused him to decide to get himself into that situation," Connor tries to clear up, though the look on Bri's face says he did anything but.

Duncan chimes in, "It means don't judge until you know the whole story."

Brianna shakes her head at Connor. "Why couldn't you have just said that? It's simple. Be simple, like Duncan."

Duncan and Connor both tilt their heads at her statement.

"Not sure that was the compliment you think it was, Bri," Connor jokes.

Duncan snuffs out his smoke under his shoe and lights up another as they wait for the EMTs to leave with the teen. A few chain-smoked cigarettes later, his hand gestures to the opening food court doors, making way for the hospital gurney carrying the teen. The body bag zipped up sends all their stomachs sinking to the ground.

"Could we have..." Bri starts but does not dare finish her thought.

Duncan wraps her in his arms. "No. Now we need to find where Rex said they all hang out. That's our only lead."

"He told you where?" Connor's hopes rise.

Duncan shakes his head. "All he could remember was that it was dilapidated. Ceiling tiles fallen, walls broken in, overturned tables. Sounded like a pretty nondescript abandoned building."

Connor takes a deep breath as the ambulance closes its doors. The lights fade out, and the ambulance drives away. Connor turns back to his friends. "I know where they were."

Allison and Vistrus sit in the living room, watching the evening news. The anchor smiles next to a generic drugs-are-bad, ominous, dark graphic, all topped off with a red circle slashed through it. Allison watches worry pour out of her father's eyes. Vistrus tries to watch the news without glancing at his daughter. He knows that she is not involved with such activities, but he also knows peer pressure ofttimes weighs more than one can bear.

"Don't you remember talking about this, dad?" Allison points to the screen.

His daughter's voice shakes him from his thoughts. "No. Yes, of course. Distractions have gotten to me lately."

Allison sees his stare fixed upon the newscaster. She doesn't have to have a child to know his thoughts. "You know I don't do that? Right. Not my cup of joe."

Vistrus huffs in amusement. "Tea, dear."

"What about it?"

"The saying is 'cup of tea' not 'cup of joe,'" he says, taking a small moment to impart some knowledge.

Allison shrugs. "Either way. Nothing here like that."

Vistrus crosses his brow at her choice of words but decides to leave it be, for the moment at least. There's always time to be a father.

An alert chimes on her phone.

[Connor: Come outside.]

A quick response back.

[Allison: Come inside.]

Only a second passes before there is a knock at the door. Again, Allison sends a text.

[Allison: Come in.]

"Were you just waiting outside for me?" Allison shouts to the door.

Connor steps inside, making his way to the living room, followed by Scarlett, Duncan, and Brianna, the sight of whom causes Allison's chest to tighten up.

"Yeah, we figured you'd just come out," Connor starts as the news exposé catches his eye. "We are checking out a new place tonight. Thought you'd like to join us."

"What new place?" Her tone less than convinced. She looks at his T-shirt. "Coma Noir?"

Connor looks at his new shirt and smiles. "New album, new shirt. I think you'll love it."

Connor watches as Vistrus is too entranced in the news to pay attention to their conversation. Connor nods in short bursts to the television. "The place our new friend from Ducky's recommended. I think you should come with us."

Duncan nudges Brianna with his elbow. Catching the drift of his poke, she chimes in, "Yeah, Al, come with us. It'll be fun."

Allison tosses glances between Connor and Brianna, caught in the emotional tug-of-war she has been playing against herself. A game she has yet to make any progress in that wears her down little by little. After an extended moment, of which the understood meaning remains unspoken among friends, she turns to her father. "Dad?"

His attention turns away from the news as the exposé concludes, cutting away to a commercial. "Have fun, dear. If you find yourself in any predicament, call me. No questions asked."

Allison hops up. "Of course."

They all exit, leaving Vistrus to his vice of cutting a cigar butt and grabbing some matches. He finishes watching the evening news.

Halfway through his cigar, a knock at the door disrupts his tran-
quil solitude.

Puffing away, he opens the door. "Mr. DeSalvo. Where is
everyone?"

Connor stands in the doorway, wearing his high school letterman jacket and a plain gray T-shirt, which he was not wearing
when they all left. The tone of his skin has faded and appears more
sickly than from earlier in the evening.

"We need to talk..." he pauses for a moment before remembering
his manners, "sir."

"You do not look well. What is going on? Where is my daughter?"
Vistrus's tone grows stern.

Connor's eyes dart to the ceiling, searching for an answer. "She's
still out with everyone else. I just had to talk to you."

Vistrus presses his lips together, not wholly satisfied with
young DeSalvo's words. "Then let us talk. Come sit." He puffs his
cigar once more as they move to the living room. Vistrus shuts off
the television. Lifting a cigar from the humidor, he makes note of
Connor's complexion, "You look very ill unlike earlier this evening,
but I am not your father."

"Must have been something I ate. I'll be fine." Connor does not
react to the mention of the deceased. "I am my own man." He
extends his hand to take the cigar.

They both puff away while they talk.

"You know your daughter's interests are lying on more than
just," Connor hesitates a split second before finishing, "me."

Vistrus upturns his brow just a hair, trying to ponder the possibilities of Connor's end game, but he remains suspect.

"Trouble in your heart?" Vistrus exhales.

Connor glances toward the ceiling as he picks the words to fish
out what Vistrus knows. "It's everything that happened."

"We had this talk, Mr. DeSalvo. She killed another human. You
cannot be that forgetful." Vistrus looks Connor up and down with
a hint of suspicion still in his eye.

"Not that, no. I mean with Brianna," Connor offers up bait.

Vistrus bites. "You better not have betrayed my daughter." His
words are determined and pointed.

"Not I, no. But it seems Allison's feelings betray me. Not the other way around," Connor continues alluding to his point.

Vistrus chews on Connor's words, trying to figure out their flavor. He is also trying to determine why he left his friends to come back and talk—and why he is so pale. The lack of flesh tone has him perplexed and a little worried. Though his thoughts wash away as the words he has been masticating finally digest with a puff of his cigar.

"She has feelings for Bri..." Vistrus exhales, "as she does for you."

Connor does a quick index finger double tap on his nose, ending with a momentary finger point at Vistrus. "There's the rub."

"Hmmm" is all Vistrus can muster.

"For a man of choice words, that seems a little too choice," Connor observes with a puff of his cigar. He savors the moment before exhaling. "Grandma Eleanor," he starts on choked words, "told me of someone she once loved."

Vistrus raises an interested eyebrow.

"She said," Connor continues, "that perhaps in another life they could have been together."

"What does that have to do with my daughter?" Vistrus lowers his brow, unimpressed with the direction of the conversation.

"We only have but one life, as long as it might be, but what if it were to change?" Connor offers up as if he is some street urchin selling magic beans or a lamp.

"Where are you going with this? I love my daughter. It should not matter who she loves," Vistrus defends.

"Exactly. We can't let obstacles stand in the way, then. That would be wrong," Connor lays out.

Vistrus nods in agreement. "That is a decision she has to make. The obstacles are hers to overcome."

"We could remove them. Make the path to what should have been easier." Connor leans forward in his seat.

"A parent's job is not to remove the obstacles in their children's way but to teach them how to navigate and overcome. Simply removing the obstacles teaches them nothing about how to live life. Only that others will do the work for you." The tone in Vistrus's voice shifts more to a parental-teaching moment than conversation.

"It doesn't have to be like that," Connor objects, leaning closer.

"We cannot simply go through life leaving young adults in the innocence and naivety of childhood. They must learn that the universe does not care. Knowing this gives us purpose and teaches them to be critically thinking adults." Vistrus shifts into calm frustration.

"But she should not have ended up with..." Connor realizes his shouting is not what Vistrus will tolerate. He calms himself with a breath, "The wrong person."

Vistrus, too, collects himself, if only for the respect that Connor recognizes the fault of his tone. "Again, Mr. DeSalvo, that is a choice she will have to make. We cannot choose it for her. All we can do is support her decision and accept whatever she chooses. This is something you should have known by now." He waits for a response that does not come. "If you want to be on The Council, you have much to learn about life. Life, as in politics, is helping people understand the weight of their actions."

"But," Connor starts before being cut off by Vistrus.

"But they are their actions to make. Only when their actions hurt others can we intercede. If they choose to hurt themselves, that is on them."

He watches Connor chew on those words for a moment.

"Do not make me think I was wrong for presenting you the path to The Council." Vistrus leans back in his chair, contemplating his actions.

"You are not wrong. Neither am I. True love should be unhindered. Whatever needs to be done should be. Imagine how different life would have been for Eleanor, Grandma Eleanor, if she had ended up with that other man." Connor continues trying Vistrus's patience. "It shouldn't be different for Allison."

Vistrus stands from his chair, snuffing his cigar. "You should leave. I have much to think about, the least of which is my daughter's love life. That is hers and hers alone. What I do need is to take time and reconsider if you have a future with The Council. You may be in The Nation. That is a birthright. But a seat on The Council must be earned. Perhaps I gave you too much credit for being Ken's son."

Vistrus walks to the front door. He stands, holding it open as Connor trudges out the door, head hanging down.

Allison, Scarlett, Brianna, and Duncan all huddle together in a dark, damp hallway. Mold and dust cover the walls in thicker coats. Yet it still holds the cold weather and all its harsh memories of finding Jack.

Duncan jiggles the doorknob. "Damn it." He tries pulling up on it, as if to lift the door off its hinges, without avail. "Damn. Where the hell did he go?"

Bri grabs her boyfriend's hand to try and calm him down. "Said he had to take a leak."

"One helluva leak he's takin'." Duncan rubs his hands together before wrapping them around Bri.

Allison looks down the hallway to the light creeping in from the warmer outside world. "How the hell is it so cold in here? It's seventy-five outside."

Scarlett hugs Allison to help keep her warm. "Old buildings are a funny thing."

"Shakin' it more than twice is just playing with it, bro!" Duncan shouts down the hall.

Connor appears at the end of the hall, wiping his hands on his new heavy metal T-shirt. "Didn't realize I had to go that bad."

"As long as it was just a leak," Duncan smirks.

Bri slaps Duncan's arm in disgust. "Gross, babe. Why would you say that?"

Duncan and Connor share a hearty laugh at Bri's squeamishness.

"We need to get through that door, Con." Scarlett points to the handle.

"Has anyone tried seeing if it was open?" Connor tosses his palms upward.

Allison steps to the door. "Gee, thanks, Con. We're just little simple sons and did'n think ta try that." She jiggles the handle to show it's locked. She snaps her finger, swiping her hand across her body. "Aw shucks, Con."

"Well," Connor realizes the unintended condescension in his words, "you could've just said, 'yes.'"

Scarlett unwraps her arms from around Allison. "What are simple sons, Al?"

Allison's eyebrows scrunch together, thinking of a way to explain the obvious. "Simple-minded folk. You know. When you look at someone and think, 'Oh, they're just a simple son.'"

They all exchange glances, unsure who needs to do the explaining. Duncan is the first to open his mouth. "I got this." He squeezes the bridge of his nose between his index finger and thumb.

"Got what?" Allison scans their faces.

"It's simpletons, not simple sons." Duncan takes a step back as if Allison will lash out.

"It's not gender-specific, Al," Bri adds her bit of spice.

"Whatever, I make up my own words," Allison says, owning her mistake. "Simple sons, simple daughters, simpletons: it's all the same."

Scarlett raises her hand. "Guys, standing here talking proper word usage isn't getting us inside." She motions for Connor to open the door. "Do your thing."

Connor steps up to the door. He stares it down for a moment, trying to summon the strength from the night he found Jack. All the memories flood back into his mind—the beeping of the monitors that watched over their vital signs, the medical equipment that decorated the otherwise dilapidated room, the smell of stale sweat and drying blood, the tears in his friend's eyes as he entered. All of it fills his mind, but his body does not change. Connor looks no different than he did moments ago. His hair has not grown, and his muscles are not hypertrophied. There are no thickened nails with which to rend flesh. Nothing. Just a kid a year plus out of high school who can't break down the door.

Scarlett steps toward Connor, putting her hand on his back. "Are you okay?"

Keeping his gaze fixed on the door, he grunts, "Yeah, just need a little more time."

Scarlett steps back, waiting on him to transition, but nothing happens. He stands, staring at a doorknob.

Duncan whispers something into Allison's ear. She returns the whisper with a hesitant nod.

Duncan steps forward. "Hey, Cons. I was thinkin' since Al is into Bri, we might borrow her. Nothing permanent."

Bri straightens her stance to say something, but Allison holds up a finger to stop her. Scarlett shakes her head, knowing what is happening. She does not think this is a good idea.

Duncan stops for a moment to observe Connor. His eyes fix on the knob as his breathing becomes more visible, getting heavier with each breath.

"Yeah, Bri was thinkin' her and Alli could do a little bonding, if ya know what I mean." Duncan watches as Connor's veins start to rise to the surface of his skin. Connor's hair starts thickening out on his limbs and face while his skin stretches over his growing muscles. "And if all goes well with them, maybe I could join in their little pow-wow." Connor's nails have thickened and grown into sharp points. Low-toned growls accompany his breathing as his clothes threaten to burst at the seams, destroying his new T-shirt. "And maybe, just maybe, girls' permission, we could trade. Like they were baseball cards or somethin'."

Connor takes one last deep breath before bashing in the locked door, sending it flying clean off its hinges. He turns back to his friends with a pointed smile. "After you."

The girls all enter first. Connor nods his head as Duncan walks past, a nod that lets Duncan know Connor knows why Duncan said what he said. Connor understands the need for what Duncan did, though it has brought to the forefront of his mind feelings and emotions that he did not know he had yet to deal with. Issues that, perhaps, he should have realized and dealt with sooner and not in front of all his friends.

Connor enters the room to see Duncan picking up something red from under some debris. Connor's breaths are slowing and more controlled. His veins and muscles start to return to his Normal state. His hair sheds as his Legendary form once again goes dormant.

Duncan holds up a red bandana. "This is the place. Rex was here."

"That could be just some random handkerchief. How do you know that's Rex's?" Connor needs clarification.

"It's the only one he ever wore," Duncan laughs as a thought enters his mind. "He could never get it to fit quite right, but he wore it anyhow."

Connor sees the certainty in Duncan's eyes. The confidence in his voice as he reminisces about Rex solidifies in everyone that this is the spot.

Scarlett stares at the boys in the room. "So, now what?"

Allison starts scanning the ground. "We look."

"For what?" Brianna decides to chime in as she, too, starts searching the floor.

"Anything." Connor takes command of the situation. "Anything that might help us figure out who Ashby is, what he wants, what Rex took." Connor uses his foot to overturn small debris. "Duncs, did Rex say anything that might be useful? Besides leading us here."

"I dunno. I didn't know what was real versus ravings of a madman." Duncan stops to appreciate the reality of his surroundings before continuing, "Except that none of it may have been ravings."

"Yeah, well," Scarlett's frustration grows, "it's too late to look back on what you could have listened to."

Oblivious to the tone of the room or blatantly ignoring it, Brianna opens her mouth, "I don't get it. It's not like vampires and werewolves are real. No more than my skin condition."

Everyone freezes. They each find themselves frozen in the denial of Bri's words. Duncan frees himself to wrap his arms around his love. "Did you not see Connor go full beast mode back there?"

"I saw." The level of derision rising in her tone. "That's Connor's thing. Like he might be this thing that my mother told me I was, am, whatever. This isn't my world. It can't be."

Scarlett steps to Brianna. "Okay, I'm cutting off your recession, or regression, or whatever is happening here. No denying this, Bri. This is real. I saw you at the funeral. Your skin looked more like dry, cracked desert sand than the lotioned, smooth skin you maintain. Sorry to be mean. Your mother loved you, still does, whatever you believe, but she needs you, we all need you, to understand the realness of this whole thing. There is no running from this to your old friends. There is no denying what your mother was trying to protect you from until she couldn't."

"I know!" Bri interrupts as tears fall from her eyes. "And when this did all happen, do you know what she did? She gave me a martini. The same martini that you have all seen her drink. The same martini she had every day, and every time I saw it, I had to wonder if it would end with a palm across my cheek. The same martini that made my mother the Jekyll and Hyde that she was, was the same medicine that helped her, and now me, I guess, control our disease." Bri sees Scarlett open her mouth to correct her. "Legendary condition, whatever. Whatever you call it, it still sucks. My mother sucked on so many levels, but now all of her shortcomings have this excuse. This condition of ours that, if she didn't have it, probably could have let her be a great mother, better than the one she was.

"And the kicker is, when she wasn't mad drunk, she was great. But all those great moments get overshadowed by the ones that weren't so great. So now, I am left with the reality that what made her such a bad mother was just a side effect of what she needed to maintain a societally acceptable appearance. And that is the worst part of it all. That in the end, my upbringing could have been avoided if society wasn't the crap hole that it is. So yeah, I get to pretend that this isn't real. I know it's real, but it just sucks. It all just sucks really, really bad, and I am not ready to admit that I am going to have to live in this world far longer than most." Bri turns to Duncan, who realizes she is talking about him. He tries to smile, but it causes her to look down. In a fit of petulant anger, she kicks the garbage on the floor, revealing two syringes on the ground.

Scarlett bends down to pick up the syringes, careful to avoid the needles on each. "Who says fits of anger can't be productive?" She holds up her findings. "This seems to be what we came for."

Duncan turns to face Bri. He holds her face in his hands. "We are all in this together. No matter how long we may live for or how much we like each other. We are who we are. You are a beautiful person, and you need to understand that. I'm not just talking about a killer body, but a deadly mind, too. You have to accept that you are an amazing person. Whether it be because of, or despite, your upbringing, your mother, you being Legend, or whatever, you are wonderful, intelligent, caring, and I love you for all of that."

Allison watches Duncan say the words she wishes she could say to Brianna. Allison wishes she had walked up to Bri and said all those words, but Connor is here. Connor is her first love, the first person she ever felt any feelings for. Connor was the first to look at her as a woman with something to give to the world. But here she is, standing in the ruins of an abandoned high school, while her best friend holds two used needles in her hands, wishing she could pour her heart out. Allison did that once before, albeit at an even more inopportune time than this would have been. But there Allison stands, watching Duncan say the words she wishes were hers. If only she could make Connor understand.

Scarlett hoists the needles farther above her head, trying to refocus the group's collective attention. "Guys, we still have a task at hand here."

Connor scans the room, finding a discarded, reusable grocery bag on the floor. "Here. Put them in here."

Scarlett drops them into the bag for safekeeping and to prevent any accidental stabbings. "Now?"

Connor steps toward the door. "Now we get outta here before Ashby or someone worse finds us."

They all exit the decrepit ruins as fast as they can while trying not to make more noise. A combination that makes them look like ninja applicant rejects trying one last time to prove their worth on the beginner obstacle course. In all their effort to be silent, they do not see Ashby making a cautious approach from a distance. The group of friends does not know what he may have heard or who he may have seen. Worse yet, they do not know if their fate may have been worse than Rex's had he caught them. For now, though, they are safe.

The friends drive away from the shuttered high school packed like salted sardines in Connor's Camaro. They sit in silence, eyes forward and unmoving, as their psyches try to grasp the gravity of the newest threat to their way of life. The thoughts in their heads hold them immobile. There's a gnawing need for Connor and Scarlett to speak with his parents about this, a luxury they no longer possess. While they have their grandparents, this is a run-to-a-parent kind of event. In her mind, Bri cries out for sage advice from her mother that she knows will be left unanswered. Even Allison, the only Legend in this vehicle with a living parent, feels lost, unable to find refuge in the fact she has an elder to lean on and seek wisdom.

Then there is Duncan, who, too, sits in silence. The only noise in the car, besides the road beneath the tires, is his fidgeting. He's fighting against his urge to speak. His need to fill the silence with something that may bring a little levity to an otherwise tense and uncomfortable moment takes control of the glaring need for the opposite. He knows this battle they fight is not his own. He knows, too, what it is like to be without allies in a war that could desperately use some. He fights the urge to speak, knowing that he stands at the ready when needed.

Duncan's urge to break the silence is put to rest as Allison finally speaks up. "What do we do now?"

They all feel the two-ton silence lifted as their glances turn to the pink-haired girl daring enough to ask the question on everyone's mind. Even Duncan's restlessness finds a calming comfort in her words.

"We have to tell your father, Al." Connor's tone is very matter of fact. "The Council needs to know."

"They could already know," Allison responds without hesitation.

"But they might not," Bri speaks up. "I think, had my mother told someone, she might still be alive. But she didn't. She kept it to herself to try and protect me. Look where that got her."

"That's what I mean. Ms. Waldgrave knew my dad. She knew the Senate or Congress or Council or whatever they're called. They couldn't protect her," Allison spouts off without proving a point on any side of the budding argument.

"You're saying this is your dad's fault?" Brianna lashes out before weighing her words.

Duncan sees Allison's rising anger and extends an arm. "I don't think that's what Allison meant, my love."

Allison feels her adrenaline start to slow as his words penetrate the mounting tension.

Scarlett turns her head from the passenger seat to them. "I think what Al is trying to say is that even if The Council knew what had been happening to your mom, they had no way to prevent it."

Allison's head bounces up and down, a smirk across her face. "That, or they are powerless to do anything."

"We can't just handle all these problems that arise," Bri argues. "We have a government, or governing body or whatever the hell they are, for a reason. They will protect us, but they need to know."

"We could tell them, sure," Allison finally agrees. "Then we sit back and watch them do what they've been doing since before we were born." Condescension seeps from her voice.

Connor glances in the rearview mirror at his friends. "You both have valid points."

"Thanks for not helping either argument," Allison snaps back.

Connor shakes his head. "Slow your roll, Allison. What I mean is that you are right. These problems can't possibly be new. Legends have been around since their stories first started. This means the problems we face have been around just as long. But, like Bri says, the government we have should have some measures in place to help protect us."

He glances once again into the rearview mirror to see both Allison and Brianna nod their heads in agreement with him.

"Then there's a disconnect," Scarlett adds.

"Exactly," Connor confirms.

"They aren't very good at counseling," Allison thinks aloud. "I mean, if they know about all these things, they should be doing something. Each of us in this car has at least one dead parent because of who we are. To me, that seems like our leaders are not doing right, whatever it is that they do."

Duncan raises his hand to speak but decides to keep silent a little longer.

"It goes back to what we were told. We live in secret to stay safe," Connor recaps.

"Except that we aren't all that safe anymore," Brianna reminds him.

Duncan spies his moment to speak up. "Imagine how much more unsafe you would be if Normals knew."

"You know and haven't tried to kill us," Bri smiles.

Scarlett lowers her brow. "But as reactionary as he can be, he is smart. And more so, understanding."

"So?" Bri still misses the point.

Allison decides to attempt clarification. "There's like half a billion people living in the US."

"Just over 330 million," Connor corrects.

Allison waves him off. "Either way, that's a lot of people."

"And?" Bri still can't grasp the point.

"Think about school. Getting a C grade is average. And C-average students are pretty dumb." Allison waits for Bri to respond but sees she is still in the slow lane. "C is average, which means of those 330 million-plus people, most of them are C, D, or F students. What do you think would happen if, like, 200 million dumb people learned their next-door neighbors, coworkers, friends, whatever, might be a vampire or werewolf?" She sees Connor lift his head for another correction. "Or whatever we actually are, then saw what we look like when stressed? Do you think they'd welcome us with open arms or come at us bearing them?"

Duncan gives her a nod. "Nice wordplay."

"Thanks." Allison smiles back.

"So why do we stay hidden?" Bri starts to get the point.

"Because revealing ourselves after centuries, or millennia, will most probably be construed as an uprising. All the average masses will see it as an affront to them and their way of life—a threat to their livelihood. When in reality, nothing will have changed," Connor adds.

A lightbulb clicks above Bri's head. "So, coming out at the wrong time will only set us back further than any advancement we hope to make."

"Exactly, love," Allison let slip out. She quickly corrects, "I mean Bri. What was that? I must think I'm from England or something saying that." In a poor British accent, she jests, "Roight. Cheerio, mate." She watches them as they watch her dig a deeper hole. "An-y-way, I used to think that hiding who we are was stupid. I wanted to shout it to the world, but you realize that sometimes, even if you do, the world doesn't hear. And the scarier part, more scary part, more scarier part, is thinking about what people's reactions will be when you finally tell them. You think about how revealing such an important detail about yourself might affect all your relationships and how life will be different after that point. And once you establish that point, you can't go back to how it was before, even moments ago. So, we stay hidden because somehow the pain of that is easier than what you might possibly feel if you told."

Melancholy washes over Connor as he realizes his relationship with Allison is on a deadline. He keeps his eyes on the road, letting the moment linger.

Scarlett turns back to look out at the passing road. She is confident this moment, surrounded by her friends, is not the moment to speak on the underlying subject behind Allison's speech.

Brianna, lost on the subtext, turns to Duncan. "So, what did we decide?"

Duncan grabs her hand and pats their joined hands with his other. "We decided that sometimes, all the parents and authority figures in the world can't help us, and we have to decide on our own how to handle the crap life throws at us. Adulthood sucks, love. Adulthood sucks."

Duncan watches Allison sit, having pulled away from her friends and retreated into her mind. As much as he is not a Legend, he can empathize with her right now. The silence from the front seat is also a quiet confirmation of their understanding.

Bri turns to Allison, still completely lost on the subtext of what she was talking about. "Is this about you becoming a lesbian?"

A collective, audible sigh fills the car as Brianna utters those words. Allison turns away from everyone with a beet-red face to stare out the window.

Duncan pulls Bri's hand to him. "Not now, love. Not now."

CHAPTER 10

"Irony is how the people we wanted to emulate when we were young are the ones we are glad we ended up nothing like."

~J. McAllister~

Inessa stands in a pitch-black doorway to a hidden room in a hidden hall. Stale air assaults her nostrils as her hand fumbles around the walls, hoping to find a switch to illuminate the room. As the dust swirling around and invading her lungs begins to ease its attack, she flips a switch. Overhead track lights flood the room revealing walls of green-and-black serpentine marble. There is nothing else within this room—no tables to sit at, chairs, or couches to sit upon—only Inessa and her backpack. She unzips it to pull out two items—a parchment of a charcoal-drawn portrait and a white glove.

She turns back to peer down the darkened hallway behind her. She sees nothing but the light from this room as it fades to black. She listens for the sounds of muffled footsteps or any noise that would alert her to the presence of another living soul. She hears nothing. Inessa stands alone in a room she has been the sole visitor to since being assigned curator at the West Haven Museum of Natural History and Art. The stale air clinging to her nose assures her that the room has not been discovered. For the moment, the thick air and unfathomable smells provide her with a sense of security in what she has set foot in here to do. Every sense about her says this room has been all but forgotten.

Even in solitude, Inessa takes immense care in making each step toward the center of the room as quiet as she can. Slow, deliberate pressure on her toes, almost as if trying not to set off motion sensors. After high-knee-walking her way to the center, she places the parchment face down on the ground, on top of which she sets a white glove. She takes time to pull out a box of matchsticks from her pocket. Inessa holds the sulfur head of the match against the flint, but she hesitates at flicking it. She peers down at the parchment and glove, then at the fire-starter in her hand, before setting them down next to the paper. Lifting the glove to turn the parchment over, she stares at the charcoal portrait on the page—the portrait of someone who has yet to grow into the face Inessa sees.

"Who are you?" Inessa stares a little longer before placing it face down once more.

She strikes the match, letting it burn between her fingers. Her eyes dart back and forth from flame to drawing, from drawing to flame, as the fire eats away at the wooden stick. She squints her eyes, unsure of the proper action to take. After a moment of long hesitation, the flame bites her finger. Instincts cause her to shake the match, extinguishing it. She licks her thumb and index finger on her other hand, pressing them against the remaining embers, before pocketing the debris. She reaches for a new match but instead puts the box back in her pocket.

At the doorway, she once again scans the room. She isn't sure what she is looking for. Her instincts tell her this room is safe and will guard her secrets. She sees no other entrances or pathways into the room. Not even so much as an air duct vent, only the door in which she stands. She takes one deep breath of stale air, with undertones of mildew, as she shuts off the lights. She closes the entrance to the room. She takes a second deep breath to convince herself she has done the right thing. A third deep breath to help steel her resolve before turning her back on the space that may never see another visitor after this moment.

At the far end of the pitch-black hallway, she finds herself once again at a hidden doorway. After taking a few, big breaths to calm her nerves, she holds one in, listening for footsteps or conversation. Trying to hear any noise that indicates she must wait in the cover of secrecy a bit longer. But once more, her senses tell her she is in solitude.

Her finger slides a small lever open, and a doorway emerges from the mortar that holds together the cyclopean architecture of the wall. As it opens, a dim light struggles against the darkness to add some illumination.

Inessa emerges in a dry, dusty basement filled with old relics and seasonal decor. She shuts the secret door again. The seams blend into the rest of the wall, save one small spot. She pulls out a container filled with a bottle of water, a mixing bowl, and some grout she had stowed away behind the old decorations. She patches up the wall, sealing the only way into the hidden rooms beyond the wall.

Inessa feels her secrets are safe. At least for now.

Duncan, Bri, Connor, Scarlett, and Allison all stand next to their cars in the West Haven General Hospital parking lot. The light gray clouds dotting the sky set a stark mood for the occasion. They all face the entrance doors, watching for a particular face to emerge.

"This reminds me of those movies where someone is waiting for a prisoner to be released," Allison notes, staring at the doors, "to draw him back into the game."

"So, we're the parolee's friends cooking up their retirement score?" Connor laughs.

"If only we can convince him to turn back to the life of crime for this one last job," Duncan adds, tightening his arms around Bri.

"Wait, what? I thought we were waiting on Rex." Bri tries to keep up.

They all chuckle and shake their heads as the banter flies over her head.

"Don't worry, Bri. Just killing some time." Scarlett scans the parking lot's few cars. "It does have that feel, though. Like having him along will somehow make dealing with Ashby possible."

Connor holds up a pointed finger as a metaphorical lightbulb switches on over his head. "Actually, that might be where this leads."

Scarlett turns to her cousin. "What are you cookin' up, cuz?"

Before Connor can verbalize his thoughts, the automatic door to the hospital slides open, and Rex walks out. Dressed in the same clothes he was admitted in, just as dirty as before, he strides to Duncan. "Did'n' realize I warranted such a welcome wagon." He wraps his arms around Duncan.

Duncan's face scrunches as the smell of old, dirty clothes assaults his nostrils. "We need to get you some fresh clothes."

Rex backs off, a smile crossing his face. "Yeah, sorry 'bout dat. So, who're all your friends?"

Duncan opens his car door, motioning for Rex to enter. "We'll do intros once we get to a safer spot."

Vistrus draws the windows in his home office shut before running duct tape down the width of each blind and length of the drapes, pressing them snugly against the wall, shutting out all light from the outside world. Not one tiny hole remains for prying eyes to spy in through. The desk lamp provides the sole light source illuminating the room. Vistrus has installed two deadbolts on the inside of the office door, locking himself inside.

The open diaries sprawled about the desk and surrounding floor are the sources of his budding paranoia, a trait he now shares with his departed wife. He sits in complete Legendary form, scribbling away in his notebook with blinding speed. The blur of his hand copies each hand-picked phrase from Inessa's diaries word for word.

The empty Mind holds only the white. One-half white. One half nor right. The empty Mind is not so right. Nor is it white. Green and black. Black and green. Serpentine. Holds only the Faoi Dhó Duine. The Mind is empty. My mind's not empty. All alone, surrounded by stone. Surrounded by those at home. At home in stone. The stone is home. He understands. He is my man. My man with a plan. I am the plan. I know it's his land. This land. This land is our land. My land. The Mind's land is his land. My land first, but he does not know. The Mind is like a snake. It slithers away in darkness. Hissing, tongue out, until it is safe. My love. My love. Falling away. Further away. So close. Just out of reach. No matter how *far. No matter. Forgotten matter. Resting. Waiting. The Mind sits empty. Almost. But now it can shine. The Mind I made so it can shine. Darkness. Light. If you please. Darkness if you don't please. These. Almost. Almost.*

My new mission started. The beauty of the swirling green and black walls was indescribable … The Mind is black and green marble.

His hand slows as he writes the last words. "The mind is the sealed room. I know this now. But what of the rest?" he whispers to himself. His eyes dart about, searching for answers in the aether of the universe around him. "What of this Faoi? What did it mean, my love? What does it still mean? Does it still mean anything? Did it ever mean anything? Was it something to throw prying eyes off the real message?"

His bony hand shifts the diary to the side and pulls another to him. He flips through to a dog-eared page. He grabs his pen to further punish the pages of his notebook. He presses the tip of the pen against the page, pausing to read the passage.

Their voice is gone. I think I know where. Not here. There. Close by, not here. Their voice. Not a choice without it. Taken away. Met a four. Never met the five. No longer alive. No longer on fire. The fire consumes if it were alive. Shall it be alive, or shall it remain at rest. What's best, the fire knows. The fire says no.

He relaxes his hand as the pulsating veins bulge out of each finger, ready to explode. Tapping the pen against the page, he asks himself, "Whose voice? Who has no voice? The Sentinels? Could this be them? We have known about them for so long. She would not need to hide this. Would she? There have always only been the two. Never four to meet. And never five. I should be writing these thoughts down. It will keep better that way."

The tapping morphs into writing as the speed returns to his hand. His hand blurs above the page as he writes the words he needs to remember.

> Who were the five? And the fire? There are five of us on the Council. Could this have been a previous? Could that room I suspect to have been, actually been a Council chamber? Were the Sentinels on The Council then? Where did she meet these four? She met a four. Metafour. Metaphor. Ha. My love. Clever. Now to figure out what the metaphor is.

Vistrus stares at the books before him. His sunken cheeks and withered features try to take in all that surrounds his desk and chair. He reaches down, picking up a diary off the floor. A dog-eared page opens, pleading for transcription.

> The silent ones who observe. Never interfering, like documentarians. I was approached. We talked, or at least I think we did. He never spoke a word. Neither did his female companion. But still, we spoke. I knew what they were saying, like holding a conversation with a house cat. People make up their cat's response, but yet it feels so real. And they responded to my inner dialog as if they placed it there. They spoke of something they called "The Legend of the Faoi Dhó Duine," after which they handed me the parchment.

As he finishes transcribing, he continues writing his thoughts as if everything is connected.

> If the person on the parchment is this Faoi, then it is real. I must protect them. No matter. Then we must figure out what the Legend is. What it means and why it is so vital that Inessa did this to herself to protect it.

He reaches for a different diary. "Let me see what lies within these pages."

Why the body count? Why leave the bodies out? Protect the home. Protect those that grow. Nations rise and nations fall. One responsible. The one behind it all. If I should fall. Chess. Like a queen. Or a pawn on a kill. I know the reason why. Why they all died. Why. Why. I. The Mind. The Mind protects her, the Faoi Dhó Duine. The hand shall light the way. Why don't they care? What isn't there? Erase it all. Erase the fall. Erase the past. Repeat the last. Hide it from all. Except from me. Under his nose. Under his toes. My love. Under it all. It is him, I know. I know why. But will they listen? Will they care? Do I dare? I must...

Vistrus flips a few pages forward.

Good Steve McQueen. Faoi Dhó Duine. The Mind. God Steve. He won't get it. I am done. I am dumb. Why did I do this? The Mind matters. The Mind is all that matters. I have mine. I have mine. No one believes me. No one understands. I have the Mind. But it is empty now. Nothing left in the Mind. Only the Faoi Dhó Duine and white. Save McQueen. Vistrus, love. Falling away. Can't explain. Hidden. Must hide. Secrets die. Can't share. Not secret. God Save The Queen.

Vistrus flips back and forth between the passages. His mind has caught onto some connection, some relevance between the two. He knows something connects them but can't quite place his finger on it. His fingers flip the passages countless times, trying to eliminate any information that seems too obvious. He tries to pinpoint the words that come across as mundane. A phrase he has read as many times as he has flipped back and forth sticks out: "The hand shall light the way." Though he knows there was nothing in the serpentine chambers except for the parchment and a glove. No hand that lights up like a neon sign in a dark alley. But the other passage mentions the word white, the color of the glove. He cannot be sure, though now he feels that this could be the key to why their homeland assigned them to West Haven, to figure out what happened to the old Council or whoever used such a secret chamber. And if his dearly departed was correct, the white glove is somehow the key to it all.

While this offers no long-term solace or comfort, a sense of calm washes over him for the moment. His withered nose starts to form again as blood pools in his mouth from the sudden, rapid teething, as all missing teeth break through the gums. His veins recede into his arms as his hair thickens to his usual lustrous mane.

He jots down a few ideas in his notebook pertaining to the possible importance of the white glove. He closes the diaries that sit atop others. A few passages catch his eye from the journals that remain open; he feels they are worth jotting into his condensed reader's version.

He was so real. A man shrouded in shadow and mystery, yet I could feel his breath as he looked down on me from beneath his hooded face. His menacing stare, blank behind the shadow, yet I know it was for me. His deep, slow breaths ... heavy. He wants me gone.

B. It's a game of chess. How to tell my love? I can't. What to do? Who is the Faoi Dhó Duine? The Faoi Dhó Duine is the key.

It is all a game of chess. And Vistrus is a great player.

A heaviness sinks back into his chest, squeezing his heart, that this was never about chess but him not learning her code while she lived. Perhaps, if had he figured out what she was trying to say, she would still be alive, still with them. A heavier feeling holds him in his chair in a realization that perhaps had he listened, Inessa might still be alive.

Reruns of some old sitcom about a short, foul-mannered alien living in the suburbs drone on the television, but they ignore it, opting to instead all face each other in the main living room of Connor's house. The conversation engrossing them is long past the formal introductions and any uncomfortableness that anyone may have felt upon first meeting the newest member of their little circle.

Rex finishes recollecting the attack on him while Duncan and Bri were visiting eliciting a hearty laugh from everyone.

Connor waves his hand to quell his laughter. "Wait, wait, wait. How the hell did you manage to avoid her after that?"

A half-smile crosses Rex's face. "Dude, dey trew' er in a closet."

Allison cocks her head. "That can't be legal."

Connor takes the helm on this. "Solitary confinement, love. Not an actual closet."

Allison double-taps her left temple. "Gotcha. I'm quick sometimes."

"Sometimes," Scarlett jests.

A jest that may have been, but Scarlett using Allison as the butt of a joke does not sit well right now. Perhaps because Brianna sits among them and Allison does not want to look bad in her eyes. It occurs to Allison that Scarlett making a joke about her, no matter how innocent, could be Scarlett's way of trying to further connect with Bri. She looks at her friends, all with smiles on their faces, laughing and having a grand ol' time. Allison can't help but think she missed something while being caught up in her thoughts, possibly something said about her that made them all laugh at her once more. Some new joke of which she is the butt.

Allison excuses herself for a moment, adjourning to the restroom. She rests her hands on the sink, staring at herself in the mirror. She sees no changes. No shrinking nose or teeth falling into the sink. No thinning hair or skin stretching over muscles too big for her petite frame. Nothing. She pulls out her flask and takes an exaggerated swig. As the contents travel down her throat, calm washes over her. She knows her friends are not malicious. She knows they would not turn on her for some cheap shot. Sure, they joke around with each other all the time, making little jokes at one another's expense, but they are never serious. They have no sharp edges meant to cut. She stares back into the mirror, trying to look deep into her eyes. She wonders if Brianna were not here, would the joke have affected her the way it did. She is curious if Scarlett would have even made that joke had Brianna not been present. Allison knows the ludicrousness of her thoughts—that she is spiraling into some loop of negativity. She takes another small sip from the flask to finish dulling down the edges of her thoughts.

She makes it back out to the living room. All eyes turn to her, but Brianna is the mouth that speaks. "We are about to discuss some serious events with our new friend, Rex. You up for this?"

Allison takes a step away from them, tilting her head a little to the side as her neck pulls back. She tosses a hand in the air. "Why wouldn't I be up for this? What the hell was that supposed to mean? You think I'm not up for whatever we are about to do?"

Brianna stands up and leans in to whisper to Allison, "Remember that time I became a little unhinged, and you told me, 'It's all good'?"

Allison nods.

"Well..." Brianna pulls away from Allison's ear, "it's all good."

Allison looks at her other friends, who all have moved on from the moment Allison is stuck in. She gives Brianna a thankful nod before sitting beside Connor with her hand on his thigh.

"' Fore we begin wit whatever we're gonna talk about, I have ta ask. What's your interest in Ashby?" As honest a question from Rex as his Chicago accent is thick. He is not in The Nation and doesn't know anything about it, so he sees no reason they would be interested in Ashby.

Duncan, Connor, and Scarlett all stare at each other. No awesome telepathic conversation takes place as they do with Raymond and December, but they know what the other is saying nonetheless. All three of them unsure of who should speak.

The only person who has caught onto the fact that one of them must speak is Scarlett. So, she does. "Rex, there are things that can't be explained. Things you have to see to believe."

Rex turns to Duncan. "Is she on religion or drugs or sumtin'?"

Duncan doesn't laugh. He keeps a serious face. "Listen to her."

"I'm not on religion," Scarlett clarifies, shifting on her cushion. "This isn't about faith. It's about mental capacity." She pauses for a moment to redirect her thoughts. "Have you ever seen things you can't explain? Things that you swear were real but logically know they can't be?"

Rex looks to Duncan. He hesitates his words. "Is … she … serious right now?"

"Serious as cancer, my friend." Duncan keeps his reply simple.

"I can't answer that." Rex holds in what he knows he saw.

"It's okay," Duncan assures him. "When we ran into each other at Ducky's, you were going off about something, which led us to Ashby."

Duncan waits to see if Rex will start talking, but he doesn't.

Connor decides to chime in. "It's all good. You can tell us whatever it is that you are holding back."

Rex still doesn't say anything.

"We've all seen things we'd rather not have until we realized what we saw isn't something that can be denied away," Brianna tosses in her two cents.

Allison knows those words were pointed at her. At least, she thinks they were. Even if they weren't, they are relevant nonetheless.

Rex looks to Allison. "You're da only one who hasn't said a word."

Allison shakes her head in slow, short, deliberate motions. "Nothing to say. But you should answer Scarlett."

Rex takes a deep breath in, unsure of his words. He toys with the idea of modifying the facts, tempering them to something more believable. Rex knows, though, that no matter how he changes his recollection, it will all seem fanciful and far-fetched. He scans his newfound friends one more time as they sit in anticipation of his words. He takes one more deep breath to steady his hand which had begun tapping out some spastic rhythm on his leg. "As I told Dunc before, Ashby gave us some blue stuff." Rex's already over-the-top Chicago accent thickens in his nervousness. "I took it. I felt like sumthin' wuz'n right. Like, da whole mood was eerie. A feelin' in da air. But I didn' know how to not, so I did."

Duncan lowers his head, guilt weighing it down. "I should have stayed."

Rex shakes his head. "I shoulda left wid you. If ya stayed, you'd be dead, too." Rex doesn't need to look at them to feel their eyes glued to him. "Ashby said da drugs would separate da men from da men." He reads the slight confusion on Allison's face but doesn't want to slow the story down. "Capital M and lowercase. He said if we took it, it would show who was worthy. Da way he spoke. It was inspirational. He knew what ta say ta make us feel … like we weren' garbage." Rex looks to the ground, shame holding him down. "If only."

"What happened after you took the drugs?" Scarlett nudges his story along.

Rex lifts his head. The uncertain memories flood his mind. "I saw 'em change. Ashby said he wasn' worthy. That's when things got real."

"How did he change?" Scarlett nudges a little more. "What happened to him?"

"He got big. Real big. Real strong. Real fast. Ashby an' him started goin' at it. He told me ta run, so's I did," Rex summarizes that fateful night.

Connor turns to Allison, Scarlett, and Bri. "He's hunting down Legends. He must be stopped."

Allison straightens herself up as a devilish grin overtakes her face. "He must be stopped," she mocks him. "A big dramatic moment from a '90s film, don't 'cha think?"

"Fine," Connor relents. "We need to stop him. Either way."

Rex raises his hand. "What're Legends? What's goin' on? Is everthin' I saw for real?"

Duncan doesn't wait for one of them to answer. "I think this should come from me. Just let me know if what I'm saying is wrong."

Urgency pours over Rex. His wide eyes beg for information. "What's goin' on, Duncs?"

Duncan takes a deep breath as he gathers his thoughts. Moments like this are not planned for. Duncan finds, in this instance, he needs a second or two to gather his bearings. "What you saw was real." Rex starts fidgeting in his seat, about to speak, but Duncan won't let him. "What happened. It's not meant to. Everything Ashby is telling you is lies. He is trying to kill many good people. People who want nothing more than to live normal lives."

"How can you say dat? I saw 'em transform. Change. Dat's not normal!" Rex works himself closer to hysterics.

"For you. No. For me. No. That's not normal. But for others, it's a part of their lives. A condition that is nothing more than a disease." Duncan winces at his choice of words. "Sorry, guys." He turns to the rest of them.

Scarlett joins in, "It is a disease."

Rex continues that thought, "One dat Ashby is tryin' ta cure."

"One that doesn't need a cure," Scarlett interjects, "It's not contagious. It's auto-immune. You can't catch it."

"It's not herpes," Brianna slips in. The rest of the group lets her choice words slide.

Rex backs up, trying to distance himself from the group, only to push against the back of his seat. "How do ya all know so much? Duncan, tell me your new friends ain't some monster squad. I saw what he did ta Ashby. Dat wasn't somethin' I want happenin' ta me!"

"You're a good person, right, Rex?" Allison asks.

Rex is thrown off by her question. "What?"

"You think of yourself as a good person. Maybe not a saint, but not some evil, mustache-twirling villain, so to speak," Allison clarifies.

Rex furrows his brow. "I like ta think so. Others may not."

"But those others. If they thought you a threat based on one isolated incident, would you feel they were justified in trying to kill you?" The clarity in Allison's words is a surprise, evident in Scarlett's smile.

Rex looks at the group. "'Course not."

Scarlett chimes in, "And you would hope that someone would understand the precarious position you found yourself in and offer a hand to ensure your safety. Even if it meant others might view them as you are viewed."

Rex is a little lost in her words. "Yeah. Yeah."

Duncan comes back into the mix. "That's all we are doing. Helping give voice to those who have none."

Rex tosses the idea around in his head, wasting no time agreeing with it. "So, whadda we do now?"

"First, you can't say a word to anyone. No family. No other friends. We do not even talk about it outside these walls. Understood?" Duncan lays it out for him.

Rex nods. "Understood."

Connor smiles. "Good. You are an integral part of this. But there's a lot to flesh out."

Scarlett leans in. "Then let's get started."

CHAPTER 11

"Ghosts are real.
Just not as you've come to know."
~E. DeSalvo~

October rust from dense woods surrounds Inessa. Orange and red-tinted leaves float to the ground as trees fall into autumn slumber. Only traces remain of any event that may have transpired in this spot. Inessa holds still, listening to the sounds of the forest around her, hearing only the pitter-patter of tiny woodland creatures preparing for the winter, falling leaves, and whistling wind. Satisfied no one else is around, Inessa lets her nose shrivel to half its size—withered and purple. She spits a couple of teeth into her hand as she slurps back the blood from the loss. She pockets them, so as not to taint the area further. Her skin turns trans-lucent enough to see the veins flow with blood beneath, but they do not bulge or pulsate.

She stands, scanning the area around her. The glow of blood and bodily fluids on the forest floor betrays the secret the leaves try to hide. Inessa's Legendary eyes can see what a Normal's eyes could not. She kicks the leaves away, revealing more and more evidence of a recent struggle. She touches the dried ground, feeling for something that will explain why the violence that arrived here did so in such a fashion.

She spies the faint glow of old blood splatter across the trees. Hanging onto the trees with silent desperation to be discovered are tufts of hair. Coarse and thick hair that would be mistaken for wolf or bear to any *passerby, but she spots the minutiae that separate fur from hair and animal from man. The tufts cling to the trees, waiting for her to save them from anonymity. She pulls them off, placing them into a cloth pouch for later examination. She kicks the leaves while checking the surrounding trees, revealing more dried blood on the forest floor. In one spot, the glow of the blood is interrupted with thick, scab-like chunks. These, too, would pass for tree bark to the untrained eye.*

To Inessa, though, they are broken pieces of fairy skin—a thick armor that coats their skin and helps camouflage them into surrounding woods. She picks over the trees and ground, managing to find numerous human teeth and one sharp elongated canine. Immediately recognizable to her as belonging to a member of the Ramdas Society or vampire for the layman. Recognizable because of the similarity to her own.

Tension tightens her body. She tingles from the knowledge that where she stands, many of her kind were killed and, under different circumstances, it could have been her. She swallows hard, trying to strengthen her resolve. She listens but hears nothing to sound an alarm.

So far, she has found evidence, to the best of her knowledge, of members from three of the Societies—Ramdas, Dryden, and Dach. If the decaying teeth are from an Undying, then four of the Societies, including Bradstreet, but she knows she won't find evidence from the fifth. That impossibility makes her assumption the best theory so far—that someone murdered a member from each of the five Societies. She knew there was a massacre to investigate, but she was not told what it entailed. A seed sows itself in the back of her mind, a seed that flew in on the winds of curiosity. A tiny seed that grows as fast as corn in peak season, asking, "Why not find who killed them? Does The Body already know? Do they not care?" She knows her mission is to make sure their secrets have not spilled. But if she makes certain this macabre event is forgotten to the annals of time and nothing more, what's to stop it from happening again?

Her ears pick up a snapping of a branch nearby—heavier feet than a squirrel or chipmunk. She loses the glow of the stained blood as her nose returns, and her skin regains its porcelain hue. The distant laughter of two young lovers echoes in her ears. She listens as they venture away from her, laughing over what she can only guess is youthful innocence. Inessa finds herself wondering what her mission is supposed to accomplish. She was given orders in her homeland—a land familiar with memories of first kisses, first loves, family dinners, and cold Russian nights. Now, she stands in a forest somewhere on Native Potawatomi land on a mission to cover up an unknown number of murders—Legendary murders presumably committed by a Legend. She knows of no other who could pull off such a feat.

A thought intrudes her mind like a midsummer rainstorm on an otherwise sunny day; suppose it was one person who perpetrated such unthinkable acts. Who would be powerful enough to take on, judging by the amount of blood, at least five Legends? She must visit the mortuary and chat with the undertaker to see what conclusions he drew.

Trails of green moss grow along the damp stone mortuary walls. The smell of mold and decomposition assault Inessa's nostrils, presumably, from the crude examination tables littered with rusted dissection tools and old bloodstains. On a few of the slabs rest the deceased, covered with time-yellowed sheets to provide privacy for the afterlife. The light, too, is faint, only lending enough luminescence to perform his job just enough to afford minimal comfort to those still alive.

"Why didn't you come here first?" The mortician wipes food on his dirty apron before uncovering one of the deceased.

Inessa steps away upon seeing the dead body, kept long past fresh. Decay has already begun to set in. Mother Nature's little helpers now obscure any features of who this once was in their effort to return him to ashes, dust, and dirt. She notices remnants of who he was—stray hairs too long to be random. A couple of three-inch-long hairs in the temple, away from the hairline, are not random placement from some unexpected ailment, nor are the numerous inch-long knuckle hairs. To the mortician not in The Body, stray hairs like these must come off as some unfortunate bit of fate. Still, Inessa knows the struggles that this man dealt with in life: the pain of the numerous transitions; the rapid muscle growth taking place in mere moments instead of years of pain-staking workouts; the need to hide his true self from the public eye, only able to be his natural self in the comfort of those like him. Hiding away for fear of what might be, or in this case, has been, done to him if someone found out. Here lies what the outside world would call a werewolf. To her, he is a member of the Dach Society.

The mortician uncovers the next deceased. Telltale signs to Inessa that what the man next to her mistook for animal attacks and feasting scavenger markings are natural changes from an Undying transition—the missing eye, even though the socket is not torn or chewed at. The skin aged and decayed far past the other bodies. The missing teeth and sallow skin of someone well past their prime, but Inessa knows he was not. He very well may have been in his prime, or worse, not even had a chance to reach it yet. She nods, and the mortician covers up the victim.

The next body was a mystery to the doctor of the dead. He could not give Inessa a reasonable explanation for why the bark, from what he assumed to be an oak tree, had fused with her skin. His best guess was that violent force somehow caused the skin and tree to bond. An explanation that Inessa is satisfied with, not because it is correct—it is far from—but because the poor mortician has no clue what lies in front of him. Inessa is happy that this fairy will get a chance to rest in peace.

Of the remaining two bodies, he skips the next in line for a moment and uncovers one whose face he cannot explain. The shriveled nose and lips thin enough to not even be considered lips are just the beginning. The large muscles, not quite as bulging as the member of the Dach Society, but varicose veins, nevertheless, with thinned hair like strings of thread and just as delicate, are all iced over with the missing teeth, save two canines.

"And the strange thing is, it's not as if this person had his teeth pulled. He only ever grew these two teeth," he says, shaking his head. "Poor soul. For someone who must have struggled with food, he sure knew how to make the most of himself." He covers the body before stepping back to the one he skipped over. "To the less educated, one might think I have monsters of some sort lying on my tables."

A sad smile escapes Inessa because, while he might not know the truth, he sees the humanity in the deceased before him—people capable of love and hate, joy and anger, happiness and sadness, not like the one who did this to them. One, she can only presume, was incapable of love, joy, or happiness.

The mortician grabs a half-eaten steak with his bare hand, ripping off a chunk in his mouth. He slaps it back on the plate while he chomps his food. "This one, though..." he catches a bit of food falling from his mouth and tosses it back in, "couldn't tell ya for sure. No bruising. No cuts. No reason to cut into her."

Inessa turns from the unblemished cadaver. "Then how did you deter-mine this woman's cause of death if you did not look beyond the surface?"

He stops chewing his food, letting it rest in his mouth. Inessa's words draw contempt from him. "Do not question my methods, ma'am. We have neither the money nor the resources to investigate every death when I can logically justify the cause." He swallows his half-chewed food.

"What did you determine the cause of death to be then?" Inessa inspects the body.

Inessa finds the mortician's observations are correct. There are no evident signs of bruising. No cuts from which she bled out. There is no trauma of any sort to indicate why she died.

Inessa extends her hand toward the mortician. "May I borrow your blade?"

He hands her a knife and watches as Inessa cuts an incision across a rib. She peels the skin away to examine the bone and taps the rib with her finger a few times, trying to measure its hardness. She spies a bone saw on a nearby table. "Do you mind cutting a piece of her rib for me?"

His raised eyebrow indicates Inessa will need to provide more reason before he starts dismantling the dead. "I'd like to bring it back to my client. I think this would provide insight into certain…"

Before she can finish fabricating a lie, the mortician grabs the saw. "Despite what the conditions around me might make one think, I do not take pleasure in dismantling the deceased for no reason. Whatever yours might be, I trust it is a good one."

Inessa tries to restrain a smile, as she knows if her assumption is cor-rect, his worries will be for naught.

The doctor of the deceased saws with all his might at the frag-ile-looking rib bone, but he makes no progress. His face tightens as he applies more pressure. "Blade must be dull."

Inessa nods her head. "Must be." She knows that while it may be, a dull blade is not the reason the bone won't cut.

He leans on the saw with all his might, trying in vain to cut her a sample. As he climbs on the unsteady table, adding more weight to the saw, it snaps. He falls onto the cadaver before catching himself.

He hops off the table and adjusts his stained clothes. "Apologies, ma'am. Seems my saw required replacing. If it wasn't before, it is now."

Inessa smiles at the man. "Thank you for trying."

He nods in defeat.

A sense of calm and satisfaction washes over Inessa. She knows that this man felt his tools were inadequate, not that the bones of the deceased Legend before him were ever going to break. Had her assumption been wrong, a poor soul would be missing part of a rib, but they are not—the dead lay whole, albeit with a small incision. The five dead laid out in front of her account for one representative from each Society of the nation: Lanier Society, now Frye Society—Bradstreet, now Tennyson—Dryden, now Poe—Ramdas, now Coleridge—and Dach, now Kipling. The worry that eats away at her calm is who out there is strong enough to take down all five Legends in one fight. She worries that someone out there, not in The Body, knows their secrets. Someone who is plotting against them. Or worse, someone within The Body that is doing the same. A deadlier opponent might be lurking out there.

Her concern here is to ensure a tragedy such as this does not occur again. To let this be forgotten in the annals of history. A gnawing bug keeps whispering to her that if pushed aside, it will indeed happen again. She knows that whispering voice is correct, especially if the one responsible is a Legend.

Realizing the mortician never answered her earlier question, she repeats, "What did you say for this one's cause of death?"

He swallows a bite of steak. "My guess is she was scared to death. Seen it a few times before." He gnaws off another strip of meat, trying to study her reaction.

Inessa holds a good poker face. "Sounds good to me. Do you think there could be any other causes of their demise, if you had to postulate?"

He tosses his steak back on the plate, once again wiping his hands on his apron. "Pretty cut and dry for those four," he says, waving a hand at the others. "Animals. No reason to suspect otherwise. This leaves just the guess, educated as it may be, for this one," he resigns, covering the last victim again.

"Hmm," Inessa says, not a hundred percent convinced of his words. "Sorry about your tools."

Further wiping dirt, grease, and blood off his hands, he admits, "They wear out eventually. I should pay better attention."

The mortician finishes wiping his hand before reaching into his pocket. "Found this on them. Can't make heads or tails of it. Maybe you can."

Inessa takes the parchment from his sullied hand and leaves without reading it.

Allison lays on her bed as the light from the golden hour outside brightens her room. She engrosses herself in the diary entries scanned by her and Scarlett a while back. Allison soaks in every word she reads. She even reads each sentence a few times to find any hidden meaning or to understand her late mother's mindset when writing her thoughts. Allison imagines in her mind that she is writing them, trying to feel what her mother felt—the worry, the guilt, the anxiety, the paranoid measures taken to ensure their safety. Allison tries to decode what her mother wanted to tell them and from what she was trying to hide. For the moment, Allison is not sure which of the two is more important. All she knows is that while reading these entries, free from her father catching her red-handed, she feels a calm sense of connection to her mother that has long eluded her.

Scarlett lies on her stomach across the foot of Al's bed, feet kicking the air as she reads some modern-day dime-store romance novel about an aging record producer as he encounters the love that he left behind for fame. A sudden laugh disrupts the otherwise quiet room. "Al, have you gotten to the part where her boyfriend comes home?!"

Allison looks up from her screen. "Read that book a few times. Very cathartic, I think."

Scarlett flips the book over to keep her page. "Cathartic? Nice word. You holding up okay?"

The corner of Allison's lip upturns before she even realizes it. "Yeah. I think so. Yeah. These entries seem to help me understand who she was. I think it's what I've been missing. So, yeah. It's what's been keeping me up and making my dreams what they are."

Scarlett sits up, realizing the seriousness of Allison's answer. "Say 'yeah' one more time. It'll make me believe you."

Allison's face scrunches into a look that could kill.

Scarlett takes a metaphorical step back from her poking. "So ... what? You don't think the dreams are as cryptic, or foretelling, as before?"

Allison exits the PDF file and closes her laptop. "No. Yeah. I think they're still prophetical. I just think knowing what they are is like finding little titbids about myself in my mom."

Scarlett tilts her head. "Titbids?"

Allison shrugs as if her word is common knowledge. "Yeah, titbids. Little, like, pieces of things."

Trying not to smile at Allison's mix-up, Scarlett corrects her, "Tidbits. No tits."

"You're no tits," Allison says, chuckling. "But yeah, whatever, tidbits," Allison resigns. "I think that's what the diary entries are." Allison shoots her head toward the bedroom door. "Dad's coming."

Scarlett turns to the door to listen. "I don't hear anything, Al."

Allison waves her hand at the door. "He'll be here. No talk about the stuff."

Scarlett nods in understanding.

"Enter, Father," Allison's voice takes on the tone of defensive petulance.

The door creeps open. "I see your hearing is getting more attuned."

"Whatever, maybe you're just getting louder in your old age." Allison takes a playful jab.

"Perhaps." Vistrus plays into her dismissal before turning to Scarlett. "I would like a moment with my daughter, Miss McAllister."

Scarlett hops up. "That's my cue." She gives Allison a quick hug. "Call me."

Allison nods. "Obvs."

Scarlett shuts the door behind her, leaving the father/daughter duo alone in Allison's room.

Vistrus stares at his baby girl, waiting for her to give him her full attention. She sets the laptop a little further from her and scooches to the edge of her bed. "What's up?" The confusion comes across in her words. Whatever his need to speak about at this moment is lost on her.

"I have to head out. Some business that must be tended to," Vistrus begins.

Allison shrugs a shoulder. "Okay, I guess. I'm assuming this 'business...'" she air-quotes the word business, "has to do with The Nation and The Council."

He nods. "It does."

"I know you didn't kick Scarlett out to tell me you're leaving. What's up, Dad?" Allison starts tapping her fingers on the bed. Nervous energy overtakes her calm.

"After due consideration, I shall help you find a therapist who understands your unique situation." Saying those words out loud causes a wave of relief to wash over him, lifting a suffocating weight off his chest. He knows this has been a contention point for over two years. He hopes Allison will find this to be positive news.

She does not react with the outward joy he anticipated. No, she looks to him without a mile-wide smile but instead, with a weak, half-smile, a portent to something less than what he will consider desirable.

"I don't want to see one anymore." She brushes off his admittance to her needs.

Vistrus takes a step toward her. "I do not understand. You fought for so long. Now a sudden change of heart?"

"I wouldn't say sudden," Allison squeaks out before being interrupted.

"It is to me," he interjects.

"I've found…" she lets that thought trail off, fidgeting while searching for the best way to say what she feels now, "I …What I was needing was a reason for my dreams to be happening. More than just the fact they mean what they can mean. I needed to find out why me. Why not Scar or Con? It's only happened to *me.*"

"Are you asking if it is something unique to the Coleridge Society? It is not." Her father offers little solace.

She shakes her head. "I think that … knowing Mom had the same dreams, well, not the same, but you get what I mean. Dreams that were cryptic in meaning. I think that has helped offer me some peace with what has been running through my mind." She does her best to convince her father she is all right. She knows that the only person she has to convince is herself, though she is not there yet.

Vistrus nods. "I thought knowing Inessa had the same dreams would make you want to see a therapist more so."

Allison shakes her head. "Sorry to disappoint, Daddy." She shrugs it off, not knowing how to react to his words.

"Never disappointed. Just surprised." Vistrus turns to leave his daughter for the evening but stops, resting his hand on the knob.

"If you ever change your mind, if there is ever anything you want to talk to me about, I am here. You will never disappoint me or make me think less of you."

"Nothing, Dad. Promise. Just been reading books on dreams and the subconscious mind. There's some catharticism to them."

Vistrus smiles; now is not the time to correct her word. Closing the door behind him, he chuckles to himself. "Catharticism. Good attempt. Catharsis, my dear. Catharsis."

Finding herself alone in her room, Allison opens her laptop to dive back into the journal entries. An itching in the back of her thoughts reminds her this momentary comfort will not last. Like the flask that she befriends so often, this, too, will only be a temporary relief from the mental demons that plague her.

Reaching between the mattress and headboard to pull out her flask, she chugs down more than a few gulps before placing it back in the safety of its hiding spot. She melts into the comfort of her bed, under her laptop, staring past the words written so long ago and into the abyss of her mind. She knows she cannot hide from those thoughts she is not yet ready to face.

The dim lights, drawn shades, and mid-90s slasher flick playing on the television provide the perfect mood for Brianna and Duncan to cuddle this Friday evening. Sure, the two young lovers have been intimate in their year of dating, but since Bri's mother has passed, her house has not been the location to get hormones coursing. Especially the living room, where they set the stage tonight and where Sylvia Waldgrave, Linda Espinoza, and that nurse were killed on prom night last year.

Duncan sits, his left arm stretched out across the top of the couch. His right arm cradles his love. She rests, snuggled into him to enjoy the romance, solitude, and movie slaying of the evening. No one to jab at her past digressions from friendships. No one to unintentionally kill the thoughts that run through young lovers' minds. Just her, nestled into his chest with his arm around her and a small bowl of movie-theater-buttered popcorn.

Bri tosses a handful of butter-dripping popcorn into her mouth. Not wanting to kill the moment nor wipe it on her clothes or couch, she rubs her hands together to soak in the melted butter that coats her hand, a move not unnoticed by Duncan.

Shaking his head, a weak chuckle escapes with his words. "Did you just lotion your hands with popcorn butter?"

Bri continues rubbing her hands together. "It's not specifically popcorn butter. It's just butter."

Duncan tilts his head. "Actually, it's butter-flavored vegetable oil."

Bri shakes her head. "Nuh-uh. The box says, 'made with real butter.' And either way, it's good for your skin."

"Oil and butter are good for your skin? Don't things like that cause zits?" Duncan is weary of her expertise on this subject.

"I was reading an old *Cosmo*. Some runway model, Letitia Something-or-other, said she did it because she figured if it's good in small amounts inside, it had to be in small amounts on the outside," Bri gives her rebuttal.

"Butter, though?" Duncan's only reply.

"Well, she used olive oil. But I had butter. Plus, it's not like I do it every day." She lays back on his chest, after tossing a few more pieces in her mouth. "Plus, I gotta keep my skin moisturized. Skin condition and all."

Duncan nods to himself. "You look beautiful, my love."

Bri smiles to herself as they return to the movie. On the screen, a small twelve-year-old boy backs up toward a window, scared by the dead body thrown like a rag doll through a picture window. As his babysitter bends down to investigate the body, a masked killer breaks through the other window, grabbing the young boy.

Duncan enjoys the movie and the closeness it brings as Brianna buries herself further within his chest. He wraps his arm around her to protect her from the scary movie.

As the babysitter bludgeons the masked killer over and over and over with a hammer to try and free the young boy, Brianna's mind is taken back to her senior prom night. The defining moment when they walked into this very room to discover her dying mother and the teacher, Mrs. Espinoza, who made it that way. Bri finds herself, even within the safety of Duncan's embrace, unable to move or free her mind from that night. With each hammer strike against the on-screen killer, Bri can only picture Allison striking down the biology teacher, claiming her love for Bri as she worked out some still unresolved inner feelings.

Brianna lays against Duncan, but she can feel the tingling sensation as her skin loosens around her jowls. The taste of iron floods her mouth more and more with each tooth that falls out. She points her head down to try and hide from her boyfriend.

Duncan runs his hand over her head, oblivious to what is happening in his lap. "It's just a movie, babe." He looks down to make sure the movie is not too much to handle, but he sees her scalp—the thinning, wispy hair that accompanies her transition. His eyes widen. "Are you okay, my love?"

Brianna jumps off his lap, hands covering her face. Something falls out from between her hands, landing on the couch. Not wanting to have Duncan see her in this state, she leaves it behind, hoping he does not see it. She runs to the bathroom, locking herself in. In the dim light, Duncan only saw the thinning hair and traces of the wrinkled, sagging skin that now covers her body. He puts his hands on the couch to lift himself but feels something wet squish beneath his hand. He wipes the slime on his shirt as he chases after Bri.

Bri turns to the mirror. No need to turn the light on. The dim light, paired with her ability to register Ultraviolet rays, illuminates more than she wants to see. Her heart drops in her chest, pounding harder than she ever thought possible, so hard that she fears it may burst from her chest while in her Legendary state. The shock and sheer horror of her sagging skin, crimson-colored gums from her missing teeth, and discovering her missing eyeball sets in. In her past transitions, it has never gone this far. She has never lost a body part, save her teeth.

A knock on the door does nothing to soothe her nerves. Tears fall from her eye and eyeless socket. The sallow yellow-green/grey skin covering her body pulls away from her bones as she weeps. Her mind races about how to explain this to Duncan. She reaches for a bottle of moisturizer and pumps obscene amounts into her hands.

Rubbing it all over her face in a frenzy, she urges Duncan, "Hold on, baby. I'm freshening up." The creaking, unsteady sound in her voice is more than that of panicked hysterics. The words took more effort than they should. Her voice sounded old, as if to accompany her looks, her aged appearance carries over to the mechanics of her form as well.

"You don't sound okay. Let me in." Duncan's voice is calm and collected. In theory, he knows what is happening. He saw it when Allison killed Mrs. Espinoza. He saw Ms. Waldgrave lying on the floor, a mix of human and tree. He has never seen Brianna transition, not into what she can become.

Brianna stares at herself with flat, two-dimensional vision. She has never seen herself become this. She rubs the lotions in, covering her arms, hands, face, and everywhere else she can reach while staying clothed. She dares not to peek under them—disgusted at the thought of her body in this form. She continues rubbing the lotion on her face but gets into her hairline. Her hair becomes matted from the excessive amount of cream paired with her rapid hair loss. She tries to shake off the clumps into the sink, but the lotioned hair clings to her hands.

"I'll be fine. Just. This night…" her voice frailer than moments ago. "You have to leave, Duncan." Her heart pounds more and more. She looks down and, through her shirt, sees her heart pounding through her chest. Each pump of blood sends her heart pushing through her skin like a baby forcing its way out. Her sternum and ribs are disintegrating inside her.

Duncan does not know what to do; he has not been around this before. His mind cannot comprehend what she is feeling or what she may look like. Her appearance matters not to him, though he knows she will not see it that way. "Are you sure you don't want me to stay?"

Her tears flow harder. A fast drip into the sink, mixing with lotion and hair. "Please, Duncan. Just go! I don't want you here anymore!" She coughs at the force of her own words. Her one good eye fixated on her heart and appearance. She stares at herself, unsure of how she will ever recover from this moment, as she hears the front door shut. A few moments later, she hears his 1000cc engine roar, and after a few more, he zooms out of the driveway. Duncan may not be a Legend, and he may not know what she is experiencing, but he knows better than to force himself on a situation he has no experience with.

Bri exits the bathroom; the pointlessness of slathering lotion all over herself has sunken in. She knows she needs her eye. The thought of being without an eye keeps her heart on the edge of exploding. Tracing her steps back to the couch, she sees it sitting there—mucus and blood surround the eye right next to where she and Duncan sat. She grabs it and puts it in a glass. She learned long ago that if you lose a tooth, you keep it in milk until you can find a dentist. She doesn't know why, but she knows that is what you are supposed to do. So, she fills the glass with milk and places it in the refrigerator to keep it cool, a moment of clarity in a night overtaken by hysterics and horrid memories.

She runs to her mother's room, which has remained untouched since her passing. Something in Brianna's psyche has not wanted to clear out this room, perhaps as a way to hold onto a semblance of normalcy from before her demise. Possibly, some feelings will arise from doing so that she is not ready to face, but at this moment, it does not matter. Right now, she needs to find something—anything—that will help her not remain in this state.

She remembers her first transition. Her mother told her to take long, deep breaths to help calm her down and return to Normal. So, she does. She starts with one long breath. Already, she can feel her heart begin to slow down. On breath two, a pain in her chest overtakes her ability to stay calm as frail bones strengthen and reform. As fast as her mind is calming, a thought invades—what if she returns to her Normal state and her eye does not grow back? She needs to know. She needs to stay in her Legendary form.

She starts rummaging through her mother's belongings. Each dresser drawer that opens sends a childish fear that her mother will burst through the door and scold her for the invasion of privacy. She carries on, knowing that such a fear is unfounded. Her mother is deceased, never to return, which is a notion that sends tears running down her face once more. Bri searches her mother's room through the pain and tears that cloud her vision. After emptying her entire dresser, she moves to her nightstand, spilling its contents.

Nothing.

Brianna has found nothing that will help in her quest to save her eye and sanity. As her hysteria increases, her skin sags more, swaying from her bones like turkey waddles. Through the tear-smeared

vision, she notices something penciled inside the dresser drawer—
an address. No town, no zip code. Just an address. But the street
she knows—8970 1/2 Milwaukee Ave.

All she wanted was something to help assure her that her current state will not leave some permanent scar. A way to talk with
her mother once more, a communication she left behind when she
was alive to let Bri know that everything will be all right. A little
slice of solace in a world that has been in a slow-motion collapse
around her. All she can find is an address. She does not know what
she'll find there. The street is familiar enough. She has never heard
of a 1/2 used in anything before. Maybe it is a strange unit number.
She needs her mother. A mother who, at times, was abusive and
cold and at other times was loving, curious, and the most caring
person she knew. Bri smiles at the complexity of the human soul,
the duality of the individual that can paint two very different pictures of who we are and who people know us to be. Sylvia was, and
always will be, Bri's mother. Right now, Bri needs one more conversation with her. One more lingering moment where her mother
holds her and says everything will be okay as she drinks another
appletini. She imagines her mother showing her how to pop her
eyes back into the socket, somehow magically reattaching itself. If
only magic were real.

Donning a combo of an oversized hoodie and baggy sweat-
pants, she puts her milk-soaking eye into a thermos to keep it cold
and heads out the door. Her lack of visual perspective eliminates
the option of driving. The last thing she needs right now is to
get into an accident and have someone see her. Instead, she pulls
out her phone and enters the address into her GPS. To her surprise, the mysterious address is only a few blocks away. She looks
at the star-speckled sky. "Nothing like a little exercise to keep my
youthful figure." A self-serving joke to try and add a little levity to
her stress-filled moment.

Duncan pounds on the door to Connor's house. The lack of lights
inside signals the futility of his actions. He hopes that perhaps they

called it an early night and are asleep. He pounds harder as the side of his fist starts to hurt. A car turns the corner, illuminating the end of the street. Duncan rests his hand, a tightening in his stomach, hoping that this car will turn into the driveway at 8898 Ottawa Street. That it will park and give him some insight to properly handle—or be there for—or whatever phrase his mind can't think of—be a good boyfriend. But the lights pass him by. They drive past and pull into a house four doors down.

He rubs his hand, debating the uselessness of knocking again, before shutting the screen door. As he swings his foot over the seat of his motorcycle, an approaching light, once again, beacons hope. He turns the key but doesn't start his engine. The light slows down, and the familiar hues of Connor's blue Camaro come into focus. Duncan removes the key from his ignition and waves to Connor.

Connor parks, turns off his car, and emerges, wearing the ever-so-flattering faded blue of his pet store, accented by the red logo and collar and with white buttons and company slogan to invoke that subliminal nod of patriotism to their customers. "What's up, Duncan?" Connor can see the tension across Duncan's face in his eyes, which are a tad wider than usual, and his clenched and uncertain jawbone.

Duncan tries to relax, but the wide-eyed craze only seems to intensify. "Something happened." Panic floods through his feeble attempt to conceal it.

Connor nods to his house. "Come in."

"I didn't know who else I could go to. I mean, it's not like it's every day this happens," Duncan begins rambling. His eyes lock on Connor's hand as he unlocks the door.

Connor opens the door, motioning for Duncan to go first. Duncan bounces from foot to foot, and his anxiety is in clear control. Connor shuts the door and heads to the kitchen. He grabs a couple of beers from his fridge. "They're old as hell, but it's something."

Duncan twists the cap and chugs down half of it, like he's been stranded in a scorching desert for a month. His face contorts as he finally tastes the exaggerated bitterness with sour undertones. "Those went bad a while ago."

Connor nods. "As I said, they're old." Connor takes a seat at the kitchen table. He pulls the cord on the kitchen blinds to shut out any chance of prying eyes or nosy neighbors. "I know how you feel."

Duncan takes his first deep breath since the evening's events began. "How?"

Connor chugs a bit. His face confirms Duncan's declaration that the beer is past its prime. "Because I was like you once. Or, at least, I thought I was. We don't know what we…" Connor catches where his words are heading, so he stops himself. "Before I knew what I know now. I thought I was just like you. Then, something happens, and your world is never the same." Connor watches the wheels turn in Duncan's head. "Your world changed on prom night. You may have had ideas in your head before then or notions of that thing just out of reach. But prom night confirmed it. Took away all doubt. Except, because you are a good guy, you keep our secret, so we stay hidden."

Duncan nods, "But what I saw tonight…"

Connor stops Duncan from saying something less than unintentionally discriminating, "…Might not happen every day for you. It does for us. For Brianna, it does." Connor forces down a long sip. "Even if we do not transition every day, we still have to live with it. It comes easier for some than for others. Not just the transition but the dealing. The realization that everything we thought we were is no longer who we can be. I am no longer the baseball star I was in high school. I am no longer important in that world. Sports, any athletic future is gone because of who I am."

"What do I do? I mean, I want to be there for her, but she won't even let me look at her. We were sitting there watching a movie; then she started changing."

"Transitioning," Connor corrects.

Duncan nods in understanding. "…Transitioning, and then she runs off. Won't let me in the bathroom. Won't let me see her. Just tells me to leave. But the worst part is, I think something is actually wrong. Her voice. It was…" Duncan thinks for a moment, understanding the delicateness of the moment, "not hers. Or at least not her normal voice."

A smile forces its way to Connor's face for a moment. "Exactly. Her normal voice and her Legendary voice will be different. Brianna has always been one to rely on her looks. She prides herself on that."

Duncan nods along but stays silent.

"When she is in her Legendary state, her looks are something that she is having a hard time dealing with. If she doesn't like looking at herself, do you think she wants you to see her like that?"

Duncan's nod grows. "I don't care what she looks like. I care about who she is. She knows that. I think she does."

"I can't answer that. I can say that you might not care, but she does." Connor fights to finish the beer. "Let's look at it this way. I'm sitting here okay with who I am—or dealing with it, if nothing else. I have come to accept that the dreams I had for my life are never going to be what I want them to be, for no other reason than who I am. Allison ... well ... she is in denial of the whole thing still. She comes to terms with it at times, but all in all, she acts like it's all a prank or a bad dream. Scarlett doesn't know what she is, so I guess she's okay. At the same time, she feels like a reject because she can't transition. Scarlett can't do what we do. Like she's a benchwarmer on the team.

"Then there's your woman who knows it's real—or at least knows it's real when it is real. But here's the thing of it all. Every day that we leave our house, we have to be careful of what we say. We have to be careful of who we say things to. We can never be who we are because of the consequences of existing. These realizations, coupled with the physical manifestations of the condition, are hard to deal with. All we want is to be normal and accepted without fear of what will happen if someone sees us or knows what we look like underneath."

"I'm trying to follow, but I'm lost in the thick of it," Duncan admits. "What do I do?"

"You'll always be a Normal, an outsider to what we are. But we need you. Someone who understands that we are people, no worse and no better than anyone else. So, what do you do? Nothing. Or at least keep doing what you are doing. Don't go overboard and become that guy who tries too hard. What you can do is listen. Hear what she is saying. Please don't read into it ... or do; it's Brianna, after all. But be there for her as she needs. And remember, if you love her, love her as you have. Not as you think she needs."

Duncan sits back, finishing off his beer. His face relaxed from when he first stood on the driveway. "When did you get so wise?"

Connor grabs the last two expired beers from his fridge. "Didn't have a choice." He hands one to Duncan. "Also, been spending a lot of time with … older Legends. Been teaching me a thing or two. I can't be too wise, though."

"Why's that?" Duncan asks.

"We're still drinking this piss."

Both young men chuckle as they settle into the moment, attempting to enjoy a beer that would have better been served dumped down the sink. Duncan stares past the closed blinds into the abyss of his mind, trying to understand something he will never have to deal with directly. An inward reflection not unnoticed by Connor.

"You've already joined on," Connor interrupts Duncan's thoughts. "You've already made your stance with us. You were there when Mrs. Espinoza killed Ms. Waldgrave. You understand things that others will not, but it is not over. We have to deal with Ashby."

Duncan sits in silence, nodding at the words he hears. He knows that for him, too, life will never be what it was before he met Brianna.

Bri's GPS alerts her arrival to the address from inside the night-stand drawer—The West Haven Historical Society. A building whose architecture of nondescript, tan brick and mortar, and sym-metrical design borders on utilitarian/industrial instead of get-ting the residents of this town interested in its history. Bri starts to question if that is the point, a small museum dedicated to the happenings of a suburb that no one will want to visit, save a Girl Scout troop or two. The second and third-story windows on either side of the entrance facade have a scalloped design built into the bricks, like the architect made a feeble attempt to make it look like something more than a cover for whatever it is that lies behind the walls. The rest of the building and windows are plain, functional in design, and easily forgettable. Even the landscape surrounding the building comes off more like a poor attempt at a nod to Roman design than actual effort. An old-time, non-functional water pump seems to be a centerpiece. Bri sees nothing that makes this place worthy of scribbling it inside a drawer.

However, the young Waldgrave knows her mother. Sylvia would not jot down a random address in an inconspicuous spot if it were not worth guarding. In this new world Brianna is getting accustomed to, she has learned that not everything is as it seems. She must find a way inside; it is her only hope to find something that may help her in her current situation. She realizes she could call Scarlett, a friend who is as reliable as she is red-headed. How would she explain this situation? How would she explain being stuck in a Legendary state?

She dials her number as she begins to walk around to the rear of the building. "Hey, Scar. Can you pick me up?" The creakiness of her voice overshadows the pleading of her words.

On the other end of the phone, Scarlett asks, "Are you okay? Duncan's just about to leave. We can all come get you."

Bri startles herself at the thought of seeing Duncan right now, "Never mind." She hangs up the phone with lightning speed.

She finds herself in the back of the West Haven Historical Society. A lone gas pump stands watch in the center of the small parking lot. That is not the strangest thing she sees. In a small, covered carport, her one good eye spots Vistrus Petrovsky's Porsche. Carrying her insulated mug of eye-milk, she peaks around his car to find it warm, but not too warm, indicating it's been here a while. She makes her way to the rear entrance of the West Haven Historical Society.

Locked.

A number pad next to the door sits, waiting for the right combination to unlock it. The lights in the building are off, but Bri's vision allows her to see just fine. She takes a closer look at the number pad. A nearby series of numbers glow, thanks to her Legendary vision: 4, 8, 1, 5, 1, 6, 2, 3, 4, 2. Not knowing what to do but needing something to help with her current state, she taps those numbers into the keypad. To her surprise, the door makes a clicking sound. Pulling the door with her free hand, she discovers the combination worked. She takes a few ginger steps inside to make sure it is safe. The door closes behind her with a click. She hears nothing in her surroundings, save the beating of her heart and air flowing in and out of her lungs.

At the end of the hallway, she sees an elevator. The down arrow has a color to it that Bri finds peculiar. She presses the button, calling the doors open. Inside, she sees the B button has the same strange coloring as the down arrow. She can't quite place the color but knows she has seen it before. It's not a hue one would find in a box of colored pencils.

She hears hushed tones from a few rooms down as the elevator doors open. A deep, steady voice whispers to the others around.

Bri calls out, "Mr. P?" She steps out of the elevator, holding her insulated, milk-soaked eye. "Mr. Petrovsky? Are you there?" Her frail voice calls out.

From the doorway's shadows, Bri sees a man's silhouette. "Who are you?"

He steps forward so Brianna can see it is Vistrus. "It's me, Brianna. Allison's friend … kind of."

"How did you get in here?" He takes a cautious step forward. The change in her voice is not one he recognizes. "I cannot see your face."

"You don't want to. I'm not pretty." Brianna's vanity slips into her words. "I need your help, please."

"Let us talk." He turns and motions for her to follow.

"But I need help," she pleads. "I lost my eye…" She tightens her hoodie so that only her eye peeks through as she turns into an innocuous-looking room. At first glance, the room appears to be nothing more than a meeting room in the basement of this building. The dim light illuminates enough for the Legends to see, but any Normal would feel the uncomfortableness of the dark. The walls are plain with a weird, plastic-like coating, giving them a texture more akin to an old-time doctor's office waiting room. But what made her stop talking was the round table in the middle of the room with four people seated at it. Vistrus retakes his seat to make the fifth.

All eyes turn to Brianna as she stares back—one eye to ten. They sit unphased by the sight of her withered, bony hand.

"Did you say you lost your eye?" Vistrus reminds her of her words.

She hesitates to speak. "My iPad." She hopes her quick thinking doesn't reveal her true nature.

"Your heart does not beat so loud for a tablet." Vistrus gestures to his companions. "Take off your hood."

"I'm afraid. I'm too ugly." Bri grips the drawstrings of her hood.

A voice from the table speaks up, "Are you in?"

She turns her stare to Vistrus, who nods that it is safe to answer.

"I am in true, whate'er befall," she whispers, afraid to say those words.

The same person stands. "I feel in, when I sorrow most." He pauses for a split second, "It's nice to meet a fellow member of the Tennyson Society."

Brianna takes a deep breath as his greeting falls on deaf ears, but her heart still races. "I need help. I need my mom."

Vistrus turns to his companions. "She is the young Waldgrave. Sylvia's child." The rest nod in recognition. "It impresses me that you found this place," Vistrus admits. A notion in his head that, perhaps, Brianna is not a carbon copy of her mother.

"I found the address. It's the only thing I found of my mom's that I thought may help. I can't go back." She finally gets to the start of her problems.

"Can't go back where?" the fellow Undying inquires.

"Normal," Bri loosens her hood and sets the travel mug on the table. With care not to disrupt her beating heart, she takes off her hoodie. "I can't go back."

"Never seen another like you, I take it?" the other Undying asks.

She shakes her head. "This skin," she swats at the waddle under her tricep, "it's beyond disgusting. My teeth, I lost an eye! I am missing an eye!" She points to her heart, which pounds harder with each beat through her shirt. "Why won't you help me?!"

The fellow Tennyson Society member takes a step toward her. Within that one step—a moment that passes in the blink of an eye—all his skin rots away. The little that remains clings to his brown and decayed muscles like a long-forgotten tattered flag on a pole of bones. His sunken face resembles an embalmed head more than a living being.

Brianna watches, her eye wide with a mixed sense of horror and odd comfort.

In another step, his eye falls to the ground, and his jaw drops open, dangling as if ripped away. As his foot hits the ground, it squishes his eye, sending aqueous and vitreous humor to squirt out from under his foot.

Brianna winces in disgust. The harder and harder her heart races, the more her shirt bounces on her chest.

He takes another step forward as skin forms over his decaying body. Tendons and sinew reattach his hanging jaw. Brianna watches his missing eyeball regrow in its socket. In one last step forward, he looks normal. His body is whole once again.

Brianna turns her attention to her insulated travel mug and back to her newfound Undying acquaintance.

"Is it in there?" He nods to the mug.

Brianna gives a shy nod.

"I did the same thing when it first happened to me." He is slow to take it from her. "I had no one to help me either. It would be best if you found someone who understands. Or, at the very least, tries to understand and wants to."

Bri runs her list of friends through her head as her heart and breathing slow down a bit.

"Do you have someone like that?" He sets her milk-soaking eye on the table.

"I think so," she halfway confirms.

He nods back. "Good. Now take slow, deep breaths."

She listens to his words and can feel an intense tingling. A sensation as if her leg fell asleep, but not the laughing pins and needles. This limp numbness hurts and makes her not want to move for fear of how much worse it may feel. A pain so intense she doesn't want to walk, fearing the ability to keep balanced. This sensation is not just in her leg: it is in both legs and arms, chest, stomach, head, and missing eye socket. She does not scream. Bri is not sure if she can't cry out or just isn't. Maybe the slow breaths are what she needs.

"I must warn you," the Undying starts, "when your eye reforms, or if you lose a limb, sometimes when they reform, they are a little different. Whether it be a birthmark that wasn't there before or your eye is a different color than before. Facial hair may grow curly instead of straight. Though I do not think that will be a problem for you."

As Brianna listens to him talk, all she can think about is her mother. She imagines what her mother would say right now. She thinks about how Sylvia would be telling her the words he tells her and fancies the idea that her mom might be mixing up a martini to help soothe her nerves. After a few moments, the pins and needles stop. She feels nothing. No shirt flutters against her chest with each beat of her heart. Her vision has depth perception once again. An overwhelming joy rushes through her as she touches her eye to find it wholly returned.

"Your condition does not make you unwhole. You will return to Normal when you are not in your Legendary state. And normal you will look," he assures her.

"How am I supposed to deal with this? Talking to my friends is great and all, but we are all just as lost in this. I need my mother. I miss my mom. She is supposed to help me. She is supposed to guide me. Give me all the tricks of the trade to make sure I stay little, beautiful me. She helped me pick out moisturizers before I even knew why. She helped prepare me without telling me. I just need to be with her." Bri starts crying again but stays in her Normal state.

The Undying puts his arm around her for comfort.

"Who am I supposed to turn to when life gets too ugly to handle?" she cries.

A person who has remained silent and covered in shadow leans forward into the light. Brianna recognizes him, though at this moment can't place from where. Nick DeSalvo speaks in his jolly manner that one cannot forget, "Those around you that you consider family. If you can't speak to them, you have us." Nick smiles, his red cheeks instill a sense of ease in her. His words help calm her crying for a moment as she tries to take in words whose lightness belie a heavy gravity.

The rest of the table, including Vistrus, listens to her cry. They offer silent condolences about her situation. They, too, understand that life is dealt to people in unusual and sometimes cruel ways. They know that it can become too much to handle, and that is when they need to be there for the young ones, even if they are not blood, because they are all part of The Nation.

CHAPTER 12

*"The toughest battles we face
are fought within ourselves."*
~K. DeSalvo~

*I*nessa hammers nails through the frames of the home office windows, securing them in place. Nail after nail pounds through the wood, demanding the two double windows forever stay shut. Bottoms and sides get the same treatment. Only the top of the windows feels reprieve from her punishment.

Her wide eyes stay on high alert with each strike of the hammer. Each smack of steel on steel sends her eyes darting from side to side, in case the sound might have attracted someone.

Though she finishes with no intrusion, her eyes remain wide as she sets the hammer and box of nails on top of a filing cabinet and slides it to block the office door. Just for a touch of added security, she also locks herself in this room. She draws the shades and blinds shut. She pulls a roll of duct tape out from the desk and tapes the blinds to the wall, banishing any trace of external moonlight from the room. She lights a single glass-jar candle on the desk. The lid sits close by as the smell of clean linen with undertones of sandalwood fills the air.

Turning to the desk and hunching over one of her diaries, she starts marking the pages with blinding speed. Her wild eyes fixed on them on the chance some ill fate awaited her dare she look away. Even through the shut windows and drawn shades, the natural noises of the outside world assault her ears. Each snap of a twig beneath the feet of woodland crea-tures makes her tense up for a moment. She holds still, as if not to be seen or heard, just long enough to convince herself she is alone before returning to her diary. Each car that passes on this or the surrounding streets makes her slow her writing.

There is a moment, she is sure, that there will be a pounding on the front door or through the window. If not a pounding, a ninja-style break-in that she will be lucky enough to be alerted to because of her Legendary senses. She continues writing out every last detail into the code she has created, hoping Vistrus can crack it one day.

She mumbles to herself between the sounds of passing cars and furry creatures gathering food, "I know someone knows. I know they know it's me. I know they know I know. They don't know I know they know I know they know. Maybe they do know I know they know I know they know. I know, I know—crazy, little Inessa talking all crazy. No one understands. Can't understand. They sent me from my homeland. 'Find out what hap-pened,' they said, never said I was going to make it all go away. Why, though? Why make it all disappear? I pushed. I prodded. I investigated. Now I know things. Things I shouldn't have known. No, things I was never meant to know. I know. They know. Now they know I know. Oh, this again. Insane Inessa knows things; I do. I write them down—no one to read them. Vistrus plays chess. Yes. But not like this. No. Allison's too young to understand. Too young to know. But I know."

The click of an opening door handle catches her ear, distracting her from her circular thoughts. She pauses her pen for a moment as the door handle opens into the house. In a blink of an eye, she shuts the diary and glides to the closet. She reaches up inside the closet track and removes a push pin. The door track hangs down to reveal a little hidey-hole just big enough to slide a diary inside. She replaces the pin, safely securing the hiding spot and secrets written upon its pages. She hunkers down in the corner of the closet where the filing cabinet usually sits. Her arms wrap around her knees, burying her head between them. She rocks back and forth, whispering calming words while listening to the footsteps roaming the hallways. Footsteps that are too light to be Vistrus and definitely too soft if he were carrying their baby.

The footsteps stop for a moment. Inessa stops rocking and halts her whispers. Inessa lifts her head, waiting to hear what happens next, when she spies the candle still lit on the desk and, in one blurred motion, blows out the candle and returns to her huddled position, as quiet as it was fast. The footsteps start up again, making her question if she was not quiet enough. Inessa listens to the footsteps approach the office door. A heartbeat echoes in her ear—not just hers, but a soft one, slow and calm, enters as the footsteps approach. An indicator that either friend or a very relaxed foe stands on the other side of the door. Inessa tries to hold even more still. The knob to the office struggles against the lock. Inessa feels a momentary relief as the handle stops.

A knock on the door sends Inessa's paranoia into overdrive. She lets out a high-pitched, blood-curdling scream that she immediately tries to muffle. She knows it is too late. Whoever is outside the door has heard. The deaf could have heard that scream. The dead could be turning in their graves from the fear in that scream.

A soft voice whispers from the other side of the locked door, "Inessa, is everything all right?"

As fast and intense as her heart was pounding away in her chest, whittling down her life expectancy with each beat, it relaxes—slows to a rate that lets her wide eyes narrow. Inessa can feel the tension leave her body. Eleanor's soft-spoken voice carries into the locked office.

"I can hear someone in there. Inessa?" Eleanor softens her tone, but still no response.

Inessa and Eleanor sit in an awkward stalemate for a long, silent moment. Inessa's heart slows to normal as her senses calm down. She can still hear Eleanor's beating heart, but it no longer overpowers her ears.

"I just wanted to make sure you are all right. I saw you earlier, but you seemed like you were in such a hurry I couldn't grab your attention." Eleanor's words ring gentle and genuine to Inessa, but she can never be too sure.

Inessa feels trapped, not knowing who she can trust with what she has uncovered, and the one man Inessa can trust she feels will be endangered if she does. Isolation starts closing in around her again as Eleanor stands guard outside the door. Inessa feels the walls getting smaller and smaller once more.

"Well," Eleanor sighs, "if you need me, you know my number. I'll be home all night. I hope whatever is eating at you gets taken care of." Her footsteps fade into the distance as she exits the house and down the driveway.

Crouched in her office closet, Inessa replays the events of the evening over and over in her head. She knows someone followed her. She sensed *someone in the shadows as sure as night is dark. Pondering over and over if that person could have been the benevolent Eleanor DeSalvo or if there was someone else. Eleanor would not do such things. She could not have. Eleanor wasn't around when the massacre occurred. Thoughts swirl through her mind, mixing and blending into new ideas about who else could have seen Inessa, who else could have possibly seen Eleanor trying to grab her attention and still go undetected or unnoticed. It doesn't matter anymore, at least for this night. The sounds of the outside world calm down. The creatures have gone to sleep, and the cars in the surrounding area have slowed to a trickle. The world rests around her, allowing her mind a moment to rest.*

Vistrus and Allison are seated at the dining room table with a chandelier hanging above it, a more formal lunch setting than their usual seat at the small, round kitchen table or even while watching television. The deep tones of the walnut-carved wood table and chairs lend an air of antique elegance to their afternoon. A bowl of Spanish-style quinoa sits in the middle of the table. Its giant serving spoon threatens to fall out, sending the grain flying everywhere. Allison cuts into her filet mignon. The center is a little pinker, more medium than she usually likes, but she finds something appealing about it. Vistrus notes that she has yet to complain about it not being medium-well to well. He cuts into his blue steak as they enjoy a relaxed meal.

Allison chews her food, lost in thoughts that weigh heavy on her mind, before speaking, "I've been thinking."

Vistrus raises an eyebrow at his daughter. "Always a start."

She ignores his statement. "If we are these Legends that you say we are, and I'm not saying we are, but if we are ... if I am, how do we grow old?"

"The same way tortoises mate." Vistrus smiles as he snaps a bit of blood-dripping meat from his fork.

"Carefully?" Allison asks, hesitating on her bite of quinoa.

"That is porcupines, dear." He sips a glass of bourbon.

"So then, what's the answer?" She stops eating to pay closer attention.

With a wry smile, Vistrus replies, "Very slowly."

"Dad..." Allison shifts in her chair, "didn't need to picture turtle sex."

Vistrus chuckles at that thought. "What brings this up?"

"If we age slowly, as you say, how come you still don't look like a teenager?" Allison points out.

"The best analogy is dog years." He stabs a piece of steak.

"So, when you say to people you're forty-three, you're really like three hundred and ten." Apparent disbelief sounds in Allison's voice.

"Something like that. You will stop aging at a normal rate, too." Vistrus chews his food. "It all depends on your hormones and genetics."

"Wait a second, Dad." A realization lights up in her head. "You've been head of the museum since I was a kid. No one noticed you haven't aged? No one ever notices?"

A hearty laugh escapes Vistrus's lungs. "My child, you never noticed. Your friends never noticed. You never seemed to notice Ken or Tracy DeSalvo not age. Plus, people move. Next-door neighbors change, as do employees."

Allison points at him with her fork. "So, you're telling me that a supposed secret society of Legends that I may or may not believe in has existed for centuries by people not staying employed too long or living in one place too long? That is complete bull."

"That is only a part of it. It is complicated." Vistrus tries to squash the subject.

"Does this complication have anything to do with whatever 21-gram vials are?" Allison throws her father a curveball.

Vistrus takes a deep breath while chewing his steak and his words before speaking. He watches the wheels of possibilities turn in his daughter's head, trying to figure out if she is right, what those vials are, and how they might be connected. After a moment of letting his daughter think, he chimes in, "When a living creature dies, they lose twenty-one grams of mass. Scientists do not know why. In Normal society, they have yet to figure out what it is or where it goes. To them, it simply disappears. A Legend has a distinct advantage. We can capture those grams. We keep ourselves safe with those jars."

"Yeah, brings a whole new meaning to 'my soul to keep,'" Allison drips with sarcasm, causing her father's head to tilt as he grimaces.

"You may not accept who you are yet, but you will. No matter how far any of us think we have come, there is always so much more to learn." He turns back to the Spanish quinoa.

"Life isn't that simple. Put your soul in a jar, and everything is all kosher," she protests.

Her father turns his attention from his food. "I never said it was simple. I also never said it was our soul."

"So, how do we die? I mean, we can die. I've seen that firsthand," Her heavy thoughts lift a little off her mind. She sits back in her chair, shoulders relaxed, as a calm settles over her that she has not felt yet today.

"If a Legend has filled their vial, there are ways to bring them back. But they always come back changed. If they have not filled..." he pauses, searching for better words, "if their twenty-one grams are still inside them when they die, then they are dead." His tone mellows, slowing his speech as he finishes. A seriousness sets in that this is not a subject to be taken lightly.

"We come back changed?" Allison sets down her utensils.

The corners of Vistrus's mouth struggle against this moment's weight to upturn. "Sometimes our eye color is different. Darker perhaps. Sometimes our hairline changes. Other times, personality shifts. The science behind it is not fully understood. Though The Council has tried time and time again to find the answers, some things are still beyond our grasp."

Allison takes a sip of her drink as she begins to speak, "If our personalities change, do we still have our old memories, or is it like full amnesia? I thought we were like legendary creatures. Beings of timeless gods, or whatever. All of us."

Vistrus looks down at his food, searching for the bite he wants before stabbing it with his fork. "All of us? There is no 'us of legendary gods.' We are not spawned from greatness. That myth, that legend behind what makes us who we are, is everything wrong with us. We are people. Humans. Diseased at its most basic form. If we die and come back, there is no shift in memories. We do not become new people. Just different." He catches his swelling anger. He knows his daughter means no harm. She is young and trying to figure out the answers to life. There is something within her assault of questions that reminds him of Sylvia, a naivety that he hopes fades with time.

Allison watches as her father sets down his fork on the table. His hands rest next to his plate, waiting for her next move. His eyes stare past his daughter, looking into some distant memory of a long-forgotten time. Allison wants to speak. She wants to know how to capture the twenty-one grams. She wants to know what it looks like. A morbid curiosity within her wants to know what her father used to look like before he died the first time, if there was a first time. Then she wonders if he hasn't died yet, how did he survive so many years when so many around her have perished recently—those who are Legends? Her curiosity yearns for answers, but her nineteen years of wisdom have taught her now is not the time to press the subject further. Now is the time to contemplate what she has learned and how it relates to her. That is, if she can ever wrap her head around who and what she truly is and come to accept it. But for now, the words her father said echo through her mind. They remind her over and over that she is "diseased at its most basic form."

Allison sits, snuggled into her bed with her black comforter wrapped around her. The pink sheets peeking out from the side, illuminated by the early evening light creeping through the drawn shades, work their way up to further envelop her in the safety of her bed. The light from her Hewlett-Packard laptop illuminates her face, casting shadows like a flashlight on a camper about to tell a scary story. However, she finds nothing frightening in what she reads. Instead, a look of calm serenity overtakes her face. Her eyes relax with an unconscious, subtle smile while reading more diary entries scribed by her late mother.

She scans passages that read more coherently than the ones she is accustomed to, reading more about her mother's love for the

infant Allison and her husband Vistrus than the nonsense ramblings of a paranoid woman. No inane words repeat over and over
as they morph into new phrases. No. Now, at this moment, she
reads expressions of clarity, passages that make her feel safe in an
otherwise uncertain world.

Allison scans the beginnings of numerous passages, all imbuing
the same sense of relief and calm. Paragraphs that speak of her
mother's love. Bits telling of what a mother had to do to protect
a young child. She reads about her mother's dreams and the hal-
cyon sensation that she found, knowing her dreams, as violent or
strange as they could be, were not a cryptic warning but a sign
that things may come.

As Allison continues scanning the entries about dreams, she
feels a connection to a mother long gone, a mother whose memories have long since faded from her mind. In that connection, she
feels she is not alone in this world, even if Inessa is gone. A joint-
ness to another being who has shared similar experiences, circumstances, fears, and joys. A solidarity that can only be felt when you
know, beyond a shadow of a doubt, that things have a chance to
end well. These thoughts let Allison realize she is not truly alone
in the universe.

Yet, it is this newfound solace in the serenity of familial bonds
that, in her excitement, keep her from finishing each entry. It may
be a subconscious voice telling her to stop while things are good
and move on. It may be a silent partner in her brain reading a few
sentences ahead that warns her to move on while the getting is
good. But whatever it may be, she does not read each passage in full.
She reads words that do not sound deranged or hysterical—only
words of lucidity and calm.

And she stops.

Each time that little voice in her mind tells her to, she stops.
Each time that unnamed feeling in her head nudges her to move on
to the following passage, she obliges, never seeing that end, never
seeing what happens or how it all unfolds.

Her eyes start to weigh heavy as sleep whispers its sweet tune
in her ears. As if on autopilot, she closes her laptop and sets it aside.
She turns on her side, resting her head on her pillow and hands
under that. Folded like a comfortable baby in a crib, she drifts to

sleep. A slumber that overpowers any resistance to stay awake. Not that she puts up any fight. A rest so solid and deep, she sleeps right through the text message alert that chimes out. A text message with words she has been waiting on...

[Scarlett: You coming?]

CHAPTER 13

*"The biggest lie we tell ourselves
is that everything happens for a reason."*
~D. Childers~

I nessa shakes off the decay and mildew as she steps out of the damp cellar that passes for a mortuary. She unfolds the parchment handed to her by the mortician.

Tá an corp marbh.

Four words on parchment paper.

Four.

Inessa gets stuck on the accent mark for a moment before realizing it does not matter. She does not recognize the language. She ponders the possible meaning of the words as she recounts the damages to the deceased.

One from each of the five Societies. No more bodies. While standing in the woods examining the scene, she estimated at least five bodies but figured there would be more. There was no sixth body. No deceased perpetrator to lay on a slab next to the victims.

Five.

One for each house.

A wave of emotion washes over her like a chill from a terrible flu. The emotional wave causes a need to sit down for a moment. She realizes they did not send her here to ensure the secrets of The Body stay safe. She was not moved across the world to safeguard the Legends in the United Colonies. The Body sent her to cover up the murder of an entire Mind.

An entire region has lost its leaders. Leaders that were supposed to keep other Legends safe. Keep the Legends of the five Societies safe from harm, discrimination, and persecution. They sent Inessa to ensure this atrocity is safe from leaking the secrets of The Body and keep it a secret from those in The Body.

Chills run through Inessa, overtaking her ability to stand. She lowers herself to the ground while the thoughts in her head start twirling faster and faster. She realizes The Body's motives back in Russia. The idea of being used as a pawn sits heavy on her. She stays put, unable to move. Her eyes start darting back and forth, trying to follow the thoughts in her mind.

"This cannot be. The Body would not do this. No. Not to me," Inessa repeats over and over to herself. "This was my mission. I accepted it. But I didn't know. Maybe they knew. Maybe they knew, and that's why they died. What did they know? What could they know? Why am I here?"

The questions pile up. With each new idea comes further questions as to why. She realizes she cannot approach The Body about this. She cannot go back to her homeland to inquire. The trip would take weeks, and Vistrus would not let her go without asking questions—questions that Inessa could not cover up without him finding out she lied. Questions about which she would not want to lie.

She sits on the stoop that leads down to the mortuary. Her head feels like she might be next to lay on his slab. The weight presses down on her neck, ready to snap from the gravity of her realization. So, she sits, thinking, pushing each new thought into her mind's blender, ignoring the sights and sounds of the world around her. Oblivious to the people around her as they pass by. She doesn't feel the rain as it begins tapping the back of her neck, saying, "Hey, time to go."

She sits.

Her mission was to make sure The Body's secrets were not spilled. To make sure that no one outside The Body could confirm the existence of their conditions. To ensure this incident stayed out of the public's eyes and ears. That if anything had slipped, she would be the one to cover it up.

A seed has been planted, making her wonder if she is being used to cover up more than what they told her. She wonders if, without knowing, she volunteered to cover up the slaughter of a Mind. A region of The Body that was heretofore untouched. A Mind that was new enough that her love, Vistrus, did not know about. She moved to the United Colonies under the pretense of starting a local chapter of The Body, had their secrets not been exposed. The convoluted nature of it all circles her mind, pushing out other thoughts. The five Societies of The Body ruled by regional Minds. So many words, so many parts, all that must remain secret. The future secrecy of it all rides on her shoulders.

Which makes her wonder more about what lies in front of her that she can't see. The abstract pieces of some more abstract puzzle might all be within her reach; if she could figure out what the whole puzzle is supposed to look like, then the pieces could fill in the details. She finds herself searching for fragments of an unknown enigma. Panic sets in at the immediate thought of the danger she is in if she lets anyone know what she helped cover up if her theory is correct. She wants to know the reason behind the sweeping under the rug. A need to understand what is so essential that this remains a secret urges her to investigate. She thinks of the possible danger she could be putting her husband in. The threat she might put any future family in, if only she could confirm that she is right.

She sits, convincing herself to let it go, telling herself to be a good member of The Body and do as she's told—to not delve into what is not hers to dig up. To leave well enough alone and move on.

Well enough alone.

She takes a deep breath, holding it in to calm her nerves. Slowly, she exhales. At the end of it, she pauses before taking another deep breath. She repeats this a few times, telling herself to drop it. To forget what she thinks and to move on. To go live a happy life. She pockets the parchment, stands, and walks away.

A gentle nudge and her father's voice cut Allison's early slumber short. "Wake up, sleepyhead. Time for dinner."

Realizing she dozed off, Allison snatches her phone off the nightstand to find a few missed texts and one missed call. "Shit."

Vistrus tosses her a stern stare but knows she is a legal adult. "Did something happen?"

"I was supposed to meet up with everyone." She keeps her response vague.

"Well, dinner is ready. You can meet up with them after." Her father's words are more a command than a request.

"I'm already late," she pouts.

"Then you can be a little later." He moves to exit her bedroom. "I want to revisit something."

Allison huffs, gets out of bed, and texts a quick apology to Scarlett while she walks to the kitchen.

The smell hits her nose, and suddenly she doesn't mind being a few minutes later. Then she remembers why they are all meeting up tonight. Now, she is locked in a battle between needing to be somewhere and wanting to eat what smells like lamb legs cooking in a mint sauce.

She picks a French fry off her plate, "Mint lamb and fries? Kinda an odd side dish, don't cha think?"

Vistrus lifts a finger to the sky. "Mint basil lamb and not just any fries. I coated the fries in a Serrano chimichurri seasoning with a smoked Gouda dipping sauce."

Allison dips the fry in the sauce before popping it into her mouth. Taking her seat, she admits, "Okay, that's a good fry." She smiles, nodding her head at her words.

Vistrus brings the lamb from the stove to the table and portions it onto their plates. "I am glad you like it."

"So, what's all this for?" Allison extends her arms to the gourmet dinner.

Vistrus takes his seat. "Partly because I wanted lamb and partly because I wanted to ask you something."

Allison cuts into her lamb. "I have to meet up with everyone. I'm late."

"As I said, you can be a little later." He takes a bite from his fork. "I have been thinking a lot about many things."

Allison freezes for a moment, unsure how to take his words. "Care to narrow that down?"

Vistrus takes a deep breath as he reaches for a fry. "One of those things was therapy. Are you positive you do not want to go? Last time we talked, I said you could."

Allison resumes her meal.

"I have found someone that would be good for you. A therapist who is also in." Vistrus relays that last bit of information to see if his daughter is listening.

"In what? The Nation? Is she some sort of freak, too?" Allison jests.

Vistrus finds no humor in her words. "You are not a freak. We are not freaks. Stop joking or deflecting or whatever you are doing to deny the reality of what you are and the world around you."

"I'm running late. Can you lecture me later?" Allison shovels more cheese-covered fries into her mouth.

"No. Our conversation is not about a lecture. This talk is about me relenting on you seeing a therapist about your dreams and you still saying never mind after years of asking. I thought that was what you wanted." He finishes, taking a sip of dark red wine.

"It was what I wanted, and I appreciate that you finally came around, but your timing is a bit behind." Allison chomps down on more lamb.

Vistrus takes another sip of his wine before setting it back down. "What does that mean, Allison?"

"I already told you I don't want to see a therapist anymore." Allison checks her phone.

"You have been asking me for years. Why the sudden change of heart?" His concern grows for his daughter instead of being alleviated.

She glances at her watch again. "I'm running late. Like I said, I've been reading books on dreams and coping and stuff. They're helping. The dreams haven't been as bad lately." Allison finds herself surprised by the words being a little more truthful than she thought. Except for not telling him the "and stuff" books are her mother's diaries.

Vistrus does not seem a hundred percent satisfied, but he surrenders. "Fine. If that is the way you want to work through your sleep issues, so be it. Just know that I will stay open to seeing a professional if you decide to."

Allison takes her last bite of lamb. "Thanks. I'll keep it in mind." She shoves the remaining few fries in her mouth before swallowing her lamb. "I'm late."

"Yes, you are." He nods to her dishes. "Clean up after yourself. I am not your maid."

Allison grabs her dishes. "Just out of curiosity, what would you say to me moving in with Scarlett?"

Vistrus chugs the wine he was sipping on. "You want to move in with Connor?"

Allison rinses off her dishes. "Not Connor. I mean, I guess since it's his house. But more with Scarlett. I don't know; it was just a question."

"You are an adult. While you will always be my daughter, I cannot force you to do anything you do not want to do, including living here. But if you want my opinion on the matter…" he lets the words trail off, waiting for an invitation to give his thoughts.

"I do but make it quick. I'm late." Allison checks her phone.

"I would give it more time to see what happens with you and him. There is no rush." This a simple answer from a complicated man.

"Hmm," she replies. "Thank you for that."

"Are you going to move in with him?" Vistrus fishes for an answer.

She willingly takes the bait. "Nope. Just a question is all." She checks her phone. "I'm late. May I take the Porsche?"

Vistrus shakes his head. "Solstice."

He watches his daughter leave; his smile masks the sadness behind his eyes. He has spent so many years trying to do right by Allison that he feels he missed her blossom into a woman—a full adult, if not fully grown. Her petite size ever an obstacle for him to look past, so he remembers she is not as young as she is small. Nineteen years. A long time for someone who is nineteen. Nineteen is a decent chunk of time for someone who is fifty-six. A third of their life is nineteen. To Vistrus, however, nineteen years is a blink of an eye. Nineteen, for Vistrus, was too long ago to remember, though he tries. He wants not to be the helicopter hovering over her, scrutinizing every move she makes. He knows he is not, at least for the most part. That makes him proud right now.

A pride that Allison found a way to deal with dreams that caused so much turmoil most of her life. Sadness eats at him because the pride he feels he knows might be false and may end up being his daughter's downfall. A downfall that would be on him if he could have done something to prevent it. There's the rub, though. He knows he can only protect his child for so long before he has to let her live her own life. Now, he can push aside the gut feeling that everything is not, nor will be, okay and hope that he is wrong.

The dim lights of The Attic, paired with the loud noise from the speakers set close to the couch, always make Duncan feel a little more anonymous than he is. He knows it is a false feeling, but he likes it nonetheless—that feeling of invisibility amongst the masses. Perhaps a little childish, but it reminds him of childhood. The notion that an unseen superhero silently watches over the people, looking for trouble to thwart.

It seems that trouble may have found him. Duncan watches as a man, a few years older than the rest of the crowd, enough to stick out, approaches him. This man is not old enough to have people question if he is at the onset of a midlife crisis being in this place. But he has enough evident years past the rest that one might question his motives. His light brown hair, combed flat against the side with a line buzzed into the part, a deep green-and-blue plaid flannel buttoned up and tucked into his dark blue denim jeans free, from any fraying or tears, is in contrast to Duncan's shaved head, random rap or metal artist T-shirt, ripped jeans, and scuffed-up shoes. Even this guy's face is shaved clean, accompanied by well-groomed eyebrows. His black combat boots laced high gleam with fresh polish, telling those around that nothing about him is less than perfect.

Duncan's eyes grow thin and cautious upon seeing the stranger's path is aimed directly at him. His eyes shoot past this stranger to see if Brianna, Scarlett, Allison, or Connor are making their way to him as well. A fast scan reveals the moment consists of only him and this stranger.

The stranger snaps his feet together, stopping in front of him. The man's stiff, para-military stance rings a bell for Duncan. A description Rex gave that is engraved in his mind—Ashby. Duncan stands to meet the gaze of the man responsible for the latest strife in West Haven. He cannot be a hundred percent sure, but if he were in Vegas, he'd place the bet.

Duncan stares into the eyes of the man before him, not a menacing, Clint Eastwood-esque stare. Duncan offers a look to say intimidation will not work. The stranger stares back. "You don't belong here," he says

A smile forces itself across Duncan's lips. "Like I haven't heard that before." Duncan waits for the man to speak, but he does not. "I've grown up my whole life hearing words like that come out of mouths like yours. 'You don't belong, boy.' 'We don't like your kind, boy.' In the end, the problem ain't mine. It's yours." Duncan points to their surroundings. "This is my world as much as anyone else's. So, you got a problem with me, deal with it. Educate yourself and move on."

Duncan stands stalwart through impassioned words. His eyes spark with not wanting to deal with what he hears and sees before him. No underlying defensiveness coats his words.

This man, however, does not sway. His feet remain steeled into the ground. His hands gripped behind his back, paired with a stone-cold stare. The corner of his lips betrays what he tries to hold in. A slight wrinkle starts forming between his eyes, a tell Duncan only sees because of their proximity.

"You misunderstand my words," the man starts, but Duncan interjects.

"Then clarify." He ensures this man knows he will not suffer a fool.

"I belong to an organization. We separate the men from the Men." He smirks.

Those last five words confirm Duncan's winning bet. He pockets the metaphorical chips to cash in later.

Ashby continues, "There are those not long for this world. It is a shame that you feel society always directs those words at you in negative tones. When I say, 'you don't belong here,' it is not because of your skin color, the god you worship, or the clothes you wear. No, it is because of the potential I see inside of you."

Duncan toys with the bait. "What is it that you see?"

Ashby finally breaks eye contact to give Duncan a dramatic once-over. "I see a man held down by society. A man who does everything he can—follows all the rules, and still can't get to where he wants to be. A man who sees others getting ahead while he is left behind. A man who sees lesser beings exploiting the system set up to help men such as you advance. In front of me, I see a man who can be everything he wants to be. All you have to do is join me."

"Join you? That's it?" Duncan tests Ashby's words.

"Join me." Ashby pulls out a business card from his pocket. "This address. Next Friday. I will show you how to become the man society has prevented you from becoming. I will show you who has been holding you back and all the ways we are going to fix that."

"Friday night? Seven days from today? What time?" Duncan fishes for information.

Ashby finally smiles. "Eight-thirty. Early is on time, on time is late, and late is unacceptable."

Duncan pockets the business card as Ashby turns to leave. "Ashby."

Ashby freezes in his steps. He never said his name and knows the young man before him possesses information he shouldn't.

He turns back to face Duncan, but Duncan speaks first. "Using the word 'is' is a mathematical equivalent of equals. So, in your own words, early equals unacceptable. But so is on time and being late. When do I show?"

Ashby's face drops. Any pleasantry he tried to put on before has left. "Sarcasm and disrespectful wit will get you nowhere. Neither will flaunting information you shouldn't have."

Duncan chuckles. "My quick wit and intelligence have gotten me this far. I think I'll be just fine. What isn't fine is you coming into my haunt." Duncan gestures to the venue around him. "This place. This is our place. You do not come in here spouting your rhetoric for weak minds and lost souls to try and strengthen a cause you know, as well as I, is rooted in your own damn insecurity and low self-image. You might be able to cause me pain right here. You might be more well-trained in your backyard, wanna-be militia crap. But do not think that for a moment your clean-cut hair and perfectly polished boots make up one bit for the little boy inside you crying out for one more hug from Mommy or a 'that a boy' from your daddy. Your appearance is as misplaced as your beliefs. You have no right coming in here spouting your rhetoric." Duncan huffs, "And your rhetoric is all you have. We're in public. You wouldn't dare take action here. It would tarnish that perfect, gilded image you project."

Ashby's eyes bulge out of their sockets. A vein in his forehead pulsates, and his face turns red, even under the dim lights of the venue.

"I know what you did to Rex, Ashby. I know what you did to my friends. I know what you are planning. I may not be what you hold so much hatred for, and you might think that gives us some connection. It doesn't. I do not hold the same contempt for people trying to live normal lives—people whose only desire is to be left alone. Anyone who says differently will have to answer to me. And I do not care if the cops arrest me or if you get hurt in the process. Do I make myself clear?"

Duncan watches as Ashby shakes—a trembling in Ashby's stance he can hide no longer. He does not answer back.

Duncan steps close enough to whisper. "And if you ever go after the woman I love, or those she considers friends or family, whatever it is that you think makes you so special and somehow gives us a connection that you think you can ruin my night with will not protect you. I will make you regret ever walking into this place, coming into this town. Do you understand? If I ever see you in West Haven again after tonight, the only way you will be leaving is in a pine box or a zip-top bag."

Ashby steps back from Duncan, still shaking in anger. "You talk big for a small man. You may even be able to get me into that pine box. But now, after I walk out, you will spend every moment of every waking hour looking over your shoulder. Every noise you hear when your house settles or the air kicks on, every snapping twig or falling leaf will send you looking around in a paranoid panic of what if's and who's there." Ashby snorts his nose. "I will be. Every minute of my day will be in preparation of how I can return the favor, not only for you but for those you love. If I am to leave this town the way you said, I will make sure others do as well. Unlike you and your friends, I have an army behind me."

Duncan smiles a sly, cocky smile, if only to stall for a few seconds. He knew about Ashby. Rex had told him what he could about Ashby, but Duncan did not know there were more. If Duncan is to take Ashby at his word, he does not realize the scope of what he and his friends have to deal with. Still, he stands stalwart. "You may have an army, but we have vampires and werewolves."

Ashby cocks his head as Duncan says werewolves. A pause in Ashby gives Duncan the feeling Ashby did not know werewolves, or members of the Kipling Society, exist. That tidbit of knowledge alerts Duncan that Ashby might not know as much as he claims, a card Duncan will play at a later time.

Ashby shakes his head and turns to leave. Nothing further is spoken as Duncan's words run through his head.

Duncan sits, saying out loud to himself, "I think I'll skip that meeting in seven days, Ashby." He pulls out his cell to send a text.

[Duncan: Where are you?]

A quick reply back.

[Brianna: Where are you? I thought we were meeting at Manic Monday's for food.]

[Duncan: Not to my knowledge, but I'm on my way.]

Duncan heads toward the exit, sending one last text.

[Duncan: Don't leave. You'll never guess who I ran into tonight.]

CHAPTER 14

"The biggest disservice we do ourselves
is trying to understand that reason."
~R. Chandler~

*I*nessa paces the museum halls, infant Allison held tight in her arms. Her tiny, little eyes look up at her mom with adoration for this stranger that takes care of her. Inessa scans the halls, not sharing in the joy that baby Allison shows. Rounding a corner before looking over her shoulder, she sees someone turn again. This is the fifth hallway she has ducked down, and the fifth time the same person has been forty to fifty paces behind her. Never more, never less. She does not know this person. She has never seen him before, but he is there. She stops a security guard and engages in idle chat about the comings and goings of the museum. She is the curator, after all; she can talk to any of the employees. This security guard does not give the conversation any thought besides the immediate content. A gesture in the direction from where she came while chatting about the employee's favorite displays scares off her would-be stalker.

After a moment, she bids the guard a fond adieu and heads to her office. She sits in her chair, rocking her baby, bottle in hand, *"Who do I tell? Who is there to tell? All these years and no answers. No, little Alli. No one to believe me. The Body back in Russia long since disbanded. Who knows what happened to them? Maybe they share the same fate as those I was sent to cover up. Yes. Maybe they do."* Inessa's voice rises and falls in that speaking-to-an-infant-like-they-don't-understand-a-word-you-say way.

She does it because it keeps the child calm and eating. "The Council is in charge now. The Council. But the others don't know they aren't the first here? Over two centuries, and still, the others think they are the first in West Haven. We say we are looking out for the betterment of all Legends, but are we?"

She slows her speech as little Allison falls asleep, bottle in mouth. The food and comfort of her mother make her surrender to sleep. Inessa moves her to a small crib set up for such occasions, then opens a diary to begin writing.

> This is the man. Is it the man? The man whose plan was to kill. The man who killed never returned— no reason why. The Body denied. They made me do it. Cover it up. Why? Protection of our kind. I can believe. But it was our kind that died. No justice. Or is that it? It is just us now. He follows me. I thought it was coincidence. Then he showed again. Again. Again. It's him. It's been so long since that day. The land has changed. The world is not the same. But it never left. The why of it all. Eating away till there is only an answer left. No questions. Only the quest. Now I have found him.

Inessa hears a noise outside the door. An accidental jiggle of the door-knob as someone got too close trying to peer in. She looks up and sees a face moved away, trying to deny they are there. A face she saw for only a split second but recognized. A face she once knew but now knows means danger. It all falls into place for the moment, but the face is gone.

She turns back to her diary to finish the entry.

> The game of chess. I still must teach V. The Adeirrig is real. He knows I am too.

The interior of Brianna's house is the same as it was before Mrs. Espinoza killed her mother. She has not changed any knick-knacks that line the shelves or windows, but has kept up with watering all the plants. She even keeps the lawn and garden manicured as her mother did. To her, these are the little things that keep her mother's memory alive. At least, the good memories of the mother she wanted—and struggled—to be. On the side of irony, she has hung her mother's martini glasses from the bottom of the alcohol cabinet in true bar-style. The vodka and apple pucker sit in the cupboard, a little less full since her mother's passing.

In Bri's mind, she knows she is not her mother and will not become the alcoholic she was. Though her mother did show her when the transitions get out of hand, a little appletini helps calm the nerves. She wonders if her mother never gained complete control of her ability to transition from Normal to Legendary, or if what started as a little to curb the pain, turned into a little more. Then, eventually, became a problem of more, leading to even more.

A bridge she will cross when she gets there. Right now, she has lotion to rub into her face, neck, arms, and anywhere else she feels isn't as soft and luxurious as it was when she started high school. A battle she knows grows more futile with each passing day, but she will not give in without a fight. She takes her seat at the table— the smell of melting cheese and tomato basil soup drawing her in.

Duncan sits next to her to share the late-teen fine dining cuisine. He watches thoughts run through her mind with no idea what those thoughts are. Duncan wishes he could jump inside her head and know everything she thinks, but he can't. Her smile reminds him of that. Besides being an impossibility, he understands that those thoughts she does not wish to share are not his to know. So, he waits for the day she can open up to him like he wishes she would. He remains patient for the day she feels comfortable enough to do what Legends do in front of him, without the worry of seeing disgust on his face or whatever emotion he thinks she thinks she'd see on him. He shakes his head at the convolution of that thought, which catches her attention.

"Everything all right?" she asks, holding back each word.

"Yeah," Duncan smiles a little wider, "Just looking at how beautiful you are."

"Beautiful? While eating grilled cheese dipped in soup?" She raises a brow.

"Yes, while eating," he defends, resting a hand on her thigh.

She dips the sandwich in the soup and shoves it into his mouth. "What are you doing?"

He bites off a sizable piece. "Nuh-ng," he says with a full mouth. "I jus' been 'hinkin'," he finally swallows.

"Thinking about what?" Bri spoons a bit of soup into her mouth.

Duncan wipes his mouth with his hand. "You. Me. Us."

Brianna's face drops. Though his words may have been said with hints of joy, she heard quite the opposite. All confidence she felt has evacuated her body. "Oh, God. Are you breaking up with me? Is this because of the other day? Just get it over with, so I can cry it all out." Her breaths grow faster and heavier.

Duncan fails in his attempt not to chuckle at her misunderstanding.

She scoots her chair away from the table. "See, now you're laughing about it."

Duncan scoots his chair to hers. "Quite to the contrary, my love."

Those words quell her anxiety, causing her breathing to become noticeably less labored.

"I was thinking about us—about you. How I wish I had the friends you have." He leans in toward her.

"You do have the friends I have." She cocks her head in confusion.

"Yeah, but only because Scarlett tutored me. Only because you said yes. Had you said no, I would've just been some guy Scarlett helped and some poor sap you turned down," he says, straightening his back.

"I feel like I'm still earning my way back in with them," Bri confesses.

Duncan shakes his head. "No way. With Scarlett, with Connor, you have earned your place. With Allison…" his thoughts trail off for a moment. "With her, well, she loves you or at least has feelings for you she still isn't ready to admit. But that's not on you."

Bri looks at the floor, cracking a melancholy smile. "You still have not told me why you are all Mr. Hopeless Romantic right now."

"I want you to know that I love you. Not you in this moment or only when you are like this. I love you. All of you and every aspect." Duncan tries to make eye contact, but her gaze remains fixed on the floor. "I can definitely understand feeling different, like an out-sider, like you don't belong. I've been told that enough throughout my life. Looks, hair, or lack of." Duncan rubs his head. "I can relate. Even if I do not know what it feels like to change, or transition, or whatever you call it—I'm still learning; I can empathize. But more so than me, your friends can literally relate."

Bri finally lifts her head to meet his gaze. Her smile widens.

"A lot is coming up. A lot of which is uncertain. I want you to know you are not alone. You don't have to be uncomfortable around me. I mean, yeah, it'll take time for you to be comfortable with yourself, but I am already comfortable with you and whatever it is you look like while not like now. I want to be there for you, with you, alongside you, whatever you want to call it because the world won't be. If I've learned anything, it's that the world does not care, so find those that do. I do. I love you, Bri."

She hugs him, and her heart begins to race again, this time with joy and a love she had prevented herself from feeling before this moment. She holds a tight embrace, inhaling this moment.

"You don't have to say it back. I know you do, too, even if it's scary to face."

She tightens her arms around him a little more.

"What do we do?" Bri finally speaks.

"About Allison?" Duncan fishes for the answer.

Bri laughs. "No. I mean, yeah, I'll have to chat with her at some point. But about Rex and that situation."

Duncan pulls away from her. "Glad you asked."

Connor sits on his bed; it is still in the same room of the house it has been for his entire life. He never took over his parents' room after their deaths. There was something about doing such a thing that would cement the reality of their passing. So, he stayed where he had always been, right here in the comfort he knows. His bed, desk, and the hiding places for magazines teens hide from their parents are unchanged: everything is as it always has been.

He sits on his mattress—an empty box rests next to his feet on the floor. He holds a trophy, rubbing it to give it a good spit polish. A way to keep things as they were—perfect, pristine, innocent, and naive. He knows that life is not so simple. Life moves on, and so must he. He has felt the urge before, that push to purge himself of his past—of dreams gone by. He finds no reason to hold onto what can never be—hopes of college ball. A baseball career cut short by a drug test he cannot contest because it would reveal his true nature. He has to keep The Nation a secret. Such things come with sacrifice, whether he wants to make them or not.

He hand-polishes the gilded copper shine of the trophy to keep his past as perfectly remembered as he can. He knows a time is coming. The past two years have been trying enough. He knows what is coming won't be any easier. No paternal advice or maternal support to help ease the burden of becoming an adult. No pats on the back or embraces to comfort him as he continues discovering his true nature and true purpose in life. He holds onto what he knew for so many years—that he would play ball, a gut feeling he had that ruled his actions for so long. He possesses an innate talent that he will never get the chance to hone. The path was clear. Today, though, he sits on his bed, imagining all the baseball games he will never have the opportunity to pitch in, to open, to close. He reminisces about what it felt like to stand on the mound fresh out of warm-up, clean uniforms all around the field, a new batter standing in the box, the anticipation of the game's first pitch, or to throw that last pitch of the game and watch the umpire make his silent signal to end it all.

Gone.

Memories flood his mind of past bus rides and make-up ones about the rides he'll never be on—the plane rides to states too far to drive. The nights in hotels, sharing stories of the women they love while playing cards when they should be sleeping.

Gone.

All he has left of that life are the trophies, those he deserved and those he got just for playing. Those are the ones he knows he can do without. The awards he never asked for. The hand-outs. The "thanks-for-playing" trophies. The accolades thrust upon kids for doing nothing—for the "just because" are the ones he has grown to hate—the ones handed out so everyone feels like they accomplished something. Trophies handed out to bolster self-esteem instead of letting the little one feel a short-lived pain that perhaps baseball isn't their game. That bowling, chess, music, or art might be more fulfilling and worthwhile for them. The trophies handed out to mask any disappointment they might have learned to handle but instead will send their future selves into the world unequipped to deal with such change, letdowns, and rejection that we are not all great at everything we do. And we are all definitely not the same. No matter how much we want to be.

He knows this. He knows this because he has to stay hidden. He has to keep from the world who he truly is because if they found out, they would drive him out of town. They would spread rumors based on pure speculation and conjecture. They would hurl insults and beat him. They would do all these things for no other reason than he is not one hundred percent like them.

He puts all his hand-out trophies in a box because they taught the youth nothing. The only thing they did was make his parents' job a little easier for a little while. All it did was delay the inevitable and leave him unprepared. When he looks at it, all it does now is point out that he is lucky he can hide what needs to be from those that need hiding from. Those gilded reminders do nothing but remind him that life does not thank anyone for playing, and each year someone expects one will only cause further grief, anxiety, and depression.

He puts those trophies away because they mean nothing. They offer no solace in what he will lead himself and his friends into—a confrontation with Ashby that has too many outcomes to narrow down. So, he puts those things away that hold no value.

A couple of boxes later and all the hand-outs stored away, he looks to what remains. The trophies he won. The reminders of past accomplishments—the perfect game, the no-hitter, the traveling team championship trophy. Things he did. Events he was a part of that he worked tooth and nail for. Acts that lasted only a moment but gave him more confidence than any material reminder of mundane times. These trophies are the ones that carried him through his rough patches. These trophies are the badges of honor that proved he was a leader and could do it again.

Polish rag in hand, he makes these shine. Not in some effort to relive his glory days. He knows those days are behind him, and that those days he revels in are not the last of his glory days. They are nothing more than a chapter that has closed—a fun chapter filled with family and friends and Jack. These trophies are his way of telling Jack that they will do right by him, that the future is not just in their hands, and that the future will be a glorious place. Whatever that future may be, it will be a good chapter, one filled with remembrances of those lost and left behind.

The remaining, fresh-shining trophies are proudly displayed, not as a way of holding onto the past but as a way to look toward the tomorrow—whatever it may bring.

A few ornaments try to bring joy to the Christmas tree brooding in the corner of the room—the only decoration Connor could work through the loss to put up. Scarlett had wanted a few more, but the sheer amount of work that goes into decorating a home for the holidays is only compounded by the loss of those no longer able to share in the joy of the season. After a loved one passes, those that remain need to learn to live again. The simple thoughts of wanting to share news, ask for advice, or have a casual conversation to catch up on the day's events are no longer an option. As time passes, the occasional thought invades the mind to call them, as if those deceased are nothing more than long-lost friends who went out of touch, but as the hand reaches for the phone, that universal reminder nudges to say it can't happen. So, Connor, Scarlett, and Bri have all learned to live again over the past few years. Each passing day does not get easier, as if the death of friends and family loses meaning; it's that each passing day numbs those that survive a little more, so it does not feel as bad.

There sits the tree, reminding them of the holiday season, the season to share with family and friends. Tonight, those friends that celebrate the eve of the eve of the holiday share in a lactose-overload of eggnog and pizza. Connor, drink in one hand and slice in the other, looks down at their go-to makeshift battle plans of a pizza box. Scarlett, Allison, Bri, and Duncan listen with skeptical ears, looking over the board with uncertain eyes.

Duncan wipes the eggnog mustache from his lip. "I say we get catapults and battering rams." He watches as the girls all glare at him, like his idea is beyond realistic. "I know that climbing the walls in black-dyed leather would be a stealthier approach, but face it. Catapults and battering rams..." an idea dings his mind, lighting up his face, "and WAR WAGONS!!!! We NEED war wagons!"

Bri looks a bit lost on the whole idea. "Isn't the point of the mission, like, to get the gold, save the slaves, and not raise suspicion as to anyone being there?"

Allison nods in agreement. "I can climb. I have the skills. Then I'll let you in the back way."

"I like her idea. Sorry, Duncan," Scarlett chimes in.

Duncan huffs in defeat. "Fine. But my way would have been much quicker. Plus, no one knows who we are, so our appearance alone won't raise the alarm on who might be behind it."

"Sorry, baby. We win," Bri smirks.

But before they can begin their assault, the doorbell rings.

Scarlett gets up to answer the door. "I must admit, this game is pretty cool. Aren't there supposed to be dice, though?"

Duncan throws up his hands in defense. "I may have forgotten them. I think we are making it work, especially for a bunch of first-timers."

"But isn't there supposed to be, ya know, like, dragons? We haven't encountered any so far," Bri pouts.

"Just in the name, babe. Dragons are more of a tool than a foe to destroy," Duncan explains.

Scarlett reenters the room with Rex. "Speaking of foes to destroy, we have to pause our assault to discuss more imminent matters."

"Sorry ta ruin your fun." Rex looks at the battle plans to see what Duncan had tried to set up. "Always wantin' a full-frontal assault. Never gonna happen, Duncs."

Scarlett's interest is piqued. "You play?"

"I taught 'im how ta play." Rex smiles.

"After this whole Ashby thing is over, you simply must join us," Scarlett smiles.

In a faux British accent, Allison doesn't miss a beat. "You simply must, darling. And the queen shall join us for some tea as well."

"Whatever, Al. It'd be cool to have another player," Scarlett defends her words.

"I'm not saying it wouldn't. I'm just making fun of you saying 'simply must join us.'" Allison backs up her jab.

Connor finishes off his slice of pizza. "That's all good and fun but pause we simply must."

The rest of the group laughs. Scarlett, too, laughs at her own expense.

"We have a real issue at hand," Connor finishes.

"What is the plan? I mean, do we even have one?" Bri jumps right in.

Rex takes a seat. "He knows whad I look like. I don't know whad good I'd be. Hell, I'm not even sure whad's goin' on."

Duncan gives Rex a reassuring nod. "We got this, Rex. All you have to learn is your role." Duncan turns to Connor. "So, what is the plan, oh captain, my captain?"

Connor's head drops like a dog caught taking a dump on a Persian rug. "See, here's the thing. I don't actually have a plan, so to speak."

"Then what the hell are we doing? I love ya, Connor, but we can't let this just happen to us." Allison starts to get all worked up. "I thought we said I'd be the one to..." Allison catches herself before she lets slip what Rex does not know, "do what needs to be done since I have already?"

Connor lifts his head a bit. "Yeah, and that's about as far as I got. It's not like planning what we are planning is something they teach in school."

"Well, didn't you watch some kid die right in front of your eyes because of this Ashby guy?" Allison's voice grows more intense with each word.

Everyone but Scarlett nods.

"That's a lot of you to see someone die because of one person. Aren't you tired of seeing the stories on the news of heroin and the growing drug problem in our city? When no one else will do the right thing, it is up to us to do it. It means that no matter what we think, no matter what we want to feel, we must do what we know is right. We must protect those around us who need protecting, since no one else will. We must be the voice for those without a voice. For those who do not have a voice." Allison begins pacing like a battalion chief from an old war movie, preparing for battle.

Rex looks around at the others, a bit confused at the display of bravado before him.

"We must put an end to the injustice that this Ashby brings to our streets. We must let him know that we will not go down without a fight. Shout to the skies that we are not some monsters lurking under beds. That he is the monster, and we are the monster slayers, hunters, or whatever we need to be to get avengement for all the wrong he is doing. We shall be the ones to beat him off." Allison firmly plants her foot in place and stops pacing. She takes a deep breath, letting her words permeate the air around them.

Rex leans into Duncan, whispering, "I don't think avengement's a word."

Duncan whispers back, "Not the point. But no, it's not."

Rex raises his hand. "Can't we just call da police?"

Duncan turns back to Rex. "Do you remember what we talked about at the hospital? About those hallucinations you had when you took the drugs?"

"He called it something else, but I remember us talking. It's all so fuzzy," Rex admits.

Connor speaks up, "I remember something told to me once, a long time ago. It stuck with me, and I think it'll help."

"Please," Rex injects.

"Forget those grand, goth romance, fright night, satin-lined coffin tales you've watched and read. The werewolves, the vampires, the demons, the Legends, the truth … they are much stranger than fiction." The tone in Connor's voice as steady and serious as he can be.

Scarlett cracks a smile. "Wow. I remember that now—Grandpa's brother or cousin or something. I always thought he was crazy. Huh, who knew?"

Rex looks at Duncan. "He can't be serious?"

The deliberate and slow nod from Duncan confirms Connor's sincerity.

Rex shakes his head. "Dat's somethin' you don't go to da police wit."

"Motivational speeches aside, got any ideas, Alli?" Bri turns the attention back to her.

Allison eyes the pizza box. "As much as I didn't like the idea in the game, I think it may be our best plan for making sure Ashby doesn't get away."

The group all nods in agreement.

"There's always a possibility that things could go wrong," Scarlett points out the worst-case scenario. "One of us could end up like … well, I don't need to say it."

"Yes," Allison agrees, "but I'd rather not, and I'd rather not see any of you, either. So, we stop this before it gets more out of hand."

Still unsure of what he is getting involved with, Rex asks, "Whad exactly we talkin' about here?"

Connor takes the floor to answer this. "Rex, things we never thought capable of until put into a situation that demanded it. Things you do not have to be a part of if you'd rather not."

Rex raises an eyebrow. "You talkin' some serious trouble, huh?"

"More than some can handle." Connor keeps his reply simple.

"More than some want," Duncan adds. "But it's doing the right thing, even when it's illegal."

Rex huffs. "Legal, illegal, dat don't matter. Fight fo' whad's right, and the universe has your back."

"So?" Allison chimes.

Rex nods. "So, I'm in. Full frontal assault an' all. Plus, I need a few more scars on my body."

"We could get arrested or worse," Scarlett relays one last out to Rex.

"I look good in mugshots." Rex smiles.

Connor takes a deep breath before realizing the ludicrousness of it all. "All right. Now, all we gotta do is find Ashby."

Bri whispers to Scarlett, "Did Al say, 'beat him off?'"

CHAPTER 15

"Having trust in people is a wonderful thing."
~I. Petrovsky~

Inessa stands in a mostly empty forest preserve parking lot, watching a gray truck drive away. A nearby sign reads "Miami Woods." The overcast skies above and moderate winds further unsettle her nerves. Her white-knuckle grip around the straps of her backpack holds tight, lest someone tear it away. Her eyes dart around the nearby woods, searching. The only car left is hers.

Each time the wind picks up or a nearby woodland creature runs away, she jumps.

A twig snaps at the very edge of the woods.

"I know you're here." She looks into the woods.

Her eyes are determined to find someone there, like a hidden picture in a children's magazine.

"You won't get away with this." She steps closer to her car.

Another branch snapping nearby echoes in her ears.

She double-times it into her car, flinging the backpack onto the passenger seat. She shuts the door while climbing in and immediately slams the lock shut. Her eyes fixate on the woods, trying to find what lies beyond the forest's edge. The car starts, and she floors the gas pedal, darting into traffic—a momentary escape from the person following her.

Her eyes look at the backpack as she drives.

"Gotta hide. Gotta keep safe. Safety first, right? That's what I always say. That's what they always say. Who's they? Hideaway. Hide. A way to hide." Her mumbling fills the time while she drives.

After countless checks in her side and rearview mirrors and using obscure side routes home to make sure no one is following, she pulls into her driveway.

She grabs the backpack and opens the zipper enough to peek inside, a quick check, making sure someone, somehow hadn't snuck into her car while she drove at sixty miles per hour and stole the contents. Yes, they are still there, but that does little to calm her racing heart.

"Find a place to hide. A hiding place, of course. Until the time is ripe. Biting the time until the time is ripe. Right? That's the words. I'm right. The time is coming. That's easier," she continues rambling, more words to occupy her mind while making her way inside.

A quick beeline to the office, and Inessa locks the backpack in the filing cabinet. Making sure she hears no one coming, she grabs the diary stashed above the closet door track. A deep breath later, Inessa sits at her desk scribbling more coded incoherency into the book that, if respected, no one will ever read anyway, which is part of what eats at her. The only outlet she has to tell anyone all the secrets she thinks she has uncovered, and all the suspicion of being followed, is a diary that no one may ever see the pages of. Her heart drops, knowing that Vistrus would never break such an unspoken promise while she lives, meaning that what she writes, and has been writing for so many years, is for when she is gone. All so a mother could protect the family she was going to have, and now, she finally has.

Vistrus stands in the middle of numerous piles of old history books, Inessa's diaries unlocked from his floor safe, personal ledgers from his years at the museum, and classic works of fiction, all stacked in piles in the middle of his home office. The drawers of his desk have been emptied and organized. Every last item he housed in the office is now in a pile surrounding him—all within eyesight. Even the contents of his filing cabinet that stay locked twenty-four hours a day, seven days a week, are now spread across the floor. He taped to the wall the drawn drapes and blinds.

"Allison!" The boom of his voice carries through the house.

A moment later, the stomping of her tiny feet blazes their way to him. Allison stops outside the door to his office. "Yes, Dad?"

His voice calms. The anger in his yell was not so much meant to portray that way. He just needed the sound to carry. The two happen to sound the same. "Do you still have one of your mother's diaries?"

"No!" The defensiveness in her voice matched only in its offendedness. "You said not to touch them. So, I left them alone."

"You are sure one did not fall beside your bed?" He stands, spinning around the piles, searching for a missing diary.

"Positive. Why?" Allison tries to turn the knob, but it is locked.

He squats down and starts handpicking each pile to see if he missed it somewhere. "I had become so enthralled with the contents I never noticed she numbered them. I am missing one."

"If I see it, I'll let you know. But I just cleaned my room not too long ago, and nothing." Allison pauses for a moment so he can digest her words. "I'm heading back up. We're planning another siege."

"Still playing that dungeons game?" Vistrus asks before realizing she is gone.

He relents on finding the missing book in the pile. He looks around the room. His hands feel the bookshelves for a false wall or some indication of a key that leads to something.

Nothing.

He searches under the desk and in the desk drawers for some hidden compartment.

Nothing.

He removes the air vent covers blowing into the room and gives the ventilation shaft a once-over.

Nothing.

He examines the drywall for a patch job he overlooked for too many years.

Nothing.

Pushing the filing cabinet back into the closet to refill its contents, he nudges the door frame while shimmying it into place on the rug. A bit of drywall dust sprinkles down from the overhead track. Vistrus looks up to see a small, almost imperceptible hole where the dust fell out, but a hole nonetheless. He turns the screw counterclockwise until it falls into his hand. As he wiggles the track out of place, the missing volume falls into his hand.

He again sits, surrounded by the volumes of diaries. With the newest find in his hand, he flips the pages, looking for anything that catches his eye. He rifles through the now-accustomed-to-ramblings he knows he must decode to see if anything stands out. Near the end of the text, he encounters a grouping of names: Oliver Thompson, Penelope Williams, Mercedes Lee. After those three names, something is written, then scribbled over so many times the letters beneath it can no longer be read.

Vistrus tries angle after angle to hold the page to the light to see if it brings the letters to the surface but finds no success. Inessa dashed any possibility of reading the words beneath. Now, Vistrus has more questions. *Who are these people?* Even more gnawing than who the people belonging to those names are or were is whose name was so unmentionable that even she did not want to read it?

Vistrus finds himself a cozy spot on the cluttered office floor. He knows if there are any clues as to the people behind the names, they may be in this diary volume. He wiggles himself into a comfortable position and begins at page one.

The smell of buttered popcorn fills the air more and more with each handful Connor and Allison shove in their mouths. She snuggles into him on his couch as they watch some '90s rom-com about a girl who accidentally becomes college roommates with two guys. As the movie plays out, Allison finds herself trying to squeeze closer into Connor. Some internalized emotion she has been pushing down boils up by the visuals in front of them.

Allison wraps her arms around Connor and leans in to plant a big kiss on his lips. Caught by the surprise of the moment, he plays into the kiss.

"Not finishing the movie, I take it?" Connor jests through their kiss.

Allison moves to straddle his lap. While kissing him, she replies, "You know I love you, right?"

Connor nods his head while continuing their kiss.

"I know I haven't always been the best girlfriend." She scoops her hands around his head.

"I think you're super," he manages to squeeze out in between smooches.

Moving her hands to his shoulders, she pushes herself away to look at him. "Good. And you know that whatever happens, it doesn't change the way I feel."

Now it is his turn to create a little distance as he tries to push back into the couch. He feels he knows what this is about and where this may head, but he needs to be sure. "What are you saying?"

"I'm ready to talk." She leans in and pecks a kiss. "I love you."

"I love you. About what?" Connor twirls a pointed finger.

"Prom night," she squeaks. Again, she pecks a kiss. "I love you."

Connor smiles. He knows not every boyfriend wants to engage in this conversation, but he has been preparing himself for many months, hoping she would finally be ready. Now, the moment has arrived.

"What you did, or what you said?" Connor won't let her do this without facing herself.

"Said. Did," Allison corrects, almost stumbling over her words. After a quick inhale and huff, she backpedals, saying, "Said." She looks at him for a moment, peering into his eyes. "Both. Everything from that night."

A smile creeps across his face. "Let's talk."

He pushes pause on the Blu-Ray remote.

"I think I might be gay," she lets out. The feeling of an elephant pushing on her shoulders dissipates. Tears well in her eyes from the release of the moment. "I don't mean gay, but bi, I think."

Connor notices Allison's hands start to tick. Her breathing picks up as tears fall from her eyes.

"I mean, I love you so much. I do. I always have. Even before we started seeing each other, I felt like this, but these feelings crept up in me. Feelings I didn't know I felt. Feelings I didn't want to feel or face or acknowledge. I especially didn't want to feel them for her. She was so mean to us for so long. Just dismissive. I wanted to hate her for that. I wanted to smash her face into the ground, grind it against the concrete, and destroy it," Allison stops, lost in thought.

The tension of the moment blocks her from staying focused.

"It's okay" are Connor's only words right now.

"I didn't actually want to ruin her face. I mean, that would be contradictating the feelings I have. I wanted to destroy my feelings. I wanted not to feel them. Not for her. I have never felt feelings like that for any other girl, female, woman, whatever. Ya know? But I did, and I didn't want to..." Allison notices the smile on Connor's face.

She stops her mile-a-minute confession to stare at him.

"Thank you for beginning to tell me all this." Connor again keeps his words short.

"And I don't know what I want to do. I don't want to lose you. I especially don't want to ruin our friendship. But I know I don't want to lose you ... this. I don't know how Scarlett will feel. I don't know how Bri will react. I don't want them to be fake around me. No one should have to walk on eggs for me."

"Eggshells," he interjects.

"What?"

"Never mind. Go on."

"I don't walk on eggs, or eggshells, for anyone, so they shouldn't for me. I think they will, though. They'll look at me and think I'm some fragile, little creature who's too delicate. I just know I want you, but these feelings are too much sometimes, so much that they hurt. It physically hurts me to be around Bri because all I can do is want to be Duncan. I want her to look at me like she looks at Duncan. I want her to look at me like you look at me. And it's wrong to want someone else when I have such a wonderful person already. I know this. But I am discovering all these new things about myself. Maybe it's the stupid disease we have. Maybe it's not. I don't know, and I don't know if that even matters.

"What I do know is that I can't just push down this part of myself that has been causing such conflict inside. But I don't know what to do. All I can do is be myself, and I don't know if I know who that is anymore, or right now, or whatever..." The tears stream down her face as she stops to catch her breath.

"They say if you love someone, you should set them free," Connor whispers.

Allison sniffles, wiping away tears that are immediately replaced. "Are you dumping me after all I said?"

He shakes his head. "It's something they say, whoever they are. I think it's true if you are holding the person you love hostage. I am not. You are a free person and always free to go. I would not look forward to such a choice, but the choice is yours to make." He watches her eyes to know she understands his subtext. "What I am saying is that I want to see you happy. While I would prefer and hope that you are happy with me, if you find true happiness with someone else, that is what matters."

"What are you saying?" She sniffles again.

"I am saying, I'd rather you be truly happy with someone else than falsely happy with me. But my wish is you find true happiness with me," Connor tries to clarify.

Allison doesn't say anything. She wraps her arms around him, burying her head on his shoulder.

"We take it day by day, and I enjoy every minute I have with you until you decide otherwise. I have no plans to the contrary." He runs his fingers through her hair.

She cries into his shoulder. The words she hears are meant to make this moment easier—to show his understanding of the situation. To her, all it does is complicate an already complicated revelation. As much as she was hoping for recognition on his part, having the compassion he does instills in her a pang of guilt that seems heavier than the feelings she had not faced for so long. She continues to sob, realizing that as one problem comes to a close, another opens.

Wet snow sloshes under feet as pedestrians stroll down Michigan Avenue. The various holiday decorations illuminate the storefronts, while headlights reflect off the melting snow, making the streets and sidewalks shine like glass. Even the store speakers resound with old crooners singing in your ear, wishing you a merry Christmas and happy holidays.

The thousands of people spending their money to keep the stores in business up and down the Magnificent Mile do not even register on Duncan's radar right now. The only person in the whole world to him, the only person in the city of over four million that his eyes even see tonight, is Brianna.

Wrapped in a white coat with faux fur cuffs and collar, Bri looks as glamorous as she looks warm. Her boots and gloves are a perfect match for the jacket. Warm winter wears that pair with her denim blue jeans and button-down blouse. Her down-do hair helps keep her head warm, but the white winter hat adds a layer of adorableness that makes Duncan even more nervous about this evening.

An uncomfortableness not unnoticed by Bri. "You okay, babe?"

Duncan blows on his hands, rubbing them together to keep warm. The cold steel of his rings nips at his attempts to warm up. Ever the macho man, he dons a leather coat sans any winter lining. He doesn't even zip it up. His flannel, usually reserved for wear around his waist, is buttoned over a nu-metal band shirt.

"Yeah, just a little colder than I expected." He bounces from foot to foot while they stop to window shop outside a jewelry store known for its little blue boxes.

"We can go home if you're not having fun," Bri offers up, hoping he declines.

He shakes his head as he blows into his hands. "I don't want this night to end. The cold is worth every second I have with you."

Bri's already rosy cheeks brighten a few shades.

Duncan looks through the window behind her. "I'm not one for mainstream establishments or giving money to some corporate monstrosity, but I'd give you everything in that damned store."

Not realizing where they stopped, she turns to see diamond bracelets, earrings, and assortments of other fine jewelry displayed in the window. "They are beautiful." She turns to Duncan. "A year ago, definitely. I don't really need any of that now, I think."

The cold seems to dissipate as Duncan listens to her ramble. The words she says warm him in a way he has never felt. A part of his mind knows that they are young. The odds in the long haul are slim, but a larger part of him never wants to hear another voice— never wants to feel the way he feels for another person. Something about the vulnerability and hesitant honesty in how she speaks makes him feel like he has found his home.

"…but you were saying something about mainstream media or something like that," Bri finishes rambling.

She only rambled on for a moment or two but long enough to lose her train of thought—a quirk that Duncan finds endearing.

"Yeah. Bri, this evening. I don't want it to end. This..." he looks at the city around them, "I want to give it all to you. I want to give you five carats and everything you deserve."

Bri's brow furrows. "I'm not a huge fan of carrots."

"Not those carrots." Duncan laughs at her innocence. "Bri, what I am trying to say is this night and every night that I am with you, I don't feel the rebel in me screaming to get out. I don't feel like I need to get back at society for the institutionalization of the youth as they indoctrinate them into their way of thinking, their values, their morals, and their money, leaving no room in our minds for original thoughts. Leaving no room for us to think for ourselves. I don't feel any of that. I want to feel that more."

"I'm not going anywhere." Bri smiles. "I did not understand half of those words, but I'm here, my love."

Duncan grabs Bri's gloved hands. "We are opposite sides of the tracks. You are very much what the toy makers wished Barbie looked like; I am a little more Garbage Pail Kids. The thing is, though, we work. We make each other want to be better people, and in turn, we are better people. I can't offer you five-star dining night after night. I can offer you dinner on a TV tray. I don't know if you'll ever not have to work or what the future holds."

He sees her eyes start to light up as he talks. Most people on the street pass by, unaware of what is happening. A few who have heard his words have stopped behind him. He remains unaware of their company in this event.

"All I know, Brianna Waldgrave, is that whatever the future holds for me, for us, I want you to be there with me. I want it me and you's. I know that a restaurant with champagne, or a hot air balloon ride, or hell, not being freezin' cold would have been more romantic. But I can't wait to ask any longer." Duncan starts to bend down on one knee, but the cold ground shoots him back up.

Brianna and the growing crowd chuckle at his attempt. He turns to see them, gives a cursory nod, then brings his attention back to Bri.

"I don't have much..." he pulls his only non-ornamental ring off his finger, "but I'll give you all I have if you let me." Duncan pulls off her left glove and looks her in the eye. "Brianna Waldgrave, will you make me the happiest guy alive and say yes to marrying me?"

Bri's face tightens as tears well in her eyes. She tries to hold in a smile that overtakes her face. She peers at the crowd behind Duncan to see eager faces awaiting her reply.

"Are you serious? You want to marry me?" The reality of his words not entirely sinking in.

"Dead serious. I know we haven't been dating for years. I know there are things we do not know about each other yet. But there will always be things we discover. I don't want to wait till the end when there's nothing left to learn. I know I want this. I hope you do, too." The cold tries to creep back into his shivering words, but he shakes it off.

The seriousness of his proposal sinks in. The smile drops away, her insides warming up to the weight of his question. "Oh my God, you are serious! Duncan, people are watching us." She gestures to them, but he grabs her hands to bring her attention back to him.

"Don't worry about them. This moment isn't about them. This is about you and me—about our lives, our way. Look, tomorrow they will forget the details. All these people will know is some guy proposed. But you, me, we'll know the details. Bri, I want to live out the rest of my life with you," he says, shivering and staring at her. The winter cold creeps back in, demanding his attention.

Bri does not think that her life very well might be decades, or centuries, longer than his. Right now, in the cold winter of the Windy City, with numerous strange eyes upon her, all she can think about is the man in front of her who has made her feel more comfortable about herself than her high school years as queen bee. She does not think about the kids she wants or how they may be affected by her condition and his normalcy. All she knows is she wants to say "yes."

A voice behind him shatters the tension, "What's it gonna be?!"

Bri snaps out of her head, her eyes squint as her lips upturn. "Yes! Of course, yes!"

Duncan slips the ring on her finger, wraps his arms around her, and swings her around. The crowd claps and a few whistle before saying their congratulations and moving on with their night. And Duncan is correct, the crowd will recant the tale, and the details will change over time until forgotten to more personal memories. To Duncan and Bri, this is their night. This is their city. And tonight, they begin their future together.

CHAPTER 16

"Wonderful things can get you killed."
~E. DeSalvo~

T he long line at the Chicago Italian beef staple drive-thru signifies
this chain's lasting impression on the city's landscape. The interior is
no less busy. Lines to both registers stretch just shy of the revolving door
that provides an entrance. The tables and booths are all sat with business
professionals on quick lunches and friends catching up over a slice of the
moistest chocolate cake they'll ever share. Busy individuals writing in notebooks, typing away on laptops, or with noses buried in texts fill the center
bar-top-style seating. Two such individuals are Raymond and December.
They sit, watching a lone Inessa nibble away on a char-burger and sip a
milkshake in a corner booth.

Inessa notices them. She noticed when she walked in, and they followed
a few people behind. She caught them earlier in the day while she was
dropping baby Allison off to spend the day with Vistrus at the museum.
Inessa has not been blind to their presence, but had noticed them since she
first came to this country before the United States was neither united nor
states—when it was still called the United Colonies and Illinois was
Native land, and Chicago was not anyone's kind of town. She noticed
them and knew they noticed her. The distance between them was always
enough that Inessa never felt threatened. She just saw the two silent ones
as residents of the same city—fellow Legends who have kept to themselves for a couple of centuries. Inessa would see them occasionally here

and there. *Shopping carts bumping corners in the local Dominick's or walking down the street. Once in a while, she would see them splitting pie and coffee at the local Baker's Square. Nothing that ever alarmed Inessa. She knows her family is not the only Legends in town. To Inessa, two strangers who happened to be Legends are no different than two who happened to be Normals.*

Lately, though, she has seen them more and more, always behind her and far enough to not be too close, but close enough to not be discreet. Inessa tries to spy on them without getting caught, watching them continue to scribble in their notebooks and watch her in return.

Even after she has left the hot dog joint, Inessa can feel their presence. A car ride later to a new record store that just opened, she can sense them. She enters inside to see rows and rows of vinyl clawing to make a comeback, cassettes that gasp for air to stay alive, and the CDs now dominating the walls, snuffing out the other media's life. But the quaint store provides a hopeful escape from the two silent ones that have been following her. Inessa pretends to peruse the records, but the door chimes as December and Raymond enter.

A soft, feminine voice resounds in Inessa's head, "Don't be alarmed."

Inessa's head bobs around, searching for who spoke to her.

"Only you can hear me," December says in Inessa's mind, trying to calm her down. "My name is December. I know who you are and who you seek."

Inessa turns to find a disarming smile on the woman's face at the end of the aisle. The man beside her, equipped with soft, soulful eyes, helps soothe Inessa's worry, as she takes a few cautious steps toward them.

"I have seen you around. For a long time," Inessa starts.

Before she can continue her thoughts, a male voice cuts her short, "Do not say out loud what you are about to. We can hear you just fine inside your head."

Inessa squints a suspicious eye their way. Thinking the words, she asks, "Are you in?"

Raymond responds, "I am in as they put out the star-light."

Inessa does not respond but instead turns her stare to December, "Are you in?"

December nods, "I am in as they put out the star-light."

Inessa takes a moment to weigh the situation before responding with a simple, "Hmm."

"If we all pretend to look at the records while we talk, it won't look so strange to those around us," December advises.

They all turn to flip CDs, "The man you are looking for…."

"I do not know what you mean." Inessa pauses on a selection, pretending to contemplate it.

"You are looking for someone, no?" Raymond cuts to the chase.

Inessa continues her faux search. "What does that matter to you?"

"We think we all seek the same person," Raymond says, showing a card or two.

"Why would you think that?" Inessa plays back.

"We have been watching you for a while now. At first, we thought you might be the one we were looking for." Raymond stops to look at a CD. "That you were looking for us. You were not."

"No. I am not. What tipped you off?" Inessa moves a few feet over to continue browsing.

"We heard you whisper to yourself. A word that has not been spoken aloud in many, many years," December looks at Inessa, making sure they have her full attention. "Faoi Dhó Duine."

The lost look in Inessa's eyes proves them wrong.

"It matters not if you know the words. The Faoi Dhó Duine is part of this. We just are not sure how," Raymond admits.

"But you are sure." Inessa's words are more a statement than a question.

December nods her head. "Yes." She scans the store to find no one around, not even a clerk. She pulls out the parchment from her coat, "Take this."

Inessa unrolls the parchment to look at the portrait. "Who is this?"

The silent ones both shake their heads. "We do not know. We tended to the one you seek. We did not know back then what we all suspect now. This will help you somehow. We suspect that much."

Inessa's confusion grows. "This will help me somehow?"

Raymond nods. "Hopefully. We have one more thing to give, but it is not on us. We shall meet later."

"When? Where?" Inessa rolls the parchment and tucks it into her purse.

"We shall contact you. Keep that picture safe. No one shall see it. No one must know you have it," December advises.

That said, both Raymond and December do an about-face and leave the store. Inessa stands alone in the wonderment and confusion of the events that just transpired, trying to comprehend the importance of what *they gave her. Even though she does not know what else she will receive, she assumes it shall be just as important, if not more so.*

"It's nice of you to help us with our spring, well winter, cleaning. You don't have to, you know." Eleanor pulls out the last of the old blankets from the hall closet, handing them to a pale-faced Connor.

"Not to … no worries … Grandma," Connor takes the blanket, setting it on the couch with the others, "Got nothing else to do today."

Nick comes around the corner from their bedroom, pushing a vacuum to clean the closet once it's ready. "I still think rest is your best bet. You look a little under the weather."

Before Connor can answer, Eleanor interjects, "I think you should go see a doctor. This is the third time I can recall you looking ill this year."

Connor shrugs it off, biding time to respond. "Just a late night is all."

Nick chuckles as he sets the vacuum aside. "I remember the good ol' days. Late nights, a few beers, and more laughs."

Agitation begins creeping into Connor. "Yeah, they can be like that. But honestly, I couldn't sleep."

Eleanor starts pulling boxes off the top shelf. "Then maybe seeing the doctor isn't such a bad idea."

Connor takes the box from Eleanor. "I'm starting to think I might have sleep apnea. Sometimes it hits a little rough."

Eleanor reaches for another box. "Then you should definitely make an appointment. Treatment for that is readily available."

She pulls down the box as the contents shift, enough for her to almost drop it. The already precariously balanced lid falls as she recovers her grip. A single white glove sits on top of the contents—no other glove to complete the pair. All three pairs of eyes notice the glove. A strange tension fills the room. Both Nick and Connor reach for the box.

Nick glares at Connor, a look that brands on him, "Let go." Connor holds on for a moment before looking at his hands. With a quick shake of his head, blinking a few times as if he were snapping out of a daydream, Connor relinquishes the box to Nick.

Nick turns to Eleanor. "I can't believe you still have that thing."

"I forgot all about it." Eleanor clutches at a talisman dangling inside her blouse. "Been so long since I've seen it."

"What's that?" Connor nods to the glove.

Eleanor rubs the amulet with her thumb. "An old gift. Something I should not have kept."

Connor takes a deep breath as his eyes widen. "Someone gave you a pair of gloves?"

A sad smile crawls across her face. She shakes her head. "Not a pair. Just one."

"You never did tell me why just the one," Nick recalls, hoping an answer now will somehow bring closure to a festering wound.

She continues shaking her head, reminiscing about days long gone by. "Lost the other. Thought I'd hang onto this one in case the other showed up one day. Never thought I'd still have it."

"Maybe it's time that goes in the discard pile," Nick offers an end to the matter.

Eleanor lets go of her amulet. "Perhaps you're right, my love."

Her mind snaps back to the present to see Connor squinting at Nick. An unclear intent on display in his eyes, accompanied by a clenched jaw.

Eleanor peeks into the box to see what is under the glove. "So many memories." She shuffles through photos that never made it into albums. "All these memories with so many more that got lost to the annals of time."

"Is our second wedding in there?" Nick takes some photos from Eleanor's hands.

"Oh, possibly. And some anniversaries, holidays, birthdays..." Eleanor glances at photo after photo of old family gatherings, friends she's lost touch with over the years—of times she cherished long ago that still hold a place in her heart, and of times she laid to rest where they were, sealed by the marching of time.

"But why throw out the glove?" Connor picks it up off the coffee table.

Eleanor turns to Connor, leaving her memories again. "Sometimes, the past is best left to rest." Her energy picks up. "Plus, the other glove is long gone, wherever it is."

Nick watches Connor play with the glove. A white glove. A white glove that has been in his house, forgotten in a closet for more decades than he cares to think about. Nick realizes, as he watches Connor examine the glove as if it's an ancient artifact, he knows the location of the other half.

Connor turns to Nick, lost in thought, though his eyes stare directly at him. Connor sets the glove down. "You know what would help with organization, vacuum bags."

"Vacuum bags?" Eleanor is unclear on what they are.

"Bags, you seal and vacuum them to save space. They carry them at The Home Store," Connor clarifies.

"Grand idea. I'll go get them while you boys give the closet a good, elbow-grease cleaning." Eleanor heads to the front door.

"Let's take a break before we clean. Did I ever tell you about our wedding? Our first wedding?" Nick takes a seat in a recliner next to the couch.

Nick begins his story after Eleanor leaves. "To start with our marriage, there is much you must understand, Connor. As Legends, we must adapt over time. If not, the world will make sure we either adapt against our will or perish. Change with the world around us. You will, too, one day. When we met, we were not who you know us to be. We change if we die. When we come back, we look different— eye color, hair color, the nose is a little smaller or bigger, straight hair turns curly. The years can get added on. We age—little things. But over the centuries, we have used those little things to adapt. To pass down family estates, houses, and the like. Neighbors don't notice. They attend a funeral for us, consoling us, thinking that we are uncles or cousins of the deceased. Never to know they are the ones grieving. Times change, and so must we.

"But to the point. Back then, over a lifetime ago, I was Nioclás. Not too far of a stretch in a name. It made it easy when Nick had to take over. But your grandmother. She was something else. Her eyes were green once. Not a pale green either. No. Emerald green, they were. Bold and daring as her youthful rebellion. Her name then was Eiley. I loved her more than anything I had ever loved. Her spirit was free. Tales were scribed about her and the hearts she broke. Stories spun into cautionary warnings."

Nick laughs at the thought of his Eleanor being anything but loving.

"She was caught. Troubled. I knew a heart like hers was hard to hold. A spirit like hers was too big to love just one man. I knew it. She knew it. I was torn. How was I, one young, naive man, going to gain the attention that I thought I deserved? She deserved more, I thought. I was no different. There are two kinds of men. The one that feels he will never be good enough for the woman he loves. Eternally struggling against the feeling that there is someone out there who could and should make her just a little happier than he could, but also grateful beyond any words that she chooses to spend her days, her eternity, with him.

"And the other type of man, the man that thinks he deserves her. That he alone can make her happy and cage her wild spirit to suit his needs. The selfish man who feels owed or somehow deserves a woman because of his actions, despite what the woman may want.

"I was not that man. I am still not that man. I have had her by my side for far longer than you could imagine, Connor. Still, I have never been able to let go of the feeling that one day she will say a final goodbye. That she will tell me that there is someone who makes her happier."

Nick turns to Connor. The pale tone of the young DeSalvo still dominates his features.

"There was a man once—someone that could have come between us. I told her that the choice was hers. I could not weigh in, for if I did, her decision would not have been made without bias. She asked about this other man—what I thought of him—this Easpag. I told her I did not know enough about him to say anything. All I told her was that I would rather see her happier with someone else than less than happy with me.

"What else could I say? Plead my case that my love for her burned with a fiery passion I did not understand? A consuming flame that ate at me every moment of every day? There is nothing noble in that. Those were my feelings to deal with and not hers to bear as some burden.

"But she chose me. Before the wedding, I saw her tell him, this Easpag, that she could not love him. I felt my heart break for the man. I knew the pain he felt, as I had imagined it time and time again."

Nick sighs. "Perhaps I did not know the pain. Perhaps the pain I felt at the thought she may have chosen him was only a fraction of what he ended up feeling that day. But I will tell you, Connor, that not a day goes by that I do not thank the stars above that she said yes. That she wanted and chose to stay by my side day after day for all these years."

Nick looks into the distance. "There was a look in his eyes, this Easpag. They did not know I saw them. He held her hands as she broke his heart. She told him 'no,' and I saw the pain. Watching from the distance I was, I saw the pain. There was nothing that would mend his heart that day. There's a reason love, war, and anger all share the same color. His shade of red was all three of those. And more. He had a look that said it was not over—an undertone in his breath. I could hear him. A pounding in his heart. A tone in his voice that said he would wait for her. Wait forever if he had to."

Nick turns to Connor, shrugging it all off. "He did not. I saw him around for a while after that. Never bothered her. Just watched from a distance. Respectful, if nothing else. The years went by, and he disappeared. She says the glove wasn't from him; it was the only time in our years together that I doubted her. No reason to doubt her. Just did. It was the only time. But here's the thing, young man. You will grow old, like us. You will learn to love and let go of the things you did to yourself and others. You will learn to forgive. You have to. If you don't, it will eat you up. Tear you apart from the inside and turn you into someone you don't even recognize. I am grateful for who I am today and love your grandmother more and more as time marches on."

Nick returns from inside his head, reliving days gone by. Connor, however, is nowhere to be found. Nick walks through the house, calling out to Connor, but no response. Nick returns to the closet, ready to vacuum. "Kids. They never do appreciate a good love story."

Bri, Scarlett, Allison, Duncan, and Rex are all seated, scattered through Bri's living room. The early evening light shines bright, reflecting off the snow outside.

"I feel like we should be sipping wine or something," Bri laughs.

"This does have the feel of a dinner party. Wine, cheese, and Kenny G on the stereo," Duncan adds.

Allison raises her hand. "Are we serious? I could totally use some wine right about now. If not wine, something."

"Not sure alcohol and assault make for a good defense should things not go as planned," Scarlett says, killing the mood.

"Well, nothing's going to go as planned if Connor doesn't get here soon. He's the mastermind of this whole thing." Allison's frustration not at all hidden in her tone. "Shouldn't he be here by now?"

Rex speaks with hesitant words, "Does ... anyone know ... where he is?"

All heads turn to one another, clueless as the next. Before anyone can ask another question that is sure to go unanswered, the door opens.

"Sorry I'm late. Got held up." Connor kicks the snow off his shoes but doesn't enter the house any further. "Let's do this."

His words are not a request; they are definitive. They are commanding the moment like the snow commands the darkness to light up. Everyone else stands, making their way to the cars outside.

"We're not all gonna fit in my car," Connor states the obvious. "So, this is how things will go. Scar, Al, you'll ride with me. Rex, ride with Duncan and Bri."

Everyone nods, but Rex speaks up, "Whose car do we take?"

Connor shrugs. "Anyone that runs. Doesn't matter. We'll call you, and we'll all be on speaker. That way, I can explain the plan." Connor takes a moment so the reality of what they are about to do can sink in. "This is it. Last chance to stay home."

Everyone shakes their head no.

"Rex, last chance to stay innocent. After tonight, everything changes," Connor warns.

A dog-sly smile crosses Rex's face. "Everything needs ta change. Let's do dis."

They all hop in their cars and take off.

Blaring out over the speaker, Connor looks for confirmation. "So does that all make sense?"

Silence.

"I need noise."

"I thought we agreed on full-frontal assault?" Brianna breaks the silence.

"Yes, once we're past the fence. We don't want the cops chasing after us while we take Ashby down," Connor clarifies.

Bri interjects, "But if we lead the cops on a chase to Ashby, then they can see what he's doing and arrest him. Isn't that better?"

Allison chimes in, "Unless Ashby goes down in a hail of gunfire, he'll be back on the streets in no time. We need to handle this."

Before a rabble of a discussion breaks out, Connor commands the speaker phone, "While I like your idea, Bri, Allison is right. I've seen too many teen movies to know a teen-led police chase won't end with the bad guy behind bars."

An audible confirmation from everyone can be heard over the phones.

"Now that we are all on the same page, we got the plan?"

Everyone confirms their understanding as they pull into a parking lot a few blocks from the old school.

They walk in uneventful silence from their cars to the abandoned school. A few cars pass by, and the clouds overhead clear from the moon to light their path. No suspicious strangers straggle behind them. No police cars following them questioning the legitimacy of a group of adults. Just a walk to find themselves in the cover of the brush, ready to cross the broken fence into enemy territory.

"So, we just walk in like it ain't nothin' and confront him," Rex confirms aloud.

"Yup," comes Connor's one-word response.

"I'm all for the Napoleonic way of show up and see what happens, but, Con, it didn't end well for him." Duncan reminds Connor of history.

"Good thing we aren't French." Connor smirks as he crosses under the fence.

"I don't think that was the proper takeaway, cuz," Scarlett talks to herself as she follows.

Then Allison, Bri, Rex, and Duncan follow, too.

They slow their approach as Connor formulates a semblance of a plan. "Duncan and Rex, you guys go in first. We'll listen and see what plays out."

Duncan stops Connor with his arm. "Yeah, remember that Ashby knows me. Knows I know, too."

"We can't just, like, send Rex in alone," Bri points out.

"I'll go with him," Allison volunteers. "If any of us can play angry youth, I think I can."

They continue their cautious approach, attempting to keep their steps as light as possible.

Their hearts are all pounding from the anticipation of what's to come. A strange unison of thumping reverberates in Connor and Allison's ears. Even Scarlett tingles in a peculiar way she can't quite place. Her hearing picks up nothing unusual. However, her awareness of the world around her is as if she can see the sounds emanating from her surroundings. Not exactly a visual representation, but she knows they are there—a unique, high-contrast hearing that separates the sounds and colors down to the slightest variation. Even her nose is sorting out the undertones of the boys' cologne and Bri's perfume.

They find themselves at the end of the hallway. The closed door at the other end leaks light out of the bottom, betraying whoever is inside. They all stare at each other and nod. Allison and Rex traverse the hallway and knock on the door, while the others disappear around the corner. A moment later, Allison and Rex find themselves separated from their friends as the door shuts behind them.

Connor, Bri, Scarlett, and Duncan all stand in silence, trying to listen to the events on the other side.

"I only hear one other voice. But three other heartbeats," Connor informs them.

"So, five, including Rex and Alli?" Scarlett confirms.

Connor nods his head, then shoots a finger up to silence them. After a quick moment, he waves his hand to usher them toward

Rex and Allison. No more time for silence and sneaking. Full frontal assault.

Connor bursts through the door to find Rex holding his chest, blood seeping from between his fingers.

"Sorry, bro," Rex apologizes.

Allison stands between two boys dressed in full para-military style gear: black steel-toes combat boots, camouflage, and haircuts to match Ashby's. Each holds a syringe filled with the same blue liquid that Rex once took.

Duncan sees Rex. "What happened?"

Rex motions to Ashby. "He knew we were friends."

Ashby stands a few feet behind Rex, a small paring knife in his hand drips with blood. He smiles at Duncan. "Do you still think I am all rhetoric?"

Duncan seethes with anger. His eyes widen as he watches drop after drop of Rex's blood drip from the knife. A war cry fills the room as Duncan charges Ashby. Ashby responds with a quick side-step, tossing Duncan to the ground. "That-a-boy."

Duncan stands, ready to strike at Ashby again, but Connor moves across the room in one swift motion before he can. He stands, heaving his chest up and down with heavy breaths; his Legend form pulsates with veins on muscles that could dwarf even the strongest of bodybuilders. Long, sparse hair adorns his body in patches, as if the growth of his body spread the would-be thick hair thin. Fangs protrude from his mouth. He turns to Duncan. "Tend to Rex. I got this."

Allison finds herself still parrying off the two young recruits. Blue liquid teases her with each drip from the needle. Her form also fully transitioned. Her nose has withered away, and her lips have thinned so much that they have disappeared. Her muscles overtake her diminutive form. Her pink pixie-cut hair has grown out and filled in jet black, thinner than it was moments ago.

The two boys each lunge at her, needles aimed to inject. In less than the blink of an eye, she grabs one of the boys, swinging him into the other. One of the syringes stabs the other boy. He drops his syringe, shattering the glass and sending the blue liquid known as the cure to wet the ground. The clank of their heads against each other sends them to the floor, unconscious and bleeding.

Brianna watches her boyfriend's hand get covered in his friend's blood. Her breathing escalates as her skin starts wrinkling. Before she can control it, it decays in front of her eyes.

"Stop it!" Guttural and lower than usual, Brianna's voice is what Duncan heard through the closed bathroom door.

Bri takes a step as she continues decaying in front of their eyes. Her jaw dislocates, hanging only by the sinew. Her eye falls out of the socket. Instinct kicks in, and she catches her eye, holding it in her hand.

Duncan turns to his woman, his eyes filling with fascination, not disgust. "I can't stop the bleeding."

Words not unheard by Connor. He pushes off Ashby, sending him to the ground in one swift motion, and leaps to Rex.

"I'll get him to a hospital," Connor scoops Rex into his arms before bounding out the door. Scarlett follows to make sure they make it back to the car okay.

Ashby brushes off the dirt from the fall. He grabs a small case from nearby and pockets it unnoticed. A wicked smile across his face as he sees the Undying and Vampire.

Allison's attention turns from the boys to a quick once-over of Brianna before resting her gaze on Ashby.

Brianna shuffles to Duncan, who takes her by her skeletal hand.

Ashby creeps closer to the group. "All of you. You are dead and don't even know it yet."

Brianna goes to speak, but her dislocated jaw only allows moans and incomprehensible mumbling. Frustrated, she throws her eyeball, hitting Ashby in the face.

Ashby stands, shocked that a flying eyeball hit him.

Duncan rubs her arm with his bloody hand to try and calm her down.

Allison keeps her stare locked on Ashby, waiting for him to make a move. "It doesn't have to be like this. You didn't have to stab Rex. You didn't have to kill that kid in the mall."

Ashby stops moving. "You can't cure disease without making sacrifices. What your friends have done for the cause is greatly appreciated."

Duncan shouts, "They didn't make that choice! You made it for them!"

Ashby huffs. "If they knew what was possible, they never would have volunteered. Informed consent stifles scientific advancement."

Ashby sneaks a hand around his back.

Allison snares, "We are not some disease that needs a cure. We are human. We are normal. There is nothing wrong with us."

Ashby's huff turns into laughter. "Have you looked in the mirror? Have you seen what sort of monster you are?" He grabs a syringe from the pocketed case. "You will never be okay. You will never accept who you are, and we will never accept you. Just be done with yourself. Let me help you." He brings the syringe around for them all to see.

Allison hears his words. A moment of defeat washes over her. All she craves is a little normalcy. A life that she doesn't have to hide or explain. A life she can accept as her own. She watches as Ashby takes cautious steps toward her.

"You can take this all away? Make me a Normal?" Allison pleads. "So, I can be who I want to be?"

Ashby nods his head. "This will take away all of it. Give you everything you want. All you have to do is everything I say."

His words echo in Allison's head as he takes one more step toward her. "Everything you want." At that moment, she sees Brianna struggle to talk. Allison sees Bri's decaying skin and exposed muscle. Allison sees Duncan holding Bri's hand, not caring that she looks different. Brianna has someone who loves her as she is: Duncan. Allison knows she loves her as she is, too. She turns her attention back to Ashby, now inches from her, ready to inject her with the cure.

Allison grabs Ashby's hand, snapping his wrist in half as she turns the syringe on him. She jabs it into him, pressing the plunger too fast for his body to take in, rupturing whatever muscle or vein she stabbed. With her other hand, she lifts him by the neck. His face goes from flesh tone to red in a matter of seconds as he struggles to breathe.

"You cannot cure us. We are not to be cured. You offer everything I want. What I want, I can't have. What I want does not want me. That is something you can't promise," Allison spits her words at him.

She squeezes his neck, turning his face from red to blue as his eyes start bulging out, petechiae form in the whites of his eyes.

"You have taken from us more than we can ever take from you. For that, you win. But this battle..." she squeezes a little tighter, causing one eye to bleed, "this battle I win. And no amount of what you have to offer can take that away."

Every ounce of Allison boils over with anger and hate for everything that has been cast upon them. Every ounce of her wants the pain of everything to go away—wants to find a peace that she has never known. In her hand is one of those responsible for everything that has caused her to drift further and further from finding peace with herself and who she feels she needs to be. In a moment of pure, unadulterated hate and anger, she flings Ashby across the room. Like a ceramic plate hitting the wall, the sounds of Ashby's bones shattering fill the room. He drops to the ground, motionless and contorted from multiple fractures and internal injuries.

Allison sees Bri and Duncan embracing each other, fear in their eyes. Before anyone can say a word, Scarlett comes back into the room.

"Well, that was fast." Scarlett looks at the bodies on the floor. "Are they all..." She dares not speak the word for fear of making it real.

No one answers her. Bri and Duncan turn their heads to Scarlett, while keeping their eyes on Allison. Allison looks at the carnage she caused, thoughts racing through her mind as to how she can cause such pain. They all stand in the aftermath of the events, unsure of what they have done.

"They make it to the car?" Duncan breaks the silence.

Scarlett takes a step toward them. "I lost him. He was too fast for me to keep up with."

"Rex better be okay," Duncan thinks out loud. "Come on, let's go find them."

Duncan and Bri take one step at a time to calm her and return her back to Normal. The fact her fiancé is not disgusted by her Legendary form helps more than she can ever express. Scarlett trails behind them, but Allison does not move.

"You coming?" Scarlett turns to Allison after Bri and Duncan are in the hall.

Allison shakes her head. "Gonna stay for a while."

"I can stay with you if you'd like," Scarlett offers.

"Go. I need to be alone." Allison looks at Scarlett.

"You okay?" Scarlett makes one last attempt.

"No. But yeah. I need to stay." Allison turns away. She crouches next to one of the boys as her Legendary form retreats.

Scarlett exits into the hall, leaving Allison alone among the chaos that ensued.

The front door swings open. "Sorry that took so long. The lines were tremendously long." Eleanor shuts the door behind her.

Horror greets her in the hallway as she checks on the progress made by Nick and Connor. The thud of the space-saving bags hitting the floor rings throughout the silent house. Laying over the hallway closet door threshold, Nick stares at his love, his mouth forming cries of help, though no sound emanates. She sees the small pool of blood forming on the floor; his blood-stained teeth tell of its source. He clutches his stomach, holding in his intestines that attempt to wriggle around his fingers.

Eleanor rushes past him to their bedroom. The wood-framed vanity mirror that was the centerpiece of their dresser lies shattered in a thousand shards—the wooden frame, broken to bits. A hole punched into the drywall behind the mirror reveals a horizontal wood shelf secured between the studs. Two small circles are evident in the dust.

Her eyes widen, knowing that their 21-gram vials are gone. Without the vials, death is permanent. Without the vials, their years and their centuries together will come to an end.

She needs to help him. Eleanor needs to keep his insides in. She needs to get him blood. She needs her Nick, who has stood by her side for too many days and nights to count. She needs to save him.

A weak cough from the hallway sends her rushing back. Still laid out, Nick coughs up blood, clinging to life.

Eleanor punches 9-1-1 into a cordless landline phone from around the corner and kneels by his side. She feels the fear-infused sweat form on her forehead. The first ring sends heart-pounding panic through her chest.

"9-1-1. What is your emergency?"

Words that she never thought she'd be so happy to hear.

"My husband's been attacked. He's bleeding. Bad. Please send help!" The panic in Eleanor's voice is not to be mistaken. The fear of losing her loved one cannot be faked.

An emotion the operator understands all too well.

Eleanor keeps vigil over her beloved as the instructions of what to do pour through the earpiece. She takes a blanket off the couch, using it to hold in his innards. She listens, knowing everything she does is crucial, and that time is of the essence.

Keep pressure on the wound to help slow the bleeding.

There is a smile on Nick's face. The pain has passed. He smiles as he stares at the woman in front of him. A woman who is centuries younger and back in their homeland. A different time, a different place. He stares at the woman he fell in love with. Her wild, emerald-green eyes that have since faded with the passing of years. Nick stares at her as she cries. He hears no sound. It is easy to pretend her cries are laughter when there is no sound. He watches as she tries to save him. He smiles.

The operator speaks words that pull Eleanor from her panic for a moment. She turns to Nick, yelling to get his attention, "Do you know who did this?!"

Nick struggles to speak, his words soft and frail, "C … on … nor." He coughs out his name, spraying his wife with specks of blood.

Eleanor drops the phone, disbelief on her face. It can't be. Her loving grandchild would not do such things. He wouldn't hurt a fly. Then she starts to think of the past couple of years and the loss he has endured between family and friends. The events he has gone through play in her mind, trying to imagine what he must have felt. But she can't believe that Connor would do such a thing.

More blood sprays from his words. "Not … who … you … think."

From the floor, a voice sounds on the phone, "The EMTs are almost there. Stay with me, Mrs. DeSalvo."

"Buh," is all he has the strength to mumble as Eleanor watches the last flicker of light and life fade from his eyes. A light that has lit her world for as long as she can remember has dimmed; only the smile on his face remains.

The knock on the front door can't save him now.

CHAPTER 17

*"There are those who benefit from
things best left forgotten."*
~B. Scott~

Inessa faces Raymond and December in an otherwise empty forest preserve parking lot. Besides Inessa's car, the only other car is the gray truck belonging to December and Raymond. The wind whips with the racing clouds above. Every tiny branch snap causes Inessa to jump a little more.

She holds a tight grip on her backpack straps. Her eyes dart around. "I don't like this. Why did we meet here? He could be here, you know."

December sounds her voice in Inessa's mind, "Everything is okay. There is no one else around. No one of consequence anyhow."

"I still don't like this. Something in the air." Inessa turns to the woods nearby. "Something in there. Tell me what to do. Tell me of this Faoi Dhó Duine."

Raymond steps forward. His voice whispers in her head, "We do not know much. We have been watching—observing for so long. We have spoken with The Nation. With a select few members of The Council about matters we felt were worth their attention."

"That's not true. Never heard of you," a hushed tone snaps from Inessa.

"Only one on The Council knows, as of now. We do have our own interests to look out for." December pulls a white glove from a small purse.

"Which brings us to this." She hands the glove to Inessa. "The other item we had to give you."

"What's a glove got to do with this?" Inessa asks them in her mind.

"He was wearing it the day we saved him. Had we known what he had done, who he was, we would have handled it differently. Now, we hunt him. He has something of ours." December holds back her words.

"I think he knows I know." Inessa jerks her head to a snapping twig. "I think he knows I know he knows."

"We thought these items might aid you in your search. Guard them well. Do not let him get them. Do not let anyone see the Faoi Dhó Duine," December warns.

"You still have not told me what that is," Inessa reminds them, eyes peering into the woods.

"The Faoi Dhó Duine came to me some time ago. Then the visual of their face. I sketched it." December joins Inessa's peering. "This came to me before the fairies split. The Faoi Dhó Duine means the twice human ... roughly translated."

Inessa turns back to them, wide-eyed with fear. "The grey fairy."

Raymond steps toward their truck. "Guard those with your life. If you find the Faoi Dhó Duine, guard them as well."

Inessa shoves the glove into her backpack, watching as they pull away. A snap at the edge of the woods draws her attention. She thinks she sees the outline of a light fairy against the tree. She is unsure, though. The transparent skin causes the translucency of the muscle tone to blend in with the wooded surroundings.

A closer snap of a twig.

The grip around her backpack tightens to white-knuckle.

Scarlett sits, legs crossed, staring at her parents' tombstones. The wind plays with her hair, as it always does on her visits here. She has grown accustomed to it, letting nature do what it will. She feels it is some sign that her parents still know she is there, even though it defies all logic. It gives her a sense of comfort that she is doing more with her time than talking to two stones.

She picks at the grass in front of her. "And I know things are not being handled well, but it seems all The Nation does is cover its tracks, keeping us hidden. Maybe I'm wrong, but that doesn't seem to be a great way to present an upstanding reputation to the few who aren't in and know of us."

Scarlett tosses a few blades of grass into the wind. "Things have really gotten complicated."

The chime of Allison's ringtone interrupts her thoughts.

[Allison: Where ya at?]

[Scarlett: Cemetery. Come by.]

"Sorry about that." She resumes picking at the grass. "I just don't know. No one prepares you for these things. There are no classes on how to live in this world. No books that seem to have the right answers. I wish you were here to help. To tell me what to do. Not that any of this is relevant to me right now. All I know is that you were Legends, and I should be. But I'm not. I watch all my friends discover these frighteningly wonderful new sides to them. They are growing and becoming more than they ever dreamed. It's scary, sure. Alli is stuck somewhere between denial and acceptance. Connor has gotten a better grip on it. Bri has come back around, but her biggest issue is how ugly she is when she's in Legendary form, or whatever it's called."

Scarlett looks to the cemetery's far reaches, ensuring she is still alone. She watches the trees dance in the wind. "Alli sure is not getting it any easier. She may be the only one who still has a parent who's alive, but she's the only one who's killed people. I can't even begin to think about what that must feel like. I think, more than her struggle with who she wants to kiss, is the guilt from the lives she has taken."

The sound of approaching footsteps breaks her concentration. She turns to see Connor standing a few yards back, pale and gaunt.

Scarlett nods to him. "Let me finish." She turns back to her parents. "The things in life no one teaches you could fill books. The things we'll never know could fill more." She sighs. "I just wish the world cared. I mean, cared but free of putting their own, what's the word, agenda behind it. I wish the world cared. Sad words to say, but then I am in a sad place." She reaches forward and puts her hands on her parents' stones. "One day."

She leverages herself on the tombstones to stand, searing pain ripping through her. She falls to the ground, clutching her neck as blood sprays over the gravestones. Shreds of skin, muscle, windpipe, and esophagus dangle between her fingers as she tries to stop the bleeding. With each passing second, her strength weakens.

Life fading, she looks up to the cousin she has known her whole life. His Legendary form, too, has become a little more familiar. But something is wrong. Besides knowing her cousin, she knows he would not snap. He would not do such a thing. Scarlett can't place a finger on it, perhaps because she is bleeding, but something is wrong. A look in his eyes, a color to his skin, even in his Legendary form, is off. If it was there when he arrived, she missed it. It's too late now. All she can do is watch as this man stands over her, watching with a dark intensity as she clings to life.

After a moment, the Legendary state recedes. The Normal form is that of Connor. Much like his Legendary form, the dying Scarlett sees something off about him. He looks ill. His face isn't his, as if someone was trying to look like him but didn't get it a hundred percent right.

"You will never lead The Nation. It is not yours to control," he speaks.

She does not understand the context of his words. The meaning is lost. Scarlett had never talked with any of the Council members about such a thing. Scarlett doesn't even know who is on the Council. She can't help but wonder if this is some mistaken identity. If, from grief over recent events, her mind sees Connor, even though someone else is standing in front of her. It doesn't matter now. She hasn't the strength to move or speak. She watches as he walks away. No rush, no urgency in his step. He just strolls away with an air about him like this is an everyday occurrence.

The lights around her dim as the distance between them grows. The sounds fade as if she is falling asleep, but she knows she is not.

Allison idles her car through the cemetery roads. Approaching in the distance, she thinks she sees Connor. The sun glares in her eyes, distorting her vision. She has not seen him since their final encounter with Ashby. She has no idea if Rex is alive. No idea how Connor feels about his girlfriend killing another person. She starts recollecting her body count—Mrs. Espinoza and Ashby. Two. Such a small number when considered in some terms. In her case, it is a rather large number. Most Normals make it through their life killing no one. Here she has killed two. Legends, for most, it is only a matter of time. Even then, it is more out of self-preservation than rage, misplaced anger, or serial killer motives.

Connor walks closer and closer with each step. Allison pulls out her flask from the glove box and chugs away, drowning her feelings. She covers up anything she does not want to feel as the clouds move to cover the sun. Connor walks past her open window oblivious to her presence. The numbing effect of the alcohol not keeping her calm.

"Connor?" She takes another swig.

He stops, taking a moment to register his name being called to him.

"Baby? Did you see Scarlett?" She puts her flask back in the glove box.

Connor walks back to her window. "Yeah. Up at the grave. Said she wanted time."

Allison looks him over. His pale, sunken features sober her up a touch.

"You holding up okay? You don't look so well." She tries to focus.

"Just feeling a bit ill," he dismisses, looking in the direction he was walking.

"Did Rex make it to a hospital?" Allison tries to see what Connor is looking at.

"Who?" Connor's confusion about her question sends up a red flag.

She turns back to him. "Poor baby. You must be taking it hard. I'll call you later. Go rest."

Connor nods and continues on his way.

Allison releases her foot off the brake to idle along the cemetery roads. She checks her rearview mirror to watch Connor walk off. She did not see the blood splattered on his clothes. Perhaps the colors were a tad too dark. Maybe she has had too much to drink, or the weight on her shoulders distracted her.

She did not see.

The sun peeks out from behind the clouds. The brightness distorts her vision as Connor changes shape, disappearing down a sloping road. To Allison, Connor changing shape is something she will have to adjust to. In some sense, she already has, but the form she saw was not him changing into his Legendary form. It looked as if he had changed into another person. She continues, dismissing her own eyes to the alcohol and blinding sun.

Her foot stomps the brakes as she spots Scarlett lying on the ground, covered in her own blood. Allison jumps out of the car and dashes to Scarlett's motionless body.

Shaking Scarlett, Allison shouts for her to wake up, over and over again, "Wake up! Wake up!" But Scarlett does not. The words do not rouse her. The life that was inside the body seems to be no more. Allison stops shaking Scarlett, pleading with her to say something. Tears stream down onto Scarlett while Allison tries to puzzle piece the muscles, flesh, windpipe, and food pipe back into place, hoping this is the magic cure Scarlett needs.

Allison rocks back and forth, holding her friend. Teardrops fall onto Scarlett. "I was gonna tell you I'm sorry. Sorry I haven't told you what's been going on. Not that you don't know. I guess I was the last to know. But I was gonna tell you I'm sorry I drifted away lately. I'm sorry I've not been a good friend. Connor…"

Her words cut her thoughts short. Connor. The last person to have seen Scarlett. Not Connor. It couldn't be Connor. Allison will not let her mind think such thoughts. Connor would never do this. No. Though, she just saw him. He told Allison that Scarlett was at the graves. He must have. Allison won't believe it.

Frantic, she lifts Scarlett like a rag doll. In the distance, an excavator starts digging a grave for some unfortunate soul. A memory springs forth in Allison's mind. A memory of a dream. One where she buries Scarlett. If there ever was a time when her dreams needed to mean something, now is it.

Allison tosses Scarlett in the back seat, her mind too cluttered to have time for care. "Sorry, Scar."

Allison speeds down the road. Her senses become more aware of her surroundings as the hysteria of what happened to Scarlett pumps adrenaline through her veins. Allison allows the dream replaying in her head to guide her as she drives.

"I didn't mean to be a bad friend. I've been dealing with things. You know. Connor knows. But we won't talk about him right now. But these things, I'm dealing. I've dealed. Dealt. You know. I think. Oh, Scarlett!" Allison rambles away, cruising to where her dream-led instincts tell her to go. Her speed and intonation sound more like what she imagines her mother must have sounded like when she wrote the nonsensical diary entries.

The residential houses pass by in a blur. The night adds little cover for Allison, who speeds through West Haven with Scarlett's body strewn across the back seat.

Tears stream down her face. Panic in her voice. "Scarlett, Scarlett, I take back what I said. That kid. The one who died in the mall. I had to tell myself those things. I had to say it. So I could do what we had to do. But he didn't deserve to die that way. I would not want to die that way. No one deserves to die like that. Not in public. He was surrounded by so many people. He had to feel so alone. I would not want that. I am so sorry."

She turns her head for a split second to check on Scarlett. "Come on, Lil' Let! Wake up! This isn't how things are supposed to end! This can't be it! We are Legends. Legends don't die. Not like this. Not while visiting their dead parents."

Allison's tires screech as she rounds a corner. "Do you remember, junior year, you helped me study for that exam? Government. We were talking afterward about that kid from gym class—the one who killed themself. I take back what I said. I wouldn't want anyone to find me dead. I don't think. No. I mean. I wouldn't want to find you dead. So, wake up!"

Allison lugs a limp Scarlett through the woods. She scans the sur-roundings, searching for her long-forgotten trail. The blowing wind once more reminds Allison of her dream. Though not as pointed a gust as in her dream, she decides to follow the wind while continually looking for a place she's never seen in her waking hours.

A few animals scurry around her as the clouds play peek-a-boo with the moon. The wind dies down. She tells herself that the wind was not guiding her, but she sure could use some cosmic help.

Allison turns to her pale, lifeless friend, stopping her expedition into the woods. Realizing she is lost, she looks to the sky above to gather her bearings, but a ship's captain she is not. In the darkness of the woods, unable to tell north from south and east from west, she is glad she can tell up from down. Panic sinks further in as the familiar sounds of ambulance sirens close by remind her of the evening's events.

A clearing comes into view. Allison double-times her pace, Scarlett flung over her shoulder. The middle of the clearing is a perfect spot. Close enough to what Allison dreamt all those nights ago that she could swear she was in this very spot in that dream. The only thing missing are the people who were there and a shovel.

A shovel.

Allison needs to bury her friend, and she doesn't have a shovel. She spins around, hoping some vagabond, vagrant, or forgetful hiker left one lying against a tree.

No luck.

Allison starts digging with her hands. Rapid stabs at the dirt to move as much as she can with her tiny frame.

It doesn't take long until frustration and anger coat the panic controlling her. With heavy breaths, she swipes at the ground, grabbing more dirt. Faster and faster. Her hands have started to rub raw and callous over. Her nails thicken into something akin to discolored talons. The blinding speed at which she digs makes for quick work.

She stands up to grab Scarlett and realizes she is the creature she has denied for so long. She sees her hands with varicose veins pulsating with each beat of her heart. Her arms have tripled in size. Pure muscle. She looks at her body. No longer petite and frail-looking. She has bulked up to the likes of which Olympian-sized Arnold would be proud. She has no time to worry about what she has been denying. No moments to take for herself right now.

She still has to bury her friend. Why? She does not know. She follows the crazy dreams she has journaled for so long—a dash of hope in a tragic time.

She buries her friend and with her all their memories. All the times they shared and laughed about having in some future that Allison questions will ever come. Buried with Scarlett are all the hopes and dreams that they held onto for a life outside of West Haven. A life that was not too provincial-feeling—a life that meant something. A life they thought would be one for the books, not one that ended with her buried in the woods.

Allison exits the woods, as the last of her Legendary form returns to Normal. Inside her car, she pulls out a flask and takes a couple of swigs. Just a little poison to kill the pain. The hysterics in her tears do not quell. She can't help the heaving cries at the thought of what she just did.

She takes another couple of swigs.

Her chest weighs heavy with guilt and loss.

She takes a swig.

She tries to calm herself, but each attempt makes her emotions worse.

She takes two swigs.

Turning on the ignition to her car, she holds a deep breath—the sadness enveloping her forces it out in a sob.

She takes a giant swig, finishing off the flask. She tosses it back in the glove box and pulls out of the woods.

The roads move from under her tires. Yellow lines in the road, not staying where they should. She sticks her hands at ten and two—thumbs pointed up to match the lines on the road. It does not help. The streets twist and turn under her. Perhaps it is she who weaves in and out of the lines. It does not matter. She is blocks from home.

All she can do is think about her best friend, lying under a pile of dirt, helpless and alone. She did this. In a reckless panic, she did this to her friend. She doesn't know why. She needs to get her. The woods are no place to bury a friend. Scarlett deserves better and deserves a better friend than Allison. Not to be buried like a camper's excrement. Not to be left to waste away in a shallow grave.

Allison turns the car around to get her friend. She'll call her dad and make everything better. Daddy fixes everything.

In the middle of scrolling for her father's number, she drops her phone. Keeping one hand on the wheel and half an eye on the road, she flails her arm, searching for her phone. Grabbing it, she straightens herself to see headlights aimed at her. Realizing she drove into the oncoming lane, she overcompensates her correction, sending her past her lane and onto the sidewalk, missing a tree by mere inches.

She glances back to make sure she didn't hit anything. She swerves back onto the road, hoping her commotion does not attract any attention.

It doesn't matter. Before Allison can gather her bearings, she sees Connor step into the road. His hands rap against his head, whispering to himself over and over, though clear as day to her Legendary ears, that Rex is dead. She slams on the breaks, but it is too late. The screeching tires snap Connor from his distraction. He tries to jump out of the way but gets clipped by the bumper. Allison jerks the wheel in her ill-fated attempt to avoid hitting her boyfriend, stalling herself in a bush.

Allison sits in the driver's seat, collecting herself. The car groans to a sleep. She doesn't know if she turned it off or if it died, but it is off. Allison stares at the lit-up house next to her with a person standing in their window making a phone call.

Outside the car, Connor is nowhere to be found. She swears she hit him. Now she doesn't know if she imagined the whole thing or if he ran off. The answer to her questions may not be found, deterred by the approaching flashing red and blue lights.

Allison sits handcuffed in the back of a squad car. The police stand outside, talking to each other as they decide what to do. A third car pulls up. No lights. No police markings. Nothing to indicate any police involvement. All she can see is the driver is wearing what appears to be a sports jersey with the number 51 on it. She can't make out his face as he talks with the officers. The cops make a few motions her way and gesture to the scene around them. She watches as a cop nods, extending his arm to her.

She turns her head to look away. The consequences of her action start to sink in. The friend lying a few feet under dirt, her boyfriend turned killer, her drinking and driving, her acting out of panic instead of calling her father first, all leading up to this moment—a moment in the back of a squad car, arrested for drunk driving.

The driver's door opens, and the jersey-wearing man takes a seat. He remains facing forward but adjusts the rearview mirror to see her. She makes out his eyes. Familiar, but she can't place them.

"Life deals harsh hands sometimes," he speaks.

The voice penetrates her like an arrow through the chest. Max Espinoza. Officer Max Espinoza.

Her breathing stops. Unsure if she is going to make it out of the car alive, she holds back her screams. The last thing she needs is officers coming to his aid.

"I should know. You killed my wife," he finishes his thought. He waits for a response from Allison but does not get the satisfaction of hearing one. "I understand. We did bad things. We did not know. It does not matter now. What's done is done."

Allison turns to look out the window. She will not let him look her in the eyes.

"What happened tonight ... as I said, life deals harsh hands. There are times we work so hard for things to become better. We take steps to ensure they do. No matter how hard we try, though, sometimes the obstacles never stop coming. Tear one down to have two more pop up. I've been keeping tabs. Well, not me, but people. It's saddening to see you try so hard to deal with your insecurities just to have those around you become killers. All that hard work to accept who you are to make the future a little safer, a little brighter, torn away by a boyfriend gone off the rails." His voice becomes sullen, "I know I did nothing to make your life easier. I did nothing to help you and your future. I was one of those obstacles that life kept throwing up."

Allison turns back to him. "You took so much from us."

"Life can be cruel. You have spent a good portion of a year trying to take down Ashby. A year of your life making all the wrongs that happened to you right somehow. All while your father deals with his demons, you and your friends are growing, becoming adults in your own right. Except everything is all wrong." Max huffs. "How little we know. Here's the sad truth. Sometimes happy endings come only in stories. Not everything always gets wrapped up in a nice box with a bow, easily concluded with no loose ends and unfinished business. Try as you may to do everything right, and somehow you still end up in the back of a squad car, arrested for drunk driving, while the man responsible for your initial troubles lectures you about life." He turns to her.

Before he can speak, Allison's lips part. "If you are going to kill me, please spare me the lecture and do it. I have nothing. My boyfriend killed my best friend. That best friend is under a pile of dirt." She catches her words and silences herself.

Max knows what Allison means. He might not know where or when, but he knows what she means by her words.

"Allison Petrovsky, you are in a bad spot. I will not say something so cliche as pull yourself up. Sometimes you can't. Sometimes you have no bootstraps. There are times when being at the bottom of life's barrel is where you end up. How long you stay there is up to you. I am not here to kill you. I do not believe I could do such a thing anymore, even if I wanted to. I came back to find you—to tell you that the things happening to you in West Haven are so much bigger than you could imagine. I've been away learning the truth. Learning that while no one thinks they are the bad guy, there are right guys and wrong guys."

"Right and wrong guys?" Allison reiterates in a less-than-impressed fashion.

"I am not a wordsmith. Right and wrong. Even those on the side of wrong won't think their acts terrorize—won't think they are bad. They will justify their actions as I had, only until someone finds a way through. Where you are now isn't where you have to stay, even if the past events have led to this seeming conclusion."

"Nice platypus," Allison snarks at him.

He forces out a laugh. "Platitude. But that doesn't matter."

"What does matter then? Please, tell me what matters anymore." Allison turns back to stare out the window.

"What matters is the conversation. You have been asking the same questions, getting the same answers since Jack was first arrested," Max offers.

She spins her head back to him. "Arrested by you."

"True." Shame rises in his voice. "No matter what the inciting incident was, the questions have been asked over and over, and all answered the same way. People everywhere echo the same maxims and the same ideas over and over, trapped in their thoughts. They never grow beyond the moment. Never moving forward to advance or strengthen the foundation of their arguments and beliefs. So, you have to ask yourself—how do you want to advance the conversation? We are stuck having the same talks over and over again, like a bad relationship. The conversation needs to move forward. What can you do to contribute to the issues at hand instead of just being noise in the background? Before every time you go to speak from here on out, ask yourself, 'Have I said this before?' If so, change what you say to add to the conversation. Do not just regurgitate the words you have heard spoken before. Make them better. Make them your own. And make sure that, above all else, what you contribute makes the future better for everyone, not just those like you. A lesson I learned too late."

Allison watches him speak. His words resonate with her.

They sit for a moment, silence surrounding them inside the squad car. He pushes the button to roll down her window, flooding the car with sounds from the events outside. He exits the car, only to lean into the open back window.

"When it comes to the human condition, someone once told me, 'There is no beginning, and there is no end. There is only where you come in and where you depart.' What you do while you're here is what matters." He opens her door enough that she can weigh her options. He turns to walk away before looking back. "So, make it matter."

DIALOGUE TRANSLATIONS

Chapter 1:

"Uisce." (Water.)

"An oiread sin corpán marbh." (So many dead bodies.)

"Níor thosaigh siad ach ar troid." (They just started fighting.)

"Is ar éigean a d'ealaigh mé." (I barely escaped.)

"Tá an oiread sin comhlachtaí fuilteacha ann. An comhlacht." (There were so many bloody bodies. The Body.)

Chapter 6:

"Это не то, к чему следует относиться легкомысленно." (This is not something to take lightly.)

"Вы понимаете все, что мы просим от вас?" (Do you understand everything we ask of you?)

"Все?" (All?)

"Да. Ваш суженый." (Yes. Your betrothed.) "Он будет на теле. Вот почему мы сказали ему, что он переезжает в Соединенные Колонии." (He will be on The Body. That is why we told him that he was moving to the United Colonies.)

"Так?" (So?)

"да." (Yes)

Chapter 7:

"Je to připravené?" (Is it ready?)

"Ne." (No)

"Pokračujte v míchání." (Keep stirring.)

"Jsi si jistý, že to bude fungovat?" (Are you sure it will work?)

"Ano, Dášenka." (Yes, Dagmar.)

"Tohle musí fungovat." (This has to work.)

"Co to je, Pasha?" (What is it, Pasha?)

"Na Zdravi." (Cheers.)

"Mrtvý. Spálit." (Dead. Burn.)

Chapter 13:

"Tá an corp marbh." (The body is dead.)

BOOK CLUB QUESTIONS

1. If you've read any previous books in *The West Haven Undead* series, how do you feel this compares? If you haven't, what are your general thoughts on this novel?

2. Do you feel any of the characters have grown since either the beginning of this book or the start of the series? Why?

3. If you've read previous books in the series, how do you feel about the ending? If you haven't, what are your thoughts on the character at the end?

4. Are there any themes that stand out to you as you read? If so, what and why?

5. Who's your favorite character and why?

6. Are there any scenes in the book that stand out in your mind? If so, what are the reasons they do?

7. Are there any quotes from the book or lines of dialogue that you find relatable in some way?

8. Given its science fiction/fantasy elements, how realistic do you find the events and characters in the series?

9. Do you find yourself relating to one character in the book more than others? If so, why?

10. If you could change anything about the events in the book, what would it be and why?

ABOUT AUTHOR

Nick Savage is an award-winning and Amazon best-selling author. He lives in the greater Orlando, Florida area with his wife and two cats. He is an avid video game nerd, artist, and musician.

Other books by Nick Savage:

Other books in *The West Haven Undead* series:
Us Of Legendary Gods
So We Stay Hidden

The Fairlane Incidents
The Fortunate Finn Fairlane
The Fragile Finn Fairlane
Finn Fairlane: The Complete Package

Coming Soon:
World Whore, D

Also featured in the anthology
Once Upon a Brothers Grimm (AMR Publishing)
Summer of '87: A Rock Anthology
(Venom Studioz Publishing)

MORE BOOKS FROM
4 HORSEMEN PUBLICATIONS

PARANORMAL & URBAN FANTASY

AMANDA FASCIANO
Waking Up Dead
Dead Vessel

BEAU LAKE
The Beast Beside Me
The Beast Within Me
Taming the Beast: Novella
The Beast After Me
Charming the Beast: Novella
The Beast Like Me
An Eye for Emeralds
Swimming in Sapphires
Pining for Pearls

CHELSEA BURTON DUNN
By Moonlight

J.M. PAQUETTE
Call Me Forth
Invite Me In
Keep Me Close

JESSICA SALINA
Not My Time

KAIT DISNEY-LEUGERS
Antique Magic

LYRA R. SAENZ
Prelude
Falsetto in the Woods: Novella
Ragtime Swing
Sonata
Song of the Sea
The Devil's Trill
Bercuese
To Heal a Songbird
Ghost March
Nocturne

MEGAN MACKIE
The Saint Liars
The Devil's Day
The Finder of the Lucky Devil

PAIGE LAVOIE
I'm in Love with Mothman

ROBERT J. LEWIS
Shadow Guardian and the Three Bears

VALERIE WILLIS
Cedric: The Demonic Knight
Romasanta: Father of Werewolves
The Oracle: Keeper of the Gaea's Gate

Artemis: Eye of Gaea
King Incubus: A New Reign

SciFi

BRANDON HILL & TERENCE PEGASUS
Between the Devil and the Dark
Wrath & Redemption

C.K. WESTBROOK
The Shooting
The Collision

NICK SAVAGE
Us of Legendary Gods
So We Stay Hidden
The West Haven Undead

PC NOTTINGHAM
Mummified Moon

T.S. SIMONS
Antipodes
The Liminal Space
Ouroboros
Caim
Sessrúmnir
The 45th Parallel

TY CARLSON
The Bench
The Favorite
The Shadowless

YOUNG ADULT FANTASY

BLAISE RAMSAY
Through The Black Mirror
The City of Nightmares
The Astral Tower

The Lost Book of the Old Blood
Shadow of the Dark Witch
Chamber of the Dead God

C.R. RICE
Denial
Anger
Bargaining
Depression
Acceptance
Broken Beginnings: Story of Thane
Shattered Start: Story of Sera

Sins of The Father: Story of Silas
Honorable Darkness: Story of
Hex and Snip
A Love Lost: Story of Radnar

LESLIE & JANICE SOMMERS
Brighde Reborn

M.E. BATT
The Syphon's Daughter

VALERIE WILLIS
Rebirth
Judgment
Death

DISCOVER MORE AT
4HorsemenPublications.com

Ingram Content Group UK Ltd.
Milton Keynes UK
UKHW010135060623
422929UK00019B/787/J